DATE DUE			

ALSO BY JULIO CORTÁZAR

The Winners

Hopscotch

End of the Game

Cronopios and Famas

62: A Model Kit

All Fires the Fire and Other Stories

A MANUAL FOR MANUEL

A MANUAL FOR MANUEL

by Julio Cortázar

Translated from the Spanish by Gregory Rabassa

PANTHEON BOOKS

New York

 Published in the United States by Pantheon Books, a division of Random House, Inc., New York, and simultaneously in Canada by Random House of Canada Limited, Toronto.

Assistance for the translation of this volume was given by the Center for Inter-American Relations and the New York State Council on the Arts.

Library of Congress Cataloging in Publication Data

Cortázar, Julio.
A Manual for Manuel.

Translation of *Libro de Manuel.*
I. Title.
PZ3.C81929Man 1978 [PQ7797.C7145] 863 77–88782
ISBN 0–394–49661–2

FIRST AMERICAN EDITION
Manufactured in the United States of America

A MANUAL FOR MANUEL

For obvious reasons I am probably the first one to discover that this book not only doesn't seem to be what it wants to be, but that frequently it also seems to be what it doesn't want to be, and so proponents of reality in literature are going to find it rather fantastical while those under the influence of fiction will doubtless deplore its deliberate cohabitation with the history of our own times. There is no doubt that the things taking place here cannot possibly take place in such a strange way, while elements of the purely imaginary are seen to be eliminated by a frequent slipping into what is everyday and concrete. Personally, I have no regrets concerning this heterogeneity which, fortunately, no longer seems to be such to me after so long a process of convergence; if, over the years, I have written things that are concerned with Latin American problems along with novels and tales where these problems were missing or only tangential in their appearance, at this time and in this place these streams have merged, but their conciliation has not been easy in the least, as can be shown, perhaps, in the confused and tormented path of some character or other. This man is dreaming something I had dreamed in a like manner during the days when I was just beginning to write and, as happens so many times in my incomprehensible writer's trade, only much later did I realize that the dream was also part of the book and that it contained the key to that merging of activities which until then had been unlike. Because of things like that, no one should be surprised by the frequent inclusion of news stories that were being read as the book was taking shape: stimulating coincidences and analogies caused me from the very start to accept a most simple rule of the game, having the characters take part in those daily readings of Latin American and French newspapers. I was innocent enough to hope that such participation would influence their behavior more openly; only later on did I begin to see that the story as such would not always fully accept those fortuitous intrusions, which really deserve a more felicitous experimentation than mine. In any case, I did not choose the external materials, rather, the Monday and Thursday news that became of momentary interest to the characters was incorporated into the course of my work on Monday and Thursday; some few items were deliberately set aside for the last part, an exception that made the rule more tolerable.

Books should take care of their own defense, and this one does so like a cat on his back with his belly up every chance it gets; I only wish to add that its general tone, which goes against a certain concept of how these themes should be treated, is as far removed from frivolity as it is from gratuitous humor. I believe more than ever that the struggle for socialism in Latin America should confront the daily horror with the only attitude that can bring it victory one day: a precious, careful watch over the capacity to live life as we want it to be for that future, with everything it presupposes of love, play, and joy. The widely circulated picture of the American girl offering a rose to soldiers with fixed bayonets is still evidence of the distance that lies between us and the enemy; but let no one understand or pretend to understand that that rose is a Platonic sign of nonviolence, of innocent hope; there are armored roses, as the poet saw them, there are copper roses, as Roberto Arlt invented them. What counts and what I have tried to recount is the affirmative sign that stands face to face with the rising steps of disdain and fear, and that affirmation must be the most solar, the most vital part of man: his playful and erotic thirst, his freedom from taboos, his demand for a dignity shared by everybody in a land free at last of that daily horizon of fangs and dollars.

NOTE FOR THE AMERICAN READER:

This book was finished in 1972. Argentina was then living under the military dictatorship of General Alejandro Lanusse, and the escalation of violence and the disregard for human rights were already quite evident. They have continued and increased under the military junta of General Videla. The testimony of torture mentioned on pages 373–84 is only the beginning of a hell that Argentines still have horrible daily proof of. Although the dictatorships have changed names, the oppression and the repression have only become accentuated; therefore the references that appear here with regard to Argentina and other Latin American countries are still as valid as they were when this book was written.

Otherwise, it was as if the one I told you had intended to recount some things, for he had gathered together a considerable amount of notes and clippings, waiting, it would seem, for them to end up all falling into place without too much loss. He waited longer than was prudent, evidently, and now it was Andrés's turn to find out about it and be sorry, but, apart from that mistake, what seemed to have held the one I told you back the most was the heterogeneity of the backgrounds where all those things had taken place, not to mention a rather absurd desire, one not at all functional in any case, not to get too involved in them. That neutrality had led him from the beginning to hold himself as if in profile, an operation that is always risky in narrative matters—and let us not call it historical, which is the same thing, especially since the one I told you was neither foolish nor modest—but something hard to explain seemed to have demanded that he assume a position he was never disposed to give details about. On the contrary, even though it wasn't easy, he preferred from the start to dole out diverse facts that would permit him entry from different angles into the brief but tumultuous history of the Screwery and people like Marcos, Patricio, Ludmilla, or me (whom the one I told you called Andrés without straying from the truth), hoping, perhaps, that that fragmentary information would someday shed light on the inner kitchen of the Screwery. All this, of course, so that all those notes and scraps of paper would end up falling into an intelligible order, something that didn't really happen completely for reasons that could be deduced to some degree from the documents themselves. One proof of his intention to get into the material at once (and perhaps to point up the difficulty of doing it) was provided, *inter alia*, by the fact that the one I told you had been listening when Ludmilla, after clasping and unclasping her hands in what looked like a rather esoteric gymnastic exercise, looked at me slowly with the help of her deep green ocular equipment and said Andrés, I get a feeling down near my stomach that everything that happens or happens to us is quite confusing.

"Confusion is a relative term, Polonette," I pointed out to her. "We understand or we don't understand, but what you call confusion isn't responsible for either one of the two. It seems to me that understanding depends on us alone, and that's why you can't measure reality in terms of confusion or order. Other forces are missing, other options, as they say nowadays, other mediations as they archsay nowadays. When they talk about confusion, what they almost always mean is confused people; sometimes all that's needed is a love, a decision, an hour outside the clock so that all of a sudden fate and will can immobilize the crystals in the kaleidoscope. Etc."

"Bloop," said Ludmilla, who would use that syllable when she wanted mentally to cross over to the opposite sidewalk—and try to catch her.

Naturally, the one I told you observes, in spite of such subjective obstructionism, the underlying theme is quite simple: (1) Reality exists or it doesn't exist, in any case it's incomprehensible in its essence, just as essences are incomprehensible in reality, and comprehension is another mirror for larks, and the lark is a birdy, and a birdy is a diminutive of bird, and the word bird has one syllable and four letters, and that's how reality can be seen to exist (because larks and syllables) but it's incomprehensible, because, furthermore, what do we mean by mean, or, among other things, by *saying* that reality exists. (2) Reality may be incomprehensible, but it does exist, or at least it's something that happens to us or that each of us makes happen, so that a joy, an elemental necessity, makes us forget everything said (in 1), and on to (3). We've just accepted reality (in 2), whatsoever or howsoever, and consequently we accept our being installed in it, but right there we know that, absurd or false or trumped up, reality is a failure for man even though it may not be for the birdy, who flies without asking any questions and dies without knowing it. Therefore, inexorably, if we end up accepting what was said in (3), we have to pass on to (4). This reality, on the level of (3), is a fraud and we have to change it. Here we have a divergence, (5a) and (5b):

"Oof," says Marcos.

(5a) To change reality for me alone—the one I told you goes on—is something old and feasible: Meister Eckhart, Meister

Zen, Meister Vedanta. To discover that the I is an illusion, to cultivate one's garden, be a saint, overtake the sacred prey, etc. No.

"You're getting there," says Marcos.

(5b) To change reality for everyone—the one I told you goes on—is to accept the fact that everyone is (ought to be) what I am, and, in some way, to meld the real with mankind. That means admitting history, that is, the human race on a false course, a reality accepted until now as real, and away we go. Consequence: there's only one duty and that's to find the true course. Method: revolution. Yes.

"Wow," Marcos says, "you're the best there is for simplistics and tautology."

"It's my little red morning book," the one I told you says, "and you've got to admit that if everybody believed in simplistics like that it woldn't be so easy for Shell Mex to put a tiger in your tank."

"That's Esso," says Ludmilla, who owns a two-horsepower Citroën where the horses seem to become paralyzed with fear of the tiger, because they stop on every corner and the one I told you or I or somebody has to push it along.

The one I told you likes Ludmilla because of her crazy way of seeing anything at all, and probably for that reason, from the outset Ludmilla seems to have a kind of right to violate all chronology; if it's true that she's been able to talk to me ("Andrés, I've got an impression at stomach level . . ."), on the other hand, the one I told you mixes up their roles, deliberately perhaps, when he makes Ludmilla talk in the presence of Marcos, because Marcos and Lonstein are still on the Métro that's bringing them, it's true, to my apartment, while Ludmilla is playing her part in the third act of a dramatic comedy at the Théâtre du Vieux-Colombier. This doesn't matter in the least to the one I told you, for two hours later the persons mentioned will have come together at my place; I even think that he decides it on purpose so that no one—including us and most especially the eventual recipients of his praiseworthy efforts—will have any illusions about his way of dealing with time and space; the one I told you would like to dispense with simultaneity, show how Patricio and Susana are bathing their child at the same moment that Gómez the Panamanian, with visible satisfaction, is filling in a set of Belgian stamps, and a certain Oscar in Buenos Aires is phoning his friend Gladis to tell her about some very grave matter. As for Marcos and Lonstein, they've just come into bloom on the surface of the fifteenth arrondissement in Paris and they light their cigarettes with the same match, Susana has wrapped her son up in a blue towel, Patricio is preparing a drink of *mate*, people are reading the evening papers, and so on.

Ludmilla
Gómez
Monique
Lucien Verneuil
Heredia
Marcos
Andrés
The one I told you
[Francine]
Oscar
Manuel
Gladis
Lonstein
Roland
Fernando

So as to shorten the introductions, the one I told you thinks of something like this, suppose that everyone is sitting more or less in the same file of theater seats facing something which could be, if you wish, a brick wall; it's not difficult to imagine that the show is a long way from being anything colorful. Anyone who buys a ticket has the right to a stage where things happen and a brick wall, except for the more or less fortuitous passage of a cockroach or the shadow of someone coming down the center aisle looking for his seat, doesn't go very far. Let us admit, then—all this in the care of the one I told you, Patricio, Ludmilla, or myself, not to mention the others who, little by little, are coming along to sit in the seats farther to the rear, the way the characters in a novel take their places one after the other in the pages that lie ahead—although how can you tell in a novel which pages are the ones that lie ahead and which the pages to the rear since the act of reading is to proceed ahead in the book, while the act of appearing is to go back in relation to those who will appear later on, details of form that are of no importance—let us admit, then, to a complete absurdity

and yet those people are still there, each in his seat facing the brick wall,

for different reasons since it's a question of individuals

but something which in some way goes against the grain of the absurd, as illogical as it may seem to the inhabitants of the neighborhood who at that same moment in the movie down the block are watching with fascination the sensational Made in USSR production of *War and Peace* in Technicolor and two parts and wide screen, supposing that those attending might suppose that the one I told you, et al., are sitting in their seats facing a brick wall,

and being against the grain of the absurd means precisely that Susana, Patricio, Ludmilla, et al., are where they are,

because that kind of metaphor into which they have all got themselves knowingly and each in his own way means, among other things, not seeing *War and Peace* (continuing with the metaphor, because at least two of them have already seen it), knowing very well where they are,

knowing even better that it is absurd,

and knowing on top of everything that they cannot be violated by the absurd to the degree that they not only face it (sitting down in front of the brick wall, metaphor)

but that the absurdity of heading in the direction of the absurd is exactly what brings down the walls of Jericho,

who cares if they were made of brick or pressed tungsten, if it fits the case. Or if they go against the grain of the absurd because they know it's vulnerable, conquerable, and that underneath it all it's enough to shout in its face (of bricks, continuing the metaphor), which is nothing but the prehistory of man, his amorphous projection (here innumerable possibilities for theological, phenomenological, ontological, sociological, dialectic-materialist, pop, hippie descriptions)

and it's over, this time it's over, no one really knows how, but at this point in the century something is over, brother, and then let's see what happens, and for that reason precisely

tonight,

in what's done or what's said,

in what will be said or done by so many who are still coming in and sitting down facing the brick wall, waiting, as if the brick

wall were a painted curtain that will go up as soon as the lights go out,
and the lights do go out of course,
and the curtain doesn't go up arch-of-course,
because-brick-walls-don't-go-up.
Absurd,
but not for them because they know that it's man's prehistory, they're looking at the wall because they suspect what might be on the other side; poets like Lonstein will talk about the millenary kingdom, Patricio will laugh in its face, Susana will think vaguely about a happiness that doesn't have to be bought with injustice and tears, Ludmilla will remember, without knowing why, a little white dog that she would have liked to have had when she was ten and which they never gave her.
As for Marcos, he'll take out a cigarette (it's not permitted) and will smoke it slowly, and I will put all those things together in order to imagine a way out through the bricks for mankind, and naturally I will never get to imagine it because extrapolations from science fiction bore me in detail. Finally we will all go and drink beer and *mate* at Patricio and Susana's, something will really start to happen at last, something yellow cool green liquid hot in mugs gourds placed in a circle and sucking tubes and seeming to fly over the imposing mountain of sandwiches that Susana and Ludmilla and Monique will have prepared, those mad maenads, always starving when they come out of the movies.

A Clermont-Ferrand

LE CONSEIL TRANSITOIRE DE LA FACULTÉ FAIT ÉTAT DE BRUTALITÉS POLICIÈRES COMMISES CONTRE UN MAITRE ASSISTANT

(De notre corresp. particulier.)

Clermont-Ferrand. — Le conseil transitoire de gestion de la faculté des lettres et sciences humaines de Clermont-Ferrand vient de publier un communiqué, dans lequel il déclare « *avoir pris connaissance, avec indignation, des brutalités policières dont M. Pierre Péchoux, maitre assistant d'histoire à la faculté, a été récemment victime à Paris* ».

Le communiqué précise : « *Surpris par une charge de police, le 28 mai, vers 22 heures, alors qu'il passait boulevard Saint-Michel, après une journée de travail en bibliothèque, M. Péchoux, qui est âgé de cinquante-cinq ans, a été soudainement matraqué, jeté à terre et amené d'abord dans un commissariat puis au centre de tri de Beaujon. Transporté, à l'aube, à l'hôpital Beaujon, après qu'on eut reconnu qu'il ne pouvait marcher, et huit jours plus tard, à son domicile clermontois, M. Péchoux souffre d'une triple fracture de la rotule et de plaies qui le condamnent à plusieurs semaines d'immobilité.* »

Le conseil transitoire de gestion a désigné une délégation qui demandera audience au recteur de l'académie de Clermont-Ferrand pour lui exprimer l'émotion de la faculté tout entière.

"Translate," Patricio commanded. "Can't you see that Fernando's fresh off the boat and that Chileans for the most part haven't got the gift of Gallic gab."

"You've got me confused with Saint Jerome," Susana said. "All right. Clermont-Ferrand. Provisional Faculty Council protests act of police brutality against adjunct professor. By our special correspondent."

"A summary will be fine for me," Fernando said.

"Shh. Clermont-Ferrand. The Provisional Administrative Council of the Faculty of Letters and Human Sciences of Clermont-Ferrand has just released a statement in which it declares, quote, that it has learned with indignation of the act of police brutality of which Mr. Pierre Péchoux, Adjunct Professor of History on the Faculty, was victim in Paris. Unquote. The statement follows, quote, caught up in a police charge on May 28 at about 10

P.M. while walking along the Boulevard Saint-Michel after a session of work in the library, Mr. Péchoux, 55, was suddenly attacked with clubs, knocked to the ground, and taken to a police station, from where he was transferred to investigation headquarters in Beaujon. At dawn he was removed to the Beaujon Hospital when it was noted that he was unable to walk, and a week later he was returned to his home in Clermont-Ferrand. Mr. Péchoux suffered a triple fracture of the kneecap and other injuries that will require him to be completely immobilized for several weeks. Unquote. The Provisional Administrative Council has named a delegation to seek a hearing with the president of the University of Clermont-Ferrand to express the faculty's indignation."

"So they've got the hospital right next to investigation headqvarters," Fernando said. "Vell-organized, these Frenchmen. In Santiago things are alvays tventy blocks avay from each other."

"Now you can see why it was useful to have the item translated," Patricio said.

"It's obvious," Susana conceded. "Now you can finally see what's waiting for you in the land of the *Marseillaise*, especially along the Boulevard Saint-Michel."

"And that's just vhere my hotel is," Fernando said. "Vone thing, though, I'm not an adjunct professor. So they beat up on profs here. It's still something positive, leaving out the barbarism. Poor old Pechú."

The phone rang, it was I, telling Patricio that Lonstein and Marcos had just come by, could we run over with Ludmilla and them to talk, we've got to fraternize from time to time, don't you think?

"This is no time to call, damn it," Patricio said. "I'm in a very important meeting. No, dummy, you should have been able to tell by my voice, a person's voice always pants a little in cases like this."

"I bet he's telling you a dirty story," Susana said.

"You've got it, baby. What? No, I was talking to Susana here and a Chilean who got in a week ago, we're giving him an indoctrination course in the environment, if you follow me, the guy's still pretty much of a hick."

"You can go to hell along vith the vone you're talking to," Fernando decreed.

"That's the way," Susana said. "While those two are exploiting Alexander Graham Bell, you and I will fix some *mate* with the *yerba* Monique stole from Fauchon."

"Sure, come on over," Patricio gave in. "My remarks were of a disciplinary nature, don't forget that I've got fifteen years in this country and it leaves its mark, chum. They're Argentines," he explained to Fernando who had already figured that out for himself. "We have to amene them as we say in France, because Marcos probably has some fresh news from Grenoble and Marseilles, where there was a donnybrook between the gauchists and the cops last night."

"Gavchists?" asked Fernando, who had palate problems. "Are there gavchos in Marseilles?"

"You have to understand that translating *gauchiste* by leftist wouldn't give you the precise idea, because in your country and in mine it means something quite different."

"You're going to get him all confused," Susana said. "I don't see that much difference, the trouble is that with you the word leftist is like a weak *mate* because of your younger days with the People's Cause and things like that, and while we're on the subject, take this one, I just brewed it."

"You're right," Patricio said, meditating with the sipper in his mouth as Martín Fierro would have done under similar circumstances. "Leftist or Peronist or whatever comes next hasn't had any very clear meaning for years now, but while we're at it, translate that other item on the same page for the fellow."

"Another translation? Didn't you hear Manuel wake up and demand his hygienic care? Wait till Andrés and Ludmilla get here, they can learn a little contemporary history along the way while they translate."

"All right, go take care of your son; the trouble with the kid is hunger, girl, bring him here and bring the bottle of grappa on the way, it's good for the *mate*."

Fernando was doing his best to decipher the headlines in the paper and Patricio watched him with bored sympathy, wondering whether or not he shouldn't find some pretext to get rid of him before Marcos and the others got there, lately the vise had been tightening on the Screwery and he didn't know too much about the Chilean. "But Andrés is coming and Ludmilla of course," he thought. "We'll talk about everything else under the sun except the Screwery." He handed him another *mate* without ideological content, waiting for the doorbell to ring.

Yes, of course there's a mechanism, but how do you explain it and, after all, why explain it, who's asking for an explanation, questions that the one I told you brings up every time people like Gómez or Lucien Verneuil look at him with raised eyebrows, and one night I was able to tell him that impatience is the mother of all who get up and go out slamming a door or a page, then the one I told you sips his wine, sits looking at us for a while, and then condescends to state or only to think that the mechanism is in some way the lamp that is lighted in the garden before people come to dine in the cool air amidst the smell of jasmines, the perfume that the one I told you had come to know in a town in Buenos Aires province a long time back when his grandmother would get out the white tablecloth and set the table under the arbor near the jasmines and someone lighted the lamp and there was a sound of silverware and plates on trays, talking in the kitchen, the aunt who would go to the alley with the white gate to call the children who were playing with their friends in the garden next door or on the sidewalk, and there was the heat of a January evening, grandmother had watered the garden before it grew dark and you could get the smell of the wet earth, the thirsty privets, the honeysuckle covered with translucent drops that multiplied the lamp for a child with eyes born to see things like that. All of that has little to do with today after so many years of a good life or bad, but it's good to let yourself fall into an association that will tie in the description of the mechanism to the lamp in the summer garden of childhood, because in that way it will come to pass that the one I told you will receive a particular pleasure in talking about the lamp and the mechanism without feeling too theoretical, simply recalling a past that becomes more present every day due to sclerosis or reversible time, and at the same time he'll be able to show how what's starting to happen now for someone who's probably getting impatient is a lamp being lighted in a summer garden on a table in the midst of plants. Twenty seconds will pass, forty, a minute, perhaps, the one I told you remembers the mosquitoes, the praying mantises, the inchworms, the beetles; it's easy to figure out the simile, first the lamp, a naked single light, and then the other elements begin to come, the scattered pieces, the shreds, Ludmilla's green shoes, a turquoise penguin, the beetles, the mantises, Marcos's curly hair, Francine's panties, so white, a certain Oscar who brought some royal armadillos, not to mention the penguin, Patricio and Susana, the ants, taking shape and the dance and ellipses and crosses and bumping and rapid pecking on the butter plate or the platter of manioc flour, with shouts from mother who asks why they didn't put a napkin over it, she can't believe they don't know that nights like this are full of bugs, and Andrés called Francine bug once, but maybe the mechanism is being understood now and there's no reason to let yourself be carried off by the entomological whirlwind ahead of time; it's just that it's nice, nicely sad not to leave that point without looking back for a second at the table and the lamp, looking at grandmother's gray hair as she serves dinner, the dog as she barks because the moon has come up and everything quivers among the jasmines and the privets while the one I told you turns his back and the forefinger of his right hand rests on the key that will print a hesitant, almost tired period at the end of what is beginning, or what had to be said.

For his part and in his way, Andrés, too, was looking for explanations of something that he was missing as he listened to *Prozession*; the one I told you ended up being amused by that obscure reverence for science, the Hellenic heritage, the insolent why of everything, a kind of return to Socratic ways, a horror of mystery, of things happening and being accepted just because; he suspected the influence of a powerful technology rising up with a more legitimate view of the world, aided by the philosophies of left and right, and then he would defend himself with freshly watered jasmines and privets, weakening on one side the requirement that the clockwork of things be shown, but offering an explanation that few would find plausible. In my case the matter was less rigorous, my problem that night before Marcos and Lonstein arrived to break my back, goddamned Cordovans (the Argentine city, not the Spanish one, of course), was to understand why I couldn't listen to the recording of *Prozession* without alternately being distracted and concentrating on it, and a fair amount of time had passed before I realized that it was being done on the piano. So that's how it is, I only have to replay a part of the record to corroborate it; in the midst of the electronic sounds or traditional sounds modified by Stockhausen's use of filters and microphones, from time to time, with great clarity, you can hear the piano with its own sound. So simple, really: old man and new man in this same man placed strategically to close the triangle of stereophony, the breaking of a supposed unity that a German musician had stripped naked in a Paris apartment at midnight. That's how it is, in spite of so many years of electronic or contingent music, of free jazz (good-by, good-by to melody, and good-by to old defined rhythm too, to closed forms, good-by to sonatas, good-by to chamber music, good-by to wigs, to the atmosphere of tone poems, good-by to the foreseeable, good-by to the dearest part of custom), all the same, the old man is still alive and remembers, in the headiest of adventures we have the easy chair, as always, and the archduke's trio, and suddenly it's so easy to understand: the piano had coagulated sounds that had merely survived before, so in the midst of a complex of sounds where everything is discovery, the color and tone of the piano appear like old photographs, and even though the piano can give birth to the least pianistic of notes or chords, the instrument is recognizable here, the piano of the other music, an older mankind, an Atlantis of sound in a full, young, new world. And yet it's easier now to understand how history, the temporal and cultural conditioning, becomes fulfilled, for every passage where the piano dominates sounds to me like a recognition that brings my attention into concentration, awakens me more sharply to something that is still tied to me by that instrument which acts as a bridge between past and future. The not very friendly confrontation between the old man and the new: music, literature, politics, the cosmovision that takes them all in. For contemporaries of the harpsichord, the first appearance of the sound of the piano must have slowly awakened the mutant that today has become traditional vis-à-vis the filters manipulated by that German so that he can fill my ears with sibilants and other chunks of sound never heard before anywhere under the moon. Corollary and moral: everything should be a leveling off of attention, then, a neutralizing of the extorsion of those outbreaks from the past in the new human way of enjoying music. Yes, a new way of being that tries to include everything, the sugar crop in Cuba, love between bodies, painting and family and decolonization and dress. It's natural for me to wonder again about the problem of building bridges, how to seek new contacts, the legitimate ones, beyond the loving understanding of different generations and cosmovisions, of a piano and electronic controls, of dialogues among Catholics,

Buddhists, and Protestants, of the thaw between two political blocs, of peaceful coexistence; because it's not a question of coexistence, the old man can't survive just as he is in the new one even though man continues to be his own spiral, the new spin in the interminable ballet; it's no longer possible to talk about tolerance, everything is speeding up to a sickening degree, the distance between generations grows in geometric proportion, nothing to do with the twenties, the forties, pretty soon the eighties. The first time a pianist stopped his playing to run his fingers over the strings as if it were a harp or beat on the case to mark a rhythm or a pause, shoes flew onto the stage; now young people are surprised if the sonorous uses of a piano are limited to its keyboard. What about books, those shabby fossils in need of an implacable gerontology, and those ideologues of the left who doggedly insist on an only slightly less than monastic ideal of private and public life, and those on the right unmoved in their disdain for the millions of dispossessed and alienated? A new man, yes: how far away you are, Karlheinz Stockhausen, most modern musicmaker mingling a nostalgic piano with full electronic iridescence; it's not a reproach, I'm telling it to you from my own self, from the easy chair of a fellow traveler. You've got the bridge problem too, you have to find the way of speaking intelligibly when, perhaps, your technique and your most deeply installed reality are demanding that you burn the piano and replace it with some other electronic filter (a working hypothesis, because it's not a question of destroying for destruction's sake, more than likely the piano serves Stockhausen as well or better than electronic means, but I think we understand each other). The bridge, then, of course. How is the bridge to be built and to what degree is building it going to serve any purpose? The intellectual (sic) praxis of stagnant socialisms demands a total bridge; I write and the reader reads, that is, it's taken for granted that I write and build the bridge over to a legible level. But what if I'm not legible, old man, what if there's no reader and therefore no bridge? Because a bridge, even if you have the desire to build one and if all works are bridges to and from something, is not really a bridge until people cross it. A bridge is a man crossing a bridge, by God.

One of the solutions: put a piano on that bridge and then there'll be a crossing. The other one: build the bridge by all means and leave it there; out of that baby girl suckling in her mother's arms a woman will come someday who will walk by herself and will cross the bridge, carrying in her arms a baby girl suckling at her breast. And a piano will no longer be needed, there'll be a bridge all the same, there'll be people crossing it. But try telling that to all the satisfied engineer builders of bridges and roads and five-year plans.

"Who called?" Fernando asked.

"Oh, that guy, the less said about him the better,"•Patricio opined with perceptible warmth. "You'll see him in the space of ten minutes, it's Andrés, one of the many Argentines who don't know what they're doing in Paris, although he's got his theory about chosen places and, in any case, he's won his right to floor space, Susana met him before I did and she can tell you about him, she might even confess to you that she went to bed with him."

"On the floor, since you say he's won the right," Susana said. "Don't pay any attention to him, Fernando, he's a natural-born Turk, every Latin American whose path crossed mine before I met this monster automatically gets on the retrospective jealousy list. It's good he's convinced Manuel is his child, because if he wasn't, the poor kid would be covered with Proustian scar tissue."

"Vhat does Andrés do?" Fernando wanted to know, a little nosey when it came to personal matters.

"He listens to a wild amount of aleatory music and reads even more, he's always involved with women, and he's probably waiting for the moment."

"The moment for vhat?"

"Oh, that . . ."

"You're right," Susana said. "Andrés is like waiting for some moment, but who can say, it's not ours, in any case."

"Vhat's yours, the revolution and all that?"

"What a way of asking, this guy must belong to the SIDE (that's our Argentine intelligence outfit)," Patricio declared, passing him a *mate.* "Hey, girl, let me have your son, since you've just stated that he's not retrospective, and translate the news about Nadine for the fellow, this Chilean has got to pick up the local political culture, that way he'll get a precise idea of why one of these days he's going to get his ass broken when he begins to take a close look at what's going on, and there's a lot going on."

"Who's coming with Andrés?"

"If you can hold off for a while, Chile boy, you'll see for yourself, and that's that, because when they pop by it's always for more than a spell. What I mean is that Marcos and Lonstein are coming, Argentines too, but from scholarly old Córdoba, if you know about all that, and Ludmilla will probably show up if she survives the Russian tortures they put on at the Vieux-Colombier, three acts of nothing but samovar and knout, not to mention that somewhere along the line the doorbell will ring for the fifth time and the one I told you will drop by, which is fine, because he usually has a bottle of cognac close at hand or at least some chocolate for Manuel, look how the little devil's eyes are glowing, come to papa, you're going to be my justification in the eyes of history, m'lad."

"Something else I didn't catch too vell vas vhat you said about the *yerba*, that somebody stole it somevhere."

"Mother of mercy," Patricio said, overwhelmed.

"It's obvious you've never read the adventures of Robin Hood," Susana said. "Look, Monique is writing a thesis, on the Inca Garcilaso, no less, and she's covered with freckles. Then she went off with a bunch of Maoists to storm Fauchon, which has gotten to be the Christian Dior for fatbellies, a symbolic act against the bourgeoisie who pay ten francs for a mangy avocado flown in by air. The idea wasn't new because there's no such thing as a new idea, in your country they've probably pulled off something similar—it was a question of loading the victuals into two or three cars and distributing them among the people in the shantytowns on the north side of Paris. Monique saw a package of *yerba* and stuck it someplace or other to bring to me, something not foreseen in the operation and somewhat irregular, but, bearing in mind what happened that night, we must admit it was sublime."

"It's a good introduction to the news item we're going to translate for your edification," Patricio said. "You know, something went wrong and the people on the street were ready to lynch the kids, just imagine, they were just people passing by who certainly never went into Fauchon because all they had to do was look in the windows to figure out that it took three months' wages to buy a dozen apricots and a slice of roast beef, but that's the way things turn out, Chile boy, the notion of law and order and private property has meaning even for people without a cent to their name. Monique got away in time in one of the cars, but the police caught another girl and even though they obviously couldn't charge her with robbery since the group had handed out flyers explaining their intentions, the judge sentenced her to thirteen months in the can, mark that, and without—without, what was it?"

"Without appeal or something like that," Susana said. " 'I want you to know, young lady, that you are going to spend a year and a month in jail as an example to others who might be thinking about new attacks on things that belong to other people, no matter what reasons are given.' And here's the piece in the newspaper, because it's about another girl Monique knows."

L'attaque de la mairie de Meulan

MLLE NADINE RINGART EST MISE EN LIBERTÉ PROVISOIRE

Mlle Nadine Ringart, détenue depuis le 17 mars dernier pour avoir participé à l'attaque du bureau de main-d'œuvre de la mairie de Meulan (Yvelines), vient d'être mise en liberté provisoire par M. Angevin, juge d'instruction à la Cour de sûreté de l'Etat.

La jeune fille, étudiante en sociologie à la Sorbonne, reste inculpée de violences à agent, violences volontaires avec préméditation, violation de domicile et dégradation de monument public.

"Vhat a lot of girls," Fernando said, enchanted.

"Listen: Attack on Meulan town hall. Miss Nadine Ringart paroled. Those are the headlines. Miss Nadine Ringart, held since March 17 for having taken part in the attack on the employment office of the town hall of Meulan (Yvelines) has just been paroled by Mr. Angevin, examining judge of the State Security Court. The young woman, a student of sociology at the Sorbonne, is still accused of violence against the police, voluntary violence with premeditation, violation of residence, and the defacing of a public monument. Period."

"Vhat a lot of v's," Fernando said with satisfaction. "If you believe that news story, the kid beats Calamity Jane and Agatha Christie, no, I mean that Agata Galiffi you people have in Argentina. Vhile you vere reading, the whole story sounded like a joke; can you imagine seeing it in a newspaper five years ago? And they say it just like that, voluntary violence, violation of residence by a sociology student from the Sorbonne. It's like a put-on, really."

"Nobel Prize winner in theology chops up wife," Patricio said. "We'd take it just as calmly, like now that they land on the moon twice a week, and what do I care."

"Don't you two start carrying on like my aunt," Susana said, rocking Manuel vigorously as he became more and more awake and glowing. "There are things I'll never get used to and that's why I take the trouble to translate these news items for you, to get the feeling of how much they show and of all the work that's left for us to do."

"All right, that's exactly what we'll be talking about with our transandean comrade here, but that's no reason to get him all worked up at the start, damn it."

"Vhat a lot of mystery," Fernando said.

"And vhat a lot of broken asses," said Patricio.

It's probably as a defense, Andrés thought, that Lonstein talks that way, making use of a kind of language that everyone finally ends up understanding, a thing that doesn't seem to please him too much sometimes. There was a time (we were sharing a cheap room on the Rue de la Tombe-Issoire, it was in the winter of sixty or sixty-one) when he was more explicit, sometimes condescending to say look, any reality that's worth its salt reaches you through words, leave the rest to apes and geraniums. He would become cynical and reactionary, he said that if this or that weren't in writing it wouldn't exist, this newspaper is the world and there isn't any other, by God, this war exists because the dispatches are here, you write to your old lady because that way you bring her a little life. We didn't see each other very much afterward, I met Ludmilla, I took some trips and I got tripped up, Francine appeared, in Geneva once I got a postcard from Lonstein and I learned about his work at the medico-legal institute, it was underlined and followed by a swarm of !'s and ?'s, and at the end of one of his sentences: Don't emplope me too much, haddy; plot me a response, sconce. I sent him a card in return with a view of the squirt on the shores of Lake Leman and made up a message for him with the help of all the signs on an IBM electric; which he must not have liked because four years passed, but that doesn't matter, what I have to recognize is that this business of words Made in Lonstein was never a game, even though no one could ever tell where it was leading, a defense or an attack, I thought it held Lonstein's truth in some way, what Lonstein was, small and rather dirty and a Cordovan to the core and self-confessedly a great masturbator and adept of parascientific experiments, fervently Jewish and Latin American, fatally nearsighted, as if anyone could be like Lonstein without being nearsighted and small, here he is again now, he mooned into my apartment twenty minutes ago without warning, like all South Americans, arriving, of course, with Marcos, who will do anything to avoid saying he's coming by, fuck their mothers.

These guys have come at a bad time, they've caught me right in the middle of a weaning mess, because ever since ten o'clock at night and it's twelve o'clock now (a very natural time so that Lonstein and Marcos, of course) I've been kicking at everything around me, trying to decide once and for all whether it's the right moment to put the record with *Prozession* back on or whether I should write a couple of lines answering the Venezuelan poet who sent me a book where everything seems to be underlined or to have been read before, polished words, just like an office master key, patented metaphors and metonymies, such good intentions, such obvious results, bad poetry, purportedly revolutionary, but if only that were all there was to it, Stockhausen or the Venezuelan, the bad part is that matter of bridges, which has my time all tied down, all that trouble with Francine and Ludmilla, but most of all this confusion for which the bridges are to blame that comes along to bother me at a time in the order of things when other people would send it straight to hell, that urge not to give in an inch (why the commonplace of an inch when we are metric decimal system? Traps, traps on every line, the little rabbi is right, reality comes to you through words, so my reality is falser than that of an Asturian priest; plot me a response, sconce), not to give in a single centimeter, which doesn't fix things up much even though we're being faithful to the metric system, and at the same time to know that I am commingling, contributing, compensating, commiserating, but in no way consenting, and that's where the confusion starts and, why not say so, fear, this has never happened to me, things would come to me and I would manipulate them and turn them around and boomerang them without coming out of my shell until one of those times precisely when I could feel myself more enshelled than ever, it's not only confusion that fills your ashtray with bitter butts, it's everything, loves, dreams, the taste of coffee, the subway, paintings, and political meetings start to twist, to mingle, they become all tangled up among themselves, Ludmilla's little ass is the speech by Pierre Gonnard at the Mutualité, unless the speech is that little ass that I don't wish to recall now, and, to top it off, Lonstein and Marcos at this moment, fuck it all.

It's something like this, the poor beasty comes out into the ring and stands very still, snorting. He just doesn't understand, here he'd been in the dark, given his feed, everything was going along fine with the aid of trucks, shaking, and habit, everything had started to be a smell, a distant sound, a total absence of the past, and all of a sudden through an alley with shouts and poles, a huge circle filled with colors and *paso dobles*, a sinking sun in his eyes, and then boff the hoof writing the cipher of confusion in the sand. *¿Qué coño?* thinks the beasty, who is Spanish naturally, since the Japanese haven't gone into the bullfight business yet the way they've done with French oysters, what the hell is this all about? I'd like to ask Lonstein or Marcos about it, for example, now that they've come by (not to mention Ludmilla, who will pop by as soon as she finishes her role at the Vieux-Colombier), but what am I going to ask them and why, since the confusion is more than can be put in a question because it's already obvious that the business about Stockhausen and Ludmilla's little ass and the Venezuelan bard are only small pieces, just a few tessellas in the mosaic, and there it is, what right do I have to use the word tessella, which probably won't say a thing to a lot of people, and why in hell not use it since it tells me all that's necessary and, besides, the context helps and now everybody knows what a tessella is, but the problem isn't that, but, rather, the awareness that it is a problem, an awareness I'd never had before and which is slowly shoving me into life and into language like Lonstein and Marcos into my place, late and without warning, half on the bias, it's obvious that I'm employed too deep, haddy. Because, to top it off, Lonstein and Marcos have started talking now and that's precisely the other tip of the problem, a kind of wager against the impossible, but they just go on, and try stopping them. Just in case, I'm going to call Patricio, if they get to be a drag I'll slowly set them adrift and listen to *Prozession* again, it would seem that the choice has been made and the Venezuelan poet has lost, poor lad.

The topic is the morgue, in plain talk the medico-legal institute, drowned people, Lonstein has let himself go tonight, Lonstein, who never talks about his work, but Marcos, behind his cigarette, is slowly going back and forth in Ludmilla's rocker, he runs his hand through his curly locks from time to time, throws back his curls and releases the smoke slowly through his nose. Andrés hasn't asked Marcos a thing, as if slipping into his apartment in the middle of the night was the most natural thing in the world, and Marcos almost enjoys that somewhat aloof procedure Andrés is taking, waits a while longer, and Lonstein going on about suicides and schedules, completely off the track in spite of the instructions received along the route of eight Métro stations and two grappas in a café. Even Andrés seems to sense that something's out of gear, he listens to Lonstein but he's looking at Marcos as if asking him what the hell and for how long, damn it.

"Turn off your hose, rabbi junior grade," orders Marcos, who is rather amused inside. "Save your Edgar Allan Poe for the people when we're at Patricio's, the women will listen to you with their souls dangling on a string, you know what necrophiliacs they are. The idea, my good man, was to use our visit to talk about things that are a bit more alive, plugging you and your little Polack girl into a cram course in Latin American informatics, something you seem a little far-removed from. This talmudic beast was told to break the ice, but you got ahead of us as soon as the gong sounded and all these fancy-dress preliminaries annoy me."

"Out with it, then," I said in resignation.

"Well, this is what it's all about, more or less."

I finally came to understand that one of the most important reasons behind Marcos's visit was to use my telephone, because he didn't trust his own those days. I should have asked him why, but if I didn't ask him, Marcos would avoid having to tell a lie and, besides, I didn't feel too keen about getting involved in Marcos's thing, at least when I wasn't at Patricio's, where politics and direct and indirect action were practically the only reason people opened their mouths. Marcos knew me, he wasn't bothered by my nonparticipation; with Lonstein and me he enjoyed a relationship like that of old schoolmates (we weren't) and no other contact was needed. He let himself go with Ludmilla, talking about everything going on at the moment, all the binds he and Patricio were mixed up in; sometimes he'd look at me from behind the smoke of his cigarette as if wanting to know where I stood, why I wasn't taking that little step forward or running off a little to the side in order to go into orbit. And so, while he was phoning an endless series of male and female characters, in French and Spanish and sometimes in a mysterious ginzoid gibberish (the one on the other end was named Pascale and was answering from Genoa, my phone bill for that three-month period was going to be hairy, mustn't let him leave without settling up), Lonstein and I were chatting, drinking white wine and reminiscing about the good, cheap semillón wine in waterfront bars. Poor Lonstein had got a raise that week and he was mournful, thinking that everything has its counterweight and that they were going to break his back with work; his misfortune had made him strangely talkative, Marcos had to keep hushing him up so he could hear somebody who must have been in a phone booth somewhere in Budapest or Uganda, then the little rabbi would lower his voice a bit and on with the drownings, the night schedule at the morgue, asphyxiated people, the ones who jump out windows, the ones burned, girls raped with previous (or simultaneous) strangulation, boys *idem*, suicides by poison, a bullet in the head, illuminating gas, barbiturates, razors, accident victims (cars, trains, military maneuvers, fireworks, construction scaffolds) and last but yes least, the beggars dead of cold or vinous intoxication as they try to defend themselves against the first with the help of the second on top of some subway grating always warmer than the sidewalk where the busy and honest petit bourgeois and working-class population of the capital walks by without pausing. But Lonstein doesn't give those statistics with such enumerative precision, for as far as his work is concerned, his versions are mainly exercises in language, making it difficult to know what belongs to Caesar and what belongs to the morgue, tonight Lonstein is outdoing himself in elocution and in his Cordovan accent he talks about such things as apwals and shellballs, which, from their early contexts, I deduce are the occupants of forensic tables, and he whimpers on from there that he has a hell of a lot of work when he gets to the icebox between eight and nine o'clock and half a dozen apwals are already waiting for him to undior them, unchanel them, peep off their things little by little, getting them slowly used to the marble, to the horizontal position where ankles, gluteals, shoulder blades, and neck will receive, to a more or less equal degree, the influence of the law of gravity for lack of any better one, what can you do.

"Pascale, puoi dire a quello là che è un fesa," Marcos is saying. "Have him send me the melons directly to Little Red Riding Hood's."

The key to those things, Andrés thinks, the melons must be pamphlets or pistols, Little Red Riding Hood must be Gómez, who shaves every two hours.

"Then the laving reannoys me," Lonstein is explaining, "if you're lucky put the case that start the passing in review, a femme between fourteen and fifteen, all talcum powder and the face of a Luna Park Saturday night except that at respiration level there's a black-and-blue ruff and on the skirt a wild double ketchup concentrated map, then I have to go about removing her dreamcovers, cutting elastics and lowering sticky tergals until I can see every foliole, every ficciore, the operation, life's impairments. Sometimes gimpy Tergov helps me, but if it's a cutey I send him to work at the other table, I prefer washing her by myself, alone, an apwal like in her mama's time, you understand, a little sponge here, a little sponge there, I leave them for you better than on the day they received their first, Tergov only slops a bucket of water over them and kind of from a distance rearranges their hair and lays their arms and underpinning straight, I, on the other hand, will turn them over, if they're worth anything, not just to look at them, I don't want you to think, but, naturally, what do you think Leonardo did and look how they respect him, sometimes it's hard to believe they've got no more urge for a little humping, going around with their whole life in their assholes, it's like you were giving them a little help, even though, of course, you end up sad, hell, they don't cooperate. The one last night at eleven o'clock, for exemplum, they brought her in while I was off to Marthe's to have me a rum, I come back and, what can I say, another job on table six, I don't know why they always put the cutest ones on table six, I lower the pink, I cut the black, and I lift the rayon, it was even hard for me to take, Tergov had the card from the fuzz, gas, you could tell that already by her nosey and her nails, but what do you know, still warm, I swear, although it could have been from the meat wagon now that they've bought some that look like Swiss chalets, there I was; she couldn't have been more than eighteen, her cute little hair bicolored and her knees softer than I'd ever seen; there was a lot to do for her because gas, I don't know whether you're aware or not, but I'll tell you about that later; well, half an hour with strong detergency, a general ablution, the phase of glove on wardsback, the froth, I hope you won't think that I'll end up as a necrophile."

"Let's just say you like what you like," says Marcos, who is listening as if from a distance as he dials another number and that makes seven.

"When they're boizy or flonde, when they still look like sundials, then they do awaken the florence-galen-night in me, after all it is a good way of getting up Death's ass, not let them be strapstepped up against the ropes, and that's why you have to be careful, my boy, denoose them and froth them, and that way, when you've hundled them well, they're the same again, just like the ones prepaired at home or at the Mayo clinic with the help of the blessed woman and the galenizers, because in the end there's no reason why my apwals, young as they are at times, should run handicapped by the grelle, you understand, I mean bad luck, if I can terminologize discepoliarily."

"Oh, brother!" Marcos says, annoyed, hard to tell whether because of Lonstein or because the line is busy.

"Let him go on," I tell him, "it's been years since he's turned himself loose like this, when a monster takes off you have to gallop alongside, let's be Christian about it."

"You're a mother," Lonstein says, visibly content. "People are like those classic torturers who ended up as neurotics because all they had was their no-less-classic daughter to whom they could recount every detail of torturocomy and leadsqueals; don't you realize that in Marthe's bistro I didn't go around declining my gig as my co-pains say, and that condemns me to silence, apart from the fact that since I'm a celibate, chaste like Onan and master of my bait, there's no exutory left for me but soliloquy, except for the privybook where from time to time I defescrape a turdscript or two. The worst part, as I was explaining to you, is that now that they've doubled my work these days under the pretext of paying me four times as much, I agreed, as an incurable outpopper and, besides the inst I've got the hosp. All Hindus, there'd been a wave of Czechs, but now they're all Hindus, Made in Madras, word of honor."

"Hindus, shit," Marcos says.

"Kidnapped right off the funeral pyre," Lonstein insists, "and hermeneutically canned in numbered containers with an indescription of age and sex, who the hell knows how they've set the racket up, but one of these days the people in Benares who sell wood for cremation are going to raise such hell that it will put to shame the blackass Calcutta hole we studied about in the Bolívar National School, Province of Buenos Aires, Jesus, the things dumb old Cancio taught us, he was a wild prof we had, oh nostalmia, oh exuborium!"

"You mean they import Hindu corpses for dissection?" asks Marcos, who's starting to be hooked. "Get out of here with your damned stories, take your drivel somewhere else."

"I sacre to you by what's most sworn," Lonstein says. "Gimpy Tergov and I have the job of opening the containers and preparing the merchandise for the night of the long knives, which is on Thursdays and Mondays. Look, at this point you get a negascientific element of the many that the gimp and I garbage away because the profs don't want to find the raw material in anything but a state of integral ballnakedness."

From his pocket he takes a paper flower with a wire stem and flips it to Marcos, who leaps from his chair and cuts him with a son-of-a-bitch. I start thinking about herding them slowly toward the door, because it's not right to keep Patricio and Susana waiting until one o'clock in the morning and it's five after one already.

Because of all that, the business that the absurd is only the prehistory of man as understood by the one I told you and so many others, and also because of the bugs flying around the lamp which is one of the many ways to answer the absurd (deep down that's what homo faber really means, but there are so many fabers and fabers number one, two, and three, sharp or dull, long or stubby), because of all that and similar things the moment will come when the one I told you will decide that there are enough beetles, mosquitoes, and mantises dancing a wild but highly showy jerk around the lamp, and then still within the metaphor he'll turn it off all at once, instantly freezing a determined situation of all the whirling bugs or starting points which suddenly deprived of light will become fixed in that last look of the one I told you at the instant of turning off the lamp, so that the largest mantis who was flying away from and above the lamp will remain situated in symmetrical relation to the red moth who was tracing his ellipse under the lamp, and thus successively the various discomfited and summer bugs will assume a condition of fixed and definitive points in something which with one instant more or less of light would have been infinitesimally modified. Some will call it choice, the one I told you among them, and some will call it chance, the one I told you among them, because the one I told you knows quite well that at a given moment he put out the lamp and that he did it because he had decided to do it at that moment and not before or after, but he also knows that the reason that made him decide to push the switch didn't come to him from any mathematical calculation or any functional reason, but was born inside of him, being within a particularly uncertain notion as anyone knows like falling in love or playing poker on Saturday nights.

Les « jeux du cirque »

Nous avons reçu de M. Etienne Metreau, jeune Grenoblois de vingt ans, la lettre suivante :

Me promenant au campus de Saint-Martin-d'Hères, samedi 6 dans l'après-midi, pour voir des étudiants et pour comprendre la raison de leur violence, j'ai été invité à venir à la « boum-barricade ».

Dans le courant de la soirée, je me suis approché de l'avenue qui longe le campus. C'est alors qu'une voiture s'est arrêtée à ma hauteur. Un commando de sept personnes en descend. L'un d'eux m'assomme de sa matraque, tandis que les autres passent à tabac deux autres jeunes qui étaient à côté. Ils m'enferment dans leur voiture et démarrent en abandonnant les deux autres sur le carreau.

Au cours du trajet, ils me frappent d'une série de coups de cravache, tout en me menaçant de mort (par injection de cyanure ou par noyade...). Après une halte dans une cour d'immeuble où ils se livrent à divers matraquages, ils m'amènent en face d'un magasin Record, où ils renoncent à continuer leurs tortures à cause de la présence de témoins. C'est alors qu'ils me remirent aux C.R.S. qui, un par un, me frappèrent. Puis ils firent un cercle autour de moi et commencèrent « divers jeux de cirque » : me faisant courir pour échapper à leurs coups, me forçant à crier : « *Vive Mao ! Vive Mao !* »

Puis ils m'enfermèrent dans un car : coups de poing, coups de pied, coups de matraque, coups de casque ininterrompus pendant une demi-heure, se disputant entre eux pour avoir le privilège de participer aux réjouissances (parmi eux se trouvaient deux gradés). Ils me ramenèrent alors dans la voiture « banalisée » qui m'avait kidnappé au départ.

Ce n'est qu'alors (plus d'une heure après m'avoir enlevé) qu'ils m'interrogèrent et que je pus dire que je n'étais pas étudiant et que je n'avais participé à aucun affrontement. Ils me déposèrent alors sur un trottoir à 150 mètres de la préfecture.

Je me trouve maintenant à l'hôpital, avec un traumatisme crânien (j'ai perdu trois fois connaissance au cours de cette aventure).

"Shall we go on a little more with what awaits this transandean if he doesn't keep to his hotel as much as possible?"

"Vell, I'm already beginning to catch on," Fernando said.

"I don't know, your eyes still show that thing that one of our better poems talks about, maybe your bean is full of sad illusions. So, Susana, translate that two-column piece for him, the one Monique gave you along with the *yerba*."

"If you two keep on pestering me I'm going to charge you the going UNESCO rate for home translations," Susana grumbled. For days now I've had my eyes on a little Dorothée Bis item and if you don't watch out I'll buy two, as the name of the couturière subliminally suggests, she must really be something. 'Circus Games,' title. We have received the following letter from Mr. Étienne Metreau, a young man of twenty who lives in Grenoble, semicolon. On the afternoon of Saturday the sixth, while I was strolling on the campus of Saint-Martin-d'Hères to watch the students and try to understand the reasons for their violence,

> You have to permit me a smile here, because this business of still not understanding the reasons for their violence almost justifies what happened to poor Étienne,

I was invited to the 'boum-barricade.' That night I went over to the street that passes by the campus. A car stopped across from me. A squad of seven people gets out,

> This change of tense is always a little rough in Spanish. "Never mind the comments, girl," Patricio said.

One of them

> Here too, you can see, from people, which is feminine, he changes to one of them, masculine and with a club. What a language, you'll have to pay me double or I'll run out of gas,

hits me with a club while the others beat up on two boys who were walking close by. They make me get into the car and they start up, leaving the others lying on the ground. They keep on beating me along the way, threatening to kill me all the while (with an injection of cyanide or by drowning). After stopping in the courtyard of a building, where they continue clubbing me,

> here I must say that it's not clear whether they were only beating Étienne or whether there were others getting it in the courtyard too

they take me over in front of a Record shop, where they hold off torturing me because of the presence of witnesses. That was when they turned me over to the CRS people,

> another change of tense, these fellows must read Michel Butor, but without any moral benefit, naturally,

who took their turn at hitting me. Then they formed a circle and started playing 'different circus games,' making me run to avoid their blows and forcing me to shout: *Long live Mao, long live Mao!* Then they locked me up in a patrol wagon: punches, kicks, whacks with their helmets, for half an hour without interruption, fighting for the privilege of joining in the fun (there were two officers among them). After that they took me back to the 'undercover' car they had kidnapped me in in the first place. Only then (more than an hour after they had grabbed me) did they question me, and I was able to tell them that I wasn't a student and that I hadn't taken part in any confrontation with the police. In view of that, they threw me out onto the sidewalk 200 yards from the police station. Now I am in the hospital with a brain concussion (I lost consciousness three times during the course of that adventure). Period."

"So you see, Chile boy," Patricio said. "And the guy is a French citizen, just imagine if he'd been a greenhorn from Osorno or Temuco for example, yi, yi, yi, said Pérez Freire."

"Vell, at least they don't kill them the vay they do in Gvatemala or Mexico."

"Or in Córdoba and Buenos Aires, angel of love, don't take my country's inalienable rights away from it. Of course they don't kill them, for the moment, but not because they don't want to, only because there's what's called a scale of values and that scale hasn't got all the way down to their trigger fingers yet because there's still heavy industry, industrial relations, façades that have to be preserved. Hey, old girl, something tells me your son is crying, what happened to that mother instinct that's always getting so much praise, those fables you people invent to keep us away at least from the critical zone of the crib?"

"With good reason, love, because you people have a tendency to knock it over every time you get an onset of loving tenderness. *Your* son," Susana added, sticking out her tongue, "you say it as if you'd been at the movies that night instead of in bed."

"Are you sure it was in bed and not on the bath mat?" Patricio asked, grabbing her under the shoulders and spinning her around until she hit the ceiling with her head, an amorous operation that Fernando watched in amazement. They seemed to have forgotten about him for a moment, kissing and tickling, and they also seemed to have forgotten that Manuel was turning up the volume of his hoarse and pissy decibels. Naturally, it had to be at that moment, when the atmosphere was a bit confused, that the doorbell rang. Fernando waited a little, but since Patricio had disappeared with Susana and he could hear them calming Manuel down with laughter and demonstrations in no way inferior to the infant's auditory outbursts, he decided to open the door himself, always a disagreeable operation when the people arriving are friends of the house and find themselves face to face with someone they don't know and there's that moment of hesitation in which everyone is so polite, but each one asks himself what the fuck is going on, have I got the wrong apartment, at two in the morning it can be kind of hairy, and when things get straightened out and the period of looking at watches and of verbal explanations has gone on to the shaking of hands and self-introductions, there's always an aftertaste of general maladjustment, of a bad beginning to the ceremony which invalidates it liturgically, the eucharist that runs into a coughing spell and ends up as a shower of dough, those things out of sequence, the way it happens to certain automobiles on the assembly line, Lonstein being the worst of all, introducing himself with: "I am highly contornate," an expression that Fernando immediately took to be French, but vhy are you standing there in the doorway, please, so we came in and there hadn't been any mistake, we were in Susana and Patricio's apartment because even from the door Manuel and what else.

Probably that endless talk about the challenge, which they called the response, was getting on his nerves a little; probably Sara's letters just rose up out of verbal association or simply because they liked rising up (why couldn't memory arrange its whims, its tides, the petulance of giving or denying according to the humor and the rumor of the moment?); in any case, the one I told you had been recalling the letters for a while now while Marcos was commenting on or criticizing the most recent forms of response along the perimeter of Paris. The letters had been coming at the time a friend of Sara's was staying at the one I told you's, where he spent a month before going back to Argentina; he left them behind when he left because they were a little much for him too in spite of the fact that the one I told you had already gone ten years without seeing Sara, who had never traveled to Europe; his last picture of her was a demitasse spoon, Sara's hand making the spoon spin slowly as if she were afraid of hurting the sugar or the coffee, at three o'clock in the afternoon in a cheap restaurant on the Calle Maipú.

During those days when Marcos and Patricio and the rest of the gang were setting about organizing the Screwery, the one I told you seemed to understand that Marcos at least deserved to know about Sara's letters and he gave them to him to read one night while he was waiting for some important news on the phone (Marcos was waiting and Lonstein and the one I told you were there as always, the little rabbi inseparable and distant and the one I told you more or less; they were stirring sugar in their mugs too but without the slightest concern). I arrived while Marcos was reading the letters and I began to notice that the one I told you was taking them back as soon as they were finished, not even apologizing for leaving Lonstein and me out of it, although damned if it made any difference to us (it did make a difference to us, but damned if we'd say so). Yes, there's nothing new in that, Marcos had commented, but that's the same way it happens with accidents, they make an impression on you when your aunt's involved. Let me see the handwriting, Lonstein said, the content unrupts me completely. The one I told you had already put them in his pocket and limited himself to nodding at Marcos's comment. It wasn't that he didn't trust Lonstein, but, rather, because those letters weren't meant to have the little rabbi go into his graphological ecstasies over them, the radiaesthetic pendulum and that kind of rather disquieting psychospeleology that he practiced, starting with the use of pen and ink, the indentations and spaces and even the way the stamp has been affixed; as for Andrés, who knows why he was denied the letters, a kind of darkly Proustian resentment, suspecting that they would have interested Andrés for reasons different from those of Marcos or Lonstein and that he would have wanted to know more, in some way bring the image of Sara to that café on the Rue de Buci that had nothing in common with the lunchroom on the Calle Maipú. The one I told you was like that, in proportion to his powers he would share the game in his own way and he was even amused at the image since it was a matter of letters and cards which would be only for Marcos that night, even though they had nothing directly to do with the Screwery. As for him, a person who threw away so many letters, he hadn't only kept those of Sara's but would reread them sometimes, and in spite of that, it had never occurred to him to answer her. First, they weren't letters that called for an answer, but, rather, a behavior; besides, he would rather have seen Sara again, the oval of her face, which was his clearest memory along with her voice and the demitasse spoon, and also that intense and clear way she had of looking. October 2, 1969, from Managua, Sara wrote dear people, I have a long story for you.* Long, confused (it might even be amusing, although it doesn't seem so to me now) and it could be entitled "Sara, Or the Misadventures of Virtue in Central America." Of course I would first have to write the beginning part of the story: "How Sara Reaches Central America Through the Panama Canal Zone." The very idea of writing all that makes me feel fatigued, so I've decided in favor of a factual letter.

I felt the first shock with (. . .). Pepe, your friends the X's are very "formal" people. Do you know what that is? It's not having a bed for you, my dear, and it doesn't mean that they didn't or that they're bad people. They're wonderful, but from a different world, a different generation, a different mentality, a different life-style, *different-everything.* Pepe, Lucio, I don't know if it's true or not, but I'm sure of it, and after everything that happened (I was almost put in jail in Costa Rica) I'm surer every day and the fact is—please excuse me, this incoherence is due to the fact that there are three of us in one room here in Managua. It's worth describing. Ángeles is a black girl from Panama, I'm me, and John is an American. We said we were cousins and since we speak a horrible stew of English, slang from all different countries, and Spanish (I've got a Peruvian accent now) and also since we have that air of being untouched by everything around us, which everybody else touches right away, and since it's a kind of family air, they believed us. Other people have brought us together. Even if you don't believe it, gentlemen, each one of us decided this afternoon that we were sick of everything.

Sara's letters are authentic; the proof is at the disposal of any doubting Thomas who might like to see them, provided that first he request it in writing. Along with a few changes in some first names, personal passages have been left out as well as any references that might be politically compromising for third parties.

What is everything? Everything means: that people laugh at us on the street, that they point at us, that they insult us, and it's true, John's had stones thrown at him and I've learned to do a little slapping, and Ángeles answers with shouts and we help each other as best we can. It's not pathetic, but sometimes we cry, just because we thought it was different here, or that we weren't so different, or because we can't understand why they hate us.

So each one of us decided separately today *no* Lake Managua, *no* walking around, no nothing. We've stayed in the room with all the heat there is, and it rains on and off, and tomorrow we're going to El Salvador, where it will be just the same as here, and I'm trying to get ahold of a dress, John goes out with a huge bandage we put around his neck in the morning to hide his hair, and Ángeles (who doesn't go anywhere) is going back to Panama to put some money together and try to go live in some other country. I have the illusion that in Mexico it will be different, but the news from other people coming down from there is frightening. Oh, I was forgetting, the whole thing is that in these countries where poverty, prostitution, sickness, and filth eat your life away, they've begun a cleanup in the name of morality, religion, and law. Down with hippies! Filth, addicts, criminals. This on the part of customs officials, politicians, and the people, I just don't know. I don't understand. But they hate me, they hate us, I've had to hide all my beads and things and I have to wear my hair in a bun, I've tried to get something else instead of my knapsack, another thing that makes them get sick; they see a knapsack and they immediately tear it open and pull everything out, shoes, dirty clothes, necklaces, *mate* gourd and sipper, everything spread all over, and they look me over down to the smallest detail because besides being a hippie I might be a guerrilla fighter. And in the end, after receiving so many blows in the name of *Reason, Morality*, and everything else imaginable, maybe they're right. Never in my life have I felt the way I do now; it isn't only hate or pain, it's a mixture, and at the same time it comes on (believe me) with compassion and pity and I don't understand *anything*, well, worse than that, I just don't understand.

10/3/69

I'm on the bus now, going on by myself. Last night an Argentinian came to see me at the boardinghouse "Costa Rica" where we were staying and, even though he was stupid, he did me a great favor. He came to buy some clothes (we sell but nobody has any money) and he took me to his group where there were two Swiss, a Chilean, and a couple from Canada. Mistrust at first, we probed and tested each other, first to see if we could be trusted, one of the Swiss told me what the Mexican border is like, the one with Guatemala. Since I didn't believe him, he showed me his passport and his head. He had a visa, a letter from the Swiss consul, and eighty dollars. In Guatemala they held his money for three days but he was able to cross (he's going to the States too), but on the Mexican side they decided that his hair was too long (he wears it much shorter than you people) and that he had to produce a hundred dollars. Can you imagine what it feels like for a person who gets to Mexico after so many months of traveling and all that's left is Mexico and he's in the U.S.A. *and they wouldn't let him through*? That's the way I feel. They cancelled his visa, beat him up, and sent him back to Guatemala. And for twenty days he's been wandering around Central America trying to find someone to lend him the money just so he can get across the border. And all that because he *might* have been a hippie. But since it's well known that money doesn't abound among hippies, on top of everything else they've discovered the money dodge. You have to *produce your money*, and if they rob you when your back is turned, that's another problem. And don't ask me about the questions, why do we have to travel, or why to the States (almost all of us are going to California). Why they hate us, I don't know, I imagine just because we're different and we might be happy. And that's why they manage to make us so unhappy! I've tried to get close to the poorest people in every country and from Colombia all the way up here all I've found have been mockery, disdain, and hate. And the other people, the intellectuals and "artists," help sometimes but they're afraid and are looking after their own and right away they ask: but you're not like those immoral dirty gringos, are you? You're not going to get me in any trouble, are you? They're in the establishment up to their ears and they've forgotten the only important thing: life and the mind and everything else we talked about so many times, Pepe, and what I know you've never forgotten, Lucio. So now I'm going to San Francisco to find my family, to listen to my music, and to paint, and *above all* because I want to live like a living creature and not like a nut or bolt among my own people, I want to have a cracker for breakfast shared with love and I want to dedicate myself to opening my mind and my body and my life to life. Period.

So last night we all decided to separate again, since we'd discovered in Costa Rica that it's easier to cross the border that way, and today here I am traveling alone to El Salvador and I'll try to get [illegible]. Let me give you a detail. John helped me carry my bags. I had to get the bus at five in the morning and we slept with the light on because nobody in the boardinghouse would wake us up or lend us a clock because they saw the knapsacks, and "gringos" (little by little they've been calling us Argentines gringos) are dangerous. Ángeles and I bandaged him up before we went out, but everybody was sound asleep. We divided up the money Ángeles had, John and I didn't have more than five or six dollars apiece, and we left, me for my five o'clock bus, Ángeles for hers at six o'clock to Costa Rica, and John was staying behind another day to see if he could get work on a ship and get to the States that way. At the office a woman thought Ángeles was Nicaraguan and said to her: Doesn't that boy look like one of those hippies to you? His hair seems to be sticking out on this side!

Ángeles warned us in English and we left the office. They'd already begun to insult John. Some guy began to make nasty remarks to Ángeles, and everybody on this bus is looking at me from a safe distance and whenever somebody passes by I can hear him mutter something like: [illegible] filth, garbage, darling, and things like that . . . In Costa Rica, since we didn't know any better, we were traveling together, and it's not worth it, I'll tell you about that miserable trip another time. Besides, I've just found out that an Argentinian is traveling on this bus. You don't hear a La Paternal accent very often between Managua and Honduras. He seems to be a nice guy and he talks about Jan Kiepura and Palito Ortega. The road is like a swamp and the mud is flying all over the place. But the countryside is beautiful, the clouds crawl over the mountains and the sun finally comes out, just as I spent my last pennies on a [illegible] and a piece of pastry. Life is a mixture and it goes on, sometimes too much for me to take, I love you both, I really do, a lot, and I miss you.

Sarita

10/3/69

San Salvador.

And here I am sitting tonight on the bed (an army cot) that the director of television news of San Salvador set up for me. I had something to eat. And I'm going to go to sleep and I have a bathroom. And in addition to this Mr. [illegible] told me that he defended hippies in a debate he was in, that it doesn't seem so terrible to him that I wear jeans, and that he loves human beings. He does go on, doesn't he? Lots of kisses, Sarita.

October 6, 1969
San Salvador, El Salvador

. . . .

. . . which isn't at all simple with the emotive-mental-physical-psychic complications I've got caught up in. I can't make it, there's no way, it doesn't come out right for me, I'll never understand the world. I mean it isn't a problem of metaphysical realities. It's a problem of too much misery and decomposition. One of these days I'm going to write to Lucio, just to tell him what the refugee camps for Salvadoreans kicked out of Honduras are like, how they're received in their native country, and the varying amount of diseases you can detect there. I'm working as a volunteer for the International Red Cross, and not because I believe in individual help, but because nobody is doing anything, somebody has to help out with a census, don't you think? Along the way I've become everybody's friend, and already the compassion and the pain, the love and the distress I feel are "too much" as they say. The whole thing is beyond me. I don't understand, but I've already said that in other letters. I'm putting the finishing touches on a disguise that will help me travel in the future and I'm going to put a part of these dollars into it. I have a full list of the charges I almost went to jail for in Costa Rica and I'll use it as a guide to cure all those aberrations: eliminate the knapsack first, get rid of the books, especially the ones in English. I don't know whether or not I told you that I had to consult the Appleton-Cuyás that travels with me to convince a rather drunken captain, every inch a man, by God, that Alice in Wonderland wasn't communist propaganda, but nobody, not even the English-Spanish Appleton could convince him that it wasn't part of the dissolute hippie system of life. Well, no more slacks, a skirt below the knees, hair in a bun, no jewelry, and still and all I'll be suspect, I don't know whether because of my gringo look or because I have the habit of saying may I come in when I want to go in somewhere. But this way at least I won't have to be insulted on the street or have stones thrown at me and other things like that. There's no way out for me. Some people think I'm an emissary of the United Fruit Company, others an emissary of Castro (horrors), and others that I'm traveling with a load of good grass. In any case, your cable saved my life, because I'm practically out of things to sell, out of money, and waiting for the money order to arrive is nice waiting and has nothing to do with the anguish of going about getting some money together in order to cross a border that you already know about ahead of time, no, nothing doing (. . .). My God, I remember everybody, I feel as if I were splashing around in the muddy bottom of a garbage can, and now, luckily, soon, away, away . . .

With things like that, it was impossible for the one I told you to be surprised that on the very days he was giving Marcos Sara's letters to read, the supercivilized *Monde* published two news items that he added without comment to that kind of general file that was being put together and which Susana (but let's not get ahead of ourselves, as Dumas *père* would say at critical moments)

● ***Trente-cinq évêques d'Amérique centrale dénoncent la « constante violation des droits de l'homme en Amérique centrale »*** **dans un document diffusé à Mexico par le Centre national de communication sociale (CENCOS). Ce document, résultat des travaux de l'assemblée de l'épiscopat d'Amérique centrale, est signé notamment par les archevêques du Guatemala, du Salvador, du Nicaragua et du Panama.**

Thirty-five Central American bishops denounce "the constant violation of human rights in Central America" in a document distributed in Mexico by the National Center for Social Communication (CENCOS). The document, which came out of the sessions of the episcopal assembly of Central America, was signed by the archbishops of Guatemala, El Salvador, Nicaragua, and Panama, among others.

Refus d'une « abdication morale »

IL SE DONNE LA MORT PAR LE FEU PARCE QU'ON L'AVAIT OBLIGÉ A SE FAIRE COUPER LES CHEVEUX.

Un jeune homme de dix-neuf ans, Jean-Pierre Souque, qui demeurait rue Maurice-Berteaux, aux Mureaux (Yvelines), avait, lors d'un récent voyage en Angleterre, adopté la « philosophie hippy ». Il avait laissé pousser ses cheveux et adopté la tenue vestimentaire appropriée. Du coup, il fut en proie aux moqueries de ses camarades et des adultes. Il travaillait cependant à la société Mingory, 128, boulevard de Charonne, à Paris, où il était entré comme aide-cuisinier après avoir suivi les cours de l'école hôtelière.

Mais voici que, mercredi dernier, son patron lui donna un avertissement à propos de sa tenue... et, samedi matin, son père l'accompagna chez le coiffeur. Jean-Pierre subit sans protester. Et pourtant... l'après-midi, il quittait le domicile de ses parents et achetait du gas-oil. Puis, il se dirigea par un chemin peu fréquenté vers une ferme voisine des usines Renault de Flins. C'est là qu'un ouvrier de l'usine, regagnant son domicile, le découvrit sur le chemin de terre, mort, à demi-brûlé. Dans le sac qui lui avait servi à dissimuler le bidon de gas-oil, on trouva un carton sur lequel le jeune homme avait écrit : « La réponse est dans la boite aux lettres. » On y découvrit une lettre dans laquelle il expliquait qu'il ne pouvait accepter cette « abdication morale ». Il ajoutait en particulier : « Vous ne comprenez pas, vous, les adultes. Vous imposez votre expérience, vous jugez votre prochain. » Dans cette longue lettre, il déclarait en outre vouloir imiter les bonzes, préférant se donner la mort que d'accepter la « dictature » de la société.

REJECTION OF A "MORAL ABDICATION"

BURNS SELF ALIVE BECAUSE MADE TO CUT HAIR

A young man of 19, Jean-Pierre Souque, living on the Rue Maurice-Berteaux in Mureaux (Yvelines), had taken up the "hippie philosophy" during a recent trip to England. He let his hair grow and dressed in the manner usually associated with such cases. He soon became the butt of jokes from his friends and from older people. Nevertheless (sic) he continued working at the Mingory Society at 128 Boulevard de Charonne, in Paris, where he had obtained work as a kitchen helper after having studied at hotel school.

Only last Wednesday his superior called attention to his appearance . . . and on Saturday morning his father took him to a barber shop. Jean-Pierre gave in without protest. And, nevertheless . . . , in the afternoon he left home and bought some diesel fuel. Then he went along a little-used road that led to a farm near the Renault factory in Flins. A factory worker on his way home found him on the dirt road, dead and half-charred. In the bag he had used to hide the can of diesel fuel there was a note in which the young man had written: "The answer is in the mailbox." There they found a letter in which he explained that it was impossible for him to accept that "moral abdication." He went on specifically: "You adults don't understand. You impose your experience and you judge your neighbors." In his long letter he further declared that he had wished to emulate the bonzes, preferring to kill himself rather than accept the dictatorship of society.

Yes, probably the one I told you hadn't let me read those letters as a way of making an obscure sign that will or will not be understood, because for a long time I had suspected that tendency to reproach me for Francine, to be on Ludmilla's side in some way (she didn't have the slightest notion of the alliance, poor thing, because if she had she would have told him to go to hell), not to understand what no one really understood anyway, beginning with me. Coming to the café and seeing how the one I told you was holding the letters before the very hand the little rabbi had already reached out a little, everything was part of the sign; one more time all I could do was shrug my shoulders and think O.K., that Ludmilla or Francine or the one I told you had every right in the world in view of the state of things which, in view of a behavior which, etc. Because later on Ludmilla would arrive all fresh with Russian soul (three acts impregnated with steppes and despair can condition even a Pole as vital and as pushy as she) and I would feel a kind of presence of Francine in Ludmilla's presence, in the same way that being with Francine was feeling Ludmilla's undeniable closeness more and more, elements that the one I told you didn't appreciate too much and with good reason since they seemed to be extrapolated from the Russian play at the Vieux-Colombier even though I, if anyone wanted my opinion, would have said one more time (how many times have I said it to you, Ludmilla?) that there was no reason for it to be that way, that there was no reason for it to be that way, goddamn it, that there hadn't been any reason for it to be that way.

Fine, but in the meantime how could I deny to the one I told you his disdainful discrepancy, letting him know that keeping some letters in his pocket in order to make me feel that my concept of life was nothing but a petit bourgeois anachronism, the same as Francine's injured goodness was also her way of keeping what I really might have wanted from her, and Ludmilla's unwrinkled camaraderie raised the gray concrete wall between her and me higher and higher. What was there left for me to do outside of music and books except carry things to the bitter consequences that were final rather than predictable; at least if there had only been something else, a shortcut, a crossroad somewhere, one last exit that would give me what was mine without shattering other people's things. At times it had made me suspect that Marcos was sticking out his finger to me so that the parrot could climb on it, Polly want a cracker, but Marcos wasn't up to individual acts of charity, up to his neck in the Screwery, in the world that echoed with dispatches and bombings and executions and Lieutenant Calleys or General Kys, but always Marcos, oh yes, sometimes Marcos, his finger held out, Polly want the Screwery, eh? As at my place now, taking his ease with Lonstein at an ungodly hour, making phone calls to Jujuy or Reggio Calabria and the little rabbi with his apwals and paper flowers stained with blood and Ludmilla's footsteps on the stairs already. What difference did my private machine make, my stubborn urge for living Francine, living Ludmilla, and *Prozession*, the piano crossing over between the electronic sibilancies? The letters were more important, and the halo of blood around Lt. Calley, and that flood of news that Patricio (the one I told you was still trying to take in his surroundings, a rather foolish intent) was offering Fernando, newly arrived from his native Talca, at the moment when Oscar and Gladis were getting on an Aerolíneas plane in order to bring the Screwery fresh reserves, not to mention a certain Heredia who was boarding BEA in London, and Gómez who, or Monique. But Marcos wasn't one to insist, just the finger held out for the fraction of a second and on to something else; like the one I told you holding onto the letters, just a sign. And the little rabbi who all of a sudden sighs thinking about his raise, in the end the footsteps on the stairs are not Ludmilla's, we can go on talking a little more.

"Shall I demonstrate the war cry for you?" Marcos proposes.

"Fuck your mother," I tell him serenely but a little alarmed, "at one o'clock in the morning, just tell me please if you want to get me thrown out of this functional, all-white apartment secured after years and years of commercial drawing, you goddamned Cordovan."

"After so many telephonemes it's become an extratranscendental phonorama," Lonstein says, "there's no doubt but what he is proposing to you is the polyhowl of a soul imprisoned by the miasmas of masmedia, by God."

"All right," Marcos relents, "then I'll explain the cry to you in a theoretical way along with other forms of response that the kids have been trying out around here, the bus one, for example."

"That matter of a response is a kind of badly used epiphoneme," the little rabbi says, "really a hateful Gallicism, a hybrid of answering and kicking."

"You just listen," says Marcos, who doesn't worry about questions of language. "Just imagine that we're

in a neighborhood movie house at ten o'clock on the night the family went to see Brigitte Bardot prohibited for under eighteen ESQUIMAUX GERVAIS DEMANDEZ LES ESQUIMAUX GERVAIS DEMANDEZ LES ESQUIMAUX the family and another family and all families after a holy day of noble work, noble and holy, yes sir, work dignifies, your father started at fifteen, learn you lazy bums, your mother

<table>
<tr><td>your mother is a who</td><td>le-hearted lady</td><td rowspan="3">} Lonstein singit in G sharp major</td></tr>
<tr><td>who has a cun</td><td>ning little smile</td></tr>
<tr><td>that's full of prick</td><td>les all the while</td></tr>
</table>

and Aunt Hilaria who went through so much and Grandpa Víctor with his legs, supporting a whole family delivering charcoal from

seven in the morning till seven at night
the neighborhood, that foul Paris magma, that mixture of strength and moral trash, that thing that isn't the people even if no one knows who the people are but the neighborhood now, families at the movies, the ones who voted for Pompidou because De Gaulle wasn't around to be voted for any more

"Just a minute," Andrés says, "what's all that about the people and the family, or the family that isn't the people, or the neighborhood which since it's the families isn't the people, stop fucking around."

"You've missed the point," Marcos says. "I'm trying to give you an instantaneous gesture painting of the atmosphere of the Cambronne movie theater, for example, or the one in Saint-Lambert, those theaters infected with half a century of leeks and sweaty clothes, those sanctuaries where Brigitte Bardot lowers her panties so that the audience can see precisely what Article 465 allows, the fraction of time set by Article 467, and that all responses have to start at the bottom if they're going to be worth anything, in May it was the streets or the Sorbonne or Renault but now the comrades have realized that they have to respond the way someone shifts his guard between the fourth and the fifth rounds and then his opponent gets nervous, the sportswriter says. Let's say that you've already grasped the description that you didn't really need but which was a way of plugging into the threshold of the satori, you can keep right up with these words, little rabbi, and then just when Brigitte starts to turn the screen into one of mankind's stellar moments or rather into two and such a two, well, that can't be challenged or responded to in any way but unfortunately you have to take advantage of the state of rapture, of ecstasy if you follow me, so that the anticlimax will be more positive, at that precise moment Patricio gets up and gives out with a frightful shriek that goes on and on and on and what's going on, lights, there's a nut here, call the police, there's an epileptic, he's in the twelfth row, a foreigner, must be black, where is he, I think it was that one but since he sat down again maybe, yes, can't you see his curly hair, an Algerian, and you, why did you start hollering?"

"Me?" said Patricio.

"Yes, you," the usher said, lowering her flashlight because the more distant part of the audience was getting lost in the ribs of Bardot who was naked and completely unaffected by what had happened, and the spectators near the scene and the agent of what had happened were struggling with an understandable indecision between going on with the protest over the foreigner's scandalous behavior and not losing a quarter-inch of the half-turned silky thighs on a bed in a luxury hotel in the Forêt de Rambouillet where a certain Thomas had taken her with the aim of making her his before it was time to face the gourmet menu which is always foreseen in that kind of adventure among the rich, during all of which the usher's flashlight began bugging everybody including Patricio, and the usher was keeping it as low as she could and the beam of light flattened out right on Patricio's fly, which he seemed to find the most natural thing in the world, as proven by

"It happens to me sometimes," Patricio said.

"What do you mean it happens to you?"

SH
SHH!!!

"I mean I can't help it, it's something that comes over me like that and then."

(*ah ma chérie, ma chérie*)

"You'll have to leave the theater then, please."

SHHH!!!!!

"Ah *merde*," the usher said, "first they call me and now they won't let me do anything, but it's not going to be that way, oh no, what do they think I am, this is all I needed."

(*J'ai faim, Thomas*)

"Why do I have to leave the theater?" Patricio asked in a very low voice and without annoying anyone except the usher but that person in a convulsive geometric proportion. "It's like the hiccups, except stronger."

"LA PAIX!"
"A POIL!"

"The hiccups?" roared the usher, turning out her flashlight. "I'm going to call the police and we'll see what kind of hiccups they are, ça alors."

SHH!!!!

"Do whatever you want to," Patricio said, ssstillinawhissss-perrrr. "But it's not my fault, I've got a certificate."

That part about the certificate had its effect as always in France, and the beam of light began to make its way along the aisle precisely when things got to what everybody had wanted to see but as a tough was saying to his buddy as soon as they start fucking the bastards cut it, just when you get to see the pri

vileged thoughts of Lonstein, who's not too interested, but Marcos smiles with a look of revelation and says aspetta ragazzo that's not all because in the third row of the Pullman called balcony here whom do we have but Susana who was a veteran of the battle of the Sorbonne and had other commemorative medals, if they didn't throw her out of Paris it was because she had a twa ddle of a record in the files of the fuzz, but unnecessary clarifications when precisely Thomas, who isn't as much of a libertine as he had seemed, decides to marry Brigitte who's now flying over Acapulco in one of those jets that comes over now with blue sky all around and whiskey flows inside like I'd like to tell you and the first-class passengers are in the middle of a lunch served by Maxim's, I don't know if you're aware, until Susana just when Thomas gets to the hotel in the middle of the night and you can almost see those little sparks in the upper right-hand corner of the screen that precede the words THE END unless it's the next-to-the last reel because why should the last one have little stars since the projectionist has already put his jacket on and lighted up a Gauloise and has his hand near the switches and right then

"I know," Andrés says, "another shriek."

"He's very smart," Marcos confides to Lonstein. "This man from Buenos Aires is onto everything."

"But what good is it, if you don't mind telling me, starting something under circumstances that we might call restricted, I mean that a standard movie house probably has four hundred seats, which, compared to the population of France, gives us a proportion of one to fifty-nine million, more or less."

"You don't seem to give a damn about what happened to Susana," Marcos says.

"I don't give a particular shit. I have to admit, though, that she's got more balls than her comrade Patricio, because the second time is hairier."

"Since she's been busted two times," Marcos says. "They couldn't do anything to her, of course, because the people started scattering as soon as Brigitte did her thing and what can I say about Thomas and the ensuing infighting, everybody getting the hell out, so only the usher was left, in a rage, and it seems that at the precinct later on she called the cops bastards because they wouldn't take her complaint right away, and her Fernand who had to get up at six-thirty to go to work and who'd make his breakfast I'd like to know."

"She was the people," Andrés says. "The cops deserved what she called them and Susana almost did too when you come right down to it. What I'd really like to know now is what good was the shriek, because from the way you told it it seems

like nothing, really nothing, but the fact is that nothing plus nothing doesn't give nothing but sometimes a little of something, when people say nothing they don't mean pure nothing as everyone knows but a tiny little amount of something, and keep in mind that if the operation is pulled off well no cop or judge can do anything about it, the second try was at the Celtic and much better done, that is, Marcos himself in person and a certain Gómez, from Panama and a stamp collector, released the shrieks without getting up in their seats, Marcos in the middle of the ads, exactly between NUTS and KUNTZ, and Gómez in that part where Bibi Andersson lies face down on a bed with black sheets and they come out like roars from different parts of a theater attended mainly by scholarship students, without moving out of their seats they let out a shriek and there was nothing that could be done, one guy tried to hit Gómez but afterwards he apologized saying that he had tried to cure his attack with one of those backhanded slaps recommended in psychiatry texts when the potatoes are too hot and the mental patient has stuck pieces of glass in his mouth for some self-punishment and to ruin the doc's reputation along the way. It was impossible to do anything serious to them, absolutely, especially to Marcos who stayed very quiet after the shriek, and four or more ladies who at first had turned red shifting almost immediately into the complementary color that foretells the worst of tortures, ended up agreeing with interfamilial whispering that the poor boy must have been suffering from although when it was Gómez's turn nobody was buying it and there was talk of unseating and out onto the street with them, but the darkness is protective and Bibi Andersson too, naked finally, if you paid eight francs for that you're not going to miss it because of some kind of chirping or other, except that

"The one at the Opéra was wild," Marcos said.

"Oh, at the Opéra," I said, refusing to marvel at anything.

"Precisely at the moment the swan comes out, I don't know if you've seen it," Marcos explained. "One of Wagner's."

"It's not right," Lonstein said. "Twisting the neck of the swan now that we've had Donald Duck for quite some time, you people have got your birds mixed up, by God."

That's how they went on, with quite a bit of gin and shrieking, until the news that after two weeks they hadn't been able to replay the number for tactical reasons, that is, people were talking about it on the street and were going to the movies with the aim of cracking the skull of the first person who yawned, people who paid their taxes and doing things like that to them, no sirree.

"A success," Marcos said. "Why stick with temples of the seventh art when you've got buses and cafés. In cafés it doesn't come off too well because in the first place everybody is talking in shouts and there's a very high decibel level, and afterwards you don't know why it doesn't matter to people to be bothered as they sit over a beer or a cinzano as much as when it's a movie, somebody should make a study of that. But on the other hand on

> "I've still got three hypogeal flowers," Lonstein threatened, "one of yellow paper and the other white, but I can saussure you that they've got some stains that you might say that

any bus line at all, let's say 94, which boasts a clientele that is rather petit bourgeois, Lucien Verneuil is the specialist and he's already taught the technique to Patricio, Susana, and the others who go around more or less giving responses everywhere. First the bell to signal the stop, properly (not to mention that you're well dressed and carrying a book or a notebook under your arm to accentuate the impression of an intellectual), and when crunch the mastodon puts on its brakes right next to the curb, Lucien Verneuil goes over to the driver and holds out his hand. The driver's glacial look or (a variant) gesture translatable as

What the hell
Eh
Is he crazy or just an idiot
Why don't you stick your hand

but Lucien Verneuil puts on an almost pastoral smile, something like a bowl of alphabet soup for a good child, an innocent smile like that can't be resisted and the hand still outstretched waiting for that of the honest driver who begins to (option) purple/ green/black/glassy/, and then

"I want to thank you for the ride," says Lucien Verneuil. I don't have to tell you what the answers are, at least Marcos doesn't bother to list them. Lucien Verneuil: "You drive this bus with a sense of responsibility that not every bus driver shows these days." Or: "I can't get off this bus without showing you my gratitude." Or: "I could never let myself end this trip without first bearing public witness to the pleasure it has been for me and I ask you to pass that on to the administration of the RATP." The variants at this moment: (1) A breaking off of contact, getting out of the seat, a catapultic shove in the direction of the sidewalk; (2) foaming at the mouth; (3) a deathly pallor and a tetanic trembling of body and extremities. Subvariants of the *environment* (especially old women and gentlemen with Legion of Honor rosettes): Call the police/there's no respect (sub-sub-variant: . . . religion) any more/The young people of today, where are we heading/He's going to make us late for work (multiple infra-variants)/Cursing and threats. While all that is going on the conductor is coming from his glass cage at the back and along the aisle precisely when Lucien Verneuil, who has a chronometer in his eyes, gives a very courteous salute to yr obedient servant for the last time and goes down the two steps beyond which begins the territory that no conductor will tread for the purpose of a kick because his prerogatives, etc.

"That's all very fine," I tell Marcos, "but the day before yesterday a boy in Lille committed suicide by burning himself alive as a protest over the state of things in France and he's the second one to do it in this country, not counting what you read about in dispatches from abroad. Don't you think that next to something like that

"Of course I think," Marcos says, "except that as the Japanese hymn says drop by drop the seas are formed and the grains of sand will become a rock covered with moss or something like that. Jan Palach was only one, there are all those Czech students and they're not sleeping, not to mention over four bonzes. You're quick to dismiss things. So just wait till I tell you about another form of response that only yesterday raised a big ruckus in the Vagenande restaurant, and it's going to be repeated for a week starting today in a lot of others as long as we've got the dough because you should see what the chow comes to in places like that. Gómez went with me at one in the afternoon, the time for fat ladies and dudes with fat bankrolls, you've seen the art-nouveau surroundings and the kind of moth-eaten atmosphere that gives it a special prestige. We asked for leeks in vinegar and pepper steak, red wine and mineral water, a responsible and proper order as you can see. As soon as they brought the leeks, Gómez stood up and proceeded to eat them on his feet, one leek after another, talking to me as if nothing were wrong. A statistic of the looks: eighty percent surly, ten percent uncomfortable, three percent amused, another three percent undaunted, four percent interested (piles acting up, paralysis of the spine, just crazy?). The waiter with another chair, Gómez who tells him no, thank you, I always eat like this. But, sir, you'll be uncomfortable. On the contrary, it's quite functional, the action of gravity is better and the leek descends to the stomach as if it were being pulled along, that's good for the duodenum. You're putting me on. Not in the least, you're the one who's come to annoy me, with laudable intentions, I'm sure, but you can see. Then the maître d'hôtel, a rumpled old man with kind of fish eyes. Excuse me, sir, but here. Here what? Here we're accustomed to. Of course you are, but I'm not. Yes, but just the same. The gentleman isn't bothering anyone, I put in, cleaning my plate with a piece of bread because the leeks were great. Not only isn't he bothering anyone, because he's eating with the greatest elegance and refinement, but you're the one who's come to bother him, not to mention the waiter, so that. The Ortegan circumstance deeply involved in it all, ladies chuchuchuchuchu in the ears of other ladies, a rolling of eyes, scandalous, people come here to sit down and chat, go eat at a lunch counter. Then Gómez, wiping his lips with Brummellian elegance, I swear to you: If I am eating on my feet it is because I have been living on my feet since the month of May. I could tell you about the row, bread all over the floor, the cashier calling the police, the pepper steaks getting crisp on the grill, the uncorked bottle of wine and everything unpaid for, you can imagine, because as long as we left the bastards would accept the loss, but then and there Gómez sat down like a count, holding the folded napkin in his hand, and said in a fairly loud voice: I do this for my fellow man, and I hope that my fellow man will learn to live on his feet. A great silence, except for two or three chuckles from guilty consciences, believe me, not many people enjoyed their lunch. Tomorrow we're going to repeat it in a bistro on Bastille, they'll probably break our asses because the climate there is different, but maybe, who can tell

Enter Ludmilla

with her third-act look and still wearing makeup, she got into her car almost before the curtain came down and she's starving, she has some wine while I prepare an omelet and Lonstein, a determined ritualist to the delight of Ludmilla, begins with the other theater for the nth time, so you're Russian? no, my parents were Polish, but isn't it true that you work at the Vieux-Colombier? yes, that's true, ah, I was wondering, because this one here is such a faker, and Ludmilla enchanted because the little rabbi always finds new variants, something that's not habitual in the Vieux-Colombier and the Polish girl believes in the free theater and things like that. Do you want three eggs and an onion? asks Andrés to see if he can get her over to his side a little, oh yes, lots of everything, Ludmilla says dropping into an easy chair and letting the little rabbi light a Gauloise for her and fill her glass with wine as he starts out on a new version of his trip to Poland two years before, probably false, Marcos thinks as he waits for one last long-distance call and is kind of distantly present at the programming of the omelet and the main square in Cracow, the violet color of the square at dusk/It's more orangey, Ludmilla says, of course I was very small/The flower stands and that café in the basement of the tower where they drink a kind of hippocras or hydromel or something hot that has clove and cinnamon and myrrh and aloes and climbs up into your head/The last time you told me it was a kind of ancient beer, Ludmilla says, only accepting the variants within a somewhat secret system/We were talking about you, the little rabbi comes back, offended, but Ludmilla feels so well and the wine after the interminable third act, the smell of the omelet as it comes from the other room like dusk in Cracow, Lonstein must be served, rituals must be fulfilled, let's see, where are you from, sir, I've been here awhile, madam, and what do you do in Paris, I, well, it's a little rough to explicate it before the omelet, but if you want me to later on

"C'est toi, Laurent?" Marcos asks almost before the phone rings.

"Neither before nor after," I request as I telepathically take care of the healthy swelling of the omelet while I set the table with meritorious speed, by table there being understood a paper napkin with a purple design and half a bottle of red wine plus a newly cut loaf of bread, tender and simple operations for you, Ludlud, for you there in your chair, tired and small although as far as small, no way, five six and what can I say about weight, but small because I want you to be when I think of you that way and even when I look at you and kiss you and you, but none of that now, and your straw hair, your ever-so-green eyes, that snub nose that rubs across my face sometimes and fills me with stars and salt and pepper, two leaves of lettuce left over from lunch, a little sad looking because vinegar tires out vegetables, come eat Lud, come quickly old pigeon-roost player, piece of eastern sky, *culito lindo*, here in this chair and now I'll make some coffee for toolemone, ristretto, yes, ristrettissimo like a little Chardin painting all substance and light and perfume, coffee that will condense the magic arts of night like those songs by Leonard Cohen that Francine gave me and that I like so much.

"When he gets started," thinks the one I told you.

"Why don't you want him to explain to me what he does in Paris?"

"After the omelet, you repulsive necrophile," I tell her. "This is the only part of the psychodrama that you two never change. Can't you see that Marcos has to describe the new style of response down to the fine points for me?"

"I want him to tell what he does in Paris," Ludmilla says.

"Hey, you're going to owe me a wad with your phone calls."

"Au revoir, Laurent," Marcos says, "n'oublie pas de prévenir ton frère. That's it, old man, and you, girl, eat hearty."

"I want him to tell," Ludmilla says, but for Marcos of course death is much less important than life, so that he goes on right there to talk about Roland's going into the little grocery store and taking a long time to pick out one of those regular-sized eggplants ("mm, mm, it smells of onions, mm, mm")

with Madame Lépicière looking at him out of the corner of her eye waiting for him to decide, watching him let go of one eggplant and immediately pick up another, *feeling it*, Madame Lépicière arguing hoarsely that the city, Roland dropping the eggplant into the basket and looking at Madame Lépicière as at a yet unclassified hairy beetle, the customers protesting over the delay, onlookers crowding around and Roland still looking at Madame Lépicière until everything begins to take on the atmosphere of a thoroughgoing row and then Roland putting his hand very slowly into his pants pocket and little by little drawing out a piece of string, pulling on the roll unhurriedly and letting it drop to the floor, pulling all the while while Patricio waiting on the sidewalk until then, Patricio coming in with an air of great assurance and determination and very pompous, going over to Madame Lépicière, articulating clearly PO-LICE, showing her a green card and putting it away before she could see that it's for the Jeunesses Musicales de France, grabbing the end of the string and looking at it attentively, pulling on the end while Roland keeps feeding the string out of his pocket, people all clustered around

"Not a word. Come with me."

"But I was going to buy some eggplants," Roland says. A great tug on the string, which already measures twenty feet between pocket and floor. Do you think you can upset the routine of a retail establishment. But I was only. Not a word, it's only too clear (inspecting the piece of string closely). And what's this. Some string, sir. Ah. So, you come along with me immediately or I'll send for the wagon. But I was only.

"Five pounds of potatoes," says a lady who would like to start the normal flow of events up again because child alone on fifth floor.

"You see," Patricio says, pulling on the string. "Unnecessary disturbance of commercial activities, you don't seem to realize that a consuming society has a *rhythm*, sir, a *cadence*, sir. These ladies have no time to waste because if they waste it and begin to look at what's around them in any detail, what are they going to notice?"

"I don't know," Roland says, feeding out more string.

"They're going to notice that potatoes have gone up five cents a pound and that tomatoes are twice what they were a year ago."

"The pair of them are in cahoots," an old man full of empty bottles and battle scars discovers. "Ils se foutent de nos gueules ceux deux-là."

"And that they have to pay for the plastic containers that aren't returnable and for the advertising campaign for the new soap powder that washes just the same every time as it did before, so it's important not to upset the rhythm of sales, you have to let them buy and buy without looking too much at the prices and the packaging, in that way society will develop quite nicely, believe me."

"And are you two putting on this act so that we can learn that everything is sky high?" asks the lady with the child all alone. "You could have saved your time, we've got troubles enough without your making us waste time on top of it, five pounds of medium potatoes, si vous plaît."

"You get out of here or I'm going to call the police," says Madame Lépicière who no longer has any faith in green cards.

"All right," Patricio says, and helps Roland get his string together and put it back in his pocket, "but you yourself have heard how this lady is on our side."

"Not on your life," the lady says in alarm, "but prices really are going up all the time."

"And you do very well in protesting about it," Patricio says.

"I'm not protesting," the lady protests, "I'm just saying it's true, what else can I do?"

They go on like that for some ten minutes and in the afternoon it's Gómez and Susana in the GALERIES RÉUNIES on the Avenue des Ternes at the time when all the fat women in the neighborhood are buying white and colored and bibs and sanitary napkins and panty hose, and at the bottom of the escalator and over every counter there is a huge sign with the slogan of the sale so well conceived by one of the two hundred thousand francs a month brains of the establishment

THE CLEAN SWEEP OF THE YEAR

and Gómez waits for the greatest possible number of people to be gathered on the ground floor and also the guard in blue who is directing the fat women in all directions, shoes third floor, graters basement, and only then does he ask him in a friendly way if in the Galeries Réunies they only sweep up once a year, in a friendly way but so that several fat women and their husbands or children can hear the question and various heads turn in the direction of the guard who fastens on Gómez the look of a camel with a convulsive cough, and of course not, sir, what are you trying to insinuate.

"I'm not insinuating anything," Gómez says. "But if they do sweep everyday as cleanliness demands, I don't understand why they put up signs where they cynically proclaim that they've done the clean sweep of the year."

"It's incredible!" Susana interrupts, dropping a pair of stockings into the basket with the slippers great bargain twenty francs. "Is this how the store fights against the danger of polio, then? Poor children! Look at that little girl over there playing with the nylon panties, contaminating herself!"

"Please, miss," says the guard who is no fool. "If you've come here to start something there's nothing left for me to do but."

"It's already been started," Gómez says demagogically addressing the girl's mother and the stupefied customers. "They themselves admit that they only sweep once a year. Can you calculate the number of germs that collect in that time? In every padded bra, in every lipstick! And we come in here and BUY! BUY THEM! OH!"

"You get out of here or I'll throw you out," the guard roars.

"You just try," Susana says grabbing one of the slippers

twenty francs. "Besides passing the disease on to us, just look at that poor child who's already turning pale, she most certainly will wake up with the symptoms tomorrow, yes, and you people there not saying a word!"

The one I told you, Lonstein, and I sat there too without saying anything while those microagitations gave us the impression that they were not worth very much, and one must admit that Marcos himself considered them more as a bit of fun with one phone call after another, because after a certain Laurent there followed Lucien Verneuil, Gómez, all people for whom twelve o'clock at night seemed to be a very telephonic hour, especially if the telephone was mine. The great defender of the shriek and other disturbances turned out to be Ludmilla who was incubating her omelet with an air of enormous satisfaction, and who must have filled Marcos with joy when she said that the activities of the group were vox populi and especially two reserve vigilantes in every theater (tot it up, in Paris, France, alone, and add Marseilles, Lyons, and all the rest), in any case and according to Ludmilla who belonged to the guild, the last shriek in the Théâtre du Châtelet precisely as the romantic tenor was melting away in an aria full of whispering and wingèd music had unleashed one of those rows that always end up with other concomitants, that is, night court, newspaper coverage, fines, and diverse civil and penal consequences.

We were still talking about those things when a fellow nobody knew and who turned out to be from Talca opened the door of Patricio's apartment for us, and so we all ended up drinking *mate* and grappa, with Manuel being passed from hand to hand because the little brachycephalic had decided upon a separate response with his own shrieks as if two in the morning, et cetera, so that turns of rock-a-by-baby/in the treetop while Susana took a break because tomorrow is a holiday/and the day after too. Thin and peevish, Patricio did not seem to find it anomalous that so many people should pile in at such an hour without any apparent reason apart from Southamericanism and all that went with it, I refer to Ludmilla's inventing a complete theatrical production for Manuel, for Manuel and maybe for me too, because that night the only bridge I'd had to her was the omelet, setting the table bridge for Ludmilla and beating the omelet bridge mm mm all those onions mm, although in any case even if we had been alone we wouldn't have talked much, the gray concrete wall would have arisen just the same and maybe worse than now with Susana's laughter and the dialogue on poisonous mushrooms between Lonstein and Fernando, with the distant calm of Marcos looking at us as he always seemed to look at what he was trying to see well, behind the smoke of his cigarette, that is, his eyes drooping and his hair in his face. Why then did it occur to me that Ludmilla's games with Manuel (she seemed to be playing the role of the Chinese emperor's mechanical nightingale or something like that for him) were also for me, a cryptic language, a last call as if in some way my long beating of the omelet had also been a call, a hoped-for bridge, those poor things that can still stay with us when we're with other people who neutralize the solitude two-fold, the direct look, the first word of the first phrase of the first interminable good-by. Then the gears of the mechanical nightingale flew off in all directions, Ludmilla clown mime saying it all with fingers and elbows and tricks which were bringing about a happiness in Manuel that was closer and closer to sleep, an occasion that Susana could not miss to lift him slowly up from the rug and, followed by Ludmilla the mime (a Chinese procession with lanterns, a triumphal march of the legitimate nightingale), carry him to the bedroom. Andrés watched them go out, slowly looked for a cigarette; Patricio and Marcos were talking in a low voice, the Screwery of course, two minutes wouldn't go by without one of them going to the phone, those people wanted to make the revolution on the basis of little numbers and don't forget the ants (they insisted very much on that), tell your brother to send the fruit, romantic telephonic cryptic cybernetic. The one I told you, who was also on that rather ironic wavelength, thought that Andrés was hanging a little behind as always, too lost in what Ludmilla had just done, clinging, in any case, to a version of the world that those others, telephonic cybernetic people from Buenos Aires and Córdoba ("tell him to call Monique at eight o'clock") understood in a different way, as in another way so many Latin Americans were finally beginning to understand everything in the world. Poor Andrés was stuck right in the middle of the previous generation and he didn't seem to get too deep into the jerk and the twist of things, to say it another way, the boy was still in the tango of the world, the tango of the immense majority even though paradoxically that immense majority was the one that was starting to say enough and beginning to move. Oh, oh, the one I told you kidded, the immense majority still hasn't understood that beautiful image, or it has understood and hasn't been able to put it into practice, for one Patricio or one Marcos there are droves like Andrés, anchored in Paris or in the tango of their days, in their loves and their aesthetics and their private little turds, still cultivating a literature full of decorum and national or municipal prizes and Guggenheim Fellowships, a music that respects the definition of the instruments and the limitations of their use, not to mention structures and closed orders, there it is, everything has to be closed for them even though afterward they applaud Umberto Eco a lot because that's what's done. "It would be better for you to wait for me at Madame Bonnier's store," Marcos was telling a guy who must have been hard of hearing because it was the third time already, Marcos's patience on the telephone deserved a prayer book with little gold corners, thought Andrés who was sleepy and was up to here with the poisonous mushrooms that Lonstein and Fernando were still cataloguing in the region of Talca, Chillán, and Temuco. I had no idea that your country was so mushroomy, the little rabbi was saying in amazement. Of course, I can get you catalogues if you vant, Fernando proposed. You've got to come see mine. You've got a mushroom? Of course, in my room. Vhere, in your room? Of course, I'm going to invite all these others too, it's about time they got interested in serious things. Like Susana and Ludmilla, busy in the more than serious task of putting Manuel to sleep as he seemed to be waiting for new performances by the mime Ludlud and would not let himself be undressed too easily, give me that footsy, take that out of his mouth, naked finally but still a twisting earthworm, face up, face down, they gave him their beads and their bracelets and made him swallow a teaspoonful of tranquilizer, Manuel was falling asleep and they stood beside the crib, smoking and waiting because they knew his wiles, exchanging impressions of Fernando who seemed to be a nice guy, a little innocent according to Susana, wait till he gets caught up with your husband and Lonstein and Marcos and you'll see what happens to his innocence. Of course, Susana said, that's really why he came, he was sent to us by somebody safe, the boy seems a little on the dummy side, but that won't last, hey, look at my son, what do you call that. Manuel was sighing in his dreams, his hand had gone down erratically until it found his little tool; he was holding it delicately between his fingers, opening his legs a little. He's got promise, Susana said twisting with laughter, but Ludmilla was watching without laughing, Manuel must have been dreaming, God knows what they dream about at his age, probably dreams that are ahead in time and Manuel is going to bed with a mulatto girl from Honduras or something like that. Maybe, Susana admitted, but you really do have a morbid imagination, it's easy to see that Chopin is your fellow countryman, those nocturnes that fill your face with cobwebs from a tomb, in any case that business of the mulatto girl from Honduras, poor little Manuel. Laughing without making any noise was deadly, especially for Ludmilla who the more she covered her mouth the more her nose became a peanut vendor's horn, Patricio had to come to put order in the ranks, what the hell is this separatist and discriminatory gynoecium, the men are demanding women, what are you laughing at so much? Oh, just like me, imagine, at the age of nine my aunt would shrivel my soul with "hands under the pillow," and God knows what she was doing with hers with the excuse of being older and single. Come, my lovelies, there's a whole thing out there about poisonous mushrooms that's beginning to give me the shivers, as they say, Andrés is either sad or asleep, come boil us up some *mate* before I have to give you a whack on the ass.

"Real macho stuff," Ludmilla said to Susana.

"You," Patricio said, "should make arrangements with this one to come by on Saturday or Sunday to give us a hand preparing the cigs and the twigs."

"She doesn't know what you're talking about, cool devil," Susana said as she looked at Ludmilla's stupefied face. But it didn't take long because they were talking about it in the living room, a microexperiment by Gómez and Lucien Verneuil in the restaurant on the Rue du Bac where Gómez sweated over the dishes he washed.

"South Americans are all washing something in this psychoputanic city," Lonstein protogrunted. "There's a sign in that, an indication I can't quite get, something hermetic in the detergents. You'll see, it'll be your turn to wash something as soon as you need some dough," he told Fernando. "Proballockly cars, it's obvious that any set of coveralls will fit you, not like me, I have a hard size to find."

"Sometimes I have trouble understanding vhat you say, but getting back to the mushroom on the lapageria vines . . ."

"Just a minute," Patricio said, "you two have got me nine months pregnant with your mushrooms, and we have to teach Ludmilla here the art of the used twig, so let's see if you can move it with that *mate* and we can turn to serious matters, you Marcos, you know the details, not to mention your hick accent which is the joy of my life."

"I was telling these people," Marcos explained patiently, "that since Gómez was always trusted in that bistro and the kitchen is right next to the corner where they sell cigarettes, it wasn't hard to replace twenty packs of Gauloises and twenty boxes of matches with the ones these kiddies had fixed. Monique was the lookout having a tomato juice at the bar while Lucien Verneuil called the owner from the telephone on the corner to distract his attention, not at all easy. Then Roland replaced Monique because at any moment the owner would become deductive and would put together telephone + tomato juice + Panamanian dishwasher, three equally disagreeable things if you think about it."

"It pains me to say so, but this is utterly inane," Lonstein said looking for a book among Manuel's latest bibliothecophagic hecatombs. "You're right, this is miniagitation, infrabatrachomiomachy."

"Let him go on," Andrés said, "then we can tell him what we think, all right?"

"It all started almost immediately, a customer from the neighborhood asked for some cigarettes and a glass of vermouth at the bar, it seems that he had lunch at the bistro occasionally and was a friend of the owner's. Just imagine the moment when he opens the pack of Gauloises and finds them all different sizes, he takes one out because his kind is never convinced that easily that the established order has fallen, and he comes up with a smelly butt. The owner comes running over, Roland becomes very interested in the customer's strange case, they take out another cig and then another and they're all butts that have been smoked down to different lengths. I have to tell you that at first it wasn't that that left them stupefied so much, but the fact that the pack had an unpolluted look about it, fresh out of the factory, since Monique and Susana have a technique that I don't have to tell you about, and let it be said in passing that you should leave your butts in that ashtray because in a few days the girls are going to fix up another round."

"They trapped me," Ludmilla confessed to Andrés.

"Grotesque," said Lonstein, "but with a certain indefimultiple beauty. I take back what I said about being inane, but not the feeling of unethicundity."

"And that's what they're up to when a kind of roar is heard at the bar and it's an old woman who's just bought some twigs and is trying to light her cigarette to soften the swill they drink there which is a mixture of beer and lemonade. A monotonous recurrence, as this one might say, but quite effective because with the fifth burned-out match the old woman lets out a roar and turns the box upside down on the bar and out of the fifty there are only three that are any good, so poor Senecta calls upon all creation as her witness and raises a row wanting to know why, and the owner doesn't know which way to turn, Gómez who looks out to see what's going on with a studied idiot look, Roland pouring oil on the fire and saying that everything's turning to shit in this country and bringing up the war of 1914, the colonies, the Jews, poliomyelitis, and hippies. A phone call to the distributor of cigs and matches, second phase of the uproar, from the booth you could hear the owner's voice outdoing Chaliapin. Now the success of the matter meant that it was time for at least three analogous cases so that it would pass on to the journalistic level, without which it would have no reality as MacLuhan has already explained

"I'm the one who said that," Lonstein said offended.

and luckily we could count on others infiltrated into like lunchrooms in Belleville and Parc Monceau, moral an article in *France-Soir* that left everyone wondering what was going on now if cigarettes, those perfect things that assure a person he is awake, normal, and with a government that has a firm hand on the tiller of the ship of state, but then it means that something's not working and it's no longer a matter of plunking down one franc fifty just like that and coming away confidently with a pack of cigs in your pocket and when you get to your modest home you find it full of slugs or spaghetti with meat sauce."

"Speaking of spaghetti and especially slugs," Lonstein said, "you're all invited to my place to watch the mushroom grow."

"It's probably still better than infantile things like this," I said, collapsing with fatigue. "Look, one of these days someone in the police is going to get fed up with you and just wait and see the clean sweep toward all borders, the postcards I'll get from Belgium and Andorra."

"It would seem that you're making a special effort not to understand," Susana said, passing me a rather weak *mate*.

"He's not making any effort at all," Ludmilla said, "he always acts like that."

Marcos was looking at us as if from afar, but Susana and Patricio were trying to start a fight with me, and it was one of those why live at all if you're nothing but indifference/it's like a line from a song/at least Ludmilla is going to help us set up more boxes of twigs/oh yes oh yes/and there's Fernando who's just arrived and already understands better than you what's going on in France/vell, it's still a little hard for me/I thought I had invihospitalitied you, but you people are logobifurcating in. a different direction/explain that business about the mushroom/impossible, the mushroom proliferates on this side of exegesis/change the *yerba*/there isn't any more/and so they began to understand that it was three-twenty and that some of them had to work the next morning, but first Patricio took out a clipping and handed it to Marcos who handed it to Lonstein who handed it to Susana. Translate it for Fernando, Patricio commanded, and in Uruguay

Uruguay

UN COMMANDO D'EXTRÊME GAUCHE DÉROBE DES DOCUMENTS A L'AMBASSADE DE SUISSE

L'ambassade de Suisse à Montevideo a été attaquée vendredi par quatre gérilleros appartenant au Front armé révolutionnaire oriental (FARO), aile extrémiste de l'organisation d'extrême gauche des Tupamaros.

Les quatre assaillants sont arrivés à l'ambassade à bord d'un camion volé. Après avoir tenu en respect l'ambassadeur et les fonctionnaires présents, ils sont repartis en emportant des documents, deux machines à écrire et une machine à photocopier. C'est la première attaque de ce genre commise contre une ambassade étrangère à Montevideo, où de nombreuses attaques de banques et de casernes ont eu lieu au cours des derniers mois. — *(A.F.P., A.P., Reuter.)*

an extreme left-wing commando group seizes documents in the Swiss embassy. The embassy of Switzerland in Montevideo was attacked on Friday by four guerrilla fighters belonging to the Armed Revolutionary Front of the East Bank (FARO), the extremist wing of the extreme left-wing Tupamaros. The reporter puts in so many extremes that you can't see the middle. The four attackers drove up to the embassy in a stolen truck. After holding the ambassador and the officials present with their hands in the air, because that business of "holding in respect" must mean hands up, they left, taking documents, two typewriters, and a photocopy machine. It is the first attack of this kind against a foreign embassy in Montevideo, where during the past few months numerous attacks have taken place against banks and army posts, AFP, AP, and Reuters. Change the *yerba* yourself, I can't do everything.

"Hairy old Tupamaros," Patricio said.

During all this Lonstein was showing a sort of project for a poem to Fernando who was tied into everything that night, while I amused myself by asking them one more time, Marcos but mostly Patrisusana, what was the sense of those bits of more or less risky mischief they were dedicating themselves to with a band of Frenchmen and Latin Americans, especially after the reading of the Uruguayan dispatch which made them look smaller and smaller, not to mention all the other dispatches that had been read that afternoon and where as usual there was a large quota of people tortured, killed, and imprisoned in several of our countries, and Marcos looked at me without saying anything, as if enjoying me the big fuckup while Susana came at me with a fork in each hand because in its own way the business of the shrieks in the movies had been just as risky as ripping off two typewriters from the Swiss ambassador, and Patricio seemed to be looking for permission or something like that from Marcos (the kids must have been hierarchically well organized even though it wasn't noticeable on the outside, luckily) to pour an Iguazú torrent of what Lonstein would have called arguminsults at me, and finally when Ludmilla had fallen asleep on me on the rug and I realized it was really time to leave, the poem or whatever it was had begun to circulate and there was no way out, apart from the fact that Patricio, a little startled by a content he hadn't expected, handed it to Susana commanding her to read it aloud. For which reason before leaving we had the Lonsteinian privilege of the

FRAGMENTS OF AN ODE TO THE GODS OF THE CENTURY

Cards to feed an IBM machine

At the side of the road

stop

greet them

offer them libations

(traveler's checks welcome)

AZUR

SHELL MEX

TOTAL

ESSO BP YPF

ROYAL DUTCH SUPERCORTEMAGGIORE*

* Its power is noise, flight, blitzkrieg. They are offered blood, naked woman, fountain pens, Diner's Club cards, weekend pleasures, haggard-eyed adolescents, poets with fellowships (creative writing), lecture tours, Camelot plans; every senator bought is good for a year's indulgence, etc.

The way stations at the side of roads
sanctuaries
snack bars and urinals
the flaccid lingams that the priest in a blue uniform and a visor
cap lifts and puts into the orifice of YOUR CAR, and you voyeur
up above who pays
FIVE GALLONS THE TIRES THE WATER THE
WINDSHIELD
venite adoremus
hoc signo vinces
SUPER: the safest
PUT A TIGER IN YOUR TANK
PUT IN THE LINGAM OF THE GOD
His temple smells of fire
TOTAL AZUR BP SHELL MEX
His temple smells of blood
ELF ESSO ROYAL DUTCH*

* Major gods (omitted are the unnameable ones, the lesser ones, the *paredroi*, the doubles, the vicarious servants; the cult of the major gods is public, ill smelling, and noisy, it is presented as *Positive*, as *Celebration*, as *Freedom*. A day without major gods is the paralysis of a nation of men. The major gods are the most recent ones, we still don't know if they will stay or will abandon their worshipers. Unlike Buddha or Christ they are a problem, an uncertainty; it is best to worship them feverishly, put a tiger in the tank, ask for the largest amount, fill the tanks with their cold, disdainful orgasm; looking is still free until a new order, but that's not sure either. The theologians consult each other: Where is the hidden meaning

of the sacred texts to be found? *Put a tiger in your tank:* Imminent apocalypse? Will the major gods abandon us one day? (Cf. Cavafy).

IN THAT CASE THE OTHERS ARE STILL THERE

Yes, we have a recourse, we are protected by

the technological temple, the spare parts

FOR A DEAD GOD A REPLACEMENT GOD

It has been seen already   and the world has not gone under*

* It seems obvious, the theologians say, that the major gods don't bother with hierarchies; if the frivolity of the faithful displaces favors and altars, if suddenly a little god of the fourth order (cf. *infra*) reigns incontrovertibly among smokers and sports fans, the great deities don't seem to notice; it's better that way, say the theologians who around the year 1950 trembled when the major god *Parker* and adlatere *Waterman* were replaced by the little gods *Birome, Bic*, and *Fieltro*.

At the side of beds

stop

greet them

offer them libations

EQUANIL

BELLERGAL

OPTALIDON

their cooing names

peace   peace   peace   peace

from ten at night to six in the morning amen

AND THE FEARSOME

the heroic ones

invoked at times of anguish

enigmatic intercessors

with the hidden Mothers, those with obscure names,
ANDROTARDYL TESTOVIRON PROGESTEROL
ERGOTAMINE
and she of the triple edge CORTISONE
At the side of streets
stop
greet them
offer them libations

THE TEMPORAL GODS
incarnate
sons and daughters of God
dead on a cross (a crashed airplane)
or beneath the Bodi tree (a Swiss clinic with a garden)
HELENA RUBINSTEIN
pray for us sinners
JACQUES FATH
CARDIN CHANEL
DOROTHY GRAY
have mercy on our freckles pimples breasts and hips, oh lady
YVES SAINT-LAURENT
MAX FACTOR BALENCIAGA
laudate adoremus

At the side of lives
stop
greet them
offer them libations

(The servants of the machine will complete the information.)

Or in other words, the one I told you thought as he went down the stairs after one of his usual good-bys which consisted chiefly in not saying good-by to anyone, at the moment of writing a text with an ideological and even a political meaning, the little rabbi drops his peculiar oral idiom and presents you with a most acceptable Spanish. Strange, strange. What would Marcos do if the fortunes of the Screwery were to raise him up one day to be what Assyrian tablets called a leader of men? His everyday language is like his life, a mixture of iconoclasm and creation, a reflection of what is revolutionary being understood ahead of any system; but there is already Vladimir Ilich, not to mention Leon Davidovich and closer to this side and this time Fidel, they certainly saw what went between word and deed, street and power. And still you wonder about the motives of that passage from a speech defined by life, like Marcos's speech, to a life defined by speech, like government programs and the undeniable puritanism that lurks in revolutions. He must ask Marcos if he's going to forget his shit and his your sister's twat someday in case the time for leadership should arrive; a simple analogy, of course, it's not a matter of dirty words but what throbs behind them, the god of bodies, the great hot river of love, the eroticism of a revolution which someday will have to opt for (not the ones already with us, but the ones yet to come, the ones who are needed, which is practically all of them) a different definition of man; because from what we've seen, the new man tends to take on the face of an old man as soon as he sees a miniskirt or an Andy Warhol movie. Let's get some sleep, the one I told you thought, the members of the Screwery do enough theorizing without my bringing them these four too-obvious trifles. But I would like to know what Marcos thinks about it, how he'd live that hour if it came.

The night was still dark but a wind that seemed to be announcing dawn was waiting for us on the little square of Falguière. Ludmilla had said almost nothing on the street, she must have been half-asleep and was letting herself be guided by my arm; I took off my lumberjacket and put it over her shoulders. If we could only find a cab, I said to her uselessly. For ten blocks, silly? and it's so nice walking through the neighborhood at this hour. But you must be tired, you're cold. Not at all, Ludmilla said. Because it wasn't that, in any case. Who could tell what it was, she wasn't in any shape to think too much after that night. I'm going to fall asleep on stage tomorrow, I'll have to take advantage of the part where the old man tries to seduce me on the couch, God what an awful play, five months of daily shit, all to great applause, even the smell in that theater is rotten. That's where they ought to go to sell their used cigarettes, Andrés, we really should give them a little help.

"I don't know," I said making her walk faster because the cold was getting to my stomach, if it was the cold. "I've stopped trying to understand them, but you've seen them with their eggplants and their string and their burned matches, they spend months on that kind of thing, and so what."

"Marcos hadn't spoken much about it until now."

"No. I wonder."

"He brought Lonstein along as an excuse to bring up the subject without its seeming too intentional, aimed at the two of us. The same with Patricio, the whole time I had the impression that he was kind of searching us out, waiting, something like that. Those cat eyes he looks at you with."

"You're cold, Ludlud. I don't know why we stayed there all that time, it's absurd with your having to go to work, you'll get sick."

"Bah, just once. I had a good time, I'm not complaining, and Lonstein is an incredible character, with his splattered flowers and the poem. Each time I find more complicated and simpler at the same time, like Marcos but on a different level although who can say whether there was that much difference between Lenin and Rimbaud. A matter of specialties, vocabulary above all, and final aims, but underneath it all, underneath . . ."

She designated underneath with her hand, pointing to the cobblestones. I squeezed her tight against me, stroked her little breasts, she felt kind of withdrawn, far away to me, I had another chill and I began to laugh, really, comparing Marcos to Lenin, not to mention the other comparison. But Ludmilla was still pointing to the underneath, she had lowered her head as if to hide her face from the cold wind and she was silent, suddenly she began to laugh and told me about Manuel, sleeping Manuel's little dicky, that wonderful bit of the two tiny fingers encircling his pink little tool without squeezing it, just holding it with infinite delicacy, dropping off into sleep. The thing you never saw in the theater, those visitations of grace, the slap in the face (but it was also a caress) that lost innocence gave to those who adultly looked at reality from the other shore, with their idiotic guilts, their yellow flowers stained by Hindu corpses.

Undressed, undone, with one last sip of *mate* that was almost cold, Patricio and Susana went to bed beside Manuel who had thrown his sheet onto the floor and was sleeping on his belly, cooing. He's getting a curl on the back of his neck, Patricio said in wonder. He's had it for two weeks, Susana said offended, it's a curl like the ones you have in that picture your mother gave me when she came to Paris. I'd have liked to have killed the old lady, Jesus, giving you that, let me see it for a minute, I want to see if it's true. Don't try to fool me, Susana said, I know you want to burn it, the fine gentleman wants to erase all traces of the past, idiot, I've got the picture hidden away with all my love letters, you'll never find it, turn out the light I've had it, what a day, what a night, what a life, ah, ah. Comedy queen. Boob. Love letters, eh? Of course, the ones from the Balkan count, the one who offered me a green diamond the only one of its kind in the world, I didn't accept it because it was obviously fake or it had fallen into the brewed *mate*. Stop laughing, you're going to wake him up, we had to give him a spoonful of tranquilizer, he was too worked up but who knows how long he's going to sleep now. At least you didn't give him the gas jet. Monster. Have a good sleep, sweety. You too, repulsive. Fernando's nice, don't you think. Yes, but he still has to lose some veight around the vaist. Stop laughing, damn it, you'll wake him up. Get your hand off my mouth, youreaogg. Sleep well, lotus blossom. You too, new match. Tomorrow at eleven at Gómez's, they canned the poor guy at the restaurant, it was predictable. I don't think he cares, jobs like that are easy to find since they pay greenhorns practically nothing. What did you think of Andrés tonight? Hum. I don't understand Marcos and his tight testing of him. A lot of t's, my ball of twine. Get to sleep, you toad. But we're going to talk some more about that picture, if you think I'm going to tolerate an iconography like that. Maybe someday, but I'm keeping it for now. Hairy megathere. A naked little boy on a puma skin, oh, wild. You asked for it. All right, pollivog, why can't the Chilean pronounce a wuh sound? Ask your Balkan count, girl. Impossible, he was killed at the end of a poker game in chapter fifteen, Eric Ambler, author. You and your bloody and bibliographical love affairs. Stop your retrospective jealousy, my only boyfriend was a hairdresser from Almagro and then you showed up one ill-fated day. Hairdressers are all fags. Not in Almagro, you better believe it. I'm from La Paternal, I've got no reason to be concerned with anything that takes place outside of there. Whatever you say. Go to sleep, love. Yes, you too, and it was already a kind of gray hallway, a waiting room, Susana was dreaming full-time during that period, Patricio's hand lost in her thighs was that pink dress that was a little tight, and Manuel who would be alone in that house full of dogs and midgets, how could she have left him like that, she had to hurry, the monotonous nightmare, but she really had to hurry, I squeezed Ludmilla's waist and I pulled her along almost on the run for the last two blocks, we were freezing to death and dropping from lack of sleep, along the Rue de la Procession we turned into the Rue de l'Ouest, home sweet home, five stories no less and no elevator, and on the third Manuel still, how cute Manuel was, his diddly between his fingers. The hurried preparation of some very hot tea with rum and lemon for her (aphony, that theatrical dread, anything but losing your voice) I thought for the thousandth time that without doubt, that in the end it was time now, that I had been too selfish, I brought the tea to her in bed and while I was getting undressed I told her.

"No, it's better we didn't," Ludmilla said. "I can talk about Manuel without motherhood coming up into my eyes. Theater and maternity don't mix too well, and besides it's too late."

"It's not too late, Lud. Up till now we didn't want to, we agreed, but I don't know, there's a way you have of talking about Manuel and afterwards what the hell, solutions can always be found, I won't be an ideal father, that's for sure."

"It's too late," Ludmilla repeated drinking the tea and not looking at me. "Too late, Andrés."

I took the cup from her, I lay down seeking warmth, Ludmilla's feet strolled across mine, warm puppy dogs. Francine, obviously. Fatal. But not just that, Ludmilla had closed her eyes and let Andrés's hands slowly stroke her, outlining her in the darkness, at some moment Andrés would turn the lamp on again, they had never made love in the dark, they had to see each other, they had to be there, denying any of the senses would have been the same as spitting into the face of life, it wasn't just a question of Francine although that too, because if they let themselves go and made a child it would be all the same because Andrés would leave and would come back, Francine or whoever else it would all be the same thing, underneath it all he wouldn't be the father of that child, he'd just said that he wouldn't be the ideal father, on that terrain he was incapable of lying, he was offering her something that he would never take on completely. What difference did it make now, it was better to go to sleep, but I didn't want her to fall asleep all tired out and sad like that, three acts every night and a matinée on Sunday, in spite of that I couldn't let her go into oblivion like that, naturally it was Francine, the red-headed incubus in the middle of the night.

"Yes, for that reason too, because of your ways and you wanting to live in me," Ludmilla said. "Francine probably doesn't want to have a child by you either, if you come right down to it, she's too intelligent, almost as smart as I am. Let's go to sleep, Andrés, I'm all done in. No, please, I feel like those packs of cigarettes of Gómez's. Oh, I promised Susana I'd go help them fix up another batch."

"All right, we'll have to save the butts," I told her, "it looks as if our activities are going to get more impassioned now."

"Don't be foolish, don't take it that way."

"It's the inevitable conclusion, having wanted so much out of life, looking for the meaning of it all, and discovering that we're heading straight toward a pile of burned matches, something like that. Words, I know, but still the truth, Ludlud, because it would have been so simple and so much better not to have told you anything, never to have talked to you about Francine or any other woman."

"Of course, silly, why bring that up again. I'm not clapping my hands in admiration for your wanting to be frank, which underneath it all is just a guilty conscience that's looking for detergents at any cost, but we've turned that problem over and over until we've been on the verge of vomiting, Andrés, what's happening is that I might have wanted to have a child by you before, when there were only the two of us and precisely because of that we didn't want to be three, we didn't want any wailing and dirty linen in the place, you needed order, calm, and Baudelaire, and I rehearsing in front of the mirror, all the scents of Araby couldn't erase, etc. Two Narcissuses in an alliance, perfect egotists signing a pact so that we would feel less egotistical too. And instead of the feared third pishy, sucky beast, voilà, along comes Francine fresh out of the university and haute couture, with her little red car and her bookshop and her freedom. I can understand it, even though neither she nor I will ever accept your scyllas and charybdises, but I don't want a child, not any more. The day my metabolism gets too strong with its demands for one, as seems to have happened tonight, I'll go to bed with the first man I get a notion to, or I'll go see Xavier so he can inseminate me like a cow. Good night, sweet prince."

"What about me, Lud? Why do you still tolerate me if you can't accept my way of life? My way of wanting to live, rather, which runs on the reef with every tack."

"Because I love you so much," Ludmilla said, and through one of those wiles of language the so much took almost all the strength out of the I love you, and it was true, she did love him a lot because he was good and merry and like a cat and full of plans that couldn't be fulfilled and records of aleatory music and metaphysical enthusiasms and little attentions, he clothed her days for her, he hung colored curtains on the windows of time for her, he played with her and let himself be played with, he would go off with Francine and come back with the complete works of Roberto Arlt, and besides he made time his own thing, habit became installed, the apartment so pretty, there was nothing more to learn or to teach, good health was enough and laughing a lot, wandering through Paris arm in arm, seeing friends, Marcos the distant and laconic Cordovan who was beginning to come regularly now, to talk, bringing Lonstein, telling them about agitprop, the shrieks, the boxes of matches, almost as if it were only for her although Andrés thought himself directly concerned, and why almost, little Polish hypocrite, he'd come to feel it he still felt it as if by touch, Marcos's listless and Cordovan voice talking mostly at her, so that she would begin to know what was going on which wasn't very much but after all the Screwery, Polonette.

I felt her move away, turn her back to me, good night sweet prince, good night, little thing, I barely stroked her on the shoulder, on her little behind, I abandoned her to sleep or to insomnia, as always after so much talk I wanted her but I knew that that night I would only find a resigned mechanism, anything but that, go to sleep sweet prince, they've gone nuts over their matches, thinking that in Biafra, but no, damn it, you won't get to sleep and Lonstein with his road gods, something's not working, brother. I could have stayed home and listened to *Prozession*, why ride Marcos's wave, they're crazy, get your hair out of my eyes, Ludlud, oh I beg your pardon, I was asleep and I dreamt something, don't be silly, I like your hair, go to sleep, forget about it, yes, Andrés, yes.

Now for example the café on the Porte de Champerret, Manuel going wild with the sugar cubes and the little spoons, ride a cock horse/to Banbury Cross/don't wear yourself out, the child won't go to sleep even with a Pasolini film, dusk among the plane trees in the square, a soft breeze that carries the one I told you off with memory holding his hand to sunsets on the pampa far away and long ago, but attent at the same time on what's going on at the table which is practically nothing except Manuel, although in some way, the one I told you thinks, something will have to be spoken about because it isn't just by chance that Roland and Marcos called the meeting without inviting Lonstein (or me, naturally, or Ludmilla either, but Ludmilla can't come because the curtain is going up and Slavic melancholy starts at eight-thirty) it isn't just by chance that it's in a café on the Porte de Champerret no less, which isn't just around the corner, it would seem, just to have a friendly chat about how the world is turning, sir, you realize, ma'am, since up till now the most striking thing that the one I told you has been able to make out is the rattle that Susana shakes vigorously to distract Manuel from all the well-pressed trousers spread around the table. And that's how they go on for half an hour until Gómez gets out of a 92 and almost without saying hello hands two telegrams to Marcos which he reads and returns without commentary so that Susana (they tease the girl sometimes) can translate them for Lucien Verneuil, Monique, and Roland, hard-core Frenchies who have made no effort to learn languages, easy as it is to understand PAPITO MEJOR STOP BESITOS COCA (from Buenos Aires) and A BANANA DO BRASIL NÃO TEM CAROÇO, filed in London, texts with a singularly idiotic meaning for the uninitiated but whose meanings gave the news that a certain Oscar

Lemos is flying into Orly bringing some items that are not exactly Argentine sweet milk candy, something that incidentally might explain why Lonstein (and I) was not invited to join the group at the café on the Porte de Champerret, because it still wasn't known whether Lonstein, although Marcos yes but there was no hurry and to the very end he will let Lonstein ask for cards or stand pat, there's always time in cases like these and the moment will come when he defines himself, the same as could happen with Ludmilla (or me, but it'll be a little wait), reasons for which the one I told you gets the impression that the café on the Porte de Champerret is something like a pointed roof, a sharp edge, and now something is going to happen even though everything seems to be going on just the same and Manuel goes about from chair to chair to the horror of Roland and Lucien Verneuil who for some time have foreseen spittle coughed up on virginal lapels not to mention piss without warning in spite of the pink plastic panty guarantees. As for the telegram from London it is of course from Heredia who for some reason is coming back from a city where according to previous letters and postcards he is getting along famously, and so the one I told you deduces on his own that the Screwery chrysalis in on the verge of becoming a butterfly although there isn't much room for hope from this lepidopteron in matters of coherence, it's enough to take a look at what's happening at the table (a mental picture by the one I told you) or

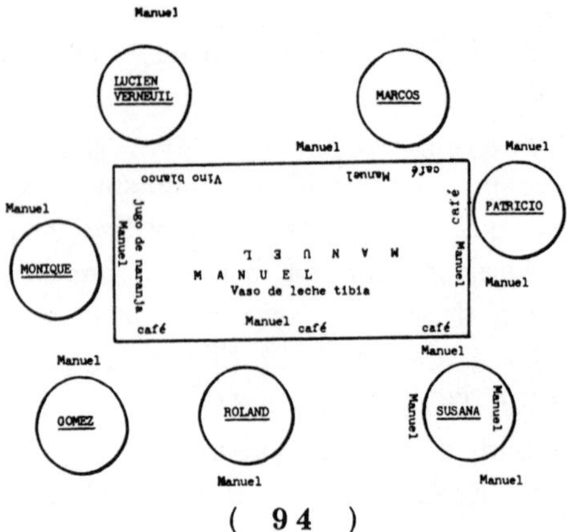

but little manages to become clear, except perhaps what the experts at UNESCO call group tensions, the fact that Lucien Verneuil is becoming visibly impatient because time is passing at that table in a way that is more perceptible for the French than for the Latin Americans, for the benefit of whom, the one I told you asks himself, and the fact is that up till now they still haven't come out of the rejoicing produced by the BESITOS COCA, then Lucien Verneuil looks at Roland who looks at Monique, quick touches of national solidarity, although the one I told you is even more amused at noting that Monique who has been living with Gómez for six months and even helps him mount his stamps in albums, has already entered a leisurely Panamanian time vainly cut in two by Ferdinand de Lesseps who wasn't a Frenchman for nothing, and she's not in the slightest hurry, not to mention that there's no one like Patricio for ordering another spot of coffee which is always like holding back the clock. Underdevelopment can be seen even in this, rages Lucien Verneuil precisely at the moment in which Marcos almost blandly lets drop the first phrase of something that they all hear in a different way, this really is the Screwery, the one I told you thinks, now it's serious, there are telegrams, ergo the thing is starting to jell, logistical problems, Oscar will arrive at thirteen hundred hours on Thursday and the Vincennes thing has to be laid on, Heredia is landing tonight at Le Bourget, get this kid off me, he's kicking my belly apart. He's caressing you, Susana explains. First off, the ants probably know all about it, Marcos says, so attenti al piato, there can't be the slightest slip-up in the Vincennes business. The screwupery has a tendency to fly off without much fluttering thinks the one I told you and he feels something that resembles pity, a vague tightening at the mouth of his stomach; so the Screwery, now yes, now the ants are going to appear with all their pincers, all their dollars; it's probably the last time I'll see them all together at a table in a café, Manuel back and forth among cups and glasses. The world is a handkerchief, Roland is telling Patricio as he tears a piece out of the *Herald Tribune* and gives it to him, the ants are going to have work down there too. No one asks Susana to translate it, the news item is in English and obviously the French are cultured types and Latin Americans we already know, English is the language of the future and your family makes you learn it even if you don't want to because you've got to think about the future, scholarships and things like that, m'boy.

Brazilian Leftists Kill Guard, Kidnap Bonn Ambassador

RIO DE JANEIRO, June 12 (AP).—Leftist terrorists kidnapped the West German ambassador last night after blocking his car, killing a Brazilian guard in a gun battle and wounding another security agent.

A third security agent and the ambassador's driver were not hurt.

Police said that four men and a woman abducted Ambassador Ehrenfried von Holleben and that five cars were used in the kidnapping. Officers said that the terrorists pulled the ambassador from his car and drove away with bullets still flying.

Later, the police said that nine men and a woman participated in the kidnapping.

The kidnappers killed a guard sitting in the front seat of the ambassador's car when he drew his gun.

They also riddled with bullets a station wagon in which two security agents were riding behind the car, wounding one of them.

In pamphlets left behind, the terrorists said that they would hold Ambassador von Holleben hostage for the release of political prisoners but they did not say how many. The demand was signed by the Popular Revolutionary Vanguard, one of several leftist terror groups that are active in Brazil. Sixteen hours later, no word still had been received from the kidnappers.

[Reuters reported that the Jornal do Brasil, a Rio de Janeiro daily newspaper, had received a telephone call, allegedly from one of the kidnappers. The caller said that a letter had been left at a suburban train station. Police are investigating.]

Occasionally the one I told you makes a mistake: instead of registering, a mission assigned and which he feels he fulfills rather well, he sets himself up at any table in a café or in a living room with *mate* and grappa and from there he not only registers, he analyzes, damnable, judges and evaluates, repugnant, compromising the not at all easy balance which until that moment he had managed in matters of compilation and filing, to Caesar what belongs to same and other tabulations and registries, as now Gómez spends ten minutes protesting about bourgeois music, including the aleatory, the electronic, and the stochastic, defending Panamanianly an art of multitudinary participation, the choral song and other ways of transplanting a canary into the aorta of the people. Not that Gómez is a ninny who sighs over Shostakovich or Kurt Weill, but the difficulties of the music that Andrés for example tries to make him listen to seem to be a proof that capitalism *lato sensu* is once more looking and will look until the last wag of its tail for the automatic formation of elites on all levels, including the aesthetic. And precisely at that moment it occurs to the one I told you to opine (instead of simply transcribing what Gómez and the others said, all braided together in Madame Séverine's bistro) that a certain Terry Riley, a Yankee, the apparently perfect expression of what Gómez is denouncing with violent helicoidal gestures, is the author of a work (and many others) whose contact with the public (Gómez's "people") is the most immediate, simple, and efficacious that has occurred to anyone since Perotin or Gilles Binchois. *Grosso modo* (the one I told you doesn't want to ask Andrés for technical details because he immediately gets encyclopedic) Riley's idea is that someone repeats interminably a single note on the piano and little by little, one after the other, anyone capable of plucking or tootling an instrument gets into the act by means of a score within the reach of a hamster. When the one playing has tired of playing his two or three notes, he goes on to play the two or three following ones, just as easy, and now there is another person or persons who in turn are starting the first series; so that each player covers in his wisdom and understanding a sequence of thirty or forty small melodic nuclei, but since each one came in when he wanted to and only changes theme when he feels like it, the result is that ten minutes after the music has begun there are already a large number of players going along on their own, and after forty minutes or so, there's almost no one left because they've all come to the last series of notes and they fall silent; the finale is always the prettiest part because it turns out to be absolutely impossible to foresee how the number is going to end, whether it will be a violin or a bass drum or a guitar that will play the last notes, still backed by the piano that obstinately repeats its soft pedal in the manner of a coagulant. All very well, Gómez says, but it must be a complete abomination, what kind of mess are you putting together for me. Who can say, admits the one I told you, but in any case you can get thirty kids together, explain the workings to them, and for an hour they'll play wild goddamned music; if you want to extrapolate they could invite everybody at the Boca or River stadiums to play Terry Riley some Sunday afternoon, distributing penny whistles and other cheap and easy horns; almost everybody is capable of reading the notes, not to mention the fact that there are systems of ciphers, letters, and other simplifications. It's completely idiotic, Gómez says. It may be idiotic, the one I told you says, but from your revolutionary point of view it's music that's closer than any other to the people since they can interpret it, there's communion and joy and universal merriment, the business of an orchestra and an audience is over, it's all the same thing now and it seems that at Riley's concerts the kids go crazy with fun. But that's not art, Gómez says. I don't know, the one I told you consents, but in any case it's people, and as Mao says very well, you can fill in the rest.

It was after eleven when we woke up, the postman had rung twice, demonstrating one more time that nature imitates art, but what art, one miserable postcard that I took back to bed with me because I hadn't yet got all the pleasure I wanted out of sleep, Andrés had taken advantage of things to steal my pillow and was sitting up smoking with his hair in his eyes. *London suínguin beri biútiful plenti náisuans, pripéar matecito, quises, Charles.* It's that damned Heredia, Andrés said, his bag isn't even packed and he's already asking for *mate*, speaking of which it must be about time we brewed up one, without sugar. We already know about your use of the plural, I said curling up without a pillow but trying to keep warm. All right, I'll brew it myself, but I have to tell you what I dreamed before it all unravels, Lud, it's so strange. Jung is listening and will interpret, I told him, I bet it was about trains.

Not trains but a movie theater and what happened there, it has to be told quickly, an almost painful need to fasten it down with words even if as usual all that was left would be a small plaster mask covering something so alive, the antimatter of the thing that was flying away at a dizzying rate of speed, leaving only shreds and maybe lies behind, I dreamt that I was going to the movies with a friend, Lud, I don't know who, I never saw his face, to see a mystery by Fritz Lang, the theater was an enormous outlandish auditorium that I've dreamed about other times, I've told you about it I think, there are two screens at a right angle to each other so that you can sit in different sections of the orchestra and choose one of the screens because the sections cut through each other in some way, the seats also alternate at right angles or something like that, better than Alvar Aalto, and I'm endlessly searching for a place I can get a good look at the thriller from, but either I'm too far away or something comes between the screen and my eyes; then I get up for a second time and I don't see my friend any more, who in the devil could he have been, it's impossible to remember. Now the movie starts, it's a courtroom scene, there's a woman with a loony face, like Elsa Lanchester, you remember, who's shouting things from the prisoner's box or the witness stand, I'm too much to one side and I try to find another seat, at that moment a waiter comes over to me, a young guy with a conventional mustache, Hilton-bar style, wearing a white jacket and he invites me to follow him. I tell him that I want to see the picture (I know that I mention the title, something with the word midnight maybe), then the waiter makes a gesture of annoyance or impatience, he points out an exit to me in an imperative way; I understand that I have to follow him. While we go from one large room into another, which I've also dreamt a thousand times, like a kind of private club, the waiter asks me to excuse his rudeness. "I had to do it, sir, there's a Cuban who wants to see you," and he leads me to the entrance to a parlor that's almost in darkness.

"Halt!" commanded Dr. Jung, "the part about the Cuban is elementary: the shrieks, the response, everything last night, the guilty conscience we have in this house, bah."

"Let me continue, Lud, it's all leaving my head, here comes the hardest part to explain, to file in the little honeycombs of our damned verbal hive. It's something like this, knowing that I'm missing the mystery film I wanted to see so much, and at the same time and for that very reason getting myself caught up in the (or in a) mystery. The waiter stops and points out to me, it's incredible how I can still see him, Lud, points out to me in the shadows of the parlor a shape on a sofa; all that can be seen are the extended legs of the man who wants to talk to me. I go into the parlor alone and I go toward the Cuban. And now wait, just wait, this is the incredible part because I know with all clarity that I haven't forgotten any scene from this part, but the scene is cut when I approach the man waiting for me, and what comes next is the moment when I leave the parlor *after having spoken to the Cuban.* A perfect montage right out of the movies, you realize. There's one thing that's absolutely certain and that's the fact that I've spoken to him, but there wasn't any scene, it's not that I've forgotten it, girl, there was a cut and something happened in that cut, and when I go out I'm a man who has a mission to fulfill, but while I know that and most of all feel it, I also know that I haven't got the slightest idea of what the mission is, I'm sorry, I'm telling it the best I can, you have to understand that I'm not the least bit aware of that interview, the scene was cut exactly when I approached the sofa, but at the same time I know I have to do something with no time to lose, so that when I go back to the theater I'm acting simultaneously inside and outside the Fritz Lang movie or some mystery movie, I am the film and the one watching the film at the same time. Just imagine now, Lud, this is the most beautiful part (exasperating for me but beautiful if you look at it as an example of a dream), there's no doubt that I *know* what the Cuban told me since I have a task to do, and at the same time I look at myself with the curiosity and interest of someone held in complete suspense by the thriller since I no longer know what the Cuban told me. I'm double, someone who went to the movies and someone caught up in a typical movie plot. But the idea of being double I'm telling you while I'm wide awake, there wasn't any doubleness in the dream, I was I and the one I always am, I have a perfect perception of the fact that while I was coming back to the theater I could feel the total weight of all this I'm breaking into segments now in order to explain it, even though it's only partial. A little as if only thanks to that act I was to fulfill could I come to know what the Cuban had told me, a completely absurd reversal of causality as you can see. We have the workings of the thriller but I will fulfill it and enjoy it at the same time, the detective story I'm writing and living simultaneously. And precisely at that moment I'm awakened by Heredia's goddamned postcard, son of a bitch of a Brazilian."

"You've had your Kubla Khan ruined too," Ludmilla said kissing me on the neck. "The idea of fate knocking on the door is a matter for a lot of meditation, think about it. But what a dream, it really gives me the shivers."

"I don't know, now that I think about it I don't think the postman's ring ruined things too much; it probably would have gone into the mushy phase of almost all dreams when they start to lose their divine proportions; remember that I don't feel it was a fatal break, the weight at that instant was on the fact that I was accepting being someone who's had a key meeting and is going to act as a consequence of it, and who at the same time keeps on being a guy who, facing the screen of himself, to put it that way, is going to follow a mysterious action that will only be explained at the end. So Heredia's coming back, well, I bet he's been going around counterfeiting matchboxes in London too or something like that, although he talked about women in the card. What about that little old *mate*, Ludlud? Are you still mad at me, my Polish dove?"

"No, bird of ill omen, but let's not talk about that, I have to study my new part and it's almost noontime, I don't know if I told you I'm a girl with sick lungs who lives several versts outside Moscow and passes her time coughing and waiting for a certain Koruchenko who never comes, I always get parts like that, but on the other hand now I can catch cold peacefully and if I push it a little I can even collect a bonus for the violence of my convulsions. Don't look at me that way, I'd really rather not talk, we're fine like this, your legs are nice and warm, this bed is like a perfumed igloo."

"I love you so much, Polonette, it's the only thing you refuse to understand, that I love you so much and still. Well, all right, another day. If there is another day, Polonette."

She didn't answer me, her eyes were lost on a pink stain on the sheet, but of course she was answering me, there were no cuts in the scenes there, it wasn't necessary to mention Francine, what for, the silence was an outburst of clarity, there wouldn't be any other days, in some way this one and many others were the last day even though we were still waking up together and playing and kissing, a ceremonial repetition that immobilizes time, the first kiss on the hair, the fingers on the back, the useless delicate truce, the first *mate*.

BESITOS COCA, although of course the signatory was not named Coca, just as Oscar was almost not named Oscar since it was his third Christian name, but apart from those details the telegram was exceedingly concrete for those in the know as the one I told you was able to appreciate in an ironic way and all at once between two kicks by Manuel on the square how the Screwery had become almost tangible, besitos Coca and banana do Brasil, people who went off in all directions to prepare decorous receptions. That's what the one I told you and Lonstein talked about in a different lunchroom, because Lonstein was better informed about the Screwery than one might have imagined given his iconoclastic and sometimes frankly reactionary tendencies. Thus, and putting into Argentine what the little rabbi defined as cryptotransfusion and cosmoassholic perianality, the one I told you finally established the parameters of BESITOS COCA, and the now distant thread with its beginning in Doña Raquela's boardinghouse in Santos Pérez, province of Entre Ríos, with the Buenos Aires assistance of Coca (whose name was Gladis) and the prescrewery of the royal armadillos and the turquoise penguin.

"The exotic opens all doors," the little rabbi had explained. "For example, offer an edelweiss to the president of Tanzania and he'll receive you within twenty-four hours, so the idea of the turquoise penguin seems to me as rather antarcticastute. Add to it the other forces that these people can't smell except Marcos and he just barely, even Oscar himself, what idea do you think he has of what he's doing, and still you can see, one day he sends Marcos a clipping out of pure picturesqueness and I have to be there to realize the latencies, the intraargentine transfundamentals. You've probably already realized that I'm referring to the matter of the reformatory in that absurd city La Plata."

The one I told you had not realized it at all, but he was accustomed to nod so that the little rabbi would go on mystifying without lifting his guard.

"Things like the full moon," Lonstein explained, "my mushroom that grows and juvenile girls who escape from a reformatory, go try to explain to guys like Gómez or Roland that that can be the Screwery too, they'll spit in your eye; that's why I'm afraid of tomorrow, when we won't be around any more, when they'll be alone. There's still contact now, you can talk to them, but the bad part is that they're the very ones who one day will hoe you out. Marcos himself, you'll see. So."

"Explain that turquoise penguin business to me at least."

"It had to be," the little rabbi said with rancor, "no one asks me about the mushroom that's ten blocks away from here and yet they get exciforated and convulverated over any common species. Penguins are abominable creatures to me, you'd better ask Patricio to explain to you what Oscar did in the Rosario strikes and the Córdoba riots."

It was a good idea because Patricio liked to tell things in some detail, and even though Oscar's role in the activities mentioned had been rather obscure, it was only so for the police and the SIDE, but not for Marcos or Heredia. The problem was to keep on doing things without getting busted, but when it became evident that any activity of Oscar's in Buenos Aires would blow the lid on a whole stoveful of pressure cookers, some responsible person saw to it that he was quickly transformed into a fellowship winner of the Argentine Zoophilia Society and sent to Entre Ríos under the pretext of studying the urinary tract of the owl and other equally respectable themes. There he took lodging with his books and his forceps in Doña Raquela's boardinghouse, horrify- the landlady's numerous daughters with flasks of formaldehyde overflowing with creatures, with stories of vampires and werewolves that he kept for nights full of courtyards and moonlight. All this time Gladis was working as an oastess delare for Aerolíneas and couldn't run just like that to Santos Pérez to give Oscar a little poodee-doo, so he was down in the mouth and there was no way out except for Moña, Doña Raquela's third, a plump little thing who had refused to go into Oscar's room at first because owls in formaldehyde but soon she was helping him bottle them and was looking at their pancreases or chromosomes, poor angels. The werewolf nights were hot and jasmined in the boardinghouse courtyards, the girls finished their cooking and sewing early, the television only functioned for the grandparents and Beany the cat, the boarders had mysteriously discovered the excellent qualities of certain easy chairs hidden among potted plants and columns, suddenly the girls would be lost from sight and around ten-thirty Doña Raquela, with the last wipe of a dishcloth on a platter, would go out to the street door crossing through the endless entranceways and courtyards, the provincial

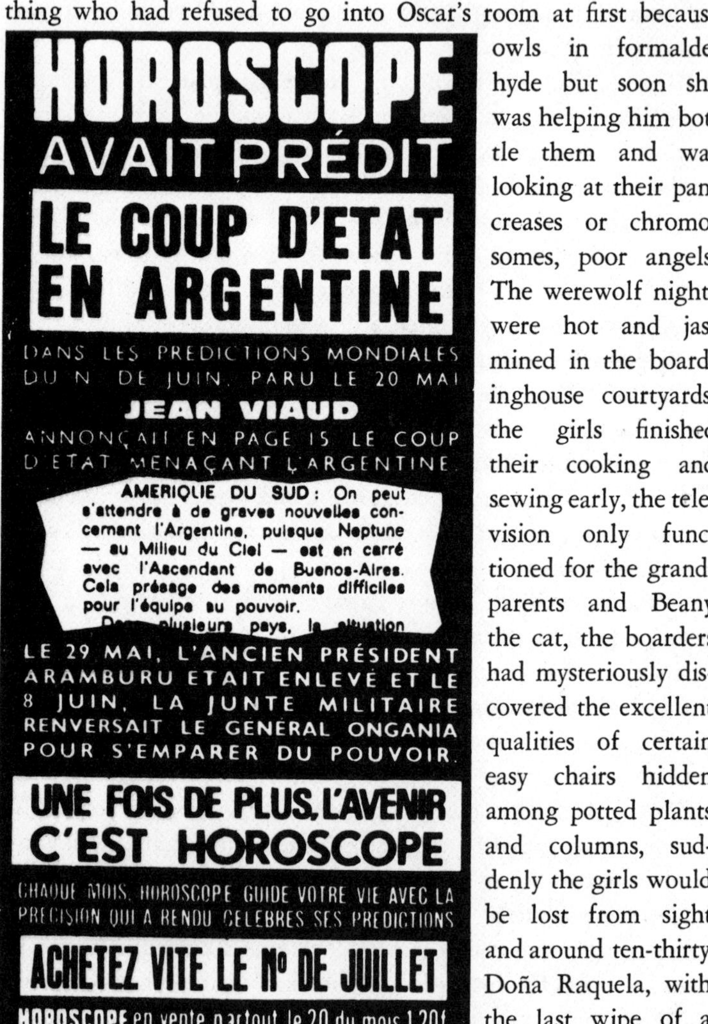

chessboard with squares of moonlight and shadow, vague murmurs would reach her from among the privets and geraniums, and finally she would go to bed outdone by events, not without first saying, as Oscar and Moña lost behind a jasmine heard her: "Son of a bitch, everybody all doubled up." But Doña Raquela was already incapable of fighting the lycanthropy and the maenadism of the full moon, and in the end what's the use since they'd all end up getting married to the traveling salesmen or bank tellers who appreciated the Sunday stews and the cool cheap rooms in the boardinghouse.

Now the full moon was not just falling on the courtyards of Santos Pérez; during those days Oscar sent Marcos a clipping, in exchange for another more astrological one that the latter had got to him along with a series of questions about the eventual use of old man Collins's talents, and that was the start of what Lonstein was mixing up in a single metascreweric salad that the one I told you had to reclassify, putting the astrological clipping from *Horoscope* on one side along with the one sent by Oscar, and on the other side the problem of old man Collins and the counterfeit dollars. In the first part were the already presented news about Doña Raquela's boardinghouse and the clipping from Oscar to Marcos that arrived together with the news about old man Collins and a first working hypothesis based on the royal armadillos and the turquoise penguin, out of all of which the one I told you and the little rabbi found most interesting the clipping about the full moon in

La Plata: Disturbance in a Youth Home

Intensive Search for 16 Runaway Girls

LA PLATA, 4 (AP).—Sixteen minor girls who ran away last night during the disturbance at the Instituto Ricardo Gutiérrez are being sought in an intensive police roundup. Approximately two hundred girls took part in the disturbance reported at the institution located on 120th Street between 39th and 40th Avenues.

"'An unexpected blackout,'" Susana read in French for Monique and Roland, "'was the occasion for the start of an infernal battle between the personnel and the juvenile girls who had shown themselves to have been extremely restless for the past few days.' Oscar talks about the full moon, but you'll soon see the official explanation, and along the way you must admire the reporter's style. 'The lack of light brought about a chaotic spectacle as in the front a group of girls scattered and quickly fled into the kitchen to force open a door and reach the street. At the same time other inmates opened a hole in the wire of a kitchen window and jumped down from there into a vacant lot on the Calle 41. The quick intervention of the police' (I can imagine how quick the fuzz were when they foresaw certain possibilities) 'prevented a mass escape and with great effort they were able to restore order.' Hum. 'As soon as the incident became known, the head of the regional section for La Plata, Inspector Jorge Schoo, with personnel under his command plus elements of firemen and police from the second squad arrived.'" "The lads were all for one and one for all," Patricio said. "This is the good part," Susana went on. "'A real pitched battle broke out' (what's a *pitched battle*, do you people know?) 'in which the police seem to have made valiant efforts to restore order with the result that the young women were found to be in a high state of restlessness.'" "Boy oh boy," Patricio said, "nine months from now the work the nuns in the hospital are going to have." "He's saying that because of the valiant efforts on the part of the police and the firemen," Susana informed Monique and Roland. "'Finally, when calm was apparently restored, 24 young women were taken to female police headquarters and attended to by doctors, remaining there until the authorities could decide upon the pertinent measures to be taken.' No one will ever know why the reporter used the adverb *apparently*, but listen to the last part, which is the best. 'The technical secretary of the General Council for Juveniles did not consider the events to be of great importance' (a trifle, of course) 'pointing out that this type of reaction on the part of young female inmates was customary just before carnival. For her part, the director of the establishment gave the information that the building has a capacity of 80 and yet at the moment it holds 196 and will get another 56 girls in the next few days.' And the bitch, that's me talking, added, here's the reporter talking 'that the cause of the trouble was the advertisements for carnival dances at clubs in the district which drove the inmates crazy.' See what the third world is like, you two, children of Corneille and Racine." Bah, said Monique, do you think things are any better in some of the "homes" on the outskirts of Paris, I know a little about that, at the age of fourteen my sensitive parents left me with the nuns in a small paradise near Strasbourg because they were sick of catching me reading Sartre and Camus, you people are aware of the immorality of modern times, the nuns were poor imbeciles full of goodwill and bad odors, in a word, the usual thing, taking baths with your undershirt on, ave maria, don't ask inconvenient questions, that's called the curse, you don't talk about it, Sister Honorine will give you something and tell you how to put it on, it was probably the full moon as Oscar says, I remember that it was hot, that they'd caught me with a novel by Céline disguised as the botany text by Hevillier et Monthéry, and they punished me and five other girls for similar things, the worst thing for the nuns was the fact that we were very popular with the younger girls, but most of all the full moon, I'm sure, because when they realized it, it was just like your clipping except without police or firemen, Maïté and Gertrude broke the lock on the classroom where we were shut up in and we ran out shouting and singing into the courtyard with the orange trees, the little ones who had to go to bed stampeded over Sister Marie Jeanne and all of a sudden we were all singing and dancing in a circle and shouting among the orange trees, just like that Polish movie, the nuns swooped down like a squadron of fighter planes and grabbed us by the hair or the clothes, they slapped us, they were as hysterical as we were, the little ones began to scream and cry but they didn't want to leave us, suddenly all the older girls dropped down along the tree that grew next to the window of the second-floor dormitory, I'll never forget that tree full of girls, white pieces of fruit dropping one after another and they ran to the courtyard, the first to appear with a strap was Sister Claudine, it was to be expected, the others brought out pieces of rope and whips from someplace, they began to lash us and drive us up against the wall of the refectory so that we would retreat through the door that opened into the main classroom and they could lock us in, the little ones had broken up crying and screaming and there were only about twenty of us older girls left against the wall, seven nuns were whipping us madly, we didn't have anything to defend ourselves with until suddenly I saw Maïté naked, she'd taken off her nightgown and had thrown it over Sister Honorine's head, Gertrude did the same and the nuns were getting more frantic every minute, their blows were leaving marks, I heard a kind of splat and it was a red piece of cloth that hit Sister Felisa full in the face, that's called the curse, four or five girls were throwing their sanitary napkins at the nuns' heads, I'd stripped naked and almost all the other older girls too, we were returning the blows with rolled-up nightgowns, we were picking up the revolting and trampled granny rags from the ground and throwing them again, trying to hit them in the mouth, the gardener had come into the courtyard with a stick, but Sister Marie Jeanne shouted at him to stay out, the idiot's dilemma was enough to make you die of laughter, how could he see us naked, a man, and Maïté ran over to the gardener and got in front of him so he couldn't get out, she was the oldest of all and had full, firm breasts which she put up in front of the gardener's face and sang to him in a loud voice, the nuns ran to protect morality and the stupefied gardener, the final hysteria began, the wails, suddenly we were tired, we fled back into the dormitories, dragging our nightgowns along the ground, and victors under the full moon among the orange trees, a week later I was back home, and if you want to know about Maïté, today she's one of the leading dancers at the Lido, that girl's career turned out better than mine.

"If you can call a halt to all that biography," Roland said, "we might be able to talk about something useful, because I still can't understand why Oscar sends those clippings or about the full moons that excite you so much."

Because he's a poet, thought the one I told you but he was mistaken since Oscar was up to his ears in prose with old man Collins and the Zoophilia Society invented for strategic reasons, the problem was to connect old man Collins effectively with the royal armadillos and the turquoise penguin (and with Oscar, of course, since it was now a question of Oscar's coming to bring the exotic animals and the rest was up to Marcos): in synthesis:

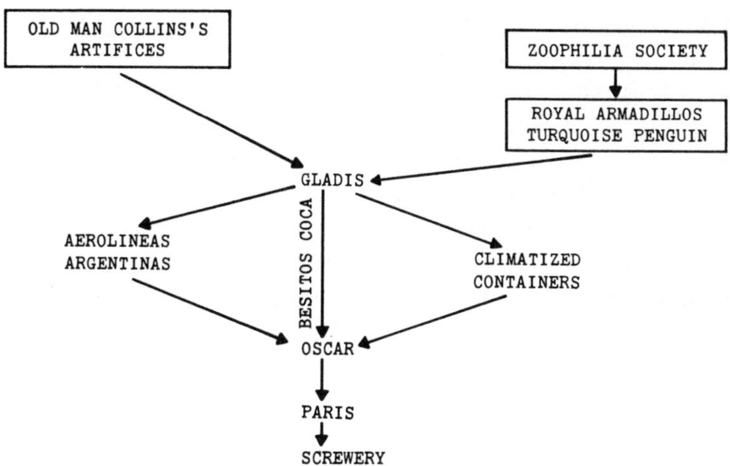

It wasn't too hard; Gladis took care of maintaining contact with old man Collins after the clandestine visit paid him by Oscar whose continued presence in Bernal might have brought on some bad deductions on the part of the police, and the old man agreed to hand over the false dollars to Gladis against an amount that the Zoophilia Society had put together with a bit of effort since there were only four members including Oscar and Gladis; the idea was that old man Collins's dollars were more than singed after an exchange broker downtown had picked up on one that was slightly less green than those Made in Washington, but the old man's artifices wouldn't receive too much criticism in regions virgin of Collins's work, and twenty thousand dollars lining the double walls of the thermal containers specially built by members of the Zoophilia Society would be able to go safely into the cargo hold of a plane of Aerolíneas, always ready to divulge abroad our most worthy cultural exponents and the great variety of things that came out of our national soil, in this case a pair of royal armadillos and a turquoise penguin which, given the delicacy of their constitutions, had to travel in said thermal containers under the constant care and supervision of the veterinarian José Carlos Oscar Lemos who would also take charge of the delicate unloading operations, the adaptation to a different habitat, and the solemn presentation to the authorities of the Vincennes zoo who in two pages on a letterhead counterfeited by old man Collins had accepted such a generous gift from the Society with great feeling, for which reason a startled functionary of Aerolíneas had ended up declaring himself most ready to authorize, which was all that was needed, the embarkation of said animals, of course, and of the one accompanying them, this last of course with prepaid passage in his hand and his ass on the ground.

"That's all there was to it," said Patricio immensely satisfied with the clarity of his exposition. The one I told you thanked him, what else could he do.

There was a dead time between ten o'clock and noon, and probably because of that, because it was dead, Marcos could think of nothing more brilliant to do than climb the five flights to my apt. precisely when I was penetrating (sic) the ninth chapter of one of those French novels they have now where everyone is most intelligent, the reader most of all, for which reason I was not too pleased to be extracted with a ring of the bell and a hi Andrés, I came to borrow your car but there's no great rush if you want to chat a while. A chat that began with a depth analogous to that of the novel, because between the grappa and the coffee it was argued how was it possible that if there was a dead time this man from Córdoba should show up saying that he'd come to kill some time, things like that or the latest speech by General Onganía which synthesized and translated by *Le Monde* had absolutely no meaning. I've always been selfish, it bugs me to have people come and drag me out of a piece of music or some reading, and that morning it was even worse because the French novel had only been a kind of soothing suppository to erase Ludmilla's see you later a little as she went off to Patricio and Susana's to manufacture matches or something like that, her distant smile between *mates* and most of all the useless hangover of the even more useless dialogue before we fell asleep last night. Who knows if Marcos was aware of those things, once or twice I had the urge to talk to him about the Fritz Lang dream, then everything fell apart in a dialogue which in some way must have had Ludmilla's absence in it, her almost profiled see you later in the doorway, her red shoes, perhaps it wasn't completely aleatory that Marcos should be talking about women, that through the tobacco smoke he should be looking at me and talking about women, the way in which we were killing time was really admirable.

An idea of the conversation:

"I've made life impossible for all of them," Marcos says for example. "We ask too much of them, probably, or we don't have any luck, we choose badly. And yet it isn't a problem of choice because in other areas I've got no complaints, quite the contrary. But enthusiasm, no, never."

"Your idea of enthusiasm has too much of the tarantula about it," I tell him. "Seeing something that attracts your attention and leaping up and waving your arms are all one and the same thing. You started the famous microagitation in your apartment, but I, for example, don't pretend that a woman will let her hair down so easily over a painting by Max Ernst or a piece by Xenakis; they have their own metabolism, my friend, and, besides, who knows but that underneath it all they may be greater enthusiasts than we are, you just shouldn't confuse emotions with gymnastics."

"I get the feeling it's Sonia I'm listening too, or Magdalena, Lucia," Marcos says, "and I won't go on and name more of them because you'll think I'm playing the Frank Harris or something like that. Look, enthusiasm is a mania, a crisis, being outside yourself so you can receive what knocked you off your hinges better, and I can't understand ataraxic enthusiasm, in every case it's something else, concentration or spiritual enrichment, whatever you want to call it, but not enthusiasm; and I can't really love anyone who at some moment of the day or night doesn't go wild with joy because the movie on the corner is showing Buster Keaton, something like that."

"Now I understand why your enthusiasm doesn't last very long, old man."

"Last night, for example, when you talked about going to the Boulevard Sébastopol for some French fries and taking a stroll through the financial district, Ludmilla started leaping, you must remember, her eyes got big and she was like a guitar, I don't know, something trembling and vibrating, and not because of your Max Ernst or your Xenakis but just over some French fries and roaming about until dawn, unimportant things."

I look at him unhurriedly, letting him finish, but Marcos lowers his head and drinks his grappa with all his hair, which is a lot, between us.

"Yes, Ludmilla almost reacts that way," I admit. "It isn't exactly what I love her for, but it counts, indeed it counts. Of course, she's just as capable of being oblivious to it all as anyone else. I've seen her come out wet like a newborn kitten, curl up in a corner of things and lick her fur for days on end until she discovers again that the sun rises around six-thirty."

"No one is claiming that a woman has to be in a state of permanent paroxysm; and if you think I don't have my depressions . . . That's not it, but there are constants, latencies, call them what you will. For me enthusiasm has to be a constant and never an exception or a kind of holiday for the feelings. That's what happened to Lucía and Magdalena and it wasn't their fault, poor things, they were simply tied to a kind of indifference, but that's not the worst, old man," Marcos says handing me the empty glass, "the worst is that they don't lack the capacity to go to extremes, how could they, but they tend to apply it negatively, that is, when they don't like something or everything is going badly in politics or in the kitchen, then they're capable of rows, indignation, an eloquence that outdoes Stokely Carmichael. They've got their motor full-speed in reverse, I mean they're champions when it comes to putting on the brakes, I don't know if you follow me. You see, if I'm here tomorrow or the next day and I hear Ludmilla raising hell because her zipper broke on her, it will seem perfectly normal to me because I'll remember the French fries, she has every right to fly off the handle since she was floating on air before and happy because you were taking her out for some French fries and to wander through the streets."

"This probably all means that you're going to fall in love with Ludmilla," I told him rather point-blank and because Marcos had every reason in the world, something that nobody likes.

"You can't ever tell," Marcos said. "And not just because of her enthusiasm, as you must know very well."

"What you really want is for a woman to be like a man in her sentimental behavior, to react the way you do to the same things. Last night you were just as enthusiastic as Ludmilla over the French fries, and you were naturally overwhelmed with emotion over the fact that she did or said the same thing as you."

"Not entirely," Marcos said. "I'm not looking for the same reactions because that would be boring; I think I've talked to you about availability, latency, which has to pop up at the right moment and the reasons don't have to be the same, women like different things, etc., as you can understand I'm not going to start fluttering over a shop window full of the latest summer numbers."

"Hum," I said.

"Hum, what?" said Marcos.

"I accept the fact that a drag is a drag, even though she may be a marvel of a woman in some other area."

"She can't be if she's a drag."

"Let me continue, all right? I would say to you that what you define as mania or enthusiasm is something particularly masculine, starting especially with adulthood, because it's notorious that the child is preserved better in men than in women."

"Whatever you say, in any case I'll always look for those women who invent the airplane or the submarine every five minutes, figuratively speaking, who can't see a pair of shears and a sheet of paper without cutting out a rabbit, who cook putting honey instead of oil in the frying pan to see what will happen to the pork chops, and who at any moment are capable of putting eyebrow pencil on their lips and lipstick on their eyebrows."

"Mutatis mutandis, you want them to be just like you, except for the eyebrow pencil."

"Not for them to be like me, but for them to make me feel like me every minute."

"Muses, in a word."

"It's not out of selfishness or because I'm going around looking for levers to move the world. Just that living with a passive woman flattens me a little, it takes away my urge to change the *yerba* in my *mate*, to sing at the top of my lungs in the bath; there's something like a dull call to order, of everything in its place, the canary is sad, the milk doesn't boil over on the stove, it's sinister."

"I know, I've felt it one time or another, but it would seem to be the price you have to pay for other things, old man. Perhaps only the most irregular adventures, high moments of love that intervene, a great flapping of wings as with Nadja or Aurélia can give you that millenary kingdom you're after. The other is two rooms, bath, and kitchen, what they call life, what lasts; some woman told me that and she was right, God was she right. So if Ludmilla and I have lived the way we live it's probably because it's not going to last, and then you can let yourself go with enthusiasm, continue with your ever-so-select vocabulary."

"You ought to know," Marcos said pouring grappa into the glasses with a kind of rage which spilled an ounce on the table cloth, fortunately washable.

"And as far as you're concerned, since women seem to have so little stimulation for you, I wonder if it might not be better for you to try what they call a homosexual experience, who knows, maybe. Look at Orestes and Pylades, Harmodius and Aristogiton, Theseus and Pirithous, you couldn't ask for more enthusiasm judging by all the trouble those boys caused in mythology and history."

"You say it as if it were like buying a different brand of liver pills or something like that."

"Didn't you ever have the experience? Judging from your characterological demands one would wonder if it might not be the answer."

"No, I never did, it doesn't say anything to me. It's not a matter of prejudice, just pure and simple libido. What about you?"

"I did when I was a boy and it was admirable and sad and it

came in very handy on the day I discovered women because the ties were nicely cut and it didn't occur to me to look for pears on elm trees as in your case. Curiously, Ludmilla had a homosexual novitiate that almost brought her to slash her wrists in Cracow on a very snowy day according to the way she tells me. But if you'll permit me a da capo al fine, all this business about enthusiasm and mania is fine as long as it aims high, because for me the enthusiasm of the fans of San Lorenzo or Nicolino Locche, not to mention French fries, leaves me rather unmoved, and if I can be frank the other night for example you people rotted my soul away with your famous vest-pocket response. When you realize that according to a responsible organization there are two hundred fifty thousand political prisoners on this shitty little rag of a world, then your used matches are not exactly any cause for enthusiasm."

Selon Amnesty International

IL Y A 250 000 PRISONNIERS POLITIQUES DANS LE MONDE

Londres *(A.F.P., U.P.I.)*. — Il y a quelque 250 000 prisonniers politique de par le monde, estime un rapport de la section britannique d'Amnesty International, intitulé « *le visage de la persécution en 1970* » et publié dimanche.

L'Indonésie, indique le rapport, détiendrait le record avec quelque cent seize mille prisonniers politiques dont la plupart, arrêtés pour leurs sympathies communistes, n'ont pas été jugés.

L'U.R.S.S. compterait « *quelques milliers* » de prisonniers, et en Afrique du Sud, où la situation « *ne cesse de s'aggraver* », une quinzaine d'entre eux seraient morts, estime encore le rapport.

Le rapport fait valoir que grâce aux efforts d'Amnesty International plus de deux mille détenus politiques ont pu être libérés depuis 1961.

Marcos lit a cigarette with a good one and looked slowly at Andrés.

"Lend me your car so I can go pick up Oscar, he's getting in at one o'clock."

"Sure, it's on the left-hand side of the corner. Why don't you give me an answer to what I just said?"

"If you yourself can't find the answer it isn't worth it."

"Well, don't think I haven't thought about you people and your games, but the only thing that occurs to me is that they're most likely a form of entertainment, let's say fraternity initiation tests for people you don't really know or who don't know themselves. The other possibility is dreary and I'd rather turn off the radio."

"You're right, save your batteries for your aleatory music," Marcos said. "Let me have the car keys. Hi."

"Hi," said Ludmilla who was coming in with artichokes, leeks, and detergents. "I'm a sad tortoise, in the time it took me to prepare two rather poor packs, Susana already had five done and let's not talk about the match boxes. By the way, Manuel ate up one of the better ones, he had to be turned upside down and then we gave him some castor oil, poor Susana is going to have a lot of work on her hands this afternoon. Can you stay for an Argentine stew with ears of corns and everything? Andrés taught me, ask him if they don't turn out good for me."

"I have to go get the turquoise penguin," Marcos said.

"Oh, Andrés, let's go with him to get the penguin."

"You go," I told her, "I want to finish a book that this guy split down the middle on me and in the meantime I'll keep an eye on the stew pot."

"What's this about a penguin?"

"I'll explain it to you in the car," Marcos said, "while you drive, something always appreciated in this benighted city. So you're not coming, eh?"

"No."

"Wait till I wash the leeks and put everything in the pot," said Ludmilla hurrying into the kitchen.

"She's enthusiastic," Andrés said, "and not over French fries."

"Have you ever seen how they feed geese so that they'll develop cirrhosis and the pâté will be more delicate? We should get one of those funnels to make this kid drink his soup."

Manuel prudently ignored his father's high-flying plans, but Susana produced four words of the kind that a true and brave Argentine child ought not to hear in his early infancy. The mimeograph machine was humming in the back of the room, soundproofed as well as possible by a screen that was backed up by blankets and a record by Aníbal Troilo, Pichuco. In the hands of Gómez and Monique it was working ten times better and the material in French and Spanish was almost ready; the one I told you took a look at them and was startled at how laconic and objective they were for documents apparently meant to provoke a more convulsive reaction; in any case, the demands of the Screwery were specified with great clarity, the people at Reuters and other Washingtonian agencies would have to use all of their rhetorical pomade to deform them. At the other end of the table where Patricio and the soup had a two-to-one advantage, although Manuel wasn't numbered among those who give up silently, Susana the farsighted kept on putting together the reader destined for a still remote literacy campaign, work that consisted of pasting up news items in several languages which would also contribute at the same time to the poor little bugger's bilingualization. The one I told you was an attentive observer of the progress of the reader and a collaborator when he had the time and he especially liked the fact that Susana was cultivating Manuel's future intuitive and inventive powers, and among other things he was the donor of an epigraph that Edgard Varèse had inscribed in *Arcana* and which according to Andrés had come down from none other than Paracelsus, but you couldn't really say much about it after all of its mutations for the one I told you had translated it into Spanish on the basis of a French text that must have come from a Latin or German original, which, in any case, said: *The first star is that of the Apocalypse. The second is that of the ascendant. The third is that of the elements, which are four. Thus there are six stars. And there is another, which is the star of Imagination.*

"Humbug," said Gómez, emerging from behind the screen and covered with Gestetner ink, "the usual illuminist, alchemist, and, in any case, spiritualist vocabulary. I don't buy that garbage any more."

"You're delivering yourself of a horsesassery," Patricio put in in a mannerly way. "The error of a system with respect to the posterior verifications of science is one thing, but its intrinsic truth, something that remains even though the base is a pile of trash, is something else. Look how much in Platonism and Aristotelianism lacks support and yet nobody can read those two old goat-bearded Greeks without coming away richer than the other one, the hubby-dubby of Maria Callas, who, by the way and in Spanish at least, couldn't have a more contradictory last name."

"Goolp," said the soup and Manuel in tight accord, broken instantly by a coughing spell that cast them in opposite directions. Watching Patricio drying his face in the midst of foul interjections, the one I told you thought thanksbetogod the little rabbi wasn't there because he would have locked horns with Gómez; a step away from taking Paracelsus's and Susana's part, he preferred to remain silent and go on inspecting Manuel's reader, remembering vaguely a phrase of Burne-Jones's in which the artist asserted that the more materialistic science became, the more angels he would go on painting. Needless to say, the incitements for Manuel's imagination had nothing angelic about them, for Susana had foreseen that at the age of nine he would already be in a position to make his entry into contemporary history through things like:

Córdoba: Four Extremists Tortured

Findings by police doctor

CÓRDOBA, 9 (AP).—The police doctor has shown proof that four extremists were submitted to torture and the district attorney has undertaken legal action against the police officers involved, according to judicial reports. Those involved are Carlos Heriberto Astudillo, Alberto Camps, Marcos Osatinsky, and Alfredo Kohn, accused of having participated in the December 29th attack on the Banco de Córdoba in which two policemen died, according to prosecutor José Namba Carmona. In his statement, the court official states that the medical examiner, Dr. Raúl Zunino, "has ascertained in his examination tremendous inhuman treatment and brutal punishment."

"All of the prisoners show," he asserts, "after a week of torture and mistreatment external bruises and scars of inconceivable dimensions. Astudillo's back is completely bruised and there are multiple marks produced by an electric prod. Osatinsky has internal injuries which seem to have affected his heart, he speaks with difficulty and walks slowly and painfully. All are in need of urgent medical attention."

"Call Marcos," Gómez told Patricio, "the buns are fresh out of the oven and nice and hot. Give me a glass of wine, Monique, this ink's got into my very soul."

Images, images; the one I told you thought about the fact that three minutes before Gómez had risen up against Paracelsus and now the ink was getting into his soul, the same imagination he had just put down was giving him that means of expressing his fatigue. Look at this, Susana insisted weeping with laughter while she pasted in another clipping for the pupil's future, it's good that in this shitty world you can still find compensations even without leaving the little corner where your existence began, even in a movie house on Suipacha, whenever I went there to see a Gregory Peck movie you should have seen the look my husband would put on, he's even jealous of celluloid. I'd better read it, it's the one that really gets right down to it:

Sentenced for Crime of Disrespect for National Anthem

The Criminal Division of the Federal Court gave a sentence of two months in prison, suspended, to Alberto Dionisio López, Argentine, 22 years old, single, employed and a student, as the author of the crime of disrespect for the National Anthem, which is set forth in Article 230 of the Penal Code, incorporated a short time back into our restrictive legislation and which sets forth punishment of from 2 months to 2 years imprisonment for public disrespect for the national flag, shield, or anthem or the emblems of an Argentine province.

" 'On July 9 last, when the National Anthem was played at the second evening show in the movie theater at 378 Suipacha, López remained seated and when questioned by an usher he said that he did not stand because he was a British subject and if he had known that it was a breach he would have gone to the toilet.' Then there are several dull paragraphs about a first dismissal of the charges and an overturned verdict, and a prosecutor appears who says inter alia: 'There is no doubt that he (López) heard the notes of the National Anthem and remained seated voluntarily and consciously as opposed to the time-honored tradition and custom imposed by a spontaneous and patriotic veneration of that symbol of nationhood. It is quite clear, then, that he ignored the admonition to stand, preferring to leave the theater and declaring to the astonishment of all that he would have chosen to go to the toilet.' "

"He probably went to hear the sound of broken chains, as the anthem says," Patricio said, "that's a joke we used to make in the fourth grade so that it would be good for you to put that chronicle among Manuel's readings too, and that way I'll avoid the corrosive reproaches of the one I told you." (Who, lost in Paracelsus, couldn't care less).

So much is done in jest and because of what we think is jest and then the other thing begins afterwards and underneath there's a kind of surreptitious recurrence of the jest or the pun or the gratuitous act, which climbs up onto the roof of what isn't jest, onto the base of the column of life to dictate hidden ordinances from there, modify movements, corrode customs, in any case,
in jest
Oscar had sent Marcos the clipping about the riot of the girls in La Plata from time to time and had forgotten about it because getting the containers ready was a slow and delicate operation in Gladis's apartment with the help of Gladis who now and then would leave off sealing up the containers to have some poodee-doo with Oscar who would give it back to her in a tumultuous way, and then they would have a shower and a drink and listen to the news and go out to eat, but the memory of the riot opened up a path again, the images created by a simple reading of a news item would become fixed like the ones in those dreams that refuse to be dislodged even though good sense must protest. Gladis who had also read the clipping had a more logical view of things and
such good friends the
Oscar's allusions appeared to her to be fatigue or nervousness,
two girls
she would get him off the subject with a little mental nudge, Oscar would laugh and hide another stack of dollars Made by Old Man Collins in the double walls of the container, would prepare the glue, would go pet the turquoise penguin who since the night before had had the run of the bathtub sharing showers with an enthusiastic flapping of wings and eating a wild amount of hake. The royal armadillos had arrived from the Chaco that night and would have to be at Ezeiza by eleven o'clock in the morning, a last-minute panic because functional readjustments

change the hostess shifts and a phone call from the assistant traffic chief to inform Gladis that she had the night flight to New York, Gladis and an unconquerable dramatic-astrological number, everybody has premonitions, Oteiza, I won't change planes, remember Marialín that time, I know, I know, you can call it crazy, but please, I've told you people many times that without five days notice I stay home, all right, fine, I'm sure Lola will take it, she doesn't care, she told me so, and Oscar in the bathroom petting the penguin so he won't let out a squawk that would why the full moon? be telephonically upsetting to the upset Oteiza who had it all arranged in five minutes so Gladis shouldn't worry. They could breathe freely, at nine o'clock Feliciano arrived with the royal armadillos and news from the north that wasn't as bad as usual; now in seat number 234B hanging at thirty thousand feet somewhere over the Atlantic and clinging to the tail of the Boeing in that always rather confused location where baskets, orange juice, toilet, paper cups, small bottles of scotch, stewardesses trafficking in perfume and cigarettes and a more or less clear space between the cupboards with trays and the last row of seats, so that the containers were between Oscar's seat and the cupboard on the port side, and Gladis would stop at every chance she had to have a look at Oscar's domain as he was scientifically strengthened by the authoritative way in which he had overseen the operation of loading the containers and proceeded to the first inspection of the armadillos and the turquoise penguin. Several ladies had already had occasion to show their enthusiasm at the sight of the penguin, which Oscar would take out of the container every half-hour to give it a ration of hake and cheer it up at such a critical moment in its life, so Oscar was having a good time turning the penguin loose in the cabin to let it the wall with broken glass stroll about and both Téllez the steward and Pepita the other airchick approved of the penguin's therapeutic walk since by consensus the passengers had proclaimed it the mascot of the aircraft piloted by Captain Pedernera, all of this amidst trays, blankets, and drinks, which made the trip an unforgettable experience, I swear to you, due to

having chosen the national airline in the course of their travels. In any case, it was time to think a little about what was waiting at the other end, to start assuming the air of the veterinarian con-
why the full moon?
scious of his important mission now, the problem would be to keep from laughing in Marcos's face when he introduced him to the officials of the Vincennes zoo (especially since one of them would be Patricio, so how could he help laughing) and there would be many spectators to witness the transfer of the armadillos and the penguin. Would there be toasts, speeches? Good Lord, Oscar thought, how can I help but rolling on the ground when I see Marcos and Patricio, and maybe even that damned Heredia is in Paris now and will show up all of a sudden to put me on, stinking monkey-chaser. In some way he understood that he was trying not to think beyond that, that was all prologue, predrome, prescrewery, afterwards there would be his first talk with Marcos, the ants, the real Screwery that must quickly follow the transfer of the armadillos because the ants must have found out about it of course, they weren't idiots, the ants, there might even be one on the plane, pointing at him like Pelé on the soccer field, what an honor, old man, Marcos would have everything synchronized and no one would be getting much sleep in Paris, he'd better catch a couple of winks between the penguin's strolls, it was impossible to get any idea of what was waiting for him there and, besides, he had so little urge to think about it, the drone of the jet and the double whiskies, the seat back into third position, taking his ease, why the full moon, maybe there wasn't a full moon that night, the clipping spoke about carnival, music,
so delicate, the reporter
dances at clubs in the district that had excited the young women, but it all came back with a full moon that made the broken glass
he'd better prepare some words
on the wall sparkle, the dirt road that went off to the city, the white nightgowns, it was flight again, the shove against the doors,
because he certainly
the shouts and the hysterical laughter, as in Doña Raquela's
would have to say something when he presented the creatures
courtyard, the full moon was an imperious call, a heartbeat that drove his breath off its track, his skin, the plush of his voice, everything was becoming a crouching and a whipping, possession

that could not be refused tightened around waists and stomachs and the glow of eyes in the corners with jasmines, over the wall over which the girls had climbed maddened by the ads for clubs in the district, the girls in love jumping in one single embrace, one watching over the other, kissing in the shadows, almost naked, already trembling at the sirens of the police cars as they came closer, the solitary ones standing, fists clenched, waiting for the first attack to fight until they collapsed, or running through the shadows of a street full of sharp objects and threats howling
there probably wasn't any moon he'd be better off thinking about his speech
hysterically without knowing at what, at full moon and carnival, at unanswered desires, until they ran into the arms of officious neighborhood people or jovial firemen who lifted them up like feathers until the first scratch cut their faces and then the big hard male slap, the settle down, dirty word, what you need is a good old hot iron, here they are, lieutenant, shit the way these fillies are carrying on. Opening his eyes and seeing the cabin windows going all the way down the compartment of the plane
Tell Sosa not to get so
and the backs of the necks of the passengers, Oscar was being
worked up with the kids
turned into something without a real base, Gladis's perfect figure miniskirted and deodorized came down the aisle with a little plastic tray and two whiskey glasses, the hostess smile which was finally her own smile, up ahead there they were quite drunk already, now I can spend a little time with you. He would have liked to have talked to her about that, the full moon and the flight toward the wall and the shrieks, but it was absurd, he had to think about their arrival, about Marcos, who would introduce him to the representatives of the Vincennes zoo, damned sure that Heredia, then Gladis translating and helping him get through without any problems, through the various defensive barriers of a
with his fatigue, he'll flip,
civilized nation that fears the contamination of exotic animals,
what do I care about that business in La Plata
and afterwards the illustrious representatives of the zoo doubling up with laughter in the car, it was wild, how are things, old man, that great big hollow that was waiting at the other end of the flight, getting involved in matters of the Screwery, Marcos and
another bit of idiocy sending the clipping to
Heredia would hide their joy that he was there, the still uncertain

Marcos
fate of the turquoise penguin once the mission was accomplished, not to mention the royal armadillos, although Marcos had probably arranged it so that later on someone would really donate them to the zoo, poor beasts, unknown parties abandon baskets superintendent's door, with the typed manual of instructions hanging around the penguin's neck because this animal is delicate and won't be satisfied with refrigerated codfish or stale vegetables, the Antarctic is Argentine, goddamn it.

let me, go, please, let me go
No, he couldn't talk about that to Gladis, better to have a whiskey together, next stop Dakar, Gladis on his shoulder and perfumed by Guerlain, whiskey absolutely scotch reserve twelve
when he told her about it in Buenos Aires it already hadn't
years old aged in oak barrels, the pleasure of finding Gladis's skin
had much effect
under the helmet of saffroned hair, tickling her slowly, feeling her tremble against him, murmuring to her you're a great chick, if only you could escape from the asylum, if only you could escape someday too, but how could he say that last bit, Gladis would have looked at him perplexed (what asylum?) and besides it would have been unfair because in some way Gladis was already halfway on the road to escape, up on the wall under the full moon, wonderful snotnose kid who was risking her job by getting
how many cut their
the animals and the veterinarian on board, if the ants got to find
hands on the broken glass on top of the wall
out someday they were capable of anything, torturing her or killing her like Rosa in Tucumán or the little Italian girl from Avellaneda. Because they would have to talk about that right away with Marcos and Heredia, the ants might already be on the plane, it wasn't very probable, but in any case they wouldn't be long in finding out and raising hell. You're a wild chick, Oscar said putting all of his face into Gladis's hair, you don't know how wild you are yourself. I haven't got the slightest notion, Gladis said, really surprised, but don't muss up my hair, please, there's a terrible restriction in the company rules. I love you very much and you're wild, Oscar insisted, and how he would have liked to have put her beside the full moon, tell her what he didn't know how to say because Gladis would have sat looking at him, something like be careful when you jump, or it's full of broken glass

up here, can't you see it shining? he was really a little flipped out because the thing was getting obsessive, it was idiotic and even dangerous, especially the idea of jumping, of climbing over the wall covered with glass and getting to the dirt road, leaving the asylum behind, seeing only Gladis among the maddened girls fleeing two by two or three by three, hollering and panting, helping each other scale the wall, the black girl had taken off her
is this what
nightgown to throw it over the glass, this way, I'll jump first, give
I'm going to say for a speech, by God
Marta your hand, can't you see she can't reach, wait till I get up first, who says that wasn't a full moon that night, actually it was
an unexpected blackout was the occasion for the start of an infernal battle
the darkness that gave them the chance to escape, it seems, I can't remember too well any more but why, then, I'm going to have to take care of myself, brother.

"I want to be with you tonight," Oscar said, "I suppose they'll leave me in peace until tomorrow after the morning ceremony. What goes on in Paris, do you have a hotel room there or what?"

"We hostesses live an extremely law-abiding life," Gladis explained, breaking up with laughter, "so the gentleman will have to find a hotel of his own."

Cooing, she received the kiss on the ear, the caress that slipped down under her blouse, she felt a little pink finger slowly lifting itself at the summit of the mound where Oscar's hand was roving slowly, circularly. Well, said Gladis, even though in principle we're not allowed to take these confidences with gentlemen passengers, I can inform you that you have a room all set with bath right next to mine, big booby, I sent the cable before we left, there's still a little gray matter here, you know. And not just that cable, because the other one, BESITOS COCA, was already causing two cars to race along the southern highway, so that three lines, one aerial and two terrestrial, were converging in a synchronized way toward the moment and place where rare representatives of Argentine fauna would be delivered to equally rare French representatives. Oscar closed his eyes and saw Gladis go off once more to do her duty amidst a dispersal of trays, what in the hell was more absurd in the end, the ceremony at the airport

or that recurring presence of something he had not known or lived, which had no reason to matter to him at all, two columns in a newspaper, a mad race brought on by a blackout (brought on by a blackout?), the girls possessed by moon and carnival, half-naked in a river of light that was driving them toward the other, the opposite shore, the beginning of something that might
and the Screwery if we think hard about it
be anything because one didn't think about that, rape or a broken nose or nightsticks on the behind, in any case no longer one hundred ninety-six girls crammed together where there was room
the director declares
for eighty with fifty-six more young women expected from one moon to the next.

It was like that sometimes, the one I told you wasn't always up on the movements of the others; for example, he didn't have the slightest idea that the austere representatives of the Vincennes zoo would choose Lonstein to drive the American car rented from Hertz with previous specifications as to color and characteristics in keeping with the importance of the ceremony. Learning about something through the little rabbi's version always called for a decoding, but this time the breadth of the Lonsteinian symphonic movement made him take to his bed for several days, although he was never sorry at having followed the disembarkation of the royal armadillos and the turquoise penguin through the view that Lonstein modestly called plurispectromutandic, or that if the armadillos seemed visibly uprooted on treading French soil, the penguin immediately showed an almost disturbing vivacity, throwing itself against the walls of the container in spite of Oscar's whistling like a trainer and the water mixed with Equanil that Gladis had given it as soon as the Boeing began its approach and Captain Pedernera through Pepita's voice wished the ladies and gentlemen a pleasant stay in Paris.

"The three of them made it megacardiac," Lonstein had resumed; "you can imagine the ceremony in the waiting room, boy, all that was missing was Haile Selassie with his black cape handing out Abyssinian medals."

I was missing too, but Ludmilla told me in the afternoon that Roland and Lucien Verneuil had got out of the car with ramrod dignity and that the exchange of greetings between the Argentine veterinarian delegated to present the animals and the representatives of the zoo receiving said beasts had seemed perfectly normal to the customs officials, inspectors, and airport cops, not to mention the local veterinarian commissioned to take a close look at the alien products and check their clinical data, all of this elegantly translated by Gladis, who was taking visible joy in the linguistic problems of the scientists present. On the way Marcos had told Ludmilla that at first there were no difficulties because the operation was too absurd not to turn out well; the only contretemps would be if some astute customs man thought that the containers were better suited for the transport of leopards than penguins, an argument that Lucien Verneuil and Roland were ready to demolish with scientific reasons based on Buffon and Julian Huxley, not to mention the influence of the imposing rented car, the whole gestalt. Not only were the customs men enchanted with the animals, but the woman who seemed to be in charge, a buxom black lady, fell in love with the turquoise penguin and promised to visit it regularly at the Vincennes zoo, a piece of news received with great seriousness by the representatives of the zoo and with particular patriotic emotion on the part of the delivering veterinarian. You missed a work of genius, Ludmilla said, Oscar so Argentine with his gray checked jacket and his hair combed at the last minute with a touch of perfume from on board that I recognized from a distance because it's more for women, and Lonstein with a leather jacket and a beret to give the impression of a typical Frenchman, the kind you can't find hide or hair of anymore, but after all.

"And what did you do there?" asked Andrés.

"I pissed in my pants, I'll never know whether from fear or from laughing, fear most likely, I think. Wait till I go change them now that I think of it, if I can find another pair."

Everything smells a little of leeks but I'm not hungry, there's Bartók's last quartet, the wine, and the tobacco, taking a look every so often at the stew pot and wondering whether I should wait for Ludmilla or go out and roam around. That story about the penguin that Marcos told me before asking for the car, probably another one of his rather idiotic microagitations; rolling through the last movement of the quartet, still taking part in an order that before and after will be missing for me (the future in the past, but yes, but of course), I prolong as long as possible that precarious interregnum of conciliation, a real product of bad faith, I let myself be until some moment when I will call Francine and take off down the stairs. Wandering about Paris is my other music, night brought no counsel, there's something like the need for a supplementary time of the quartet, never written by Bartók but latent in some region of the duration that clocks don't include, a demand for order that makes me restless, a knowing without knowing that brings back the aura, the restlessness of the dream about the movies on Fritz Lang night; going along as if feeling my way down the street with no pre-fixed destiny has something of an opening about it, a potentiality that at some corner or hour one will hear the first phrase of that musical piece that would reconcile me with so many fleeing or precarious things, Ludmilla mine and not mine, Ludmilla more and more among penguins and agitators, the dull nausea of losing her through an accumulation of behavior patterns that can't be reconciled and at the same time that feeling that it has to be that way, that we've reached the limit and that something is going to break silently leaving us on opposite sides of the fissure, the huge crevasse of the present, with useless friendly signals, tears and handkerchiefs, naked in a black wind. And so once more any subway opening at all will carry me to my favorite neighborhoods or will suggest to me through phonetic association, vaguely magical, a still unknown station where another direction of the infinite carpet that is Paris will be born, another mystery box, other chances. Otherwise that somewhat lugubrious notion that has driven me for sometime now to lose myself in the city as in music, in going back and forth between Francine and Ludmilla (why going back and forth, why that dissociation that I reject, that I've tried to erase so much, that belongs exclusively to their points of view?) is being translated into curious discoveries, vaguely in accord with the state of mind that serves me as a rhythm. Yesterday, after crossing the sad Place Clichy with its alienated and bitter crowds and losing myself in the Rue Coulaincourt, I saw for the first time under a slate-gray sky the prow of the Hotel Terrass, its six or seven stories with windows and balconies opening out over the Montmartre cemetery. In the middle of the bridge hanging over the arches and tombs like a sad flea-market last-judgment sword, I leaned on the railing and asked myself if it were true, if it could be true, if every morning the tourists and provincials staying at the Hotel Terrass would just open their blinds over a petrified sea of gravestones, and whether it was possible after that to order breakfast with croissants, go out into the street, start living a new day.

I'll have to go spend a night in that hotel, listen in the darkness to the sounds of Montmartre which slowly give way to silence, hear the last bus on the resonant bridge, the suspension over death, the balcony breathed in by that other immobile and secret noise that life rejects with words, with love, with obstinate oblivion. I'm going to take you along, Francine, so that you can have your first authentic lesson in pataphysics, little French girl, bookish and Cartesian (like me) and not that easy literary acceptance that you confuse, we confuse so many times with what runs beneath the skin of the day. And some afternoon I'll also take you to that gallery near the Palais-Royal where the dust has been falling as if time were depositing its cinerary matter on the glass cases and the hallways, a dust that smells of gloves and feathers and dried violets, and I will show you without ostentation, almost furtively, as one must do in *inhabited* zones, the showcase with the ancient dolls. There they have been since God knows when, dusty with their little capes, their bows, their conventional perukes, their black or white shoes, the stupid sadness of their smiling faces where tiny fingers touched, fingers that today are also dust or perhaps love sonnets in some bourgeois memory book. The shop is very small and the two times I looked in the window I couldn't see anyone inside; there is a suspicion of a stairway in the rear, dark curtains, more dust. Some kind of shameful traffic must be taking place at other hours of the day, people probably come to sell their family dolls, the best ones, made of ceramic or porcelain, and others probably come to choose for their collections, to stroll through that minute rigid brothel with Dutch showcases, looking at thighs, touching throats, making the blue eyes roll in their sockets, necessary rites amidst exclamations and long silences, commentaries from the saleslady whom I imagine old and withered, and perhaps visits to an attic where loose heads and legs, interchangeable clothing, coiffures, and shoes have most likely been accumulated, Bluebeard's crypt for a doubtful innocence of tea and cookies, a gift for the aunt who collects dolls to conjure time away. And perhaps

"It could be like that or quite different," Francine said, rubbing her finger along the shop window, drawing back as if displeased by something. "Why don't you put an end to your doubts? We can go in, look around. You prefer the mystery, of course, any definition disenchants you."

"The same as any doubt bothers you," I told her, "the same way that everything looks like a demonstrable theorem to you. I don't want to go in there, I've got nothing to do there, I don't need that knowledge that makes you sleep well with your hands under the pillow and without dreams in which madwomen in white wigs throw themselves from the balconies of a hotel that overlooks a cemetery."

"You'll never stop being silly, never stop refusing to understand me."

"You see: understand you. What have we done but understand each other in the only way possible, by the flesh, eyes, words that weren't only meanings? My little eye-bee-em machine, light-oriented bee, no one understands you better than I, reddest of heads. I don't need your reasoning to understand you or to go into that shop in order to know that it's a trap made of distorting mirrors."

"Yes, illusions," Francine said, pressing against me, "the happiness of preferring imagination over truth. You're right, I'm sorry. You're so right, Andrés."

Her damp lips, always a little anxious and so different from what they said. We began to laugh, to wander through the neighborhood until fatigue and desire started leading us to Francine's apartment in Le Marais, above her book and stationery shop; I liked going into the establishment that Madame Franck was taking care of at that time with the look of the perfect responsible partner who sees the younger partner arrive with her friend almost as if they were customers, I liked to thumb through the latest things, buy a pad or a book from Madame Franck and pay for them in front of Francine who would have liked to have given them to me so much. By an inside stariway one could go up to the apartment which was orderly and precise like Francine, perfumed with lavender, indirectly lighted, a purring cat of a parlor and two rooms, blue-carpeted cat, library cat with the Pléiade collection and the Littré, of course, Francine and the refrigerator, Francine and the cut glass, Francine and the scotch, Francine moving faithful to a mental honesty that brought her into confrontation with me the twisted one, the dishonest one with shop windows and hotels with balconies overlooking cemeteries. Francine in her precise cage, the other side of my life Ludmilla, the incarnation of an old nostalgia, a design defined in the days and things of life, and at the same time the almost immediate rejection of so much intelligent and reasonable convention, symmetrical to that other rejection Ludmilla from the disorder of a kitchen where pieces of leek were hung all over the place, the transistor vomiting up Radio Montecarlo, a disgusting dishrag wrapping the only healthy cup of a tea service like a hand of infamy before running out to pick up a penguin.

"But you love her, Andrés. I'm your counter-coup, the thing that gives you back to her for a little while. It's not a reproach, I love you, you know it, I keep you the way you are, in your world, from the other side where I don't recognize anything, don't recognize anyone, none of your friends, the life you lead with them, the South Americans I only meet in novels and movies."

"It's not just my fault," I tell her gruffly, "that whole tribe includes Ludmilla too and the pair of you have decreed that you can't and you shouldn't ever meet, ever."

"I wonder how we could meet, what basis could a relationship with what surrounds us have, with this world. You go back and forth, the way I could go back and forth if I had another boyfriend; once, it's so long ago now, I thought vaguely that it was possible, but everything stayed that way, vague. You really don't love us, Andrés, it's the only explanation possible, I'm sorry, I know the psychology of love and all that disgusts you, everything that doesn't really suit you deep down disgusts you, I'm sorry again."

"That's not what disgusts me, it's what lies behind, the absurd resistance of a world that's cracking up and keeps on furiously defending its most decrepit forms. To love, not to love, formulas. I've been happy with Ludmilla, I was perfectly happy with her when I met you and saw that you were a different pleat in the fold of happiness, a different way of being happy without renouncing what I was living; and I told you that right away, and you let me come here without any conditions, accepting."

"One always accepts," Francine said, "time is long and a person tells herself that. Maybe. Perhaps one day. Because love."

"The deduction is the same, of course; the two of you are the ones who really love while I, et cetera. Look, everything's become a shambles between me and Ludmilla, you know that, because she hasn't accepted either, because my being honest didn't serve any good purpose, I know in my own way that being honest for me means that she and you know that there are you and she, that's all, but it didn't work, it'll never work, we're living at a time when everything is leaping through the air and still, you see, all those schemes are still ingrained in people like us, you can see now that I'm talking about the petit bourgeoisie or the workers, people who are nucleated and familiated and marryated and hearth-and-homated and proletated, oh shit, shit."

"And you," said Francine who was almost having fun, "are playing U Thant between Ludmilla and me, the conciliator, the bee between two flowers, something like that; I'd like to see you having coffee with both of us at the same time, or taking us to the movies one on each arm. Oh, you shake me up."

"I hope so, love, I hope so."

"No, U Thant, I love you this way, on my side, and one day you'll leave me or I'll leave you, without talking about Ludmilla's having gone off after the penguins from what you tell me, but you still haven't explained all that to me."

"You don't like me to talk to you about her, I know that only too well."

"And Ludmilla must get all upset when you mention my name to her, it's obvious. But here we have the penguin business, you've got to admit that it is out of the ordinary, we could easily make an exception."

"You're a good girl," Andrés said, "much too good."

"Now you really are going to shake me up. It's bad enough already for things to be stupid and absurd, you know that I can stand it, that you sought me out, that I gave you the key to my place and fine, I accept us as we are, I accept myself at the other end of the yarn and Ludmilla is probably doing the same, I imagine, my sister on the other side, holding the opposite end of the yarn."

"And she said that last bit with a sarcastic, an almost cruel laugh," I told her, kissing her on the shoulder, hugging her until I hurt her. "Yes, of course, your sister at the other end thinks the same even though she says it with language that's more low-down than yours. And that's how the three of us go along and that's how the three of us are going to go along until the ball of yarn falls into the claws of the cosmic cat or Marcos's penguin, it's time I explained his entrance on stage to you, today at precisely thirteen hours on the Orly side. It's probably a political secret so don't say anything to Madame Franck who as we well know is a reactionary dogging runner."

"Exit U Thant," said Francine, "and enter the smiling torturer."

It had been some time since we'd got deep into the ritual dialogues, the perfect exutory which with Ludmilla were a kind of verbal delirium ending in attacks of rug and laughter, and with Francine the back and forth of soft arrows aimed ever closer to the neck veins, the meeting of the thighs.

"The torturer," I told her, "presents you with this little ancient piece of perfection: *Y para más despacio atormentarme/llevóme alguna vez por entre flores*, which translated from the Spanish means and to torture me more slowly, sometimes he took me among flowers."

"That poet already knew us over the distances of time," Francine said with the ritual voice.

"Oh yes: Francine Sacher-Masoch, Andrés de Sade."

We could go on like that, prolong the ritual, sadness and desire gradually exchanged their gloves and mists, making love with Francine was more than abolishing differences, establishing a brief territory of contact, for then Francine not only rid herself of everything that raised her up against me but on her own, a river of copper leading her by the hand, entered a zone of incredible storms, and how else could it be said, she would call to me in a broken voice, she would give herself like a flood of cymbals and nails. She was always the first to raise her hand to the switch that turned off a time of affronted figures, of enemy words, to turn on for us another light where a vocabulary made up of a few quite intense things created its sheet language, its pillow murmur, there where a tube of cream or a lock of hair were clues or signs, Francine letting herself be undressed by the side of the bed, her eyes closed, her reddish almost kinky hair against my face, shivering with every movement of my fingers on her buttons and zippers, slipping down to a sitting position so I could take off her stockings and lower her panties, not looking at me, all by touch, even when I abandoned her for a moment to take my clothes off in that silence of a cord stretched out between two lovers waiting for each other, who fulfill previous movements, Francine slipping until she was on her back, her feet on the rug, already moaning with an anxious and broken murmur, skin music, answering through her moan the mouth that was climbing up her thighs, the hands that were moving them apart for that first deep kiss, the muffled cry when my tongue reached the clitoris and that suction was born, that diminutive, localized coitus, I felt her hand going into my hair, pulling it pitilessly, calling me up and at the same time making me linger to the limit, giving her a pleasure that wasn't mine, the slave on his knees, on the rug, clutched by the hair, obliged to prolong the salty warm libation, my fingers searching deeper inside for the double petal of the retracted sex, the index finger slipping to the back, looking for the other entry, hard and firm, knowing that Francine would murmur "No, no," resisting a simultaneous double caress, concentrating almost savagely on her frontal pleasure, calling me now with two hands gripping my hair to slide up, dragging her with me to lay her on her back in the depths of the bed, she would straighten up, rolling over onto me, wrapping my sex with one hand and possessing it with her dry, harsh mouth which slowly filled with froth and saliva, tightening her lips until it hurt me, impaling herself onto an interminable panting which I had to get her out of because I didn't want her to drink me, I needed her more deeply than that, in the tide of her womb which devoured me and gave me back while the tainted mouths came together and I encircled her shoulders, burning her breasts with a pressure that she sought and made greater, lost now in a strangled and continuous cry, a call in which there was almost a rejection and at the same time the wish to be taken, possessed with every muscle and every gesture, her mouth half-open and her eyes rolling, her chin sinking into my throat, her hands running over my back, clutching my behind, pulling me even harder up against her until she began to arch in a convulsion, or was I the one who first sank as deep as I could when the liquid fire reached my thighs, we were conjoined in the same moan, in the freeing of that indestructible force that once more was spurt and tear and sob, the slow whiplash of an instant that was plunging the world into a roll toward the pillow, sleep, the murmur of recognition amidst uncertain caresses and hot sweat.

Thistledown, thirsty, unquenchable music of Francine's body in heat, how could I tell her some time that she only gave in to freedom in love, she decided upon or respected the wildest imagination of desire without those vigilant shears with which, before and after, she would recut the shape of the present to readjust it to ideas and give it that neatness that so much vigilant intelligence demands. How could I tell her that that bed, that white redhead skin, that blonde fuzz, were the gates through which one really had to enter the doll shop without the demands of sane reason that were slowly waking up, becoming a cigarette and a profile on the pillow, a sated and maybe bitter smile, the first watchful glance around the four walls of the room, at the night that was beginning to fall with some phone call to make, with shower, deodorant, the movies at nine on the dot, the rest of the day with Madame Franck in the impeccable bookstore office where no one ever found leeks on the floor or cups wrapped up in dirty dishcloths. How could he tell her in some other way that he loved her when all the rest was back on this side again, when U

Thant, of course, when Ludmilla. Waking up, looking at her still asleep, the vague light of the lamp slipping along her red almost kinky hair, a hand that was so white upon her throat; awakening her with caresses that made her contract and coo a vague smiling protest still mixed with threads of sleep; and knowing that in the end that moment would come when those eyes would look at me as from afar and become fixed on mine then, intense and regretful, run over my face, my head, as if doubting it was I. And kissing each other, and knowing that thirst, that whiskey on ice, that dinner, that outside, already on the way back in absence, back from a long trip with stops at restaurants, at shop windows with dusty dolls, talking about the penguin.

In any case Oscar had gone through a rather tight half hour and even though he was lucky enough not to be called upon to say more than four words that the Argentine Zoophilia Society and all the rest, the moment of getting into the car and leaving the customs people behind was one of alleviation which can only be expressed by opening one's briefcase and taking out the box of Córdoba pastries for Marcos, the recipient immediately ignored by Ludmilla and Gladis who proceeded to gobble up the lion's share while the victim and Oscar exchanged first impressions about the Aramburu mess and General Levingston's sudden coming to the fore. What about that damned Heredia, Oscar wanted to know as he breathed in the air of the expressway as if it were pure and felt incredibly happy. He's getting in from London tonight, Marcos said. They have sweets like this in Poland, Ludmilla observed, but no sweet milk candy, never. I can teach you how to make it, Gladis proposed as she too was being reborn after the half hour of protocol, if we can get some cane sugar, because beet sugar is for the birds, so you're Polish then? In the back seat names and rapid references were passing in review, Oscar exuding bits of news like flies, the most urgent part all covered before they reached the gates of Paris. No, at first I didn't think there were any ants on board but you know. They're hard at work here, Marcos said, Heredia's last message was a bit grim. Two hundred yards farther on the car carrying the representatives of the Vincennes zoo passed a police van and Lonstein returned to the right lane with an impeccable observance of the traffic laws while the two representatives clutched each other so as not to break up with laughter on the broad rear seat as they went back over the outstanding parts of the ceremony of delivery and acceptance, all of it with a certain shock for the armadillos stored in the trunk and the sleepy disdain of the penguin on whom the Equanil was having a wild effect. Drop us off at the Porte d'Orléans Roland proposed, I imagine that you'll be able to manage by yourself with the animals. As you wish, monsieur le directeur, Marcos has already told me that the less you two are seen around my place the better it will be from the formicological point of view. The problem is whether you can get the containers up by yourself, said Lucien Verneuil. My janitrix weighs two hundred fifteen pounds, Lonstein pointed out, and that has its somatic effect on the stairs even though it might seem to violate the law of gravity, when the fat lady lifts off to bring me up a telegram the Apollo rocket is a laughingstock. In that case, Roland said, I imagine Marcos told you not to take the animals out of the containers, Lucien Verneuil felt constrained to add. What you mean to insuggest is that I don't have to throw the containers into the trash, angel of love, Lonstein said, relax, because when Marcos explains something to me the Trinity comes within easy grasp of Kaffirs. Farewell, messieurs les directeurs, a happy rejoinment with the dromedary and the hippocentaur. Oh, damn, I forgot, the mushroom has grown a centimeter and a half, it will be something to come see when we have outdistanced this epoch of containers and other screweries, no allusion meant. Why do you insist on repeating that idiotic dialogue for me? complains the one I told you. Because it's not idiotic, Lonstein says, it was fitting that those lads, I mean those gentlemen representing the zoo, should be aware that I was just as much up on the matter as they, something they didn't like one whit because they're technocrats of the revolution and they believe that merriment, mushrooms, and my janitrix have no place in the dialectics of History. In brief, says the one I told you, who is not a technocrat but is in a hurry, you brought the beasts up to your mansion and you returned the car. Yes, the little rabbi says, and the mushroom had grown another three millimeters.

Along the Boulevard Raspail it was evident that Oscar was about to collapse from lack of sleep. Go get some sleep, Marcos said, we can talk tonight when Heredia gets here, and be careful with the telephone. I've got a pile of things to tell you, Oscar said coming out of the tenth yawn. But Marcos thanked him for the Córdoba pastries amidst the boorish laughter of Gladis and Ludmilla who had just finished the box, and he left Gladis with the logistical details for the evening's regrouping. On the sidewalk by the Hotel Lutetia Oscar stood for a moment watching the traffic on Sèvres-Babylone, his suitcase in one hand, Gladis on the other.

"Why did they leave so fast? We could have eaten together or something, I've got so much to tell Marcos."

"The boy knows what he's doing," Gladis said, "when you take a look at yourself in the mirror you'll understand, come on, I've reserved a high-class room for you; as for me, I need a shower, love, even though we won't have the penguin in the tub this time."

The girls made an opening in the wire

"So this is Paris, then," Oscar said. "Is this the center of town?"

"There's no such thing as a center here, the center is a little everywhere like the definition of something or other," Gladis explained. "I'm all in, let's stop all this Paris-by-Day stuff and go up and bathe and get some sleep, it's obvious you didn't have to serve three hundred meal trays and take care of fourteen kids with troubles at both ends."

"I'm sorry, I'm rambling, I must be missing the dampness of

get them

the estuary back home. Hey, but you and the Polish girl finished

over here they're going to get away

off all the pastry, you ought to be ashamed."

"They're nice but too sweet," Ludmilla commented turning at the end of the Rue Raspail to go down the Rue Delambre. "Why didn't you stay with Oscar? He seemed a little upset to me."

"He was probably more sleepy," Marcos said, "and in that state you can't talk about anything. But if you want the truth, I have to try to understand one or two things better, and now that everything's come off so well I can think in peace for a while. Stop over there, will you have a drink with me?"

Even before, when leaving at noon for Orly, Marcos had wondered why Ludmilla. He was pleased that she had volunteered to drive, that she hadn't tried to influence Andrés who was deliberately concentrating on the record player, his back to them. Explaining the turquoise penguin to her didn't take long and it gave Ludmilla such a laughing attack that she almost ran into a 94 bus when she heard about Roland and Lucien Verneuil and especially Lonstein. But afterwards, when they got on the expressway, Marcos sensed that she was beginning to withdraw, that she was thinking about something that was changing her way of driving, brusque suddenly, kind of tormented. He looked at her out of the corner of his eye, lit a cigarette and gave it to her.

"Like life," Ludmilla said, "a kind of joke or farce, and the other thing waiting behind it. Two things, don't think I'm not aware, two things are very clear. First, this penguin business is no joke, and second, you've filled me in on things. You've filled me in. Now I can put these two things together, you see. And it's logical for me to ask why you've talked to me about this, why me."

"Just because," Marcos said. "Reasons aren't always too clear in this business."

"Did you tell Andrés?"

"No, we talked more about women. I only mentioned the penguin and it didn't seem to interest him too much as you could see."

"But you, now . . . Why? Because I volunteered to go to Orly with you? I didn't have to. You think that I . . . shit, whore, I can't find the right word, blow."

"You've got a nice balanced mixture of European and Argentine Spanish, Polonette."

"I have the advantage of not being too sure what it all means," Ludmilla said. "In the beginning Andrés would make me repeat things to get a laugh out of Patricio and Susana, *concha peluda* and *pija colorada*, things like that, they have a pretty sound to me."

"They are pretty," Marcos said, "just that sometimes people don't use them the right way, they ruin them. Of course I trust you, it's one of those hunches. You've got no reason to be thinking about anything so extraordinary."

"Yes, but . . . Well, it's fine for me to help out a little, the cigarettes with Susana and things like that, but for you to tell me about this penguin business on just any old street corner and the twenty thousand counterfeit dollars, that's something else."

"If it bothers you that I told you we can just forget all about it, you know. Nothing compromised, nothing changed."

"No, on the contrary. On the contrary, Marcos. The fact is . . . Shit, you understand."

Marcos put his hand on her shoulder, took it back.

"Let's keep things clear, Polonette. Don't think that you're directly compromised by what we're doing. You can imagine that if I'm telling you all this it's because one day you may want to come in with us, but it has to be something like wanting to go to bed or playing or going to the movies, something that just comes out, like a cough or a curse. And most of all there's no hurry. If you're not interested, it's enough not to talk about it any more and that's that. Don't think I'm forgetting about Andrés."

"He's got nothing to do with whatever I decide," Ludmilla said. "I was working with Susana and it didn't interest him in the least, not that he's against it, but he thinks what you people are doing is childish and it annoys him. I did too at first, except that it amused me, but now I'm beginning to see other things. Yes, I'll have to think about it," Ludmilla said, passing with care a Belgian car that insisted on hogging three lanes to the great scandal of several native drivers.

"Down there's not your country," Marcos said. "No one could pretend that you were getting involved out of a sense of responsibility, what they call patriotism, for example."

"Or the directors of the Vincennes zoo either," Ludmilla said.

"Of course not, but it's not easy and you can't pretend that everybody thinks that way."

"The international brigades, eh?"

"You've got it. They weren't any worse than the others, as I see it."

"Five minutes to one," Ludmilla said. "The penguin must be landing."

Partly because of all that and also because just Ludmilla, the café on the Rue d'Odessa had quiet corners, green stools, and a silence that called for white wine, cigarettes, and memories. Now it was Córdoba, the friendship with Oscar in a Buenos Aires boardinghouse, old man Collins, the whole confused and tangled skein that Marcos was straightening out for Ludmilla, answering her questions or silences without being surprised that Ludmilla should want to know if there were other kinds of pastries, whether Lonstein had been at the university with them, and that at one moment when he was explaining the reasons that gave birth to the Screwery to her, Ludmilla put her chin on her hands and looked at him like a gypsy over her crystal ball just before some fateful announcement.

"I don't understand very much," Ludmilla said, "and the fact is it doesn't matter for now. I'd just like you to tell me one thing."

"I know," Marcos said. "An hour from now you'll be back home and then."

"Yes. Because I don't like to lie if I can help it, and at this moment more than ever. Andrés has never lied to me, although the advantages of his system remain to be seen. So there's the penguin, old man Collins, all those things. But there's also the stew we're going to eat together tonight, we always have to talk about something between one swallow and the next."

"As far as I'm concerned you can tell him everything, Polonette, I always hoped he'd make the first move, but you see. I probably should have spoken right out to him come on old man the way I did with you, he probably would have reacted all right, you never know. With him it's a question of a hunch too, if I didn't do it I didn't do it, and that's all. But you're free to talk to him of course. I know he won't open his mouth, whether he accepts it or not."

"All right," Ludmilla said. "As for me, I don't know why, I'm very happy. Don't look at me with that face. I always say silly things like that."

"That's not why I'm looking at you," Marcos said. "I'm just looking at you, Polonette."

Yes, but who are you, who have I got in my arms, who gives in and refuses, complains and demands, who takes over this hour? And that's how she agrees to everything (but who are you, who have I got in my arms?) except that when I want to lower her panties little by little she refuses, tightens her legs together and refuses, she wants to do it, it has to be her hands that take the elastic band and little by little let the pale pink panties go down to mid-thigh, just barely lifting her legs and passing them over her knees, then her soft piston rods begin to work, the warm bicycle that casts off the panties while the hands remain on her flanks as if lost, the panties roll up, it's inevitable, useless for me to try to help her, she'll insist no, use her hands again and her thighs will rise up a little more until finally ankles, feet, the last movement and the panties like a pink puppy dog all curled up and tiny at the feet of the woman recumbent on her tomb, feet that reject it as they stretch out and precisely then the sigh, exactly then the sigh, the acceptance of nakedness, looking at me from an angle, just barely smiling.

I don't understand but I love those repeated rituals, who knows why you won't let me take your panties off while you arch up like a dolphin, floating on the bed until my fingers pull them off with one tug, the little pink chihuahua next to those cold, tight feet that I will kiss toe by toe, that I will lick carefully, tickling you and you will refuse and twist away laughing and will call me a fetishist and make me do it again before yielding to the body that seeks yours out from bottom to top, the mouth that runs along your skin, a clumsy member that gets entangled in your knees and your stomach wetting you, the preludes that are invented with every repetition, with every stop on the route, your smell under fingernails, the doubly prolonged search for what has been found, the incomprehensible discovery of what has been known, your fingers losing themselves in my crotch, encircling my sex, the slipping of one over the other satiating that thirst of mouth-full flesh, multiplied by hands and teeth, primordial hydra, soft androgynous cephalopod, a substitution of means and ends, the mouth a sex, the anus a mouth, your tongue the phallus that seeks me, my lips the vagina into which you sink it, the music of silence in red, a sonata that intertwines its two voices, the serpents of the caduceus clinbing up to the final resolution, the last chord that I won't hear because you will have denied me this time, this time and so many other times will be like those panties that only you can take off, I'll roll you on your side, kissing you on the neck, slipping down your back, you will be motionless, in surrender and so almost brusquely I will only have to imagine what I desire to feel my strength bunching up again and demanding, you'll accept everything, bland and lost with your face on the pillow, you'll let yourself be kissed, you'll murmur your lax and outstretched pussycat, I will imagine your closed eyes and your hands up high, far away from your body, all of you with the profile of the swimmer springing on the edge of the board before the perfect dive, I will go down your back, you'll let yourself be opened up and detailed, you'll feel the tongue's interminable inventory as it reaches the deepest part, the suction of lips that fasten themselves to the ring of fire and musk as they feel it contract and give way, dragging it to its daily secret servitude, calling it to a ceremony that will wipe away the routines of that distracted hand that every now and then goes down to clean and wash, that almost nonexistence which only illness will rescue at times for more attentive hands, a mouth with fusiform medication, temperature, and you let yourself be licked and petted and fingered until that instant when you will have folded up, denying, you will arch, quivering, not that, you know not that, you will return to my side complaining because I have sunk my hands into your thighs to hold you back and open you up, you will reject me with a push and I will see your lips tightened, the will not to give in, I will hear that metal voice through which century-old interdictions return, and one more time it will have been the gate of horn and the gate of ivory, the angels of Sodom with their hair in the wind, slipping between protective sheets, all of you face up again offering me the canonical womb, defining yourself in yes and no, Ormazd and Ahriman, the absurd veda, the pouts from the no from mama and catechism and Holy Mother Church all piled up into one single no, my little tailor-made gazelle, mold of your god, your homeland, and your hearth, laughable key to so many things, come-eel-foe girl, irreproachable little fashion model, amen, amen, unless, of course.

"We spend all out time meeting these bastards coming from overseas," Patricio protested smack in the middle of a traffic jam on the Boulevard de Sébastopol at seven in the evening, "and naturally Heredia had to land at Le Bourget which is death three times over."

"Don't get all worked up on me, lodge brother," Gómez said. "To hear you you'd think I wasn't busy with my collection of stamps from Gabon and then Marcos with his phone call. Well, if you'll turn on the light I'll read you the news and that way you'll get over your edginess, which always gives you the look of a corpse."

"I don't like to drive with the light on, you know that, people will think we're a couple of fags, and to make things worse you with that blue jacket, you've always got to be the Panamanian, I swear. All right, all right, there's the light for you."

"You youngsters," said Gómez, who was twenty-three, "think that going around in a shirt or sweater helps you destroy society. Well, let's see what you think about these items."

"Tell me all about it while I duck down this street, it seems less crowded. What, La Calera?" Gómez off at full speed

Argentine

DES GUÉRILLEROS INVESTISSENT UNE LOCALITÉ DE DIX MILLE HABITANTS PRÈS DE CÓRDOBA

Buenos-Aires. — Une quinzaine de guérilleros circulant à bord de cinq véhicules ont investi mardi La Calera, une localité de dix mille habitants, située à 25 kilomètres de Cordoba. Divisés en plusieurs groupes, communiquant entre eux au moyen de walkie-talkies et agissant, selon les témoins, avec beaucoup de sang-froid, les assaillants ont occupé le central téléphonique, le bureau des postes et télégraphes, la mairie et, après avoir soumis la garde, le commissariat de police.

ARGENTINA: GUERRILLAS OCCUPY TOWN OF TEN THOUSAND INHABITANTS NEAR CÓRDOBA. On Tuesday some fifteen guerrillas traveling in five vehicles took over La Calera, a town of ten thousand inhabitants located 15 miles from Córdoba. Split up into several groups who communicated with walkie-talkies and, according to witnesses, acting with great coolness, the attackers took over the main telephone office, the post office and telegraph building, the city hall, and, after overcoming the guards, police headquarters. Jesus, said Patricio, what a piece of news we've got for Heredia, who certainly and literally is up in the clouds. Bursting into a branch bank they took possession of ten million pesos (twenty-five thousand dollars, good lord, how that's going to upset old man Collins when he thinks about those real dollars, and just think, by the way, how neatly it coincides with the penguin and armadillo affair, if we go on like this we'll end up as millionaires), let me read, damn it, with an aim to underwrite the revolution and ease the hunger of the auto workers in Córdoba, who have been on strike since early in June. The daring operation recalls that of October 8 of last year when Tupamaros occupied Pando, a small town in Uruguay.

There was no doubt that this was a priestly piece of news for Heredia, too bad they couldn't give it to him right away because on the passport line already they saw him talking to a tall, skinny guy, probably another Brazilian. Heredia greeted them from afar, waving a briefcase and a bottle of whiskey in his hands, a rather useful maneuver to transmit at the same time a wink, duly recorded by Patricio and Gómez, who, as was natural, greeted the traveler with embraces and exclamations that were meant to have no meaning whatsoever, while Heredia introduced them to Mr. Fortunato who had been his ephemeral traveling companion and who declared himself to be enormously. A reason for which Gómez stuck by Fortunato's side while they went to pick up their bags, and Heredia with half a mouth and Patricio all ears attenti al piato he's an ant, I'll explain later. Fortunato thought it was a fine idea for them to leave the luggage at the baggage stand and go have a farewell drink since Heredia was only going to spend a few hours in Paris, his esteemed countryman had already told him about his old friendship with Gómez and Patricio, the wild times in Montmartre, la vie bohème, ah those penniless years were the best, and Patricio informing the traveling ant how Heredia had sown lechery and debauchery the whole length of the Rue Blanche while Gómez, more decent and industrious, worked on his stamp collection, which had earned the admiration and envy of Paris's succinct little Panamanian colony. The matter of La Calera could wait for later and then the traveling ant suddenly seemed interested in the news and bought the evening papers while waiting for the second whiskey, but his comment about the fact that a thousand students in Heidelberg had just raised holy hell over McNamara's presence only found a

Allemagne fédérale

A Heidelberg

UN MILLIER D'ÉTUDIANTS MANIFESTENT CONTRE LA PRÉSENCE DE M. McNAMARA

Heidelberg-*(A.F.P.)*. — De violentes bagarres ont éclaté vendredi à Heidelberg à l'occasion de la conférence internationale sur-l'aide au développement. Les manifestations étaient dirigées notamment contre la présence de M. Robert McNamara, président de la Banque pour la reconstruction et le développement (BIRD) et ancien secrétaire américain à la défense.

Un millier d'étudiants et de lycéens d'extrême gauche ont encerclé le grand hôtel où se tenait la conférence. Ils se sont heurtés à d'importantes forces de police, qui ont fait usage de canons à eau et de grenades lacrymogènes. De nombreuses personnes ont été arrêtées. Plusieurs blessés, manifestants et policiers, ont été hospitalisés.

courteous echo in Gómez and Patricio and a purely alcoholic enthusiasm in Heredia who had already decanted three London scotches and two more in flight over the Channel, and who seemed most joyful when he thought about the fact that the students had broken glass windows and mirrors all around a gentleman who presided over a bank destined, no less, for reconstruction. When Fortunato got to La Calera on page three of *Le Monde*, it was logical for him to ask Patricio if he knew about it and for Patricio to answer yes, everything was going very badly in Argentina, poor old homeland. Fortunato had always been interested in Argentinian problems because he was from near the border and had lived in Resistencia and Buenos Aires, they could see that he spoke Spanish rather well, of course not as well as his friend Heredia who denied it modestly because he'd never been able to eliminate an accent full of bumps and grinds and with a kind of African rhythm in the midst of full Castilian prosody, so that since Patricio lived in Paris it would be great to meet him sometime and have him introduce him to other Argentines to talk about those things, but of course, let me have the name of your hotel and I'll give you a call, Patricio said. With the third whiskey, the topographical and onomastic information having been exchanged with a great opening of notebooks and datebooks, they talked about the world cup and Pelé, the greatest, the earthquake in Peru, the Cuban sugar harvest about which Fortunato had direct information while the other three didn't seem to be too up to date, and about the new atmosphere in London where Heredia had spent an absolutely orgiastic month if it was a matter of believing him, and it was. That didn't seem to interest Fortunato so much even though the pleasant manners of his new friend obliged him to listen and savor, *Le Monde* already folded like a rag on the knees of the traveling ant who after one or two attempts to draw out current events had resigned himself to the transmission of the information Heredia was giving his dear friends from bygone old bohemia, there was no place to insert the slightest reference to any socioeconomic context and Fortunato understood that the best thing was to leave but there was nothing he could do, Heredia into memories of the district of Earl's Court, S.W.5, if you go someday I'll give you the names of the good hotels, kid, there's no comparison with this puritanical town, London forever, goddamn it, you must have got yourself wet too, eh, and Fortunato denying with a little smile of understanding too well and Gómez giving him an elbow in the ribs, oh these carioca studs, well, I'm not a carioca, it doesn't matter, all of you are more or less, it's the climate, and Heredia going into abundant detail on the way to undress them when they don't want to or pretend they don't want to which is worse still because they keep a clear head and it's always nails, slaps, and knee uppercuts which are particularly ominous, in any case the most functional way is gentleness aided sotto voce by the force of gravity although it won't get you very far if the chick isn't already sitting down and if possible lying on the bed, and then Heredia softly presses her while he undoes her hair and kisses her and loosens her bra because they generally allow that in London and anywhere with no great show of terror, and when he's got her titties loose under the blouse there's nothing to do but raise it and softly count them, peck them, circumnavigate them with a finger and then the whole hand in the immemorial and moving gestures of one grasping a brandy glass, which can be either right side up or upside down in this case because the lips will come to drink from the pink little mound that loves to be drunk, that stiffens into an active little volcano even though Diana or Jennifer says no no no and hides her face in the pillow and is a storm of copper-colored hair lashing Heredia in the face as he softly reaches the beginning of the zipper on her skirt, and it's the crucial moment, sic, because Diana tightens her legs or turns on her side and even turns completely face down and you have to concentrate on the back of her neck and her shoulders, sketch out a tiny highway system along her back with caresses that acupuncture and cartograph her, calming her with a mouth that visits her ear and slowly wets it, bites the lobe and murmurs the sillys the whys the turn overs and let mes the don't be like thats, and Diana or Jennifer will sigh and say no but will let herself be turned over little by little and the zipper will go down, it has to be done as its name implies zip and there it is, but at that moment it is time for the strategic genius that gives us an Austerlitz or a Chacabuco or a Gettysburg, because if it's Heredia everything will be one conglomerate of action, the zip will run down to the lowest part and at the same time the skirt will drop to the thighs and here Heredia points out the capital detail on which everything else depends, the panties must go down with the skirt and that's hard sometimes because sometimes Diana will tighten her legs or it could happen that the fingers only pull on the skirt without being able simultaneously to grip the elastic of the panties, but when it's Heredia everything comes together in the same structure of descent as they would say in *Tel Quel* if they dealt with matters like this, and then that admirable thing would happen, that metamorphosis disposed by the immortal and peeping gods who watch over us in bed, and the panties are lowered with one single astute movement to mid-thigh but only to the middle point and not just lowered but rolled in the same movement with which they are lowered, and that isn't fatal except that it's necessary to help the process along with the palm of the hand as one rolls dough to make meat pies, they are converted into something very much like mutatis mutandis a set of handcuffs, which means to say that a pair of rolled panties turns into a double elastic nylon ring that hobbles the play of the piston thighs, a defense man in soccer kneeing back the forwards, it neutralizes them like the fists of the dangerous hoodlum held by the servants of law and order, it turns them into two kneecaps of useless, warm, pink resistance that becomes a complaint up above because Diana or Jennifer knows that she can no longer use her great silky abelarding shears on the mental and/or physical level of Heredia who now comes to lie down half on half against, slithering a long kiss that starts at the mouth and is lost on the little stomach, exploring the navel that smells softly of wheat and talcum powder, returning to the breast which had ceased waiting for him in the course of those advances and forays and mines and countermines, and with a free hand he will proceed to his own disrobement without attempting the adamic state or anything like it at that moment because such an aim has probably cost perfectionists many battles that had almost been won, just his pants halfway down and his shorts if he can and if not it doesn't make any difference for now, a grave moment because he has to envelop Diana's face and attention completely with kisses and hands and her hair itself which is not an end in itself, a desperate attempt to free the thighs from the restrictive handcuffs when Heredia's fingers run across an electrified fuzz to enter the dark and purloined territory, there where Diana will feel that it's too late and she can't open her legs and she will moan for Heredia to release her, she will still say no because she can't say anything else but she will be waiting for what he will do in another eagle movement of the panties that will open wide the scylla and charybdis of the knees where they still try to hold together, continuing on down, preferably to the ankles and stopping as a last precaution almost always unnecessary because there's that deep breathing now, that temperature that tells all, that arching that slowly returns to horizontal, that face profiled as it sinks into the pillow with a sob where the complete acquiescence of the Commonwealth is concentrated, and then it's best to run them down and off completely with the help of a foot, free the imprisoned albertine, and when the legs feel themselves free the whole weight of Heredia is already covering the territory that murmurs and wiggles because no, because I don't want to, because you're bad, because you're squashing me, but it is the darwinian return now, a soft velvety return to the frog, the cadenced separation of thighs, the knees that come up on their own, the unresisting moment of offering the musky key, Heredia archimedically will know that all he needs is a fulcrum and he will dig his knees into the proper hollow and his fingers will rise up to the mouth to fetch the saliva that is tonight's password at the postern, the cipher of the secret combination, Diana will moan, impaled and sobbing little frog, and once more the syracusan will know that now he can move the earth, that everything is starting to spin and rise and float and sink with all physical and chemical properties in a torrent of colors under closed eyelids, amidst murmurs and hair. Whereupon Fortunato decides that the moment to take leave is at hand and gets up all full of effusive welcomes and have a good time with the French girls, not without first reminding Patricio that nothing would please him more than to meet him again to talk about South American problems, a desire that Patricio returns as he should, what else could he do.

"See that?" Gómez observes. "So the traveling ant pounced on you in the big balloon."

"Let me rest up a bit from my disquisition," says Heredia, who otherwise had done his number with visible pleasure since he rarely gets a chance to go on at such length. "They are dumber than they look when you come right down to it, they really should have known up front that I don't suck my thumb and have my sources of information. Do you remember Ruy Moraes who landed in Buenos Aires once with a bagful of pistols? He's in London doing a little job for Lamarca, he gave me some definite information on the side that will please Marcos. The traveling ant tried to get himself introduced at a party of friends, you know how people drift in, and Ruy pointed him out to me from behind a glass of gin and a black girl's ass, there were so many people at the party that visibility could be considered down near zero, but I did make out that Egyptian hook of a nose he has. To play it safe I left before any possible introduction and there you have it, this afternoon I meet him on the plane, he sits down next to me and starts out with his excuse me but aren't you Brazilian too, et cetera. I was a little worried thinking that Marcos would probably be waiting for me, and you can imagine I wasn't a bit pleased to see the pair of you, but luckily you're not as thick as you look."

"Let's get over to Marcos's right away," Patricio said. "You already heard about the La Calera affair, we were saving it for you but the traveling ant always so polite and industrious got the jump on us, son of a bitch and bastard that he is."

"We'll have to be on the qui vive," Heredia said. "In any case, the guy doesn't know what to think, every Fortunato gets the Montrésor he deserves."

He said it mostly for himself, because neither Gómez nor Patricio were very well read, the proof being that they looked at him as if he were a glyptodont, after which the bags and hop it, with first an inspection of the horizon naturally completely devoid of ants amidst all that technical advance and doors that opened and closed if you just looked at them from a distance.

"So you're going to fill out your membership application," I said to her.

"Yes. The theater leaves me more than enough time for other things and I haven't had too much fun these past few months."

"I know, Polonette, I know. I neglect you, I go wandering around, I don't take you to see the bears."

"Don't make yourself so important," Ludmilla said, threatening my calf with the rather sharp heel of a shoe. "I know how to play alone, but now it's something else, a game that could have some purpose, you never know."

"You're doing the right thing, Ludlud, besides you always did have a big warm spot for penguins."

Ludmilla ran her hand over my face, kissed me on the back of the neck, and took my cigarettes. Her seahorse habits, her smell of clean hair, the merry disorder of all her movements; we began to smoke together, to share a glass of wine; I thought how I'd like to hear *Prozession*, right there within reach, but at the same time I preferred having Ludmilla go on with her telling about the expedition to Orly in the midst of laughing attacks and incredible bifurcations and digressions, for the first time the impression that something was changing in the perspective, suddenly clear lines, directions, and escape routes (this last was probably literal), a precise feeling that Marcos and Patricio and the others were facing up to tangible things, that Marcos was no longer the sluggish or distracted visitor of that morning. Of course neither Ludmilla nor I had a clear idea of the aforesaid Screwery, we only had a suspicion of what Lonstein would have called the epiphetents prolegomenists, but it had been enough for something in me to sense Ludmilla's drawing closer to the Screwery so that at the same time so much abstract foolishness should take on body, a brusque "the fun's over," which as a counterpunch was changing me, placing me in a different position with respect to Marcos and the others, especially with respect to Ludmilla who would not take long to pay for the broken dishes, to get involved in the unnameable mixups with her Polish innocence, her tiny feet precisely in the middle of the boiling soup, fuck their mother. With tenderness, he was thinking it almost tenderly because he loved Patricio and Marcos and Gómez, now something really was happening, the three-ring circus was on its way (royal armadillos and a turquoise penguin, please, Polonette); now it was the Screwery, and the devil take the hindmost, something quite different from shrieks in the movies and cigarette butts.

Who knows what kind of a face Andrés had put on at that moment in his cogitations because Ludmilla kept looking at him and started stroking his cheek again, a gesture that was suddenly cut off although it wasn't anything more than the fact that she needed both her hands at once to clutch her head:

"The seven-thirty rehearsal! My God, I completely forgot to remember!"

"Don't cry, pussycat, have another drink with your sinner of an Andrés who doesn't understand the anxieties of contemporary history and tell me a little more about that ant business that was on the tip of your tongue."

"*Concha peluda* and *pija colorada*," Ludmilla said, "this time they'll kill me for sure!"

"Bah, it's no use twisting your hands, girl, it would have been all the same in the end, when you got there they'll all be dead or married, let's eat the stew instead, it tastes very good, I swear I followed your instructions vegetable by vegetable."

"You're right, they can go to hell," Ludmilla said, "they could have called me again at least, don't you think?"

"They called you at six o'clock, love, that was the first thing I told you when you got back from the reception for the penguin."

"Then they screwed me, but my emotions are to blame, the dollars . . . Oh, the ants, of course I'll tell you, but first I've got to calm down, give me a glass of something. And how is Francine?"

"Fine," I said with the same inevitable change of intonation that there was in her voice, that diagonal way of putting the question and then answering it, back to the pit, to the useless ping-pong game.

"I thought you would have gone to see her," Ludmilla said, "I thought you would have when you told Marcos you weren't going to Orly."

"Tell me about the penguin's arrival."

"For all you care about the penguin."

"O.K., let's talk about Michelangelo if you prefer. Oh, Ludlud, how can it be that

Interruption due to higher forces

The one I told you is becoming impatient to be done with Francine and the stew and Ludmilla sad and other filigrees of liberal mentality breaking up in a drunken mess (yes, yes, I think, come with me now with those advanced schemes, you who are even worse) and with all that not a cunt hair of coherent explanation of the Vip, the ants, and the Screwery, because of which, before anything else, the one I told you gets an image (from imagine rather than from magic) of the following

VIPERO-FORMIC ORGANIGRAM

N.B. Like all organigrams, this one is not too easily understood.

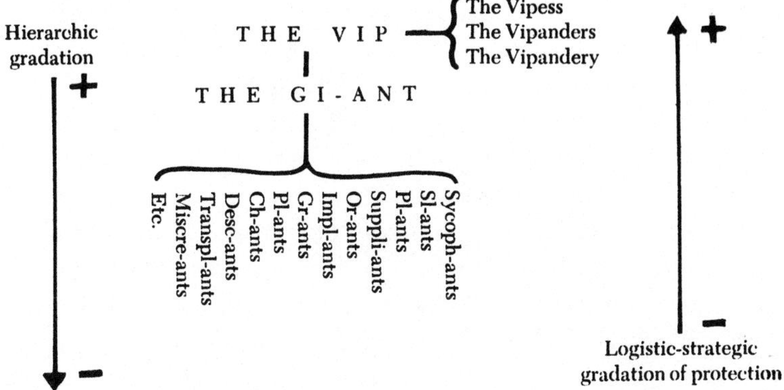

The one I told you had got quite a bit of use out of a kind of robot-portrait of the Vip put together by Gómez and Lucien Verneuil and which fell within these lines:

1. The Vip is South American (Argentinian? Bolivian? Diverse options in alphabetical order).
2. The Vip is pleni:
   —potentiary
   —lunar (an astral detail that Lonstein judges to be as important as it is ill-fated)
   —potent (cash coming from the whole purported alphabetical order *supra*, via (hypothesis) OAS, CIA, BIRD, Nelson Rockefeller, foundations, etc.).
3. The Vip operates in Europe.
4. A paramilitary group protects the Vip: the ants, under the command of the Gi-ant. In the case of the ants the ecological order is almost totally valid (Fortunato, for example, is Brazilian, and the Gi-ant is supposed to be Salvadorean, although his identity is kept hazy).

Room 498 had a radio on the night table and Oscar turned it on with great precaution so as not to wake Gladis who had one finger in her mouth Baby Doll style and her little ass in a Baby Doll position too except that it was completely uncovered. Sitting down on the bed he lit a cigarette with the technique used in the trenches of World War I, learned at the age of thirteen in the Roca de Almagro movie house and consisting of screening the hand and striking the head of the match on a surface no longer than two inches inordertoreducethenoisetoamerescratch which of course would not reach Gladis in a sleep well earned from plastic trays and poody-poody. The worst part was that the hotel radio was one of those that only has three choices, two of which are always a piece of shit and on top of it all in French, and the third had *Turandot,* act two, the princess's aria. Manipulating the volume control the way he had done with the match before, Oscar the astute found that Turandot could ventilate her poorly disguised sexual repression on a level that would not wake Gladis, and leaning back on a prodigiously soft pillow he let himself be carried away by the tobacco and the music, the unreality of that moment in which only Gladis could still connect him with the other side of the world, that Argentina so suddenly and incredibly far away and lost, Doña Raquela's boardinghouse what in hell was that doing here, and along the way Moña's little breasts in the midst of jasmines and a full moon. He wasn't completely awake, the Puccini melody that he had known and loved since he was a boy had a bit of the smell of the jasmines in Santos Pérez about it and the smell of Gladis asleep and sated, a smell that preceded the shower and the raising of the three enigmas, the memory of something read who knows where, Toscanini conducting the dress rehearsal of *Turandot* in Milan and stopping the orchestra after Liù's suicide scene to say with his face bathed in tears, "The maestro stopped writing here, Puccini died when he got to this point," and the musicians rising in silence, all of that so that Oscar should know incidentally that Franco Alfano had taken the notes left by Puccini to finish *Turandot*, it was impossible not to wonder how many things like that there were, museum statues that you admire without suspecting that the third part of them had been recomposed like the skeleton of the diplodocus, starting with some tiny little bone, Ameghino, things like that, and newspaper stories too that are put together from whole cloth, other inmates made an opening in the screen of a kitchen window and slipped out into a vacant lot on the Calle 41, who can say that the opening wasn't already there, that the girls really had escaped through a vacant lot bathed in moonlight, running frantically toward the wall, toward the carnival on the other side, in despair from alienation and crowding, greasy stew and slaps or more subtle pedagogical outrages. Why in hell do I keep coming back to this like a fly to a scrap of meat, Oscar said to himself, not having any prejudices in matters of metaphor, but it wasn't a metaphor, it was coming back in a different way, like an obedience to an obscure likeness, and Turandot was promising love or death in the final repetition of the aria, that admirably simple phrase that would probably seem unbearable and pedestrian to Andrés after *Prozession* which he had finally managed to hear in peace while Ludmilla curled up on the sofa followed the music in her own way, that is, reading poems by Lubicz-Milosz on whom she had a recurrent fixation.

Sometimes it interested the one I told you to see Andrés kind of perched on top of a pointed roof; in other days he might have been capable of jotting down a note putting people like Andrés and for example Henry James analogously on horseback between the world of his generation and the first quivers brought on by the telephone, the automobile, and Guglielmo Marconi. But now he was more interested in a different type of limiting situation in someone like André; it was on the level of an awareness that being on horseback in one's own life provoked autophagous behavior, real catoblepas butchery, almost always laughable attempts at fracture on the level of language, of relationships, or ideological currents, all of which tended to become a bit diffuse, a moment which the one I told you would take advantage of to raise his magnifying glass and murmur something like just wait till Mao gets his claws on you and you'll see about Francine or sentimental liberation or your easy chair with stereophonic earphones.

All of this seemed as obvious to me as to the one I told you, especially after the Fritz Lang dream which in some absolutely incomprehensible way was at the same time a different and obscure form of that blind alley but with the double name of Ludmilla and Francine. In that total darkness everything was most clear, because in those days I had a daily collision with the stubborn necessity of getting rid of the straight line as the shortest distance between two points, any non-Euclidean geometry at all would have seemed more applicable to me to my feelings about life and the world, but how could I make Ludmilla and Francine understand that from so much wandering and waiting all that was being left was nausea and frustration, the reproaches always along orthodox lines, remorse and a bad taste in the mouth of the slave from his occidental and petit bourgeois baptism, the feeling that there was something to be done and that it had not been done, an abolished task, the black hole between the moment the waiter took me to the room where they were waiting for me and the moment I came out again, knowing that I had forgotten, having to do something I wouldn't be able to do since I couldn't remember. Like that every day and, of course, the vigilant superego, the superstructure of the diurnal elbowing its way into position, the man on horseback on the roof trying to take in the Ludmilla world and the Francine world (and more, much more than that, a whole compass rose that had completely destroyed any locatable notion of the horizon) until touching at some time with a hand of the most extreme desire a Ludmilla Francine world, and, of course, running into the binary with every step, the unreconcilable double view from the peaked roof.

"You know," Andrés said, giving Ludmilla more wine, holding the record of *Prozession*, looking for his pipe, "you know, Polonette, as a boy I was fascinated by that terribly idiotic thing called horseback riding, going along and being present almost simultaneously at the displacement of the double lateral landscape, the house on the left, the grove on the right, shacks on the right, pretty little brook on the left, and almost nothing in front, the horse's two ears, the horizon which in the distance already begins to place itself to the left or to the right, you know that at some moment that ombú tree in the center will move to the left while the small owl perched on a dry log will be an owl on the right in spite of its undeserved legend."

Ludmilla had closed her book of Lithuanian poems and was looking at me with eyes that were still a little lost in a world of images that had little to do with what she was seeing, with that man just back from a piece by Stockhausen and a listless rumination, because look, Lud, the terrible thing is your not making a choice, people make more choices every day, it's inevitable, you're going to jump into the Screwery and I've taken the side of the Arab countries, cum grano sablis, it's true, and only mentally, even more true, that isn't the difficult or risky part even though it entails all sorts of problems and mine with the Arab countries is particularly sandy, the bothersome thing about all water divisions, my dear child, is that only innocents believe that it can be cut with a knife, that this stays here and that there. Naturally you don't understand a word of what I'm saying, Polonette.

"How do you expect me to understand," Ludmilla murmured, coming over and putting her hands in my hair until her nails scratched me as they would a cat, something that has always produced extreme pleasure in me, "when you start to talk from the end of the tunnel, bird of ill omen. And still you can see that I'm intelligent, I think I'm following you and I don't need to get out the Michelin map."

"It's not difficult per se, Ludlud, I was thinking that the problem of choosing, which is more and more the problem of this mangy and marvelous century with or without Maestro Sartre to set it to mental music, resides in the fact that we don't know if our choice has been made with clean hands. I know, choosing is a lot even though a person might be mistaken, there's a risk, an aleatory or genetic factor, but in the end the choice itself has a value, it defines and corroborates. The problem is that most likely, and I'm thinking about myself, when I choose what I think is a freedom-giving way out, an enlargement of my circumstances, I am probably following impulses, coactions, taboos, or prejudices that emanate precisely from the side I want to leave behind."

"Bloop," said Ludmilla, who always said that to encourage me.

"Aren't we, a lot of us, trying to break our bourgeois molds with nostalgias that are just as bourgeois? When you see how a revolution doesn't take long in setting in motion the machinery of psychological or erotic or aesthetic repression that almost symmetrically coincides with the machinery that has supposedly been destroyed on the political and practical level, you start wondering whether or not we shouldn't take a closer look at most of our choices."

"Well, rather than contemplating my navel, which is what you're doing, what we should aim for is a kind of super-revolution every time it's needed, and I agree that we need one every day."

"Of course, Lud, but you'd have to do a better job of showing the infiltration of the abolished into the new, because the strength of received ideas is almost frightening. Lonstein, who as you know has made an art of masturbation even though I don't think he's ever spoken to you about the subject, showed me a Victorian scientific textbook with a description of the symptoms of the masturbating child which is exactly the same one handed to us in Argentina in the thirties by our parents and teachers. Dark rings under the eyes, yellow skin, stuttering, sweaty palms, weak and evasive look, etc.; the portrait still persists today, certainly in the imagination of a lot of people, although generational mutation won't be long in doing away with it. Lonstein laughed because it wasn't only because he had never fit that description between the ages of eleven and fifteen, but also because he remembers quite well that at that time he was considered a miraculous exception and was most happy that his old man hadn't been able to catch him on that side; that is, if you consider it well with him there had finally been an acceptance of the traditional clinical picture which led him to believe that his was a privileged case."

"At the age of eleven I masturbated with a comb once," Ludmilla said. "God, it almost turned out bad, I must have been crazy."

"Combs are for good children to wrap in a piece of tissue paper and play pretty tunes on, don't you forget it. And now that we're on sexology, the book in question refers to something else that has always caught my eye in libertine novels from de Sade on down, and it's the story of the supposed ejaculation in women/Ejaculation in women?/That, my dear, must mean that you've never read *Juliette* or her numerous progeny./Yes I have, well, no, not *Juliette* because I couldn't get ahold of it, but I've read *Justine.*/It's the same thing on a rather smaller scale, but the women there ejaculate too, and the profound reasons for that conviction shared by all medical eminences of the time is another problem that touches on sexual discrimination and the primacy of a masculine world that becomes a model to be imitated, and so woman accepts or perhaps invents an ejaculation of her own which in turn man takes for granted since he is the one who imposes the model./The things you know./Not I, a certain Steven Marcus who's a regular hawk, but it's not a question of that but that one day talking to a French violinist, a friend of libidinous confidences, he told me about one of his mistresses, a mysterious Caucasian named Basilique, and he told me that she made love with such a frenzy that at the end she would ejaculate in such a way that his thighs were all soaked./Bloop./Keep in mind that that fellow knew a lot more about women than I and yet he seemed to believe that Basilique was only the supreme manifestation of something that he took for granted in all of them. I wasn't too keen on bringing up the problem but you can see how certain beliefs can jump the barrier and keep on being active on the opposite side, in a guy who's onto everything no less. I wonder if the things I'd like to change in myself I'm not trying to change unless underneath it all nothing changes to any large degree, whether when I think I'm choosing something new my choice isn't secretly governed by everything I'd like to leave behind."

"In any case, you've made a choice and what a choice," Ludmilla said and you felt she was like a piece of cloth being folded in two, in four, in eight. I kissed her and tickled her, I squeezed her until she protested, still thinking, still talking, still Andrés duplicated, out of himself, kissing me, tickling me, squeezing me until I protest, still thinking, still talking, listen to me, Ludlud, I know all of this is Francine, listen to me, Ludlud, I go out looking, I have to go out looking, then Francine or that trip to London when I stood you up because I had to be alone, but everything must be in knowing whether I'm really looking, whether I really go out looking or whether I'm only preferring my cultural heritage, my bourgeois Western world, my own little hateful and marvelous individual."

"Ah," Ludmilla said, "now that you say it I don't think you've changed so much since you started going out, as you say. Just the opposite, rather, then quod erat demonstrandum, how about that?"

"Hmm," said Andrés, looking for his pipe, which was always a delaying action on his part. "Why have you changed then?"

"Because you deceived me, because you're not authentic, because underneath it all you know quite well that you don't want to change at all, that that pipe will always be your pipe and God help anyone who messes with it, and at the same time you're ready to bring this house tumbling down in the same way that you'd probably bring Francine's tumbling down, because every blow here or there has repercussions in the opposite direction without our having to phone each other in order to get the news."

"Yes," Andrés said, "yes, Ludlud, but they're two different homes, and carrying your metaphor farther, try to understand me, two homes are sixteen windows, not eight, they're a different taste in the sauces, one light that comes from the north and the other from the west, things like that."

"In any case your ubiquity and your sixteen windows aren't doing you much good, you suspect that yourself, but in the meantime there are things that will never be what they were before."

"I tried to get you to understand, I hoped for a kind of mutation in the way we loved and understood each other, it seemed to me that we could break up the pairing and at the same time enrich it, that nothing had to change in our feelings."

"Nothing had to change," Ludmilla repeated. "You can see that your choice didn't want any profound changes, it was and is a luxurious game, an exploration around a wash basin, a dance step where you land on your feet back where you started. But with every leap you've broken some mirror, and now you come out with the fact that you're not even sure that you break them for the sake of changing something. There's not much difference between you and Manuel."

"One thing has been useful in this conversation, Polonette, and it's the fact that you're desanctifying it rapidly, you lead it over to Manuel's side, for example. You're so right, I make up problems until I get drunk on them, and what's worse I have my doubts about the problem itself. You shouldn't feel sorry for me, you know."

Ludmilla didn't say anything but once more she ran her hand across my face, almost without touching the skin, and it was something that seemed so much like pity. After all, how was I to know which one of the two pitied me more because Francine too would keep looking at me sometimes like someone who wants to console but tells herself it's useless because there isn't even any disconsolation, there's that other nameless thing that I can't stop looking for or being, and that way da capo al fine. Nothing ended there since we were all right, according to our lights. Nothing ended there but nothing seemed to begin either; at the end of every dialogue with Francine, with Ludmilla, there would be the opening up of a new precarious deadline where caresses and smiles were like furtive and courteous inhabitants, walking on tiptoe; to convince oneself, then convince oneself (break your head but stay mounted on the pointed roof, over two worlds, trying to make them one alone or ten thousand), to convince oneself then that TRIANGLE: Figure formed by three lines that mutually cut each other. No. Even if they cut each other, and you can bet they cut each other before and after the caresses. No, Euclid, no, goddamn it.

Almost incredible that so many foreigners can come together in an apartment in Paris without having the concièrge bring pressure to bear as diverse types gather and in the great majority ask for Mosyoo Lonstein as if his name were not among those on the directory at the entrance, not to mention that said questions are most often put in a language that few French concièrges deign to interpret, but in this case it so happens that the fat woman not only does not raise the slightest row but is content and placid, in the case of Oscar and Gladis, for example, coming for the first time, she shows them the stairway at the back of the courtyard and accompanies them to the first landing, commenting that it must be Mr. Lonstein's birthday and that it's very nice for people to have birthdays from time to time because there aren't many joys left to us with so much war and the floods on Saturday in the Loire valley where her mother lives surrounded by fruit trees, just imagine what a disaster. Oscar, of course, didn't understand a word of this oratorical overflow, and it is up to Gladis to insert the oh oui, bien sûr, mais certainement, followed by several merci beaucoups, vous êtes gentilles and other lubricants of a society where no one passes someone on the stairs without begging his pardon, I swear it's true, says Gladis as she rings the bell, you're putting me on, girl, although I must say that the number of hands I've shaken in the course of the day for one reason or another is something that has left me a bit astonished.

The poor fat woman is mistaken about the little rabbi's birthday but not so much in the end really because it is a kind of party even if no one knows the reason that has brought it about (here come Gómez and Monique making the stairs shake with shoes, exclamations, and laughter completely devoid of meaning); in any case and in the course of the afternoon Marcos and Heredia have stopped by the little rabbi's, the containers have been duly stripped, and the dollars are already biding their time in some other part of Paris, so if the ants attempt any reconnaissance they will only find wine bottles and Latin Americans in every corner; the one I told you, one of the first to arrive, has the feeling that the fat woman is right and it is a birthday, probably that of the mushroom which continues to be the main topic of the little rabbi's conversation, but in a little while things get mixed up for the one I told you because simultaneity is not his forte and it is well known that in Spanish-speaking gatherings it is never a matter of listening but of making oneself heard, an unavoidable Spanish inheritance, with which the only methodology possible is to fake reality as always and adapt the simultaneous to the successive with the presumable losses and errors of parallax. But just take a look at this bunch, Lonstein says mournfully, you invite them for something important and all they can think of is talking about the Screwery, for an hour and a half they've been discussing the kidnapping of the Vip. But didn't you know? the one I told you is surprised. Hell yes, but they should settle that business during office hours. Still, since I put the penguin up for them I can bear with them a little longer, don't you think. Speaking of penguins, says Gladis after a great distribution

ACCORD ENTRE BUENOS-AIRES ET LONDRES SUR LES ILES FALKLAND

Londres *(A.F.P.)*. — A l'issue de négociations laborieuses, les gouvernements britannique et argentin se sont mis d'accord le 1er juillet pour « geler » la question de la souveraineté sur les îles Falkland (Malouines). Situé au nord-ouest de la Terre-de-Feu, et colonie britannique depuis 1834, l'archipel est revendiqué par l'Argentine.

Aux termes de l'accord, le gouvernement de Buenos-Aires permettra aux deux mille habitants des îles — isolés jusqu'à présent du continent sud-américain — de se rendre librement en Argentine. Ils y seront exempts du service militaire et jouiront de certains avantages fiscaux et douaniers.

D'autre part, le gouvernement argentin s'engage à établir des services aériens réguliers, ainsi que des communications postales, téléphoniques et télégraphiques, entre l'Argentine et l'archipel. La Grande-Bretagne se charge, de son côté, de créer un service de navigation entre Port-Stanley, capitale de l'archipel, et le continent.

of kisses, I don't know if you saw the news. Nature imitates art Patricio oscarwildes, already in the know, but not so Gómez and Monique who in accordance with well-established custom drop like lumps onto the floor so they can give vent to their laughter, and Ludmilla, who reads the item in turn, remembers that Andrés may have been the inventor of a definition of the Falklands that had also made her laugh in her time: Shitty islands, all full of penguins. We should give the news to the chief interested party, Susana says, although for the moment the only thing that fills him with passion is playing with Manuel in the bathtub. In *my* bathtub, says the little rabbi, soaking *my* towels and spattering *my* tiles. Take a look, he adds looking angrily at the one I told you, you invite them to see the mushroom and it all ends up in a repugnant naumachia. I don't know whether you all realize it or not, but the treaty saves the penguin from military service, Patricio says, and he'll enjoy tax and customs benefits. If we'd only known we wouldn't have raised such a ruckus at Orly, Oscar says. And if someone Lonstein for example would only start passing around some drinks, Gómez says. There's wine and soda, Lonstein says severely. Then the one I told you retires to his neutral corner, which is anywhere although it doesn't have to be a corner, and there he remains watching and listening to them, those people he knows and loves, those people from his own country chatting and laughing, more and more involved in something that's going to explode and which has nothing to do with anything funny, nothing to do with penguins and telegraphic coincidences and wine and soda. As always the problem is to understand without any deforming simplifications, and to make people understand perhaps, but this last isn't too important for the one I told you, who limits himself to showing what he believes to be true and real and even necessary, without the staging that is de rigueur for such things. Historically speaking, the secret chapter meeting had begun way back, first with a minority, Marcos and Heredia busy stripping the containers and entrusting Lucien Verneuil with the dollars; then Patricio and Gómez dropped in, and when Oscar arrived without any sweets but rested, they could talk in detail about what would close out the operational phase Friday night. It was Monday, a night of mushrooms and wine that was most likely watered; on Tuesday you don't get married, don't start a trip, but on the other hand it's a great day for exchanging the dollars simultaneously in some twenty banks and agencies, a task under the care of the aboriginal group commanded by Roland and Lucien Verneuil, since the fewer South Americans approaching the tellers' windows the better, the ants were sharp enough to have dossiers on the darker skins and they operated with a touch of a wink from the French police, which complicated matters on the bank side. It was up to Patricio to explain a series of advance maneuvers which would take place all through Wednesday and Thursday and they were just reaching Friday morning when the doors of the little rabbi's dwelling thundered and he opened in somewhat of a fright to give simultaneous passage to Ludmilla and Susana, the latter practically dropping Manuel to hang on Heredia's neck, while Heredia looked out of the corner of his eye at Marcos with an unequivocal reference to Ludmilla who had just seduced the young student in the second scene of the last act, curtain and a taxi without taking off her makeup, so she was strange and very beautiful and Marcos looked at her and then winked at Heredia to go on explaining about the Vip without any preoccupation, something that Patricio and Gómez accepted with a reprimand because it was Marcos and probably also because it was Ludmilla. Calming Manuel took its five minutes, this child got terribly excited as soon as he felt himself the center of the universe just like everyone sort of but with even more innocence, and the secret chapter meeting was in session as if by magic after the intervening recess destined to filling the bathtub and making the introductions between Manuel and the turquoise penguin who immediately proceeded to lose interest in the Screwery and undertake a bath followed with particular delight by the women while the chapter reopened the session and it was Gómez's turn to give some precise details about the great Screwery, to wit: (1) the Vip and the Vipess, his legitimate spouse, would leave a semi-official dinner before midnight; (2) the Vip's protection, under the care of the Gi-ant (elementary my dear Watson) would almost certainly consist of the presence of two Sycoph-ants in the car, one as driver and the other just in case and also armed; (3) the area was good, near the Parc Monceau; (4) the time was also passable; (5) the itinerary for the interception and leaving Paris presented no traffic problems at that hour; (6) the distinguished ex-representatives of the Vincennes zoo, reintegrated into activities more in keeping with their nature, had everything prepared to receive the Vip at a place in the suburbs that answered to the awesome name of Verrières.

"Go in and take a look at the mushroom," proposed Lonstein who was becoming enormously bored.

"What about the Vipess?" Oscar asked.

"We'll bring her back to Paris as soon as she sees that the guest has been put up in the style he deserves and that no one is going to do to him what he would like to do to us," Marcos said. "Two birds with one stone, she'll be the one to give the news to the papers so that the great Screwery can be unleashed. I've got some other things to arrange with you and with you, but this is the main thing for now."

"What do you think about my getting them into the other room," Lonstein asked the one I told you. "Would the members of the Privy Council like a bit of wine?"

"Yes sir," Gómez summed up, "let's pass on to the buffet, gentlemen."

"I had to take him out of the bathtub," Susana announced as she came in dripping soapsuds, "the penguin gets too excited because Manuel wants to wash his belly."

"Come to uncle," Marcos said catching on the fly a naked and shiny Manuel who preferred trying to climb up the knee of Gómez who was most alarmed out of concern for the Panama crease in his pants. "Jesus, this kid is getting bigger-headed every day."

"Your grandmother's another," Susana said, and Manuel's ruffled up choephoroi, viz. Monique, Ludmilla, and last but not least Gladis: You're jealous, you'd like to have curls like that/ Such eyes/And that cute little snout/Look at those pretty little feet/and Manuel enchanted with ride a cock horse to Banbury Cross, hanging onto Marcos like a horse-breaker on a mustang, because tomorrow's a holiday and the day after too, and Friday most of all, Marcos thought letting himself be whipped by the horse-breaker from the pampas, taking a quick look at Ludmilla who after collaborating with the other choephoroi had curled up on the favorite chair of the little rabbi who looked at her with displeasure but who brought her a glass of wine just the same and something that must have been a cheese sandwich although it looked more like a blotter. A terrible squawk came from the bathroom and Gladis ran to open the package of fish she had brought, knowledgeable woman that she was, the gathering was beginning to take on a definitely pleasant rhythm.

The chair was big enough for a cow, lost in burlap and red wine Ludmilla was listening to the last fringes of the Screwery but even later, when they talked penguin or Carlos Monzón bouts she kept on wondering how Marcos and the others could trust her that far: Friday, Parc Monceau, Sycoph-ants, Verrières, all the elements. The molds that had been rigorously extracted from so many spy novels were piling up to convince her that it couldn't be, that Marcos had been having fun with Patricio and Gómez; maybe later on when they were alone, they would really talk. At some moment Marcos came over to her, squatted down beside her with two glasses of wine and a cigarette in his mouth.

"Why didn't Andrés come?"

He said it in a low voice, just for her, beyond the bounds of the Screwery; all the more absurd, thought Ludmilla.

"He didn't want to come. We talked about a whole lot of things and he went out."

"But did you tell him about this afternoon. Oh. It's O.K. then; if he didn't want to come that's his business."

"I don't understand," Ludmilla said very softly, although in any case they were isolated and protected by the voodoo rites of the choephoroi with Manuel (and Heredia involved now and most happy to buck), "I don't understand anything, Marcos. What Patricio and the others just said, that business about Friday."

"Yes, my Polonette."

"But me, Marcos, how is it possible for you . . ."

"It's all right, Polonette. You're not a member of the Screwery but you can see that there are things people know in their own way, and this time I know what I'm doing. Don't feel obligated about anything, just keeping your mouth shut is enough. Because that's for sure, you can't tell Andrés about this now."

"Of course not."

"Too bad," Marcos said brusquely. "I thought he was going to come, in that case I would have felt just as sure as with you."

"It had to be," Ludmilla said. "It had to happen sometime, now he's on one side and I'm on the other. It seems like a joke, but we were talking about it all afternoon, I mean about separations, distances. And now it's my turn to stand aside."

"Too bad," Marcos repeated. "But I know a little bit about that too, my wife is a secretary in a ministry in Buenos Aires."

"Oh?"

"Don't be sad, Polonette. If you would only just forget what you've heard and go back home as if nothing had happened, I'd call it perfect. Now, what I explained to you this afternoon and what you're hearing is up to you, so much the better. You can see that I've taken the trouble to lay out both possibilities in detail."

"I'm sticking with you people, Marcos."

"Fine, Polonette. Come on, come on, slow down, the mushroom won't dry up for at least a half an hour."

"The moment is ripe," Lonstein said, "because from midnight on the fungic phosphorescence starts to decline. If you've finished with logistics, come into my chamber."

The chamber was the adjoining room, as tacky as the first. When Ludmilla autoextracted herself from the chair, Marcos remained beside her as if he still wanted to tell her something, until the choephoroi rolled over them with Manuel half-asleep but still capable of knocking over glasses and putting cigarette butts in his ears. Heredia was the first to fall silent when they went into the chamber, ironically the idea of the mushroom was winning him over as a turn to other things, going from the first room to the bedroom was something more than a physical displacement among laughter and jokes, the choephoroi and Manuel had lowered their voices, Oscar was looking at Gladis with newcomer's eyes, looking for an explanation that Gladis was unable to give him; Patricio and Gómez, more experienced, limited themselves to putting their hands in their pockets and acting serious. As for the one I told you he was busier than ever in the task of putting all that in order, which wasn't easy. In short, let us say

Lonstein beside a table
the table in the back of the chamber
the chamber in darkness
no chairs   no furniture

a beam of greenish light coming down from the
ceiling and landing on
the contents of a flowerpot placed
on a teacup saucer

the mushroom in the center of the pot

purply vertical cyclinder
bigheaded but not too much
inevitably topically phallic
weakly phosphorescencing under
a stimulus greenish   photophilic

Don't get too close, Lonstein ordered, the nitrogen and the smoke from the butts can do it harm. A mushroom, Heredia said, all we needed here was a hallucinogen. This mushroom has nothing hallucinogenic about it, Lonstein said indignantly, it's a *lapsus prolapsus igneus* as any fool can plainly see, and considerably poisonous. But what is this, some kind of ceremony? mutters Oscar. Not even that, said Gómez, just a waste of time. Don't be silly, Monique said, we can use a little fun. If it's a question of having fun I could be putting hinges on the ones I got from Morocco or the new set from Finland, said Gómez. Oscar still couldn't understand, everything falling down on top of him in so few hours and now this mushroom, of course Lonstein was to be trusted and anyone can have his little moments of madness and it must have been something like that that Marcos was thinking because he was looking at Lonstein with a face on which there was a kind of repose, a loosening up after the other business, although in the shadows the one I told you could not make out the expressions too well and he was probably falling into full subjective projection. This is a good night, Lonstein was saying, there are a couple of nice fat conjunctions so that the *lapsus* is growing better than ever. I don't see it growing, Susana said, or the choephoroi either, it's impossible, plants grow imperceptibly, etc. This mushroom is not a plant, Lonstein made clear, plants are green and common, the very lumpen of botany. If you put out your butts you can come a little closer to take a look. But this is most scientific Heredia said, appreciating the tape measure that Lonstein was slowly drawing out of its case, he held it parallel to the *lapsus* and called Monique over as on vaudeville stages to verify nothing in this hand and nothing in the other. Exactly eighteen centimeters two millimeters, Monique said imbued with her importance. You, the exact time, Lonstein said to Marcos. Twelve forty-four and twenty seconds moreorless, Marcos informed. Let us know when it is exactly five minutes, you can skip the seconds. It really was like a ceremony, Oscar drew close against Gladis who was softly sleeping on her feet like a pony, he lighted a cigarette at a respectful distance from the mushroom and said to himself that from this moment on until Friday, and especially starting with Friday things were going to be fast and hot, in any case the mushroom and Lonstein and Marcos's rather strange condescension didn't bother him, on the contrary, there was a kind of alliance that was inexplicable but felt nonetheless, a meeting that was momentary and therefore perhaps precious because of so many diverse things or things that many people thought diverse, Gómez for example, the man of action who felt he was wasting his time, or Heredia twisting with laughter, but it was good for Oscar, this absurdity of a green light and millimeter measurements, Lonstein's looking at the mushroom and explaining that it was an extreme case of accelerated cellular multiplication, I saw it born in a ditch near the river there where I fix the forelock on my apwals. My what, asked Heredia. Dead people, Lonstein said, it's all right, I'll simplify for the outlanders present, I was looking for a bench, at dawn I get tired of the work and I go out for a breath of air, suddenly I see a small stone moving in the ditch, I say a mole! a mole! but there aren't any moles in Paris, then I say a big hairy caterpillar, an astral levitation, the pebble gives half a turn and I see the *lapsus* appear like a finger pushing up, no imperceptible growth as these women here say, a shove and out, that couldn't be an asparagus, next to the morgue just imagine, then I went to get an old can and a knife and when I took it out with great care it was already two centimeters above ground level. Five minutes, Marcos said. Measure it, Lonstein ordered, and Monique carefully applied the metric tape making sure not to touch the *lapsus*, incredible, Monique said, nineteen centimeters exactly. What did I tell you, figure it out and get the internal working of the mushroom, Lonstein said. It's enough for us to be informed, Patricio said, sleeping on his feet, the ocular observation isn't exactly maddening. They're all alike, the choephoroi protested, it's worth looking at, it's an extraordinary mushroom, a scientific phenomenon, but no one said it was beautiful, that it was growing like the thing on everyone's mind, and naturally Heredia was the one enjoined to establish the analogy, it's exactly what happens to me when I see a good miniskirt, the *lapsus* grows immediately, great celebration on the part of the choephoroi. Mention dick to them and they get all excited. Red dick and hairy snick, *pija colorada y concha peluda*, Ludmilla said, earning simultaneously the respect of Heredia and the stupefaction of Oscar who was coming out of his half-dream leaning on Gladis who was going completely to sleep, with which a brusk return to laughter, a movement of retreat because the bedroom was a little depressing with its darkness and its green light, or maybe the mushroom was giving off soporific emanations, better to keep on drinking wine in the other room where Manuel was sleeping on a rug sucking three fingers.

"You shouldn't lose sight of the mushroom," Lonstein said to the one I told you, "you understand me."

The truth was that the one I told you didn't understand much of anything, but Lonstein kept on looking at him with ironical insistence, and finally it was as if the one I told you and Oscar each in his own way were understanding better what was going on (and Marcos too, but Marcos had understood it from a starting point, from the entry of Lonstein into the Screwery, otherwise the little rabbi wouldn't have had access to something that in practice was getting too big for him), and that's why later on when the one I told you recounted the visit to the mushroom I agreed with him and thought that Marcos knew how to see things from more than one side, which wasn't the case with the others who were resolutely oriented toward the Screwery. In that idiotic comedy there was perhaps something like a hope for Marcos, that of not falling into total specialization, preserving a bit of play, a bit of Manuel in his conduct. God, who could say. It could even be that types like Marcos and Oscar (about whom I was getting to know things via the one I told you) were in the Screwery because of Manuel, I mean that they were doing it for him, for every Manuel in every corner of the world, trying to help him so that someday he would enter a different cycle and at the same time saving for him a few remains of the total shipwreck, the game that made Gómez impatient, the superfluousness of certain things of beauty, of certain mushrooms in the night, by means of which he could give complete meaning to any future project. Of course, the one I told you felt obliged to participate in the final synthesis, few people in the Screwery, in all Screweries big and small on the face of the earth would understand types like Marcos or Oscar, but there would always be an Oscar for a Marcos and vice versa, capable of feeling why it was necessary to be with the little rabbi at the moment of going into the bedroom to look at the mushroom.

With all that it looked as if they were already on their way and that was when they naturally stayed another hour, some choephoroi asleep where they could, the other people hanging on the wine and the news Heredia brought, at that time Lonstein had put out almost all the lights for reasons that the others presumed to be talmudic, the little rabbi's yawns were ignored or simply imitated while Rosario, the meeting of Pug-Nose Pérez with the people of the PROM in Honduras, the latest word from London or Uruguay, and the best of all

No News of Guerrilla Women Who Escaped from Córdoba Jail

Operation brought off by ERP. Organization and Training Shown

CÓRDOBA, 12 (AP)—The investigations undertaken by the police to shed light on the bold assault perpetrated last night by an extremist commando group on the women's jail and the freeing of five urban guerrilla women have brought forth no positive results as of the moment. A female employee of the jail who opened the door to take out garbage was being held incommunicado, because there is an investigation as to whether she played any part in the episode, as yesterday she neglected to advise the police guard that she was going to open the door as she did every day.

while Oscar and Marcos jealously defended their glasses of wine from the soda with which Lonstein was trying to improve them according to a completely stupid recipe of his mother's, Marcos explaining to Heredia and Oscar some of the things that would happen during the next fifty-eight hours, Oscar half-lying between Gladis who was snoring ever so slightly and two cushions, his elbow like Trimalchio's on a pile of old copies of the *Gaceta* (of

Tucumán), the comments about the ERP operative heard as if from farther and farther away, veering slowly to another angle, plays of sleepiness and shadows and wine, something else in that drowsiness where a high moon and the gallop of horses on the dirt roads, that noise forever of hooves digging up clods with a squeak that could be felt, again the vision of the wall shining with the glass from broken bottles, the girls taking off their nightgowns on top of the wall to protect their hands, the pileup, the shouts, the first whipping, the flight through vacant lots, nothing to do with that room on the other side of the world with its mushroom, and yet, yet, an effort to skip to the news item Patricio was reading to Heredia, and Heredia suddenly surprised,

This afternoon new details of the episode attributed to the "People's Revolutionary Army" (ERP) were learned that gave evidence to a high degree of organization and training on the part of this terrorist cell.

The members of the commando group that undertook the blow showed singular boldness, for the women's jail is located in the very center of the city, three blocks away from the Federal Police and four from the Central Police Department.

Tactics

The evidence gathered allows one to establish that the terrorists acted with a thorough knowledge of the terrain and early in the afternoon undertook actions aimed at distracting the attention of the police so that they could act with impunity.

Early yesterday afternoon the extremists attacked the residence of Commodore (Ret.) Patricio Ferrero who occupies the position of Secretary of the Treasury of the city and previously was Minister of Economics and Treasury.

A few hours later some individuals set off bombs at the intersection of the Avenida General Paz and 9 de Julio, and threw stones and Molotov cocktails at the place of business of Argencor, Inc., the Fiat agency.

The bombs started a fire and the stones broke the windows and windshields of a car.

Several police units were involved when the acts were reported, while the high command of the division was gathered at headquarters holding a press conference concerning the capture of four extremists who had attacked a policeman and had taken part in attacks on wholesalers to distribute clothing and food afterwards in low-income districts.

While the officials were showing the newspapermen the weapons and ammunition seized with the four in question, they received news of the attack on the Asylum of the Good Shepherd.

The Women Freed

Susana Liprandi Sosa de Vélez, Silvia Urdampilleta, Diana Triay de Johnson, Alicia Quinteros, and Ana María Villarreal de Santucho had just been freed by an extremist commando group. The first belonged to the Montoneros, the rest to the ERP.

The five were accused of having engaged in guerrilla activities.

hey, Heredia said with a leap, I know Alicia Quinteros quite well, and Gómez from a corner harshly now the social register starts, this guy knows everybody. Fuck you (Heredia) and Patricio enjoying it showing Marcos that in the reporter's language a garbage can is transformed into a waste container, how many garbage cans scattered along those alleys through which the girls had fled without anyone waiting for them in a car ("they showed organization and training"), splashing through mudholes and hiding in ditches from where they were probably dragged out, lifted up onto the saddles by the hair or by an arm, receiving insults in the midst of laughter and slaps, but it was the same, from his wine lookout Oscar felt that it was the same, a liberation, a necessary flight, little girls from an asylum or Alicia Quinteros, lumpen or lady lawyers escaping from the lure of the system, running naked or unhurriedly getting into the car that was chronometrically waiting for them, crazy from the full moon and carnival music or responding to an operation which, Patricio read, shows evidence of the high degree of organization and training of the terrorist cell. Terrorist cell, snorted the little rabbi, what a shitorrhea. I'm quite sure I know her, Heredia said, she's got green eyes, you don't forget something like that overnight, old man.

y se la m

ta la man

ras cómo llo

orcía y me sup

--Hicistes b

al cabo. --Así

derán esas p

"I'll go down first and take a peek," Patricio said, "just in case."

"Be careful," Susana was going to tell him but she swallowed it, incredible sentimental commonplaces coming back like flies, ridiculous to imagine that Patricio would run out into the street just like that when it was precisely important not to show yourself too much at an hour when everything is at rest and muscles are asleep, because then they can blow snot on you on the sidewalk and nobody will open the blinds except to shriek a decent person can't get any sleep any more, sacré nom de putain de dieu.

Manuel was inspecting things, partly awake, dragged from the rug by the choephoroi in concert and wrapped in a muffler loaned by Lonstein with the pledge of its return, when Patricio came back to report that the coast was clear. Heredia went down first, with Monique and Gómez who would drop him off at his hotel; eight steps behind and carrying the two baskets Marcos and Oscar sent on their way by Lonstein with an air of obvious relief at the idea that they were carrying off the royal armadillos and the turquoise penguin. The rest of the choephoroi and Patricio joined them near the door, Manuel whimpering softly in his father's arms; the Rue de Savoie was deserted, they saw Gómez who was opening the door to the car and suddenly he turned toward them and gestured in the direction of the corner of the Rue Séguier. Getting into the car, he started the engine but didn't move off. Marcos stopped in the entranceway, leaving the women and Manuel behind in the shadows; the basket with the penguin was against the door. Heads up, Marcos said, something's going on with Gómez and Heredia, don't anyone move. Oscar and Patricio had stuck close by and Marcos took out his blackjack, two figures were crossing diagonally from the Rue Séguier and two others seemed to be waiting farther back barely visible in a doorway. Fortunato, Marcos said, certain that he had had Heredia followed, they're not so dumb. If they go for the car we'll have to give them a good one and then beat it. Patricio had another blackjack, he looked back to where Susana and Manuel were one single bulk with Gladis and Ludmilla. Let's go, Marcos said and ran toward the corner. Oscar followed him, turning up his coat collar, an instinctive movement that had already amused him in retrospect other times, the wild thing was that he didn't even have a penknife, he heard Patricio running behind, now the first of the Sycoph-ants was struggling with the car door and the other one was picking something up to break the window with, but he wouldn't have dared, it all had to take place with the utmost silence at that hour and in that neighborhood because the police could appear at any moment and they wouldn't distinguish between Montagues and Capulets until much later, everybody inside just in case, Marcos fell on the neck of the one at the door just as Gómez opened from inside to get back out onto the street. Oscar stood facing one of the ones coming from the corner dragging himself out of the doorway where he had been covering the others, what the fuck do they want, Oscar said, get the hell out of here you goddamned shitty Sycoph-ant sons of bitches, he felt the club on the elbow that he had lifted in time and he gave the kick with all his heart and experience from playing soccer on hostile fields. Patricio had become locked with one in a white raincoat and curly hair, they were rolling on the ground just as Marcos dodged the two closest to the car and attacked them with his blackjack, Monique's face in the rear window, Heredia who was jumping out behind Gómez and plunged in and fell to the ground, something hit Oscar on the shoulder and sent him tumbling, two of the Sycoph-ants were running along the Rue Séguier, Gómez and the first attacker on the ground near Patricio and the other guy, from the doorway Ludmilla and Gladis couldn't distinguish the outlines, Susana hugged Manuel and murmured something, Ludmilla stood in front of her to stop her from going out just in case, they saw two who ran by the doorway and went in the direction of the Rue des Grands-Augustins, Oscar holding his arm on the corner and Gómez and Patricio after the guys, still silent, one or two exclamations, a kick at a garbage can in passing, a very fast silent film, Patricio grabbing Manuel, let's get to the car quick, they might come back with others, run, Ludmilla and Gladis hesitating until they saw Gómez and Heredia standing on the corner, Gómez half bent over and Marcos against a wall, motionless and as if out of focus; they ran to the corner and Marcos made an effort and said get in, we can't stay here, Heredia and Gómez jumping into the car with Monique half hanging out the window looking at Marcos, what happened, Marcos, what's going on, and Gladis hugging Oscar who was rubbing his elbow with the hand of his good arm and his shoulder with the hand of his wounded arm and the ten-whored mother that bore them if this is the city of light I shit on Lamartine, Gómez started up and went the wrong way along the Rue Séguier to the Seine, let's get to your car fast, Marcos said to Ludmilla, it's on Grands-Augustins, O.K., let's go, but as soon as he left the wall he staggered a little and Oscar and Ludmilla grabbed him in time, Oscar whore-cursing again because his elbow ached up to his ears, he was all elbow, a kind of pile of splinters and the thousand-whored mother who double-thousand bore them, said Oscar who knew the therapeutic value of whore-cursing, then Marcos stood up breathing slowly and was the first to walk held by Ludmilla who wasn't talking, there was no sense in talking at that moment, holding Marcos around the waist until Marcos pushed her away softly, It's O.K. now, let's go, quick, and to Ludmilla, you go on ahead and get the car started fast, these guys are going to come back, I know them. But there was nobody on the Rue des Grands-Augustins except for a black cat who studiously ignored them, Oscar was already feeling better, you're sure you haven't got a broken arm, tell me, hostess girl, he hit me on the funny bone but it's going away, and Marcos still a little hunched over, getting into the car beside Ludmilla who was racing the motor, in front of it was the space that had been occupied by Patricio's car, that's better, Marcos said, at this point it could have been dangerous, by God. But what were they after? Oscar said. Leave him alone for a while, said Ludmilla starting up better than Fangio, can't you see he can barely breathe. What a night, like a Bardi tango, Oscar muttered, rubbing his elbow like an octopus with hives, and with that tinkle-bell moon, tell me if that isn't a scenario. You can bet your ass those Sycoph-ants come from Río de la Plata country. There was at least one Brazilian, Marcos said, Heredia noticed it and gave him an extra-special kick, but the other one must have mushed in his face because Heredia couldn't find his corner when he tried to get back to the car. What about you, Ludmilla murmured making a fast turn down the Rue du Bac. Me nothing, Polonette, a kick in the stomach, the kind that makes you puke up your first communion, difficulty in breathing as a consequence and let's change the subject. You want to know what they were after, me too, brother. They thought that Heredia and Gómez were alone with Monique, with the four of them it was easy, what they call teaching a lesson, we're going to teach him not to come from London to raise hell, goddamned monkey, you know how it goes. But it couldn't be just that, Fortunato was coming from London too and probably brought information on Heredia, the kind that calls for severe measures, you understand, five broken ribs or a leg, a stay in the hospital. Well, have a good night's sleep, you've earned it. Wait, I'll stop right in front of the Lutetia, Ludmilla said, I think Oscar needs a double shot of whiskey and lots of adhesive tape. I'll take charge of it, Gladis said, especially the whiskey. What about the penguin, Ludmilla asked. Good Lord, said Gladis. They can stick it up their ass, said Oscar. It hurts, said Gladis.

The black cat on the Rue des Grands-Augustins turned down the Rue de Savoie, passed the store on the corner and when it reached the doorway it arched its back and, when it discovered it, leaped up onto a platform across the street growling loudly. Out of the basket that had tipped over the penguin emerged slightly perturbed but with a definite feeling that it was cool and that the moon up there was the same one out of its antarctic nights, something that gave it the courage to go down the Rue de Savoie to the Rue Séguier where some bloodstains contained Heredia's and Patricio's rhesus formulas, and borne along by its hydric atavism it headed for the Seine passing along the bank, turning the corner of the Rue Gît-le-Coeur and coming out on the corner of the Place Saint-Michel where a drunkard and a pair of lovers saw it and acted the way they were supposed to, and what can I say about a doctor who was passing in his car on the way back from attending to a little old lady and coming upon the penguin he slammed on his brakes upon which the van behind him smashed into his rear bumper, an accident which under other circumstances would have brought on the mandatory five minutes of insults before insurance cards were taken out, but naturally no one thought about that because a group of absolutely stupefied nightwalkers were already standing around the penguin and one could hear the whistle of the policeman coming on the run partly because of the accident and partly because it was no time to be careless what with the Maoists and the social unrest. In the center of the circle the penguin was enjoying his immortal hour, waving his flippers he let out a kind of grumbling discourse which not even Gladis could have translated for the policeman who was paralyzed by the lack of any regulatory parameters governing exotic birds and other transgressions.

"Drop me off at a taxi stand and go on home to bed," Marcos said. "You've got a puss that looks like the middle of Lent, Polonette."

"I'll take you home," Ludmilla said. "It's near the Panthéon, I think."

"Go down Vaugirard and I'll show you, but it'll be a thousand o'clock by the time you get home."

"Are you really feeling better? We could stop and get something at a drugstore, I don't know."

"Well," Marcos said, "we could buy some flax powder and you could put a bandage on my belly and take my pulse."

"Silly."

I eventually learned about some of these things from Ludmilla as time went on but mostly from the one I told you starting with the moment he retraced his steps along the docks and returned to the Rue de Savoie without understanding exactly why, a vague desire to chat with Lonstein alone, a confusion of perspectives which at that time made him nostalgically remember Capablanca no less. Could it have been true that Capablanca could foresee all the possible moves in a game and that one night he had announced to his opponent on the fourth move that he would put him in checkmate on the twenty-third, and that he did it and not only did he do it but afterwards he showed analytically how there was no other possibility? South American legends, thought the one I told you who furthermore barely knew how to move the pieces and was always twenty-three moves behind, but how useful to be able to get a little bit ahead in that Screwery business because things were falling into an ever more palpable confusion. Out of that some of the drawings or sketches or nonsense with which the one I told you tried to catch so many mental flies, besitos Coca and other variants on various café tables:

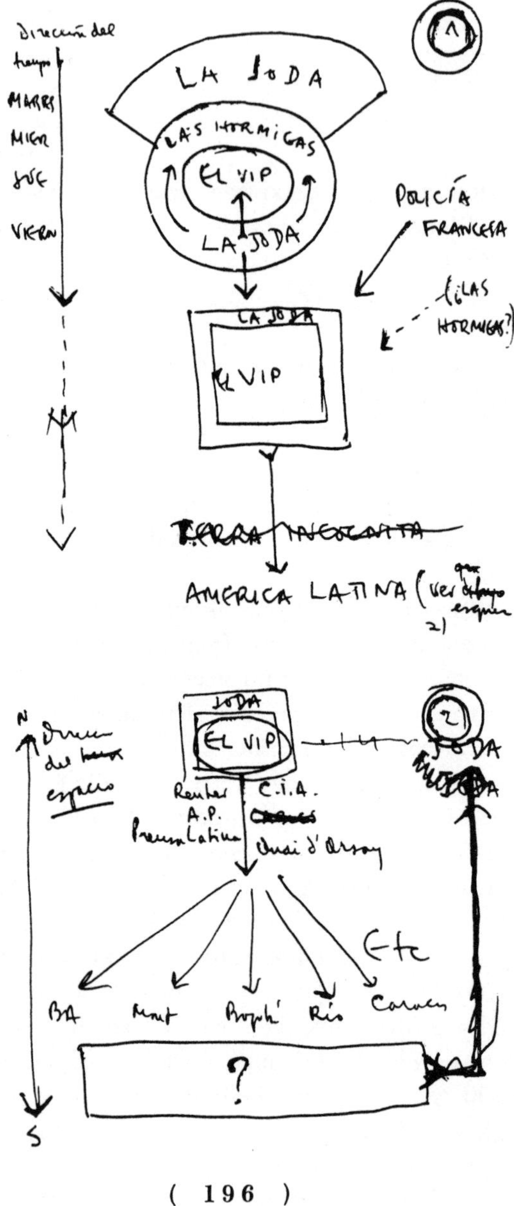
LA JODA
LAS HORMIGAS
EL VIP
LA JODA
POLICÍA FRANCESA
LA JODA
EL VIP
AMERICA LATINA
JODA
EL VIP
Reuter
A.P.
C.I.A.
Quai d'Orsay
Etc
BA
Rio
?
N
S

For Oscar, a rather swollen but bandaged elbow and bed, tinkling whiskey and Gladis naked and converted into a fragrant drink of incestuously maternal attentions, the dream that was winning him over was no longer so different from what had just happened on the Rue de Savoie, on any street with walls or fences, everything always so quick, hit and be hit, curse and be cursed, violence in an unknown quarter of an unknown city (he didn't know La Plata either, or almost didn't), territory where they had taken him and hauled him out by car, with names of streets and stars impossible to retain; there were ants, of course, but the ants too formed part of that strip without names that could be remembered, they were anonymous too and they had been lost on the run like the people in the ERP operation or the mounted police chasing the little-women-maddened-by-the-full-moon; as for Gladis she couldn't explain much either, the best thing would be to go to sleep and let everything get all mixed up since there was no way of separating so many things out of memory or the present, poor thing look at your elbow, hmm, it's nothing, wait till I turn out the light, hmm, stay just like that, oh no, behave yourself with me you're hurt, hmm, I'm not even moving, on my side like this, you're unbearable, let me, a little this way, oh Oscar, Oscar, and at some moment the moon filtering through the blinds with the vague sounds of dawn on the Boulevard Raspail, a distant tinkling, the shout of a drunk or a madman, the almost inconceivable sound of horses' hooves, most of them have probably jumped over the wall by now, to take refuge somewhere, to get lost in the city, it was the pair of girl friends again, the blond and the brunette in embrace, the gallop of a mounted policeman, the shapeless mixture, Gladis's thighs against his, the blond against the cemetery wall and the mulatto squeezing her waist, looking for the zipper, the blind getting grayer, a prison light always like dawn, a chiaroscuro of sadness and defeat, a maid at the asylum who had opened a door to take out a can of trash was arrested and held incommunicado because they were investigating if, and Alicia Quinteros, with green eyes according to Heredia, always flight, always jumping the wall over the glass, always flight like

piled up in
ory with the be
only bath for
and the guar
favorites, of course,
ing crying and
visitors, but nobody

now the dawn dream with everything mixed in together, La Plata and Paris, the telegrams and that thing that now had precise names for Marcos and Patricio but for him, simple words, Parc Monceau, a house in Verrières, the Hotel Lutetia, the corner of the Rue de Savoie. On the other hand the one I told you was not sleepy and knew Paris deeply, so that he began by picking up the basket with the royal armadillos, who unlike the penguin had followed events with resolute indifference, and he carried them back up to Lonstein's apartment because the fat woman wouldn't be prepared for a spectacle like that when she put in an appearance at seven o'clock in the morning. Lonstein stiffened naturally when he saw the one I told you and especially the armadillos who were grunting in the basket while a summary of the events on the street took place.

"Preballedictable," Lonstein roared. "Patricio was never outstanding as a Boy Scout, and here I am again as baby-sitter for these stinking beasts, at least the penguin pecked them. I have the pleasure of informing you that the mushroom has reached twenty-one centimeters, a measurement that is perfectly standard and acceptable in the best of circles. Come on in, I've got some hot coffee."

"Thanks, Polonette," Marcos said. He opened the door with a gesture of good-by.

"I'd like to fix you some tea," Ludmilla said.

Marcos didn't say anything but he waited for her beside the car and helped her lock it, looking once or twice down the Rue Clovis white in the moonlight and free of ants. You've got an elevator, incredible, Ludmilla said. I'm pretty sharp, by God, Marcos said, but the apartment was already beginning to contradict him, a cross between a monk's cell and a cheap bar, with dirty cups and glasses everywhere, books on the floor and ponchos covering cracks in the walls. That yes, the telephone that Marcos used immediately and in French to give news or instructions to Lucien Verneuil and finish the details about the exchange of the dollars that were called melons on the telephone although at that hour it seemed hard to believe that any ant was listening, from the kitchen Ludmilla caught clips of sentences and was looking for a can of tea as if all tea had to be in a can in order to satisfy its functional definition and all telephone conversations had to be understandable and everything that happened that night owed her explanations and keys. Idiot, idiot, idiot, Ludmilla said in triplicate her head stuck in a cupboard, as if it weren't enough for me to hear his voice, knowing that he trusts me, that they've all let me hear their voices (Gómez a little less, that's true) and being there while they talked about Friday night. Shit, there's nothing but some tapioca and chunks of cheese, the tea must be in the shoe closet. But she found it in a bottle that had once held bouillon extract, and she thought that she deserved it as a systematic person, tea in a tea can, Screwery in the framework of Aristotelian logic, everything in its place, like Andrés who was probably sleeping with Francine or listening to records with the stereophonic helmet he had bought for nights of insomnia. Poor thing, Ludmilla thought vaguely, suddenly Andrés was far away, poorer, he wasn't part of Friday night, he hadn't been beaten up on the Rue de Savoie. Four years were fast growing slim with all their days and nights and trips and games and gifts and scenes and weeping and kaleidoscopes, it wasn't possible, it wasn't possible. It isn't possible, Ludmilla said aloud looking for the teapot, a tree doesn't lose its leaves all at once, frailty thy name is woman. Frailty or debility? An argument for translators, in any case its name was woman, this tea is moldy and time is moldy too if I can be allowed a similar abolition, I'll wake up, it's certain that I'll wake up, I let myself be dragged along by the moment and by joy, by joy most of all because the Screwery is joy and is absurd and I don't understand anything and for that very reason I naturally want to be in this place there are five jars of pepper but not a single cube of sugar, oh men, men, I'll end up finding a condom in the spaghetti can.

Marcos had taken off his jacket and with his shirt open was rubbing his stomach, Ludmilla saw the enormous greenish welt, red on the edges and with yellow and blue spots. For the first time she realized that he had bled from the mouth, a trail that was dry now ran down his neck; leaving the teapot on the floor she got a towel from the bathroom, wet it, started to clean Marcos's mouth and chin as he lay back in a chair and breathed slowly, as if it hurt. Ludmilla looked at the splotch that disappeared into his pants. Without saying anything she began very carefully to loosen his belt which dug into his flesh a little; one of Marcos's hands reached up to her hair, stroked it lightly, fell down again onto the arm of the chair.

"I'm working on the prexpress," Lonstein stated after a ration of grappa in normal-sized glasses. "The good thing about you is that out of the whole mangle you're the only one who doesn't get surprised at my neophonemes, so I'm going to explain the prexpress to you to see if I can forget a little about those repulsive armadillos, listen to them grunt. The whole thing begins with the fortran."

"Ah," said the one I told you, ready to deserve the good opinion he had just been vouchsafed.

"Well, no one pretends that you know, after all. Fortran is a meaningful term in the symbolic language of scientific calculation. In other words, *for*mula *tran*slation gives fortran, and I didn't invent it but I find it to be a pretty expression, and why then not say prexpress for pretty expression, something that economizes phonemes, that is, ecophone, I don't know if you're following me, in any case, ecophone would have to be one of the bases of fortran. With these synthesizing methods, that is, synmets, one advances swiftly and economically toward the logical organization of any program, or the lorgprog. On this little piece of paper you can see the covering and mnemonic poem that I have prepared to retain the neophonemes:

Seek an ecophone with a synmet
but never shall a fortran
miss the date, if you want
a lorgprog of great coherence.
Prexpress!

"It sounds like one of those *jitanjáforas*, those nonsense poems that Don Alfonso Reyes talked about," the one I told you ventured to the evident annoyance of Lonstein.

"There you go, you too refuse to understand my ascent to a symbolic language that can go beyond or come beyond science, let's say a fortran of poetry or the erotic, everything that's nothing but a bag of groats in the rotten words of the planetary supermarket. These things are not invented systematically but if we made an effort, if each one could find a prexpress from time to time, I'm sure there would be an ecophone and an ilorgprog."

"Isn't it lorgprog?" corrected the one I told you.

"No, old man, outside of science it would be ilorgprog, that is, the illogical organization of any program, catch the difference; anyway, I've dried you out enough, so if you want to see the mushroom again all you've got to do is come into my chamber. So they got their asses busted on the street caught between the Milit-ants and the Concomit-ants, even though they were the Minim-ants. You watch and see how badly all of this is going to end up even if it's all right, lad, Marcos is a searcher, he's on the side of what happens in the street, though, and I'm more on the side of the graffiti on the walls, but only imbeciles would fail to see that everything is street, you know, and Marcos does and that's why he trusts me, something that has surprised me more than once because after all I'm me, a searcher after poetic sponges or something like that, a programmer of ilorgprogs."

"When all's said and done," said the one I told you, "I unfortunately lack a whole mess of synmets, fortrans, and prexpresses to help me understand certain things, but I'm glad in any case that in Marcos you see something more than a programmer without imagination, I hope that everything that's going to happen will match your neophonemes or the arrival of the turquoise penguin, even though comrades Roland and Gómez as always would accuse me of being frivolous, in any event if anyone is vaccinated against that accusation it's me."

"They'll bust our tails, that's for sure," Lonstein said, "that's what ants are for and they won't fail. And yet you're right, we still have to go on showing fortran, an unpublished image of human desire and hope; as Bukharin said I think, binary revolutions (I'd like to say Manichean, but it's a word that's turned me off ever since *La Nación* made it popular some twenty years ago) are condemned from the start because they accept the rules of the game, thinking they can break it all up they become deformed if you catch my meaning. Any madness that's necessary, little brother, intelligent and penetrating madness that will end up throwing the ants off balance. Liquidating the notion of the efficacy of the opponent as Gene Tunney used to say, because as long as he's the one who imposes it he condemns us to accept his semantic and strategic scenarios. You'd have to do something like that sketch by Chaval where you see a ring just at the moment when the bull is about to come out, but instead of the bull a tremendous gorilla comes out, and then what else can I say except that the brave bullfighter and his crew split holding their asses in their hands. That's it, it's a problem of conditioned reflexes, preventing the acceptance of hopeful and logical structures. The ants expect a bull and Marcos turns a penguin loose on them, in a manner of speaking. Well, come see the mushroom and let's change the subject."

Changing the subject, for example the clipping that Heredia had passed around and which Monique was saving in extremis from Manuel who was determined to put it in his mouth with obvious masticatory intent. Heredia knew "Cid" well, his name was Queirós Benjamin and from Algiers he was explaining one of the operations he had directed in Rio to a reporter from *Africasia.* At that moment the one I told you had not understood too well why there was a kind of example in "Cid's" story. Example of what, apart from its intrinsic importance. Afterwards, talking to Lonstein during those dawn hours he saw more clearly what for others had seemed to be just one of many guerrilla activities. "Cid" was talking about an operation against a certain Almeida, a majority deputy and a millionaire to boot, with a booty of seventy million dollars plus thirty thousand in jewels, some deputy. One of our sympathizers (in translation by poor Susana

J'ai dirigé l'opération contre le député millionnaire de la majorité Edgar Almeida. Cette affaire nous a rapporté 70 000 dollars plus des bijoux évalués par une banque suisse à 30 000 dollars.

● Une opération considérable !

● **Oui. C'est un de nos sympathisants qui nous avait informés que le député cachait dans un coffre de sa demeure des bijoux et des dollars.**

Ce fameux député collectionnait également des toiles de maîtres et ne répugnait pas à une certaine publicité.

Nous lui avons envoyé une de nos séduisantes camarades qui s'est présentée comme reporter de « Realidad », hebdomadaire brésilien de grande diffusion.

Tout heureux de faire connaître au monde ses trésors, Almeida accepta avec plaisir de recevoir une « équipe technique » pour la photographie. Et tandis qu'il répondait aux questions, tout en servant des flots de whisky, les techniciens photographiaient les tableaux... et je pouvais repérer le coffre.

C'est alors que nous avons sorti nos armes. Almeida en eut une crise cardiaque. Mais nous étions accompagnés par un camarade médecin qui le remit sur pied rapidement.

Une voiture nous attendait dehors. Les précieux dollars nous ont été d'une grande utilité pour nous équiper ultérieurement. Et notre « victime » n'avait même pas osé nous dénoncer.

always the one caught in cases like this) informed us that the deputy kept the dollars and jewels in a safe, and that in addition he collected the works of great painters and appeared to be susceptible to publicity. Because of which we sent one of our women comrades who was extremely seductive (a tradução é um mal necessário, Heredia had grunted, what's this seductive business, I know very well who that chick is, to call her seductive is to insult her and her mother and all Brazil, because she's the most imponderable monument imaginable and she doesn't have to seduce anybody since all you have to do is take one look at her to fall flat on your face, this newsman doesn't understand it at all, well, keep reading), who introduced herself as a reporter from *Realidades*, a Brazilian weekly of wide circulation. Most happy to let the world know about his treasures, Almeida was happy to receive a "technical team" to photograph his works of art. And while he was answering questions as he served them rivers of whiskey, the technicians were photographing the paintings and I was locating the safe. At that moment we brought out our weapons. Almeida had a heart attack but one of our comrades was a doctor, and he brought him around quickly. A car was waiting for us outside. The precious dollars were very useful for equipping us later on. And our "victim" didn't even dare report us. Good work, Lucien Verneuil said. Work, thought the one I told you, that's all he sees, work.

"It's so easy to deny order or logic," Francine had summed up looking at me either from her cat side or from the accumulation of Gallo-Romanic wisdom + descartes + pascal + encyclopedia + positivism + bergson + professorship of philosophy. "The worst part, Andrés, is that you're not here tonight to deny it but quite the contrary; something is breaking up in your order, something is going wrong in your logic, and the poor little casualty has come to cry on the shoulder of his number-two girl friend. Now you'll probably say no, and then we'll drink some coffee or some cognac, Madame Franck will leave, we'll go downstairs so you can browse through the new things in the bookstore, we'll come back up for more cognac and then you'll feel better, you'll go back to being the marginal man, the liberated man, you'll kiss me, I'll kiss you, we'll get undressed, you'll put the lamp on the floor because you like this violet half-light around the bed, my flesh sketched out in chiaroscuro (you said it the first time, things like that stick), you'll embrace me, I'll kiss you, we'll deny time from the repetition on, the old system. And it'll be all right, Andrés, but I had to tell you in any case, I don't want you to come here as if I didn't understand what weighs you down and makes you deviate."

"Tennis," I told her. "Singles."

She looked at me, lost a little bit behind the smoke of her cigarette, waiting. Yes, my love, tennis, singles, first Ludmilla and now you, the ball goes back and forth between two velvet rackets, once, again, brushing the net, hitting the most difficult places but always stopped and admirably returned, a hard, subtle back and forth, two female champions pitilessly airing the question.

"It's all right, Francine, I haven't come to cry on your shoulder as you say, I simply told you what was going on; I can see again that it's a mistake, that we have to compartmentalize and that nothing is held in common on these grounds."

"Nothing," said Francine. "If anything were common, Ludmilla and I would have gone to the movies and shopping together, we'd take care of you when you had the flu, one on each side of your bed, and we'd make love the way they do in libertine novels, by threes, fives, or sevens. I know that you're not looking for that kind of community, indeed, the one who parcels it out is you, the one who decides and points is you; don't talk about mistakes, then, since that's the very basis of your system."

"You mean I should shut up, here and back there, come looking for you as if everything were immutable, and when I go back home do the same, not say anything to Ludmilla, give in without the slightest concession, kill the one in the other, every day and every night."

"It's not our fault, I mean Ludmilla's and mine. It's a question of system, I repeat; neither you nor we can break it, it comes from too far back and takes in too many things; your freedom has no strength, it's a tiny variation of the same dance."

"Cognac, then," I told her, up to here with words. "Let's say I just came in and I didn't tell you any of this. How are you, sweet? Did you work hard today?"

"Clown," Francine said, stroking my hair. "Yes, there was an awful lot of work."

"You'll probably reproach me too for seeing or looking at everything from the bottom of the funnel," Lonstein said. "Marcos himself, who knows me better than anyone, gives me a hard time sometimes, finds me too radical. What do you want, what I always liked about the little kike is that he really did bring a sword, he latched onto Galilee and flipped it like a pancake; it wasn't his fault that they built a church for him later, you're not going to reproach Lenin either for the Soviet Writers' Union, are you. The wrong ones are always the epigones, the Diadochi, or whatever you want to call them. Look, tell me if that isn't a thing of beauty."

The mushroom had reached a height of twenty-one centimeters at exactly five o'clock in the morning, and it seemed prepared to stand there at attention awaiting a new order; Lonstein put away the metric tape and watered the base of the mushroom with a liquid that the one I told you thought was water but you never knew with Lonstein. Then, if he had understood correctly, what Lonstein meant/Look at that blue phosphorescence/You were saying that/It's not the lamp, if I turn it off it keeps on phosphorescing, look/All right, if you don't want to talk it's all the same with me/Jerking off, for example, I know that everyone gets all worked up when I declare that I jerk off, they would prefer a little decorum, a little discretion, and you, I'm sure you're just like everyone else/Well, yes, I mean that after the age of thirteen it doesn't seem like such a fascinating theme/A pig mistake, as the left forward of Benedetti's soccer team said, but let's let the mushroom get some sleep, it's had it interrupted a lot tonight and it needs darkness; we'll brew some *mate* if you want, I think I've still got some grappa left.

The one I told you knew full well that from that moment on he would have

LONSTEIN ON MASTURBATION

and so it was and for the one I told you the whole problem was in hanging on to what Lonstein was saying or repeating it if it came to that. Rather surprised at himself he realized that if it came to that he would repeat it, that in some way it would be necessary to repeat it even though some people would cross themselves. It's not a question of going around looking for reasons of which there are many, Lonstein said, that's what the sons of Siegmund are for, and they're not always the sons of Sieglinde for which reason they remain several bodies behind Siegfried, if you'll pardon me these Wagnerianalytical evocations/If you're going to go on pretending that I understand you, the one I told you said energetically, you'd better stop bothering me with all your prexpresses, neophonemes, and other contractions of your semantic sphincter/ Too bad, Lonstein said, but after all. We were on the subject of its not being a question of knowing why I masturbate instead of fucking, but grabbing the matter by the handle, without any pornographic allusion meant. The couple for example, that universal significant of eroticism, naturally I looked for it on the streets, on Florida and on Corrientes like everybody when I was young, but it was the same with me as with Titina in the song. I'm an extreme case although nothing that unusual, that is I never managed to form a couple, not even changing five or six times in as many years. I even tested myself with a mailman who used to bring me *Sur*, a magazine I subscribed to in those days, seventeen years old, the mailman of course. Observe my scientific seriousness, the decision to attack the problem from all angles. Result: the certainty that I would never be able to live as the mate of a woman or a man, and at the same time I needed women in friendship and in bed. The mailman left my life paradigmatically because the living experiment showed me that homosexual relations didn't interest me, and I'll even go so far as to tell you that I cancelled my subscription to *Sur* so that he wouldn't come back anymore. But woman, yes, impossible to do without her and then as I have already told you five or six youthful attempts, all very fine at the beginning because on both sides ostrich technique and great enchantment, there's no defect that at first blush isn't an interesting and characteristic trait that stamps a person's peculiarity, or a discrepancy that isn't a dialectical incitement to the mutual enrichment of the spirit, cf. Julián Marías. I'm not laughing, then, because it's quite well known and said with those same rotogravure words, but it's also well known that the day comes when a defect is just a defect and that's the end of that. In this case the statistically habitual thing is to bear it, go on to marriage and take advantage of the good things which sometimes are greater than the bad. With me the system didn't work, I made three attempts at coupling and on the third we had a son and everything, he's studying now so that his mother can show off a dentist in the family, you know that in Villa Elisa the water is very conducive to pyorrhea. So I won't have to tell you about more than one case, the second time with Yolanda, after six months the reciprocal verifications were so obvious that we decided to live our own lives but without separating, those were days when you couldn't get an apartment just like that. What can I tell you, old man, it was like satellite transmission, we came and went at home as if the other one wasn't there, but literally, you understand and not the way it is when a couple fights and there are those uncomfortable hours that follow when the two have gotten over the fight, they're sorry for almost everything they've said not because they think it isn't true but there's the vocabulary and the hidden meanings and the old story and about that time even the threat of a slap, so they go about like dogs who've been dipped in flea-killer, all of it with good manners and a gentility that's like a blue sash, would you like a cup of tea, all right, but I can make it, no, let me, all right, thank you, let's have it in the living room because it's hot in here, that's right, this room gets stuffy at this time of day, don't you think we could put in some kind of insulation, I saw an ad in *Claudia*, get it so we can take a look, that's probably the answer, well but first let me make the tea, fine, in the meantime I'll water the plants on the balcony, and on like that until after the tea comes the little smile, you're hateful, you're the hateful one, you started it, I started it because you dragged out the old vacation stuff, you're wrong, I brought it up but not with that intention, oh well, I thought, see how bad you are, and you're a regular little fighting hen, your aunt's the hen, my poor aunt, she'd barely make a good owl, and with that the first laughter, then the nuzzling, and then bed it goes without saying and it's fine because every well-ended fight is a pre-erotic act, I know that for a fact. Brew me a *mate* I'm suffocating.

"So with your Yolanda it was different," insinuated the one I told you, a specialist in digressions when the moment offered itself.

"Why do you say your Yolanda?" Lonstein was offended. Buenos Aires people have even lost their ears, goddamned wop talk. Her name was Yolanda and she still runs a dry-goods store in Colegiales, the question is that I wanted to see if we could keep the couple setup without even saying good morning to each other, you have to recognize that there are germs of anthropological mutation in the idea. Maybe everything could be reborn spontaneously and by dint of not seeing each other we would see each other as we really were, but in the meantime the apartment was like a puppet show with one going out and the other coming in, one eating at twelve and the other at one, except that around about then both of us decided to eat at one-fifteen and then we would set the table and cook at the same time, there were some terrible collisions because at any given moment we would both grab for the salt shaker or the frying pan, a fraction of a second determined who the winner was and the other one was left with an empty hand in the air, or the time I was defecating and Yolanda came in and when she saw me announced after weeks of silence: 'Either you get out or I'll do it all over,' without my being able to tell whether all over meant on her or on me, a reason for which I jumped up cutting a turd in half. You know, we interpreted the sexual in the only way possible at that time, that is to say we needed both of us for love and that raised a problem, which was resolved one time, however, because when the great blind black god stuck his javelin, one would approach and put his or her hand on the other's shoulder and that one would obey immediately. The variations, the repetitions, the whims were expressed with a first movement that the other one understood and respected; it was really horrible."

"Oh, well," said the one I told you with relief, with the feeling of having heard the confessions of a spider or a rabbit.

"It was during that period, when I failed with Yolanda and she went back to old men that I began to masturbate in an organized way, not the way I did when I was a kid any more. Now there were other quite vivid experiences, a total knowledge of the limits of pleasure, of its variants, of its byways; which many take and above all pretend to take as an ersatz form of eroticism as a couple, began to change gradually into a work of art. I learned to jerk off the way a person learns how to drive and control an airplane or to cook well, I discovered that it was a valid erotic act on the condition that one did not turn to it as a mere replacement."

"Tell me, isn't it painful for you to talk about this?"

"Yes," Lonstein said, "and that's just why I think I have to talk."

The one I told you studied his profile, three-quarters face; Lonstein was a bit pale but he didn't avert his eyes; his hands were occupied in taking out and lighting a cigarette. He understood that he wasn't talking to him out of exhibitionism or perversion. "That's just why I think I have to talk." Why because of that? Because it was painful and against the grain of the etiquette bookshelf? Go ahead, said the one I told you, it's not exactly one of Cleopatra's nights for me, you five-level motherfucker from Córdoba in Argentina, but go right ahead at least until Phoebus puts in an appearance.

During those hours or those days—Wednesday or Thursday, I'm no longer sure—the dialogues it was my turn to get involved in were about switchmen, handfuls of words or gestures slowly moved some levers, trains that previously ran from east to west turned toward the north (there was one that left Paris for Verrières, a trip that under normal conditions would have taken twenty minutes and lasted two days this time, but let us not imitate sphinxes in disuse now or—but this was what the one I told you thought—Puccini princesses appearing through hotel loudspeakers); the truth is that one enters a dialogue as a café or a diary, one opens mouth, door, or page without worrying about what's coming, and then *boing.* With Ludmilla I knew it but the hand on the switch was too brutal, the train went onto the new track with a squeal of front-page catastrophe, I don't know what braking maneuver the engineer made to avoid jumping the track, if he did avoid it, those mental trains can break into pieces falling down a ravine with no one's realizing it. Curiously (an adverb always comes forth to mask something, that's certain) I had just reread some pages by René Char on the days of the resistance against the Nazis in the south of France, and among the pages of his diary and poems a simple phrase had remained in my memory: *Certains jours il ne faut pas craindre de nommer les choses impossibles à décrire*, and suddenly the one I told you told me about his night with Lonstein and it seemed to both of us that Lonstein was simultaneously talking about something concrete that he had to say even if it hurt him, but it didn't stay on the level of a confession because he hadn't meant it as such given the kind of fellow the little rabbi was, and rather it had to do with things that were quite distant in appearance and which to me would have appeared heterogeneous and even incoherent if the one I told you hadn't insisted, he knew them better, in joining them together and making a chain of them, Oscar for example, the fact that Oscar was also in the Screwery with a kind of totally disconnected intervention in light of reasonable principles or C.P. directives. That's why the one I told you began culpably to mix it all up, and at some moment he had tried to separate the herd and put the piebalds on one side and the palominos on the other; now he was realizing that things were not separable, in any case they weren't for Lonstein or for Oscar either (or for Marcos, but Marcos didn't talk much unless he was dipping into the gin as at the time of his praise for enthusiasm, a theme that otherwise had been Ludmilla, and that's how we went), and on the days when he showed his hand to Andrés the cards were all mixed up and Andrés thought that between the one I told you and Ludmilla there was no longer one single timetable of trains that could be consulted as before, because the switches had changed the tracks all around and between Tuesday and Friday there had been a kind of general dislocation of traffic. For me it was a personal thing and I had no reason to project it into a kind of clarity for third parties, but the one I told you was on a different track, and the Screwery, which at first had seemed idiotic to him and then amusing but always simple and even primary, was beginning to slip through his fingers like a flow of tapioca and that's why he was looking at Lonstein with a rather disagreeable feeling.

COMMENT FUT ENLEVÉ L'AMBASSADEUR AMÉRICAIN ELBRICK

In fact, when the one I told you told me about the

Lonstein dissertation, I was at the point of understanding what Ludmilla had already understood, what Marcos had understood from the beginning, what Oscar was trying to understand from a different angle, what so many others would probably understand at some time; but it was still early, and besides there was the movie dream that kept coming back with its gadfly and its oppressive hollow at the door of a room where someone ("a Cuban, sir") had been waiting to tell me something; it was probably too early for that dream too, but meanwhile Char was right and one didn't have to be afraid of naming things that were impossible to describe, just as Lonstein was right when he described so many things impossible to name to the one I told you. Without mentioning any of that, history went on, as was so easy to prove for a few cents at a newstand.

AMÉRIQUE LATINE

ARGENTINE : QUERELLES DE GÉNÉRAUX ET LUTTES POPULAIRES

PAR ISABEL ALVAREZ

Andrés knew it already, and Ludmilla could have come back and been silent, or not come back and telephoned from Marcos's place, or not come back and not telephoned (postal and telegraphic variants, diverse friendly interpositions); when she came into the apartment on the Rue de l'Ouest it was almost noon, but no leeks this time. Andrés was asleep naked, one hand lost between the alarm clock and other objects on the night table; maybe a nightmare had made him throw off the sheet and the blanket that lay theatrically at his feet and to one side of the bed, and Ludmilla thought of an historic painting, Géricault or David, Chatterton poisoned, titles like

"Too Late!" and its possible variants. She looked for a moment at that body on its back, shameless and as if alien to itself, she smiled a silent good morning to him and closed the door; she would sleep too but on the couch in the living room, after moving a half-dozen records that Andrés had left everywhere. With a glass of milk, wrapped in one of Andrés's bathrobes, she thought that she ought to get a little sleep, that at three o'clock she had to go to Patricio's for instructions.

The belt had loosened easily because Marcos made the task smoother by contracting his stomach with a look of pain, and Ludmilla had been able to undo the first three buttons until she found the elastic of his undershorts. As long as you haven't got any internal hemorrhage, she had said on seeing the blue and green map of Australia that continued on down. Come on, Polonette, can't you see that I haven't any trouble breathing, it's just a bruise. I know, Ludmilla said, a cloth soaked in alcohol, it's just the thing. It'll have to be with grappa, Marcos said, because that's the only shape alcohol takes on in this house. When he kissed her slowly on the ear, interrupting the scientific examination of the damaged area, Ludmilla rested her head on his chest for a moment and remained very still. They weren't talking, the tea was growing cold in accordance with various thermal laws.

"It doesn't have to be just routine, Marcos," Ludmilla said.

"I was thinking the same thing, Polonette."

Holding his breath he sat up slowly to take his shoes off. Ludmilla helped him, made him drink a sip of tea, and went to look for the grappa but rejected the idea of a cloth because this grappa really smelled too much like grappa and because Marcos, walking slowly, was going to the bedroom and taking off his pants and shirt, he lay down on the bed in his shorts and from there made a sign to Ludmilla who turned out the lights in the kitchen and living room and returned with glasses and the grappa which could be utilized internally in any case. With a cigarette in his mouth, Marcos began to tell her about the Vip; Ludmilla had sat on the floor next to the bed, and could see Marcos's curly hair shining in the glow of the night-light. Soon it would be dawn but neither of them was sleepy. It doesn't have to be just routine, as Ludmilla's blouse came off while Marcos explained to her what was going to happen Friday night it doesn't have to be just another gesture in a recurring ceremony, that taking off her sandals and lowering her stockings should have a different value, or no value outside of feeling closer to fatigue and sleep. In the corner of Marcos's lips a touch of dried blood remained. There was a sponge in the bathroom, a strange light; through the tobacco smoke Marcos saw Ludmilla's naked silhouette rise up, her back, her thighs, a dark, tight body that started walking toward the door in search of the sponge.

"Some identification, please," the cashier said. With slight variations the request was repeated at the same time in twenty-three bank branches and exchange offices in the Paris area; Lucien Verneuil and Roland's group knew how to do things and between 2:30 P.M., the time banks opened, and 2:45 P.M., old Collins's masterpiece changed hands and was transformed into French francs. There was only one alert, at the *Cosmique* agency on the Place de l'Italie where a clerk in a blue dress and myopic eyeglasses began to examine the bills with an insistence that seemed exaggerated to the customer, a moment at which the clerk let him know that it was her obligation, while the customer replied that for his part he was only an employee of a travel agent and that if there was any doubt she had better call Mr. Macropoulos at once, GOBelins 45.44. To the surprise of the customer, who had invented Macropoulos simply to gain time and see what happened before he had to beat it, the lady exchanged the money immediately, not without some further reflections on her professional duties. The first report was received by the police at five-fifteen from a branch of Crédit Lyonnais; by nightfall the prefecture had almost all the counterfeit bills and a quantity of clues as well, since Lucien Verneuil's commando group was made up of people who never in their lousy lives had gone into a bank to take money out, much less deposit it. Lucien and Roland foresaw a space of four or five days before the first slip or the ever-possible informer; Gómez and Monique on one side, and Patricio and Heredia on the other, were already busy with the necessary purchases.

perto M. Levingst
ident of the Rep

Jeneral. Will Take Power Thursday, 18

150 Men Could be Placed on Armed Footing with Weapons Stolen in Uruguay. Worries.

MONTEVIDEO, 30 (AP)—The police arrested in the lodgings of recently thirty people with government connections such as with the spectacular theft yesterday at a naval arsenal under ion, having fulfilled orders and plans by Tupamaros due to the official confirmation, it has been impossible to obtain. Mean

To finish off Onan seemed paradoxically one of the reasons why Lonstein kept on talking, Onan as one of the so many mental ogres that no one had been able to liquidate, the piling up of profound ogres, the true masters of the diurnal harmony that so many people called morality and which then became on any day, individually, neurosis and the analyst's couch, and which also on any day, collectively, was fascism and/or racism. Well, old man, murmured the one I told you flattened by the subjacencies and subtendencies of the little rabbi's discourse, but it was useless to inject a turn it off or knock it off, baby, with Lonstein's drive to go on talking, his Raskolnikov side of solitary ceremonies, he was sketching out something like a grotesque saga, the descent of Gilgamesh or Orpheus into the underworld of the libido, it was useless for the one I told you to laugh in his face at some points or at others to withdraw a little less than offended at four in the morning and five-grappa exhibitionism, and little by little it could be seen that Lonstein had not wanted to bring Onan up to the surface just for the pleasure of giving him a legal statute or something like that, to haul Onan out to his inner cluster was to kill at least one of the ogres and beyond that to metamorphosize him by contact with the diurnal and the open, de-ogre him, change his sad clandestine skin for plumes and bells, the little rabbi was suddenly becoming lyrical, insisting and giving details and he was turning into a kind of public relations man and agent for the ogre who was after all a prince like so many ogres, except that he had to be helped so he would finally cease being an ogre. The one I told you was beginning to realize that Lonstein was proceeding rabbinically through a demonstration, choosing one ogre among many and proposing new descents to the cluster below to liquidate the other ogres gradually, a kind of subterranean subscrewery, and he ended up understanding that his role that night, if he played it honestly, was simply one of activating and goading and infuriating the little rabbi so that the hunting down and the metamorphosis of Onan might serve some purpose when he became his chronicler, something Lonstein had taken for granted and in which he wasn't wrong because the one I told you wasn't long in talking to me about the matter (I had got up after a bad dream toward the end of morning, Ludmilla was asleep on the couch and no one had had any lunch or was thinking about making any), and even though I didn't understand anything at first and even did the same as the one I told you had, put Lonstein down, after turning it over and over I finally respected that mad exorcism, I too in my mean little way had thought about talking from a balcony and doing away with some ogres, except that mine was a little courtyard balcony with flowerpots that only faced Ludmilla's and Francine's windows, individual and selfish exorcism, a small plant, a dead bird, evidence of its poor results. But maybe Lonstein was right and one had to get involved in the Screwery in different ways (supposing that he or I had a clear idea of what it was all about), in any case, the little rabbi had not spoken to the one I told you about Onan out of pure pleasure but was looking for the best possible way of projecting parabolically into the Screwery (a fortran, of course!) that delirious degree of nakedness of the word which would show to what point the strip-tease he had submitted himself to in front of the one I told you was basically an indispensable condition for Verrières on Friday night, for the other ogre hunt, and even though it looked like a plan laid out by madmen, the one I told you and I began to feel that in Lonstein's almost unthinkable, almost unprintable conduct there was something resembling a vigil of arms before the night of Verrières. And what now seemed only a demented association of heterogeneities might perhaps be cleared up someday for a few men and for new Screweries, by which the one I told you and I were like seers and vest-pocket prophets, knowing and not knowing, looking at each other with the air of one who suspects that the other one has sneaked out a fart, an always reprehensible relief.

Dive into
3CV happiness;
in Citronort:
260 down and per month.

Susana plays with Manuel while she washes and dresses him, looking at Patricio out of the corner of her eye as he has a rather swollen eye and a painful wrist. Luckily one of his most precious Buenos Aires treasures is a wristband from the days when he played paddle ball at the Laurak Bat, and the sunglasses cover the other imperfection perfectly. It's three in the afternoon but with such an agitated night the family has stayed in bed, including Manuel who appears strangely docile and doesn't try to smother himself in talcum powder or cotton. Lunch is a coming and going from kitchen to bed with salami, glasses of milk and wine, bits of cold omelet and half a dozen bananas, father, mother, and son feel particularly good over the open infraction of the rules of good behavior, and when Ludmilla arrives they receive her in their underwear and cognac and coffee, they invite her to

Heredia and Gómez roll with laughter reading the newspapers and looking at their swollen snouts which Monique cares for with an air of red cross and plenty of mercurochrome. The disconcerting presence of the turquoise penguin on the banks of the Seine at the hour of dawn had unleashed two theories, because the police were not long in establishing a certain causal chain that begins in Orly although it later tends to break up everywhere, or that at the Quai des Orfèvres they already suspect the true nature of the containers and that brings them to

One paper talks about the smuggling of weapons, another about drug smuggling. Marcos has already telephoned Oscar for them

to leave the Hotel Lutetia in case the ants, and Oscar who is ingesting his last deluxe breakfast snug in bed while Gladis waits for the serving girl to leave so that she can come in with her own tray and snuggle up to him to do her thing, he states that Marcos expects them at ten-fifteen at Patricio's and that any hope Gladis might have had left of resuming her activities as stewardess are greatly prejudiced by the causal chain that they are talking about in

"Poor Pedernera," Gladis says, "who's going to bring him his grapefruit juice to the cockpit. Pepita's going to have a lot of work."

"That Pedernera had his eye on you," Oscar says.

"Because no one handed him the juice so delicately, so he didn't have to take his eyes off the controls."

"Well, it would seem that you finally leaped over the wall, little snot-nose," Oscar says, slipping down into the bed while the last croissant slips in a parallel way down his throat. Gladis looks at him without understanding that business about a wall, but Oscar kisses her on the hair and has a sort of vague feeling of contentment, it's probably just the half-moon croissant but the full moon too, the implacable machinery of plays on words opening doors and revealing entranceways in the shadows, Gladis hasn't had the slightest negative reaction on learning the news, that's how it is then, she leaped over the wall like the girls in the full moon, she's really in the Screwery and that, Oscar thinks, is the wall and the open street even though all the police in Paris and all the firemen in La Plata are running after the girls maddened by carnival, after Alicia Quinteros, after Gladis who is throwing well-paid position with retirement benefits into the face of Captain Pedernera.

agreed, but I don't understand why you were so quick to consider yourself defeated after your Yolanda/After Yolanda, all right?/After Yolanda, and you turned to onanism with everything you've got if such can be said/I understand, you would have backslid rehopefully/But of course, what else is love but backsliding/That's not where the problem lies, man, more than fifty scholars have spent their lives asking Gogol's ghost why he preferred jerking off to marriage, not to mention Kant once a month under a tree, and naturally in each case there's an oedipal or chromosomatic explanation, and in mine I no doubt lack or have too many beta molecules, but that's not what interests me, although you, of course, you grab onto a notion of normality as if it were still a life-jacket/Look, even if we only reduce it to statistics, we have to have a certain notion of normality in order to maneuver/As you wish, put the case that I'm abnormal and judge me that way, neither your notion nor your judgment concerns me now, if I'm talking to you about this it's because you and all the rest of normal people are perfect hypocrites and somebody has to fill the office of buffoon every now and again, and not out of sacrifice since I'm not sacrificing myself for you, normal male, but for something I don't know what to call, let's say a new foundation/Don't get metaphysical on me/Oh, no, kid, I'm not talking to you about an ontological foundation even though there too they could use a few buffoons to turn over more than four hundred omelets cooked by Madame l'Histoire, I'm talking about a different kind of foundation, if you want a little of what Sade must have proposed, a foundation that presents itself more like a destruction, a turning over of idols so that afterwards, someday, the horrible workers will come as the one from Harrar said, or that new man who worries Marcos so much and that Screwery bunch, and then I open the door and say we're all Onan, at first for obvious reasons from childhood and then because solitary pleasure might be everything imperfect, unilateral, selfish, and sordid that you could call for but it's not a lack or most of all a denial of virility or femininity, quite the contrary, but right here I can see your crest rising and you're looking at me as if you'd never jerked off after the age of fourteen, you shitty ostrich/Hey, I didn't even open my mouth, boy/All right, no one expects you to notify the public and the clergy of your sexual activities of any kind, it's better doing them than talking about them, but the Screwery, to give you an example at hand, has set itself up as an enterprise for the liquidation of phantoms, of false barriers, with all that Marxist vocabulary that I lack but which you right now are probably adding mentally to the ennumeration of social and personal errors and scars that must be liquidated, and if that's how it is I understand that I must make a parallel contribution, because defending the legitimacy of onanism is not only worthwhile for that reason, which is nothing great in and of itself, but because it helps the many other fractures that one must practice solo in the whole scheme of anthropos/Well, all right, but the same can be said of lesbianism and so many other things, postal savings, the lottery, how should I know/Of course, but you've got to admit that the taboo against homosexuality has been broken down in part and that not only is its praxis more evident every day but that the verbal presence of the viability of the act forms a current and showy part of vocabularies and themes at dessert time, something that doesn't happen with masturbation which everybody falls into but which only enters the language as a theme of the end of childhood/But do you really believe that part about everybody?/Of course I believe it, married or single it's all the same to me. As soon as the couple draws apart for any momentary reason which can be a trip or a stubborn case of flu, most of them take care of themselves, and as for celibates you don't need any barracks tales or those that come from jails or sailors' bunks to know it, you can make your own vest-pocket Kinsey yourself, ask the women of your confidence if when they're alone before falling asleep they don't use their finger a bit, they'll tell you yes because it's not as spectacular as among us and because to say so doesn't affect their good name and honor while on our side to admit that we masturbate now and then emasculates us morally and personally both the one who says so and the one who gets caught at it, and the idiocy is precisely in that, in what lies between doing it and admitting it, in continuing doing it under the taboo, and so everyone is Onan again when Judah tells him to go to bed with his brother's wife in order to give him a false posterity, and Onan refuses because he knows that his children will not be recognized as his and he masturbates before going to bed with his sister-in-law, something that technically must have been a simple coitus interruptus, and then Jehovah throws a fit and wipes him out; that's where it is, Jehovah mocks him and strikes him down, ever since then we carry that inside, coitus interruptus is fine but masturbation is the Onan taboo and from there the idea that it's evil, that it's shameful, that it's a terrible secret. Out of all that, said Lonstein breathing as if he had just come up from the bottom of the maelstrom, I have made a considerable work of art, a prexpress and a technique that I don't think many people can dominate because since they masturbate under the feeling of guilt they do it primarily and out of necessity momentarily, as others go to bed with whores, without the refinement of autonomous and satisfactory sexual activity. The eroticism of the couple has given us this literature that duplicates, reflects, and enriches the reality to which it alludes, the fascinating dialectic between making love and reading about how it is made; but since the couple doesn't function for me and women are boring for me on all levels, I have had to create my own onanist dialectic, my still unwritten fantasies but yet just as rich or richer than erotic literature/All that?/All that/ Well, when I masturbated at the age of fifteen or sixteen I did it imagining myself in the arms of Greta Garbo or Marlene Dietrich, something which as you can see was not foolishness, so that the special merit of your fantasies escapes me/It isn't so much on that side, although I can also admit more dizzying developments than what you imagine with your Gretas and your Marlenes, but what counts is the execution, and that's where the art lies. For you the whole thing is a hand properly used, you ignore the fact that precisely the first step up toward the true summit of the fortran consists in the elimination of all manual help/I know all about the accessories, the rubber dolls, the well-treated sponges, the fifteen uses of the pillow according to Herr Doktor Bahrens/ So why do you get so petulant? Imaginative couples also use accessories, pillows, and creams. Heredia was going around showing that manual of positions that he brought from London and which is really very good; if I had the means and above all the desire, I would publish a manual of masturbatory technique and you would see the possibilities not to mention the best-seller it would be, but in any case I can describe them to you/I'm leaving, it's getting late/In other words you don't want to listen to me/It's just that you're boring me, boy/You bastard, Lonstein said, I thought I'd made you understand why I was talking to you about this/I follow you, old man, I follow you, but I'm leaving just the same/You bastard, you coward, you and all the rest; and then you want to make the revolution and pull down all the idols of imperialism or whatever the fuck they call it, incapable of taking a real look at themselves in the mirror, quick on the trigger but as shitty as strawberry ice cream (which is the kind I hate the most) when it's a question of a real fight, the speleological kind, the one that's within reach of every well-placed stomach/Hey, I never knew you had these proclivities for a better future in you/In what concerns me, you don't even know the color of this shirt I'm wearing, false witness of equally false Screweries/So you think the Screwery is false?/It's not that, Lonstein said a little repentant, it's half-false because once again it's going to be an incomplete link in a chain that's just as incomplete, and the sad part is that great kids like the ones you know will get themselves killed or will kill others without having first looked the truth in the face, the one every morning's mirror offers them. I know, I know, I see what you're going to say, we can't hope that everybody can start off by knowing himself in the Socratic way before he goes out into the street and starts kicking against this rotten society, etc. But you, pretending to be the witness of the Screwery, you draw back yourself at the moment of truth, I mean the moment of jerking off, I'm referring to the real man, the one there is and not what others see starting with *Das Kapital* and what follows/Lonstein, the one I told you said seriously, and it must have been very seriously for him to start calling him by his last name, I may be as big a dummy as you want to make me out to be, but for more than half an hour you've been making me perfectly aware of your prexpress, your fortran, in a word, of the allegory you've been shoving up my nose in the shape of onanism/Oh, well, said the little rabbi like someone disconcerted dropping his guard/And if I'm talking about leaving first of all it's because I'm falling asleep on my feet, and second because once your hermeneutic intention is understood I don't see why I should still be interested in masturbatory techniques/Oh, well, the little rabbi repeated, but there's just one thing I'd like to know, and that's whether your indifference toward these techniques is the ostrich again or is it simply because you like it better as a couple/The second hypothesis is the better one, but since we've already come so far and so you'll know me a little better too, lay off the ostrich and the bastard stuff, let me say to you that I have no antionanistic prejudices and that more than once in the absence of someone who should have been present and couldn't or didn't want to be I was consoled by the unilateral route, without the perfection that your disquisitions have let me glimpse, naturally/Oh, well, tripeated the little rabbi who for the first time was beginning to smile and relax, then you will forgive me for the obviously antifortranesque and contraprexpressive epithets/I won't deny the fact that you were beginning to get me mad by calling me bastard every two minutes/Let's brew another *mate*, Lonstein said, it would have been even shittier if after so much gab you took off convinced that the theme was only worth something as a theme or something like that/The sun's coming up, said the one I told you with a yawn that was more like an eclipse of the aforementioned star, but just the same give me a *mate* with beaucoup booze in it and then I'll split/And besides we can talk about other things, Lonstein said, happy, with a face that was completely new and awake and seemed washed by the rather dirty and ashen pink that was slipping through the blinds. You see, we can talk about other things, old boy, old boy.

It was also dawning on the Rue Clovis and Ludmilla who was coming in with the damp sponge saw the first gray dimming the night-light, smudging the face of Marcos who had closed his eyes and was letting himself go to sleep on his back. Silently, Ludmilla sat on the floor, the sponge in her hand like a lamp in the catacombs; moving only slightly, she turned the night-light off, watched the window become outlined in the shadows, heard the vague sounds of dawn find definite places in the hot, thick silence of the bedroom.

"I'm not asleep, Polonette," Marcos said without opening his eyes, "I was thinking that starting Friday we're going into a no-man's-land and that you still don't really know why."

"The Vip," Ludmilla said, "but the truth is that beyond that I don't understand too much."

"There's nothing original in what we're going to do, unless it's the rather unusual geographical location and a kind of multiplied effect. In exchange for the Vip the governments of five or six countries will have to free a number of comrades. It's almost not news any more, as you can see, except for us, because it's going to start a shit-fit here for reasons of national prestige; all that having to do with the immediate future, and I'm remembering that you live and work here. Think about it."

"I'm here, sure, but it's the same as my work, I mean I go through life changing comedies, right now I'm in one that's vaguely Slavic, tomorrow it will be a play by Pirandello or vaudeville with dancing and music. Yes, Paris. Paris, of course. It won't be easy getting used to something else but you can see, deep down I've got the habit, it's not so hard to change roles, you know."

"I can imagine, but just the same I had to tell you. The others have foreseen the possibilities; Patricio and Susana have friends in Louvain, and Gómez can live in Monique's parents' place, they're from Luxembourg, Heredia's got places to hole up in everywhere, Roland and the other Frenchmen are veterans and are playing on their home field."

"What about you?"

"Well, that's no problem, or for Lonstein either. That poor devil there might get himself picked up, because he's got nothing to do with it unless it's in some way that no one really understands, not even him. So there, consider yourself informed, Polonette."

"You've still got blood on your mouth," Ludmilla said, kneeling by the bed and wiping Marcos's lips with the damp sponge. When he finally looked at her in the vague light of the sheets and the air, Ludmilla was smiling at something that could be anything, far from and close to the gesture of wiping his mouth, of sliding down against him when he took her in his arms and kissed her between her breasts, sinking her head in a sea of curly hair which Ludmilla softly bit, lost in a vague smell of bath soap and fatigue.

At a certain point in the disorder the one I told you begins to realize that he's gone too far in his spontaneity, and at the moment of putting the documents in order (impossible to describe the kind of trunk or giant tureen into which he has been tossing what he calls entries and which in reality are any piece of paper he has at hand) it so happens that some things that in their moment had seemed significant to him become skinny and ugly while about that same time four foolish bits on Manuel's way of eating or something that Gladis said about a hairstyle fill up the tureen and his memory as-if-engraved-in-bronze. The one I told you half closes his eyes and admits, because you can't accuse him of idiocy on this side, that forgetfulness and memory are glands that are just as endocrine as the hypophysis and the thyroids, libidinal regulators that decree vast sunset zones and most brilliant carats so that everyday life doesn't break its head too much. As far as possible he goes pinning up his specimens in order and Lonstein, the only one privileged with relative access to the tureen or trunk of clippings, will end up admitting that all together there is a coherent Screwery, there is a Screwerine prelude, lude, and postlude, there is satisfactory causality, for example the penguin who appears in his place and at his moment, a capital detail. The worst part is finding unidentifiable entries, seeing the one I told you pressing his temples with converging thumbs and then saying I don't know, damn it, that happened to Heredia, I think, or was it Gómez with Monique, wait a bit, turning the entry all around, cursing his self-censorship, South American shamefulness because always or almost always it's slippery material and the one I told you would like to follow the footsteps of the little rabbi and never be quiet, the proof is that he's written it, that it's there and precisely then the glands begin to secrete forgetfulness, and there's another thing besides and Lonstein is the first to notice, even by making the entry the one I told you has cheated, facts tend to happen all dressed up in words, sometimes you don't know who did this or that to whom, later on the one I told you will be able to argue that he was in a hurry or that he had to complete the information but Lonstein will look at him with pity and will want to know why at a certain point, on a certain precise entry, everything turns into limp lettuce or goes on to be a great ikebana as suits the moment. But be aware that things are not simple, bellows the one I told you in exasperation, be aware, goddamn it, that it's one thing to describe aesthetically without being at all false to the truth, but *this* is something else, I mean extracting eroticism and the other concomitants from aesthetics, because if you leave it at that you're still in literature, you make the game easier, you can say or tell the most incredible things because there's something that serves you as a curtain or an alibi, there's the fact that you're telling it well and prettily, that you're once more the lettered libertine or the panegyrist of the left or the right, even though you might laugh up and down at this language. Easy, easy, advises the little rabbi, easy does it, baby. Then think about it a little, stresses the one I told you sincerely afflicted, why the fuck can't I keep the names quiet or forget who the ones doing it were when what I wanted to rescue is the noumenon, the no-distanciation or mediation as they say now, placing the Screwery the way the cubists used to place the theme of the painting, all smooth on a single plane without volume or shadows or valuational or moral preferences or con- or unconscious censorship, you can understand that it's almost impossible in Spanish, you can understand that the ballpoint drops out of my hand because I'm not writing with daring or freely or like any other kind of jerking off like that, I'm looking for man, I'm a seeker, I'm looking for the smoothness of the bread, brother, I'm sticking a finger up an ass and it has to be, it absolutely has to be the same as asking for a ten-peso ticket or blowing my nose in the lobby of the Rex. And then, of course, you forget the names, says the little rabbi, even I getcha, you betcha. Am I wasting time, the one I told you wonders all inflamed, am I making a mistake from the word go and it's not worth anything, can there be acceptance of forbidden territory because that's being a man, not going out onto the terrace naked? But then I'm sick because here in my rib cage it tells me that I have to go on, that even without names or with blank spaces I have to go on, that fear or shame and especially failure don't matter, someone's knocking at the door old man, look at these entries when you feel like it and tell me if I should have written them down or not, if these moments of the Screwery could have been kept elegantly quiet or described as something more than four liberated people from the Río de la Plata would have described them, covering them with the same words they think they're uncovering them with. Bah, says Lonstein, you finally hit it there, it'll always be a question of words basically, what you're really looking for is just a change in form. No, old man, I would have known how to have done that without creating problems for myself, you've got more than enough. The thing is closer this way, it's looking for something this way like not realizing when you go from one territory to another, and we're still not capable of that yet; what's forbidden is given to us paradoxically as a kind of privilege, it deserves special treatment, you-have-to-go-carefully-in-this-scene, then words call your bet as always, set up the great shell game. If I could only manage not to change when I go from a street corner to a bed, if I didn't change myself, understand, then I'd begin to feel that everything is the Screwery and there are no personal episodes between one moment of the Screwery and the next. Ah, says the little rabbi lighting up, once more you're leaving the context and you're projecting the facts of the Screwery onto Argentina at least. Much more than that, advises the one I told you modestly, I'm projecting them onto the very idea of the revolution, because the Screwery is one of its many squares and this chess game will never be won if I'm not capable of being the same person on the corner as in the bed, and I'm fifty or eighty million guys at this very moment. Agreed, says the little rabbi, but the bad part about you is that you feel these things and look for them in writing, which as Mao says is good for nothing unless. Unless what? Ah, ask him that yourself. You're wrong, says the one I told you dispiritedly, I don't care about writing except as the mirror of something else, of a plane from which the real revolution could be feasible. There you have the kids, you're watching them play, and then what; if they manage to do their thing, and here I extrapolate again and I'm imagining the Almighty Definitive Screwery, then the usual thing will happen one more time, ideological hardening, rigor mortis of daily life, prudery, don't use dirty words comrade, a bureaucracy of sex and sexuality on a bureaucratic timetable, all so well known, old man, all so inevitable although Marcos and Roland and Susana, although those formidable people who love each other and undress each other and fight altogether, I'm sorry for not completing the sentence because that's precisely where the incomplete leaps in, the Marcos of the future won't be the one of today and why, old man, why? Why? asked Lonstein. Because right now he isn't equipped for the aftermath of the Screwery either, he and so many others want a revolution in order to attain something that they won't be able to consolidate afterwards, not even define. Everything perfect in the ideology, of course, theory and practice at the same point, there'll be a Screwery at any cost, because this humanity has said enough and has started to move, it's been proclaimed and written and lived with blood; the bad part is that while we may be going along we're carrying the corpse on our backs, old, the terribly old rotting corpse of time and taboos and incomplete self-definitions. Oy veh, said Lonstein, all that knowledge. Agreed, the one I told you accepted, that's why I keep my mouth shut as much as possible, apart from the fact that I'm not at all qualified to talk scientifically about our lacks, insolvencies, and archsufficiencies, I'm not even an oracular madman like Wilhelm Reich or a goddamned precursor like Sade or José Martí, please excuse the combination which inevitably sounds disrespectful; I'm none of that and therefore I keep quiet but I keep on filling in my little entries, I drop my ballpoint and I pick it up again, these hairy cheeks turn red because it's hard for me to talk about putting a finger in the ass, each time I get the impression that I'm sticking my foot in and not my finger, if you'll pardon the nonsense, because underneath it all what I'm doing is bad and, for example, the libido isn't that important to our destiny, etc.; but I pick up the pen, I pick off the hairs, and I start writing again and it disgusts me, I have to go take a shower, I feel like a slug or when you slip on a pile of shit and it sticks to your overcoat, I'd like to be anything else, a tax collector or a hardware salesman, I've got a terrible admiration for pure novelists or Marxist theoreticians or poets with a strict agenda, even the erotologists approved by the establishment, those who have carte blanche like old Miller and old Genet, the ones who give their shove and reach the street door and no one can hold them back any longer even though they're banned in a whole lot of countries, I feel myself so much a pampa person, so damnably Spanish-American with my *mate* at four o'clock and my literature full of dirty words and couples in bed in parentheses, always above or below the final assumption of a different vision of man, not counting what I already said before, the fear of being mistaken, of the possibility that it could really be that the revolution can be done without that idea I have of man. Bah, said the little rabbi, you're fooling me, by God, I'm beginning to see that your famous file is written with one eye on the entries and the other on future readers, and it's them, the present or future witnesses, the judges of today or tomorrow who frighten you, tell your uncle the truth. By God you may be right, said the one I told you, I've spent my life without thinking about anybody beyond what I wanted to do, doing it not just for me but because of a kind of undefined otherness, without faces or names or judgments, but maybe with the years I'm suddenly getting softer and I'm afraid of what they'll say, to use the cliché. I can't do anything against that except to throw the file out the window along with myself one of these days, unless I go to the movies or to an art gallery, but you can see that up till now I've kept on with the entries, they don't work out for me and they're full of cowardice and shame and a bad conscience but they're there and you've read them and there are others in the works already and I'm still wound up enough even if I feel bad and every five minutes my pen jams and my stomach hurts. You're doing all right, said Lonstein handing him a *mate* which was like a pool of green consolation, after all even if you forget quote the names unquote and are more ashamed than a novice in a gynecology ward, I think you've got more than enough right to go ahead, mistaken or not, right or wrong; maybe what went through Marx's head while he wrote is a question of responsibility and I understand it, the stakes are big and I think it's worthwhile, all in all winning or losing has no importance as such, history is a wild amount of grabbing all around, some grasp the handle and others are left with their fingers in the air, but when you put it all together sometimes you get the French Revolution or the Moncada Barracks.

They were extremely satisfied after that dialogue, as anyone can understand, not to mention the fact that afterwards the one I told you spent a night putting in some names where previously there had been some blanks, and he discovered that it wasn't all that hard for him.

A person's manner of perception gets more and more like the montages in a good movie; I think Ludmilla was still talking to me when I thought of the Hotel Terrass, on the balconies overlooking the graves; or maybe I'd vaguely dreamed about the hotel and then Ludmilla, waking me up with a glass of fruit juice, became part of the last images and she began to talk while something of the hotel and the balconies over the cemetery were still present. Then the Métro took me to the Place Clichy as if only it had made the decision and organized the necessary changes of station. We hadn't talked much, Ludmilla and I, it was after midday and we didn't even think about lunch, it was hot and I was naked on the bed, Ludmilla wrapped in my bathrobe in line with her customary bad habit, both of us smoking and drinking fruit juice and looking at each other and Marcos, of course, and the Screwery, all of that. So that. Perfect. Yes, Andrés, I told him, but I don't want everything to be like an unplugged refrigerator with things slowly rotting. He looked at me lovingly, naked, half-asleep, from so far away. You're learning Ludlud, that's precisely my method and you'd come to the conclusion that it was only good to damage things more. It's not the method but the things themselves, I told him, I was always grateful to you for the truth but it would have been better if you hadn't reached the point of telling me about Francine. I can say the same for you, Ludlud, I wish you hadn't come to me with this news all smelling of Screwery and grapefruit juice, but you see, you see. I thank you too, of course. We're so well-mannered, it's obvious.

Later I couldn't even get to the Hotel Terrass, it had been a mechanical impulse that was being fulfilled as if to give me time to enter that new time, the ratification of something presumptive but still not taken on; I know that I got out of the Métro at the Place Clichy and that I walked the streets, drinking cognac in one or two cafés, thinking that Ludmilla and Marcos had done perfectly well, that there was no sense in raising future problems since others would probably decide for us as almost always. But the switchman had pushed the lever all the way down and everything was speeding off on a different track, impossible to accept all at once the new landscapes through the windows, to assimilate them just like that. Nothing could have seemed more horrible to me than introspection on a café terrace, an easy and repugnant interior monologue, the after-bite of vomit; facts simply presented themselves like a poker hand, perhaps it was necessary to put them in order, put the two aces together, the sequence from eight to ten, to ask one's self how many cards to ask for, if it was the time to bluff or if I've got a chance for a full house. Cognac in any case, that's for sure, and to cling to the new tracks with all wheels all the way to the next switch.

Ludmilla got into the shower the same way that she went on stage, she didn't need the audience at the Vieux-Colombier for the robe to drop to the floor with the movement of a great white wing. The tiled wall had a perfect transparency, even though that might have been against the intrinsic nature of tiles, and in her way of looking at them beyond the heaviness something was born that was like crystals beating against a brilliant and violent beach sky, a time reborn, the new phoenix of the Screwery. It was impossible not to smile at the exaltation in which there was as much puerility as amorous fatigue, the worst part was that the soapsuds got in between her lips as soon as she stopped holding them conscientiously tight as the sponge came and went over her thighs and waist carrying off the trivial, persistent signs of night. That's what had happened to Andrés too, like a mote of dust that the shower drags off to the drain, without saying anything after everything had been said, which proved his clear intelligence; the silence of the apartment without Xenakis, without Joni Mitchell, without Juan Carlos Paz, the triumph of the shower resounding beyond the open doors, was slowly staining Ludmilla's vision as she finished drying herself without pleasure, put herself into Andrés's bathrobe again, and walked through the apartment smoking, a cup of already cold coffee in her hand and the transistor turned on mechanically as she went through the living room and the market was down. It was the boundary, she thought, hanging on the word, turning it over like a piece of mental fruit, boundary, rebound, raybound, boundray, roundbray, ray of the bound, bound of the ray. She turned off the transistor with a flick, went over to the bed and pulled up the sheet that Andrés had left wrinkled and confused; on the Rue Clovis, too, she had straightened the sheet before leaving, while Marcos made coffee and telephoned Gómez and Lucien Verneuil. Boundary, one bed on the Rue Clovis and another on the Rue de l'Ouest: a short history of sheets, a new and giddy time that was being born between one bed and another, and the only possible word refusing to be spoken, thought of at every instant but behind the threshold of words, thought like a warmth, a wind wrapping up the body, and why not, why not if that's how it is, I love you, now I know why and how much I love you, I say it and I say it again and it's the boundary because it's you and it's the Screwery and because everything is filling up with leaps and shouts and joys and expectations and used matches, little girl, incurable snot-nose, I love you, Marcos, and I'll love you too always but from so far away now, you the spectator from now on, looking at me from an orchestra seat, maybe applauding me when I have a good part. Boundary, ray of the bound, the great die has been cast and it's two in the afternoon, having to eat something, go to Patricio's, the rehearsal at seven-thirty. Everything was apparently the same, Patricio or the rehearsal, eating or smoking, but now from the other side of the boundary, transparent and rough like the sea breaking against the sky on the shower tiles. There was an abandoned record on the couch, something by Luciano Berio; Ludmilla put it on the turntable, reached out to turn on the amplifier but didn't complete the movement, she saw Marcos's eyes in the shadows, his voice was reaching her with the news of the time of the phoenix, everything that was awaiting in those days, in all the days they would live together.

"We don't count for much," Marcos had said stroking the face that Ludmilla was hiding against his shoulder, "any personal reference is superfluous I think until we've come out of this, if we come out."

"If we come out? Well, I know that it's risky and difficult but I think that you, you the people . . . All right, what matters is the Screwery, you're right, we can wait."

"No, Polonette," Marcos said, and Ludmilla heard him laugh silently in the darkness, a quiver of his skin that was like a total smile that entered her and brought her even closer—we can't wait, as you've seen, and it's good that we didn't wait. Why that mania for going around slicing things up as if they were salami? One slice of Screwery, another of personal history, you remind me of the one I told you with his organizational problems, the poor guy doesn't understand and would like to understand, he's a kind of Linnaeus or Ameghino of the Screwery. And it's not that way, a salami can also be eaten by bites, without dividing it into slices, and I'll tell you that it's even tastier because the taste of the metal ruins that of the donkey."

"Does salami come from donkeys?" Ludmilla was amazed.

"Sometimes, I think, it depends on the season. Look, Polonette, tonight, the two of us, this is all the Screwery too and I hope you believe the same as I, even though the one I told you bangs his noggin against the wall. What's important is not to give any emphasis, just simply include it in the greater Screwery without losing sight of other things, having your sights well set until you get the brush-off and probably until long after."

"It's easy," Ludmilla said slipping her hand slowly down Marcos's chest, getting onto the map of Australia which was getting greener and yellower, caressing his sex which was sleeping to one side, feeling the electricity of the fuzz on his thighs until stopping on the hard terrace of a knee, "yes, it is easy, Marcos, for me it's basically nothing new, I think it's been that way ever since you came to our place, shook my hand, and in doing it squeezed mine a little. You're right, let's not talk about Andrés, let's not do what's usually done, what I no doubt will have to do with Andrés this same morning, putting the house in order in a manner of speaking. Talk to me about the ants, Marcos, that's the real subject I want to learn about. And you, Marcos, you, but I think I'll have plenty of time for that, right?"

"Polonette," Marcos murmured, "you talk like a bird."

"Don't pull my leg, ugly."

"I'll pull it because it's soft like a loaf of bread, Polonette, maybe someday I'll show you our wheat fields where it comes from and you'll appreciate it."

"Bah," said Ludmilla, "do you think we haven't got bread and wheat in Poland?"

La Commission internationale de juristes publie son rapport sur les tortures

Genève. — La Commission internationale de juristes (C.I.J.) a publié mercredi un rapport d'une rare violence sur les tortures infligées aux opposants et aux quelque douze mille prisonniers politiques qui, selon elle, existent au Brésil.

Le rapport, qui se fonde principalement sur des documents et des témoignages sortis clandestinement des prisons ou remis aux rapporteurs de la Commission par d'anciens détenus évadés, affirme que la torture, devenue une « arme politique », est appliquée systématiquement pour faire parler les prisonniers, mais aussi comme « moyen de dissuasion ». La mère d'un leader étudiant rapporte que les responsables du camp d'internement de l'« île des fleurs » ont l'habitude de placer dans le parloir un garçon mutilé, « dont les mouvements disjoints et la marque des supplices endurés doivent inciter les parents en visite à conseiller à leurs fils ou filles une collaboration empressée avec les enquêteurs ».

Le rapport relève que la torture est généralement appliquée de manière scientifique, et fait état des méthodes les plus couramment employées : supplice de l'eau (la tête du prisonnier est plongée de façon répétée dans un seau d'eau sale ou rempli d'excréments ou d'urine), supplice de l'électricité (application d'électrodes aux organes génitaux, aux oreilles, aux narines, aux seins ou aux revers des paupières, tortures d'ordre moral (un enfant étant supplicié devant sa mère ou des conjoints torturés dans une même pièce).

La Commission signale, d'autre part, que la prison militaire de Belo - Horizonte possède des chiens policiers spécialement dressés pour s'attaquer aux parties sensibles du corps humain. Dans les locaux de la DOPS (police fédérale civile) de Salo-Paulo, on compte parmi les méthodes « courantes », l'arrachage des ongles ou l'écrasement des organes génitaux. A Sao-Paulo, Curitiba et Juiz-de-Fora, des prisonniers ont été brûlés au chalumeau.

Le rapport, qui énumère dans le détail les services du gouvernement chargés de la répression, conclut : « Une libéralisation de l'appareil de répression ne peut être espérée du fait du nombre toujours croissant des agents, fonctionnaires et officiers se rendant coupables de supplices sur leurs concitoyens. La seule façon pour eux d'échapper à la punition, pour ne pas dire la vengeance de leurs concitoyens, est de poursuivre, voire d'intensifier encore la répression. Mais la torture a besoin du silence complice, de la pudeur des témoins, du masque de la normalité. L'opinion publique des pays civilisés possède aujourd'hui une chance réelle de faire cesser par des dénonciations répétées et précises les pratiques inhumaines dont sont l'objet tant d'hommes et de femmes au Brésil. »

"Translate it for the boy here, he doesn't dig Gallic," Patricio ordered, "I, in the meantime, will feed Manuel his soup. Hey, this kid's already fallen in love with Ludmilla and Gladis at the same time, he's going to take after his old man, what a fate we have in store, old lady."

Manuel was demonstrating his purported love by hurling spoonfuls of tapioca in the direction of the aforementioned. A stewardess, after all, although presumed to be retired, Gladis relieved Patricio of the plate of mush, of Manuel, and of the spoon in a synchronized movement that saved Ludmilla from getting sprayed full in the face. From the best chair in the room, Oscar watched the homesweethome, still not out of that general jumping of the track that had started with the disembarkation of the penguin and the armadillos at Orly and which the events of the evening and the morning had not helped to dissipate; he wasn't displeased, his soul felt like a tango singer floating in the middle of reality and baubles all of the same color, a poet above all as he was called by his comrades of the Zoological Society now probably kicked into dissolution as they pissed with laughter.

"The International Commission of Jurists publishes its report on torture," Susana translated. "Geneva, semicolon. On Wednesday the above body (I.C.J.) published a report of rare anger, and why rare, would you please tell me?/Translate without commentaries, goddamn it, Patricio ordered/Phukayu mukayu, said Susana who had a good command of Volapuk along with five other languages, of rare anger about the torture inflicted on opponents and some twelve thousand political prisoners who, according to it, exist in Brazil."

"Twelve thousand?" said Heredia opening up an enormous package of candy for Manuel, who was handcuffed by Gladis's aeronautical technique and erupted with a considerable amount of tapioca on learning that what was behind that pink paper with a green ribbon on it was not at all comparable to what he had been expecting. "I'd say twenty thousand, but that's fine for an international commission. Go ahead, girl."

"The report, which is based principally on documents and testimony smuggled out of prisons or handed over to investigators of the Commission by former detainees who managed to escape, affirms that torture, converted into a 'political weapon,' is applied systematically to make prisoners talk, but also as a 'means of dissuasion.' The mother of a student leader says that those in charge of the internment camp on the 'Isle of Flowers' have the custom of putting in the booth a mutilated boy 'whose incoherent movements and marks of torture suffered must incite the parents who are visiting their sons or daughters to advise them to cooperate actively with the investigators.' "

"It must be a beautiful land,/America, father dear," Heredia recited, "*Would you like to see it from near?/No greater pleasure at hand./Well, screw yourself with your hand,/I'm going to keep you right here.* That final parody carries a warning note, fuck their mothers, begging Campodrón's pardon. Go on, little sister."

Oscar was listening to Susana's voice, he saw Gladis's hand playing with Manuel's hair getting him to polish off the tapioca with an irresistible skill, he sensed that Patricio was all up tight, now Gómez and Monique entered and everything slipped into quick questions, glances at him and Gladis, the great victims of the penguin, children of the full moon because from that day forward everything for them would be wall and broken glass, holding hands they would have to run, open breaches, live off loans, goddamned shitty penguin, Oscar thought depressed, looking at Gladis with something that resembled pride, the confirmation of a hope. The report points out that torture is usually applied in a scientific way (what a prostitution newspaper language is, the one I told you thought petulantly, they confuse skill or technique with science, that poor word is the shit it really deep-down really deserves when it forgets that it's there to do something worthy of us and not turn us into robots, etc., oh, oh, look what you've come to), and takes into account—Susana translated, raising her voice in a clear warning that they should either quiet down a little or she'd turn off their color TV—takes into account the latest methods: water torture (the prisoner's head is dunked repeatedly into a bucket of dirty water or one full of excrement and urine), electrical torture (the application of electrodes to the genitals, ears, nasal passages, breasts, or the inside of the eyelids), tortures of a moral order (as torturing a child in the presence of its mother, or husband and wife in the same room). And to think that if this came out as a simple dispatch from the correspondent of *Le Monde*, the people in my cute little embassy would holler that it's all a calumny, Heredia said. They already have, Marcos corrected him, having come in like a cat and sat down on the floor by the window, today no less *Le Monde* announces that the International Commission asked your embassy in Geneva to send them the note in which the minister of justice of Brazil, a laughable post in the light of all this, virtuously protests the report and says that there are no political prisoners in Brazil. Here, look at the rest of it.

"Would you please be so kind as to let me finish?" Susana said. "The Commission points out elsewhere that in the military prison of Belo Horizonte there are police dogs, how's that for a good name, specially trained to attack the sensitive parts of the human body. At the offices of the DOPS (the federal civilian police) in São Paulo, among the 'current' methods of torture figure the pulling out of nails or the crushing of genitals. In São Paulo, Curitiba, and Juís de Fora, prisoners have been burned with soldering irons."

Isolating himself from the noise, from Manuel's shriek in quest of candy, from Heredia's instinctive movement as he softly ran his hand over his left forearm which a year ago in São Paulo, of all places, had been slowly broken in three places, the one I told you manages to make a hollow in which to read for himself the conclusion of the report, the simple final sentence that should have been repeated day and night on all wavelengths, on all presses, from all pens (even if quills weren't used any more, goddamned backward language)

THE PUBLIC OPINION OF CIVILIZED COUNTRIES HAS A REAL POSSIBILITY TODAY OF FORCING AN END, BY MEANS OF REPEATED AND PRECISE DENUNCIATIONS, TO THE INHUMAN PRACTICES OF WHICH SO MANY MEN AND WOMEN IN BRAZIL ARE THE OBJECT.

Madame Franck went up to get her, Francine's voice came into a broken-down phone booth in a café on the Rue Lecluse, her voice as if recently deodorized and glowing reaching me in the booth that smelled of the latrine next door, of course she'd come but why Montmartre, well, yes, she'd take a taxi, incorrigible, but yes, in half an hour. And I knew all about that half hour: a personal inspection, hair stockings bra teeth maybe changing her underwear or debating over a skirt or blouse, settling matters of the moment with Madame Franck. I waited for her with the fourth cognac half-full, night was coming on and it was almost warm, and people, the groups of Algerians heading toward Pigalle or the Place Blanche, night in its neon routine, French fries, whores in every doorway and café, time of the alienated in the most personal city in the world, the one most anchored in itself.

"I'm going to sing you a tango," I announced when we decided on one of the bad restaurants on the Boulevard de Clichy. "Right now I've only got the words, but you'll see how the music will come with dinner, it's only a matter of time. The first part I stole from something that Rivero used to sing, you don't know him, naturally, a guy from Buenos Aires: 'I found her at home and in someone else's arms,' let me translate it for you, it's simple and neat but starting there the plurifundium begins as Lonstein would say. You don't know him either."

"It might be one of the reasons you're drunk," Francine said, "but it was wrong to call me, I'm no good at Salvation Army work, I end up ordering one benedictine after another myself and I can assure you that it's not very pleasant the next day."

"Thank you," Andrés said kissing her on the hand that smelled slightly of blue or green atomizers. "You're good, old comrade, here you are beside the gravely wounded man, ready for the transfusion and the long watch. Don't be afraid, I won't bore you too much, I called you so that at least you'd know that you people were right, as always. Oh, oh, no little questioning pouts, you people are Ludmilla and you, you people are the good sense of the city, the serviceable hand that opens the umbrella, pushes away the sewing machine, and slowly passes the feather duster over the dissection table."

"I'll leave, if you want."

"Of course not, love, quite the contrary, I've already sung you the pertinent part of the tango and now we're going to tie ourselves up with two dozen oysters who are patience itself as Lewis Carroll points out and they'll listen to us talk about more agreeable things, I hope."

"It's all right with me if you don't want to talk. I'll have a drink too, obviously that's the least I can do."

Francine has always been like that, when I call her old comrade I am giving her the sweetest name possible, precisely the one that bothers her because if terms like lover or dear are no longer used in French, they're basically the ones she'd like to hear between the lines when I talk to her and give her a name, and of course we are lovers but I think that I can only reach her in her best part (or mine? Watch out for camouflaged egotism) when things happen like tonight, when I'm soaked in time, without any goal that isn't my little Pierre Boulez or Lutoslawski or Japanese movie fulfillment, and I need Francine as a discontinuance of reality, the subtle marijuana that lets me float on my back for a few hours, far from myself but facing that heaven that I can't renounce, my beautiful nineteen-seventy world so horrible for millions of people as newspaper articles tell me. The old comrade puts her face against mine, she knows that I'm sick from being healthy in a world of sick people, she thinks precisely that from the young Werther to the not so young Andrés Fava there's less distance than there seems to be, myths, taboos, and reasons for scratching one's chest change, yesterday the vexed individual in his violent high-summit willfulness, today the borderline man between two worlds (three, Patricio would have said and since that morning Ludmilla), and she feels a courteous and melancholy pity for me because the guilty conscience of people like her is controlled by a rational dialectic that helps her to live, to love without illusions, just like now, *au jour le jour*.

The oysters pass patiently one by one, the friendly chronicle of the Screwery passes, Marcos passes, that uncertain operation passes, the one I now know is going to end up in a place in Verrières in a few hours where I won't be naturally but Ludmilla will on the other hand from near or far, and Francine listens and delicately draws each oyster out of its last absurd line of defense, she drinks some chilled white wine and drinks again, the old comrade is true to her word, we're going to end up drunk. But I suppose Ludmilla knows what she's doing, Francine says. I agree, girl, but let me add that all the time I had the impression, which in some ways is a consolation, that Ludmilla was explaining the Screwery to me more for my sake than for her own, almost as if it were a message from Marcos, except you've got to wonder a little whether anyone's up to messages with all that's happened lately. They're still waiting for you, Francine said running her hand over my face, you've still got time in any case, I'm here to fill it with words while you go on missing her. I'm leaving, I told her, I don't want you to feel Salvation Army in a sinful neighborhood. I'll go with you, Francine said, I'll make great speeches to you on every corner, too bad the band didn't come and I don't have any pamphlets or a bonnet with ribbons. Old comrade, silly girl. It's better that way, Francine says, this last oyster is yours, don't put any lemon on it, it already has a teardrop.

In his rather meandering way the one I told you could have helped Marcos explain the ants to Ludmilla, a most intent student face down naked softly drowsy but lucid, bloop, of course, not missing a single word of Marcos's as the cigarette sketched ferns on her face and hair, the slow ascent of a hand along the little ass the waist the neck of Ludmilla bloop, and precisely the one I told you would have thought about the meeting of the Vip and the Gi-ant at twelve-thirty in a restaurant on the Champs-Elysées (a piece of information from Lucien Verneuil who was shadowing the Vip and it was costing him rather dearly in that establishment), out of all that would come a multilenticular and quadrichromatic picture of the ants and the Vip himself, not to mention the Vipess and the Gi-ant, in which the one I told you's way of imagining things would join with the sparser information of Marcos and Ludmilla, for example that the Gi-ant had been trained in Panama by the Yankees, a background that had already produced five deaths by his own hand, active participation in repression with techniques learned in school, and a clandestine headquarters (with long winks on the part of the prefecture of the French police, already advised by no less eloquent winks from the Quai d'Orsay) somewhere in the seventh arrondissement of Paris, the capital of France and cradle of the revolution inspired, it was necessary to recognize, by that of the United States which had so efficiently trained the Gi-ant to fight against Latin American revolutionaries, how about the logic of history, Marcos muttered, but let's not get into philosophy, Polonette, because we've got Toynbee and four others for that. Of course, thought the one I told you as he got the lunch business in order, the Vip was the supreme and supranational boss, supra everywhere, while the Gi-ant was only for the ants of the different categories already laid out in the vipero-formic organigram where tremendous terminological liberties must have been permitted, as for example speaking of Dilett-ants and Hieroph-ants and Philosoph-ants who didn't seem to have any real existence while the specific functions of other ants allowed them to be classified as Sycoph-ants, Minim-ants, or Microphon-ants. But where do they come from, how do they live? asked Ludmilla. They come from so many anthills that you'd need all the little flags of Cristoforo Quilombo and Henry Whoreson's continent to cover them all, it's thought that they were born like a kind of international brigade, with apologies to the authentic one, at that meeting in Barquisimeto attended by Latin American military leaders and a certain Pilkington W. Burlington, the latter on behalf of Lyndon Johnson and with his briefcase loaded with dough. The idea was to set up a mechanism for the control and eventual elimination of agitprop centers and revolutionary bridgeheads in Western Europe, where as you've seen there be a bunch of us passing in review with fellowships, papa's money, or washing dead people like Lonstein. The first Vip was a certain Somoza, who in spite of his name had nothing to do with but was a son of a bitch too, and the ants took care of him like a mother for three years. Now we've got another who's already been in Paris, France, for two years, and naturally

"Oh, Beto, what a difficult city," the Vipess complained, "I can't understand these menus all in French, you pick something for me without cholestorol so I don't get all puffed up like that time with the minister."

"I'd recommend these cutlets of anyo, ma'am," said the Giant.

"What kind?"

"Hog, girl," the Vip translated, "follow Higinio's advice because I'm going to have a casoolay tooloosen as they call it, it's a little heavy but I've been given to understand it has good effects, you get me, Higinio, look how the madam's blushing, come on, come on, we've got no secrets with Higinio."

"Oh, Beto, you've got such a filthy mind," the Vipess said.

"Don Gualberto knows how to live," the Gi-ant said, "now, as for the cutlets, they're lamb, ma'am, fingerlicking good, you can believe me. And for desert I'd recommend

It's a problem but the one I told you doesn't take it too seriously and is having a little fun after his fashion, because at the moment of bringing to life the conversation in the restaurant (Fouquet's, of course, where else) what kind of language are the Gi-ant and the Vip going to speak, in what cultural categories (and acultural above all), in what linguistic estates or zones

Ibero-
Luso-
Italo-
Maya-Quiché- etc. } American 1970
Yoruba-
Ural-Altaic-
Incaic-

is the one I told you going to listen to them, because after all he's from Buenos Aires and in matters of oral contests he cuts the Gordian knot with a slash of his gaucho knife, and so it is that in the sector of his friends, Heredia as well as Gómez or Marcos (and sometimes even Roland or Monique) all speak the same talk as that in the one I told you's notes, as for the Vip and the Gi-ant they're not friends of his, no one's going to spend a fortune at Fouquet's to find out how they talk, not to mention the danger of a Sycoph-ant's laying them out with a right cross to the chin in the lavatory of such a refined establishment, so the one I told you amuses himself by doing whatever he feels like on that terrain. And besides there's another problem and it indeed is serious and bothersome

"They know perfectly well that we're setting up the Screwery," Marcos said, "one of Lucien Verneuil's men took off for Morocco five months ago, Lucien warned me but it was already too late to cover a few tracks, the guy sold out to the Gi-ant, it seems, but at that time he couldn't give him too many names."

"Are they that powerful?" Ludmilla asked. "In a European country it seems incredible that a commando of foreign killers, you understand."

"Bah, think about the Ben Barka affair, or the Corsicans who are foreigners too in their way and are organized like hawks to exploit the whores and junkies of Paris. Think about the ex-colonials from Algeria, an enclave inside another enclave, the ancients were right, Ptolemy saw it exactly, everything is concentric, Polonette, Copernicus goofed if you take a good look at it. As for us it's all the same, we've managed so far

serious and bothersome, and it's the matter of the political topics that the Vip and the Gi-ant touch upon almost continuously, not to mention Gómez and Patricio who never talk about anything else, because at those moments the one I told you absolutely refuses to take them down for reasons that are valid although also rather frivolous; he's really obeying a necessity that's vital and aesthetic at the same time since the things that Gómez or Marcos talk about (and their counterpart that the Vip and the Gi-ant are talking about now) are public and current topics, newspaper stories, items on the radio, socio-cultural material within reach of anyone, and then the one I told you withdraws and thinks for example about so many novels where in exchange for a more or less banal story you have to pass through conversations and arguments and counterarguments about alienation, the third world, the armed or unarmed struggle, the role of the intellectual, imperialism and colonialism

"Without much butter, please," the Vipess said.

when all this (1) is unknown to the reader, and then the reader is a sluggard and deserves that kind of novel in order to learn, what the hell, or (2) he is perfectly aware and especially placed within a view of daily history, for which reason the novels can be taken as understood only too well and he can advance toward terrain that is more proper, that is to say less didactic. And since the one I told you only thinks about books and novels as a mere metaphoric base for his points of view in matters of mnemonic register, he quickly tosses in that towel that has been overhandled in Latin America, after having reached the conclusion that everything already known is boring and that on the other hand one must be alert on the plane of facts because things are going to happen and I don't know if you saw the item, Don Gualberto, said the Gi-ant handing him the newspaper precisely at the end of the tray of cheeses which were, the Vipess said, deevine.

« L'OSSERVATORE ROMANO » CONDAMNE SÉVÈREMENT

les enlèvements de diplomates

Cité du Vatican *(A.F.P.)*. — *L'Osservatore romano* a publié lundi soir un éditorial sévère consacré aux enlèvements et aux meurtres de diplomates étrangers.

Le commentaire, signé du R.P. Antonio Messinone, vise, semble-t-il, les actes de violence commis, en Amérique latine, contre des représentants de l'Allemagne fédérale ou d'autres pays. « *Ils violent,* écrit le religieux *les droits fondamentaux de l'homme* », et constituent une « *agression contre la souveraineté de l'Etat que représente l'agent diplomatique, comme l'avait déjà compris la civilisation grecque, à une époque reculée* ».

« *Aucune raison, aucune volonté de protester ou de contester des structures politiques et sociales, même considérées comme oppressives et injustes, ne peuvent justifier moralement et juridiquement, par exemple, la séquestration d'ambassadeurs et de diplomates,* estime l'éditorialiste. *L'agent diplomatique qui se maintient dans les limites du droit international ne contracte aucune responsabilité à l'égard de la population de l'Etat qui l'accueille. Ce n'est pas son rôle de corriger les défauts d'un système (...). Son meurtre ou sa séquestration à des fins politiques est un crime particulièrement grave par ses incidences sur les relations internationales.* »

"You better read it in Spanish because Madalena doesn't capeesh much Frog," the Vip said.

"All right, the *Osservatore Romano* severely condemns the kidnapping of diplomats."

"Wonderful!" said the Vipess claspingherhands.

"Yes ma'am, the Vatican has reacted, a little late but after all. Here's what Father Messinone says, I don't know who he is, *about the acts of violence committed in Latin America against representatives of the Federal Republic of Germany and other countries. They violate the fundamental rights of man, the priest writes*

"That's right," said the Vipess.

and constitute "an aggression against the sovereignty of the

State represented by the diplomatic agent

"It's about time," said the Vip. *as Greek civilization understood many years ago."*

"The colonels know what they're doing," said the Vipess.

"It's typical," Patricio asserted. "Keep on translating it for the boy here, and you Manuel since you've torn up the newspaper on me again I'm going to make you eat it starting with the book section which is the dullest part."

"Leave my son alone," Susana said. *"They violate the fundamental rights of man and constitute an attack against the sovereignty of the State represented by the diplomatic agent, as Greek civilization understood in ancient times."*

"What you're telling us," Oscar said, "is the same old story, as soon as the sacrosanct order of things is touched, out comes immortal Greece, age-old India, imperial Rome. It's all right, girl, don't set the laser of your big black eyes on me, keep on because we're like in church here, if this is the time to say so."

"You can all go to hell," Susana advised, "at least I'm a saint of a translator, to keep in the spirit of things. O.K., listen: *No reason, no desire to protest or answer political and social structures,* excuse the mistakes in agreement but the words were gone with the wind, *even if they (the structures) are considered oppressive or unjust, can justify morally and juridically, for example, the kidnapping of ambassadors and diplomats. The . . .*

"Clear as mud," Marcos said. "Morally and juridically, of course. The statutory organization, an elegant way of hiding the fear of the great flap of the wing and the scrubbing of the floor. If there really was such a thing as a will to defend the law as a guarantee of society's smooth functioning, O.K. then, I know a lawyer from Santa Fe in Argentina who was quite happy that they hanged Eichmann but at the same time was purple with rage because he thought the guy's kidnapping was a juridical monstrosity. I won't say that his position fills me with enthusiasm, but it is logical and coherent. The disgusting part in this case with these clerical crows is that underneath it all they're not defending the law but are archshitting with fear of the Tupamaros and other guerrilla groups, and as for that business of morality that the old raven refers to, we already know what kind of morality they're defending. Go ahead, Susanita, the best part's coming up."

"*A diplomatic agent*

"*. . . who stays within the limits of international law,*" the Giant read, "*takes on no responsibility with respect to the people of the State that receives him.*"

"That's all we'd need," said the Vip.

"*His role is not to correct the defects of a system.*"

"That's great," Heredia said. "Nobody's asking them to correct anything, let's see if they try to convert them into apostles for me now."

"The last sentence," Susana roared. "*His assassination or kidnapping with political ends is a particularly serious crime because of its effects upon international relations.*"

"He means the international relations among the Pentagon, Siemens, the colonels, and the dough in Switzerland."

"Of course," said the Vipess. "Where will we end up if they start off now with what happened to the Limber baby, remember Beto, we were young but what an effect, mother of God, give me some water I'm getting upset."

"Sleep, Polonette, listen to the recess bell ringing, that's enough questions for the teacher."

"Bloop," said Ludmilla curling up, "but first explain the ransom to me, I mean who are you going to demand to be freed and what's going to happen if the other side doesn't follow through."

"I'll show you the lists tomorrow, Oscar and Heredia brought the missing names, you know how quick these things go. Monique is getting the documentation ready for the newspapers."

"Yes, but just in case . . ."

"That case is still far off, Polonette. Go to sleep."

"I don't want any trouble with the Central Bureau," the Vip said, and the Gi-ant understood at once that everything that was going to follow was an order even though it came wrapped in *glace au parfums des îles* and coffee with the best cognac. "They're worried about mass kidnappings or what comes close to it, and they know that there's a group hard at work here."

"Inhuman," said the Vipess looking at the dessert cart but not referring precisely to its contents.

"Be still. At first they didn't take them too seriously, they thought it was a matter of contacts, of getting some money together, and alliances with other Commies to create a favorable climate in the European press that's sold out to the Russians or the Chinese, but now they tell me that it's worse than that. Goddamn it, if it wasn't laughable, you'd think the Bureau was afraid of a landing like in Cuba, what do you think?"

"Don Gualberto, the fact is there are all kinds of landings," the Gi-ant said. "I think the Bureau has every right to be nervous, and believe me we're going to do everything possible to stop these degenerates in their tracks, begging your pardon, ma'am."

"It's in the southern cone where they're most nervous, Higinio, especially because of what's going on in Montevideo and now with that gang of Brazilian criminals in Algeria, you can imagine, they think that one of these days they'll set up a coalition of the whole mass of leftists on this side and that'll strengthen the ones back there, who've always felt a little lonely."

"I'll be damned if it makes any difference to me if they're lonely," the Gi-ant said, "I've seen the reports on the latest troubles in Uruguay. But I understand, just like you, Don Gualberto, that we've got to lay it on here without holding back in order to get rid of the leaders, you leave it all up to me."

"Oh, Higinio, don't forget that Beto is the one who's in most danger here, don't relax his protection," said the Vipess from the depths of the currant ice cream with whipped cream on top.

"Let us talk, sweetheart, Higinio knows what he's doing. Tomorrow I'm going to take advantage of that dinner to strengthen our position, so you won't have any problems if you let your boys get a little heavy-handed."

"That would be very good, Don Gualberto."

"So let's have another cognac, that's what we're in France for."

"Don't drink so much, Beto, afterwards you break out all over with that eczema."

"It's good you like to scratch it for me," said the Vip, nudging the Gi-ant with his elbow and winking at the Vipess who was bashfully staring into the bottom of her empty dish, stingy Frenchmen with their midget portions of ice cream.

Those things that come out just right, the voice of Maurice Fanon on a record, at the low tide of a conversation that is unravelling, that needs more wine and cigarettes to hold on, the voice of Fanon like a bitter summary, *me souvenir de toi/de ta loi sur mon corps,* he sings well, Francine said, you don't often hear something like that in a restaurant.

"*Me souvenir de toi/de ta loi sur mon corps.* Yes, baby."

"Don't be sad, Andrés, you'll forget her, you'll forget both of us, you'll go back to your music, you never really loved women, there's nothing for you but that inner space, I don't know how to describe it, where you prowl like a slow tiger."

But was she really telling me that or were they still talking to me out of that song? Distracted, going along like that across from Francine who'd come for my sake and was accompanying me on my sad night (I'd never made her listen to the tango by that name and in any case she wouldn't understand), going away leaving her with a smooth and even attentive face, filling her glass before going far away, wandering from block to block, Rue Clovis, Rue Descartes, Rue Thouin, Rue de l'Estrapade, Rue Clotilde, and back on the Rue Clovis, for what reason now, why, since I'd wanted to myself. Poor Francine, even more abandoned than Ludmilla at that moment as I poured her another glass of wine stroking her hand and we listened to Fanon, *me souvenir de toi/de loi sur mon corps*, and everything was flight and distance, a courteous system of hollows and absences, Francine in the restaurant, Fanon's voice, my turning the corner of the Rue Thouin, my pouring her another glass of wine and stroking her hand, a vague system of trains along tracks that cross and separate, useless handkerchiefs at the windows, useless nearness, too distracted and drunk, at the same time the train and somebody lost on it and looking for someone, the words taking on an order one more time so as to name the disorder, listen, baby, listen to these

WAYS OF TRAVELING

The dusty nighttime sleeping car
that shunts us into this nameless station
where one of the two of us will get off
with a suitcase dirty with the past
while the other
(was it 14, 8, the upper berth?
the porter asleep, everybody asleep)
wanders through the passageway
where every door is rejection and that smell
of the sweat of time, of dirty socks,
searching one more time for
what already far away
comes out onto a moon-mirror square
searching one more time for
taxi and hotel until train-
time, the sleeping car
(9, 34, 5?)
where maybe they will meet
for the last stage
searching one more time
along the passageways where
every door
the taxi and the hotel
one more time
with the dirty suitcase
along the passageways where
the taxi and the hotel
along the passageways where
searching one more time.

"Everything has to be invented all over again, Polonette," Marcos said, "love has no reason to be an exception, people think that there's nothing new under the neon, we wear routine like footwear, kids holler for Carlitos shoes, you size six and me nine and a half, it's laughable. Look, every time I go to buy a shirt at a Monoprix, the first thing the old saleslady asks me is my neck size. Don't worry, I tell her, I want it big and roomy. Silence, owl eyes, tight lips, that can't be, you can see her thinking and raging clearer than if there was a TV screen underneath her bangs. But sir, your neck size tells the size of the shirt/No madame because I like them long and loose and with my neck size you'll give me one of those fitted tight shirts that look all right on Alain Delon but make me look like a corkscrew/How strange, it's the first time/Don't be upset, madame, give me the largest one you've got/It's not going to look good on you, sir/ Madame, with this shirt I'm as happy as a well-fed puma/And on like that for five minutes but you have to keep a tight rein, everything is yet to be invented and unfortunately I won't see it but while I can I'll do my own inventing, I'll invent you, Polonette, and I hope you'll keep inventing me at every moment because if there's something I like about you besides that damp little belly it's that you're always up in some tree, and you get more worked up over a box-kite than a well-tempered clavier."

"Bloop," said Ludmilla. "That's a lie, I like the clavier much more."

"Because you listen to it as if it were a kite, wind and the wagging tail and the bows of a kite, you're not one of those people who get dressed for music, get dressed for the theater, get dressed to fuck, get dressed for tomato salad. When I think that it wasn't two hours ago that you were taking off my pants as if I were Manuel and needed a sponge bath or something of the sort, and that afterwards you tried rubbing me down with the alcoholic towel, by the way I'm afraid you used up my best grappa, Polonette, you'll pay me for that."

"And then you fingered my titties," Ludmilla said.

"I'm not as original as you, you can see, but I try," Marcos said hugging her until he made her give a complaining mew, "and not just your titties but here and here and there and right between this and this."

"Oh," Ludmilla said, "don't invent too much, bloop, but it's true. I want it all to be new too and different and kite as you say, your province back there must be full of kites and young goats, I can tell by the cakes that never lie, by your hands, oh shit."

"Polonette, my province is in an old and tired country, it will have to be made all over again, believe me, it may look great to you but that's how it is, old and tired because of false hopes and even falser promises that nobody believed in anyway except Peronists of the old guard and they for rather different and rather legitimate reasons even though the end result would be the usual one, a slew of colonels, starting with the eponymous hero."

"So why do so many of your friends and those newspaper clippings and Patricio talk about Peronism like some kind of force or hope or something like that?"

"Because it's true, Polonette, because words have a terrible force, because Realpolitik is getting to be the only thing we've got left against so many Pentagon gorillas and so many Vips, you may not understand today but you'll see soon enough, think of all the juice they've got out of the word Jesus, the image Jesus, try to understand that today we need a thaumaturgical word and that the image that corresponds to that word has qualities that make cortisone look weak."

"But you don't believe in that image, Marcos."

"What difference does it make if we can use it to bring down something much worse, our grandparents' ethic no longer obtains, Polonette, not to mention the fact that our grandparents had two ethics when it came to facing up to whatever might be, you can be sure of that. You're right, I don't give a good goddamn about that old man who thinks he can telecommand something that he was basically incapable of doing in his day and that was when he held the best cards in his hand; but the fact is he's really out of the game, except that names and images last longer than the thing named and the thing represented, and they can put in better hands what they didn't put during his moment, listen to the speech I'm making to you."

"I'd like to understand better," Ludmilla said, "I'd like to understand so many things but it's so far away, you can't see things very clearly with so much water in between."

"You can't see clearly over there either, I'm not going to bother you with anything more complicated than the rent-control law, just understand that for us, for the Screwery let's say, any weapon that works is valid because we know that we're right and that we're surrounded from without and from within, by the gorillas and by the Yankees and even by the passivity of those millions of people who are always hoping that others will take their chestnuts out of the fire, and also because the very fact that the enemies of Peronism are who they are seems to us to be a more than legitimate reason to defend it and make use of it and one day, you know, get out of it and out of so many other things by the only possible path, you can imagine which one."

"And then you and I will go to Córdoba in Argentina," said Ludmilla who had her *idées fixes,* "and I want it to be full of balloons and birds and goats and cakes."

Marcos understood that fatigue was behind all that, poor Polonette with so much information piled up in her head. He asked her for something to drink, watched her go and come back naked, stepping with the step of an actress, mistress of her body, of every movement that outlined her in the shadows. Everything will be like you someday, Marcos thought, calling her, everything will be more naked and more beautiful, we're going to get rid of so many greasy overcoats and so many dirty underdrawers that something will have to come out of it, Polonette. But it would be necessary to love that desired image until you got dizzy, in spite of Realpolitik or the other necessary weapons, not always clean or beautiful, in spite of the worst inevitable options, like a surgeon's hands getting covered with shit and bile in order to remove the tumor and send an adolescent back to life, with all that and when all's said and done against all that when the moment came, only in that way would they emerge from the night.

"You're hurting me, not there."

"Hurting you? I'm sorry, I didn't realize, talking politics made me careless."

"It's just that it's very sensitive, and I wonder whose fault that is."

Marcos stretched out on top of her feeling her burning against his body, he slipped down until his mouth reached the meeting of her thighs, he began to kiss her softly, to slip his tongue into the soft salty opening; Ludmilla straightened up murmuring, moaning, he heard the call but continued searching down to the bottom, his hands clutching her hips with the gesture of one quenching a long thirst. Lost in the pleasure that others had also known how to give her, Ludmilla felt that it wasn't the same, that everything was changing now and that everything was the same in the end, her sex, Marcos's mouth, her hips, Marcos's hands, inside her the other thing was rising up, what he'd tried to tell her, something like the hope of a difference in similarity. Sinking her hands into Marcos's hair she called him up, she opened up like an arc murmuring his name where something was beginning, from other limits, on the other side of the border, where everything could be almanacs and kites and little goats and theaters, where someday the Screwery would be able to have all those names, all those stars.

Pages for Manuel's book: thanks to her friendships that lay somewhere between touching and mocking, Susana gets clippings that she pastes up pedagogically, that is, alternating the useful and the pleasant, so that when the day came Manuel would read the album with the same interest that Patricio and she in their time had read the children's magazines *El tesoro de la juventud* and *Billiken*, going from lesson to game without too much trauma, except that who was to say which is the lesson and which is the game and what Manuel's world will be like and what the hell, Patricio says, you're doing fine, old girl, you're pasting down our very own present for him and other things too, so he'll have something to choose from, he'll know what our catacombs were like and probably the kid will be able to reach and eat those ever so green grapes that we stare at from so far down.

Reflections like that don't make them melancholy but rather cheer them up enormously, and, for example, Susana decides that it would be good for Manuel, in the middle of Argentinean primary school, to find out that right next door things are said that other equally South American kids babble out with no problem at all, all of which will contribute pestalozzily to lessen the compartmentalization and the provincialism of the kids in question, and without further thought she anoints a whole page of the album with abundant mucilage and places on it a Chilean sample donated by Fernando (otherwise vanished from the map after his likely suspicion that this was a hot potato and he'd better visely vait it out in his qvarters in the hotel because fellowships are a delicate matter).

A first step on the boulevard crawling with people, fly-catching neon signs for provincials, the narrow stairway painted red and gold, the smell of a collective paid enclosure, a closet with a toothless old woman and kneaded greasy numbers, it had to be hoplessly sad, Francine thought as she went up first, to decide to go into places like that; a step away from refusing, asking Andrés to put her in a taxi and go on alone with his cheap night, she continued on up, the white wine wrapped her in a fatigue as musty and sluggish as the room on the second floor full of smoke, vague male figures in a few rows of chairs, a platform where one green spotlight and another blue one move a hot aquarium air, a great golden fish who smiled for no one, who had just taken off the spangled bra and one more time, for the fifth time that evening, put it on the back of a chair where her blouse and skirt already rested, where now she would lightly drop the red panties to leave Mademoiselle Antinéa naked ten feet away from Andrés and Francine who were beginning to make out shapes and colors in the iridescent haze of the aquarium.

"Well," Francine said, "since you had this crazy urge we might have gone to a decent place."

He looked at her with pity, too dressed and different for that place, the only woman in the audience. How could I tell her that we hadn't come for the strip-tease but to be present one more time at her pathetic, instantaneous, obstinate self-definition when facing every unusual situation, morality as automatic as deodorant under the arms or the perfection of her hairdo. How in the devil to get her and get me out of the compartments, the castrating rhythms of our daily bread, at that time when everything was

Ludmilla and the pit, a trip on the mean little train of jealousy and something like a drum, a distant cymbal, most likely tachycardia from so much white wine, a tam-tam behind his eyelids, Fritz Lang, the way the waiter both servile and authoritarian at the same time had come over, perhaps a pistol pointing from the pocket of his very white jacket, and that total blackout in which everything was waiting since something in me knew it and had dreamed it, had lived it, that is, and now having to explain to Francine no less why the fuck he'd dragged her to this sad pigsty where in all ways Mademoiselle Antinéa was the only thing (with Francine at the other pole, in the other reality equally unreal) that deserved being called beautiful, enduring, what Ludmilla had been for me, the precise facts, the summary of events in the course of a night, everything so clear on the edge of the tam-tam that was still scanning his answer like verse and then to tell Francine but old sweety, silly chick, don't you realize that we didn't come for the strip-tease, look at that fat Algerian who most certainly is spending his week's savings, look at that little old man in the starched shirt who sat in the front row so as not to lose a single detail, something that I think is an obvious mistake because it's quite well known that any magnifying glass puts an end to Cleopatra, take a look at those boys over there half-asleep, their idea of masculinity consists of playing it indifferent, they roll their eyes and peep through their lashes at Mademoiselle Antinéa who's really better than what you might imagine at such a price, don't you think.

"They revolt me, she and all of them, and especially us."

"Oh."

"A farce for hypocrites, for impotent and frustrated people."

"Ah."

"Why, Andrés, why. I can understand that today, after all, but why this."

"A pocket-size peregrination, girl, let's call it a balance in the face of the total cessation of activities, Nerval's long night under the lamp post. Don't look at me that way, there's nothing suicidal about me, it's all metaphor. Listen to the music they've foisted on poor Antinéa, they were playing that in Acapulco exactly twenty years ago, I had the record in my younger days. No, she isn't half-bad from the rear with that nice little self-contained ass of hers. Ah, yes, now, yes, that smile is sweet and good like you, girl."

"You're depraved, you and your self-contained little ass, your black-humor eroticism."

But his hand against my thigh, hot and contracted, was the beginning, as so many times, of the pilgrimage for her too, a reproach that leads to tenderness, tenderness to a kiss, a kiss to love, love to awakening, awakening to reproach, the brusque and sad separation of the capsules until the NASA of bodies gives the order to approach once more and effect the union (Reuters). Serious, secret, weary, Mademoiselle Antinéa was finishing her number with a side step that gave considerable value to her breasts, the blue curtain with stars fell over the instantaneous vision of a minutely depilated sex on which the minimum concealment ordered by municipal morals in article A-2345 seemed to disappear so that a pink flash would appear, and the brilliantly green spotlights coincided with a collective movement in the seats, some grudging applause and the howling hula-hula that didn't augur anything good, what you'll see come out is a vahiné of forty-five, when they're exotic you can forgive them their age and their bellies, I don't know why.

"An expert, obviously."

"No, child, pure conjecture. But look, if you can't adjust to circumstances in spite of all we've drunk, there's nothing left but to leave and I'll find you that taxi you were talking about a while back since it's been written that I am to spend this night alone."

Nothing, something that made her voice husky or that way of looking at her cigarette for lack of anything better to do, better to tell her shh, don't distract Mademoiselle Doudou, who, furthermore, had nothing of the vahiné about her. Andrés's fingers closing until they hurt her elbow, the grimace through the smoke and then the slow smile, how good you are, girl. And none of that could distract Mademoiselle Doudou now that she was starting her operation of undressing in open polarization to the music, as if having decided to put each movement in opposition to the form of the melody so that when the song rose in pitch, Mademoiselle Doudou lowered her very black polished body to touch her fingers to a pair of punishment boots, and on the other hand she would rise up every time the bass spun its deep cobwebs for her. She's pretty, Francine said with her voice of a cultured bookseller, she has very delicate thighs. The problem is her mouth, Andrés said, you'll see. Then you know her. No, it's the first time I've ever been here, I've been in others, of course, there are a lot in this neighborhood as you know from the guidebooks you sell Americans. What about her mouth? Just wait, you'll see it's not going to stay that way. And it didn't, because the little old man in the front row moved his head and buzzbuzzed a long incomprehensible discourse that amused the boys sitting in the row behind immensely, and Mademoiselle Doudou looked at the old man and winked, her smile filled his face with something that had no name, an eruption, an outpouring, the admission price and the customers' clothes and the curtains on the stairs and the civilization that made all of that were there in her smile, and now the little old man enthusiastically half rose from his seat because Doudou had just dropped her panties and was offering him a black and red and tobacco-colored totality still smiling at the old man, exciting him with a twisting of the hips and suddenly turning around and shaking her tight buttocks toward where the old man's hands were, his arms outstretched, Doudou naked facing the old man and it wasn't possible, but of course it's possible, girl, people come here so that these things can be possible, Doudou pulling out a pubic hair and blowing it to the old man as a good-by kiss and the old man leaping up and grabbing it in the air and putting it in his mouth, swallowing it, people falling out of their seats laughing, Doudou depraved cupping her hands over her sex and offering it to the old man who had fallen suddenly into his chair and was shaking as if under the shower, the mocking applause, the blue curtain, let's go, Andrés, please right now, so you see, girl, you ought to think about the fact sometimes that this is located exactly twenty blocks from your place, from your well-seasoned catalogues and your subscription to *Les Temps Modernes*. But that old man must be paid by the house, it's impossible that. Of course, girl, if that version makes you feel better he's paid, seeing is to stop believing as my private book of proverbs says, come on, let's go, we're thirsty, of course we'll probably miss the prettiest girl of them all. Put me in a taxi and go on back. I deserve it, girl, but no, tonight we'll stay together, two perfect little machines for turning out verbal crap, what do you expect, and to think that the way it seems I could have had a mission to fulfill and on the contrary you see, Mademoiselle Antinéa and now Doudou so demure. What mission? asked Francine. Shh, Andrés said, they're announcing the pearl of Bolivia, Señorita Dola, listen to that sort of *quena* cut in Montparnasse by a Polish Jew, I know the record, I even think the guy's name is Brinsky, you couldn't get more autochthonous, could you.

In his sluggish way Marcos had followed the manufacture of Manuel's book rather closely. Between Maria Montessori and him there were obvious differences, which did not stop him from giving the opinion that there were other good items too, and to Susana's horror he gave her some blue pages of a *télex* that he had been given by a comrade at Prensa Latina and which according to Marcos had to be pasted just as it was in the album because the telegraphic fantasies, the mistakes, and the general look of a *calligramme* and disorder helped give the information its deepest truth, which was born of all the inconveniences and mistakes and delays and clumsiness of underdevelopment, a little flower in the midst of reinforced concrete, a kitten playing among high-tension wires, hey, Patricio reined him in, when you irradiate on me you leave the little rabbi way behind. Fuck your mother, Marcos said austerely, paste in the *télex* so the kid will get something out of it someday, upon which Susana, intimidated, grabbed the mucilage once more and there

ATTENTION P
ELA PARIS *R*R*R*R*R*R*

PLS RPT ORTEGA MATERIAL FROM WHERE SAYS:
IN 1950, LEBANON IMPORTED SAUDI OIL AT A VALUE OF 10
MILLION................ETC ETC..........

THANX ER *R*R*R*R*R*R*

PL-4

BY LUIS MARTIRENA

HAVANA, MAR 27 (PL).- A RECENTLY ARRIVED VISITOR TO CUBA, ESPECIALLY IF HE COMES FROM A COUNTRY LIKE URUGUAY WHERE THE GOVERNING GROUP LIVES BEHIND CLOSED DOORS, CANNOT HELP BUT BE SURPRISED AND HAVE AS AN IRREPLACABLE EXPERIENCE THE
TESSSSSSSSSSSSSSSSSSSSSSSSSSSSSSSSSSSSSSSSSSSSSSSSSSSSSSSSSSSSSSSSSSSSSSSS
SSSSSSSSSSSSSSSSSSSSSSSSSSSSSSSSSSSSSSSSSSSSSSSSSSSSSSSSSSSSSSSSSSSSSSSSSS
HE EABILITY
ENCE THE
EABILITY TO ATTEND ONE OF THE USUA

PL-4

BY LUIS MARTIRENA.

HAVANA, MAR 27 (PL) .- A RECENTLY ARRIVED VISITOR TO CUBA, ESPECIALLY IF HE COMEX XX U COUNTRY LIKE URUGUAY WHERE THE GOVERNING GROUP LIVES BEHIND CLOSED DOORS, CANNOT HELP BUT BE SURPRISED AND HAVE AS AN IRREPLACABLE EXPERIENCE THE ABILITY TO ATTEND ONE OF THE HABITUAL DIALOGUES BETWEEN FIDEL CASTRO AND HIS PEOPLE.

AS IS HIS CUSTOM AND AS HE DOES WITH FREQUENCY, THE CUBAN PRIME MINISTER ARRIVED RATHER UNEXPECTEDLY ON WEDNESDAY AT THE UNIVERSITY OF HAVANA, WHERE HE CARRIED ON A LONG DIALOGUE WITH STUDENTS AND PROFESSORS, WITH WHOM HE DISCUSSED PROBLEMS AND THE REALITIES OF THE REVOLUTIONARY SITUATION.

WHEN THEY HAD FINISHED A WELCOMING CEREMONY FOR THE BRIGADE OF YOUNG CUBANS WHO HAD SPENT MORE THAN A MONTH OF VOLUNTARY LABOR IN CHILE AND PEOPLE WERE BEGINNING TO LEAVE, SOMEONE SHOUTED: -THERE HE COMES-, THERE WERE TWO SMALL EUROPEAN CARS IN WHICH THE PRIME MINISTER AND SOME OTHER MEMBERS OF THE GOVERNMENT WERE RIDING.

THE CARS STOP BY THE STEPS LEADING TO THE PRESIDENT'S OFFICE AT THE OTHER END OF THE MAIN SQUARE OF THE UNIVERSITY, THE SAME SQUARE WHERE THE SAME FIDEL CASTRO HAD HARANGUED HIS COMRADES IN STUDENT STRUGGLES IN OTHER TIMES.

THE YOUNG PEOPLE CAME RUNNING FROM ALL DIRECTIONS AND QUICKLY SURROUNDED THE PRIME MINISTER WHO REMAINED STANDING BY ONE OF THE VEHICLES. SOME, TO GET THERE MORE QUICKLY, CLIMBED OVER A SMALL TANK CAPTURED FROM THE BATISTA ARMY DURING THE FIRST MOMENTS OF 1959, WHICH REMAINS IN ITS PLACE AS A LIVING MONUMENT.

CONTINUED/MP10,25GMP

PL-5

FIRST ADDITION TO PL-4 (WITH FIDEL CASTRO

A FRESH AND NATURAL DIALOGUE RAPIDLY TOOK SHAPE. FIDEL CASTRO INDIDIDUALLY QUESTIONS THE BRIGADISTS ABOUT THEIR CHILEAN EXPERIENCE-. WHERE DID THEY WORK? WHAT DID THEY DO?- THE BOYS AND GIRLS ANSWER AND BRIEFLY TELL ABOUT SOME EXPERIENCES AND EMPHASIZE THE LOVE WITH WHICH THEY WERE RECEIVED AND TREATED BY THE PEOPLE AND GOVERNMENT OF CHILE.

A COMPACT HUMAN MASS HAS FORMED AROUND THE CUBAN LEADER COMPLETELY COVERING THE STAIRS AND THE ESPLANADE WHERE THEY ARE LOCATED. THE DIALOGUE BEGINS TO TAKE OTHER DIRECTIONS, THOSE WHO LISTEN OR ASK QUESTIONS ARE IN ALMOST ALL CASES VERY YOUNG AND HAVE HALF OF THEIR LIVES INTEGRATED INTO THE REVOLUTIONARY PROCESS. THEIR SPECIFIC PREOCCUPATIONS ARE DIFFERENT FROM THOSE THAT THE PRIME MINISTER'S STUDENT COTEMPORARIES REVEALED. THEY REFER TO THE INTEGRATION OF YOUTH INTO THE NEW SOCIETY, THE PROBLEMS OF DEVELOPMENT IN A COUNTRY UNDER SIEGE, ECONOMIC AND SOCIAL PROBLEMS THAT HAVE ONLY RECENTLY BEGUN TO BE SOLVED

CONTINUED/TLM?MP10.30GMT

PL-6

SECOND ADDITION TO PL-4 (WITH FIDEL CASTRO

-THIS YEAR WE ARE SOLVING THE SUGAR-CANE HARVEST WITH HUNDREDS OF THOUSANDS FEWER CUTTERS THAN LAST YEAR-, THE PRIME MINISTER OF CUBA EXPLAINS TO A QUESTION. NEXT YEAR FOR THE WHOLE HARVEST WE WILL NEED ONE HUNDRED THOUSAND LESS PEOPLE THAN IN 1970-.

THEN HE WENT INTO THE HISTORY OF CANECUTTING IN CUBA, THAT THAT CHORE THAT IS COMING MORE AND MORE TO BE DONE BY MACHINE FREEING MEN FROM A BRUTAL JOB-. THE CANE PROBLEM WAS SOLVED HERE FIRST WITH SLAVERY, THEN WITH IMMIGRATION, LATER THERE WERE THE FIVE HUNDRED THOUSAND UNEMPLOYED, WHO WORKING

EIGHTEEN HOURS A DAY BROUGHT IN THE HARVEST, IT CANNOT BE DONE THAT WAY NOW.

PEOPLE MUST WORK A REASONABLE SHIFT AND ALSO RECEIVE THE FOOD AND CARE THEY NEVER HAD BEFORE–.

THE EXPLANATION IS FLUID, DIDACTIC, AND SHOWS A THOROUGH VIEW OF THE
PROBLEMS AND THE
PERSPECTIVES OF THE REVOLUTION.

CHILE GETS BETTER RESULTS OUT OF LABOR THAN WE
THIRTY THOUSAND WORKERS IN THE COPPER
MINES, WHILE WE NEED HUNDREDS OF THOUSANDS OF PEOPLE
TO CUT SUGAR CANE BY HAND, ONLY WITH THE MECHANIZATION OF THE CUTTING CAN WE FIND THE SOLUTION TO THIS PROBLEM–.

IN ANOTHER ANSWER HE RECALLS A PHRASE OF MARX
IN A SENSE THAT THE BUILDING OF SOCIALISM IS
ONLY THE PREHISTORY OF HUMANITY. –THE WHOLE HISTORY IS STILL TO BE WRITTEN AND THEN C
RTAINLY
THERE WILL ALSO BE PROBLEMS. BUT THE PROBLEMS WILL BE DIFFERENT. CAN WE CONCEIVE OF A SOCIETY WITHOUT PROBLEMS?. FIDEL CASTRO AS WITH A SMILE.
CONTINUED/MTLM/MP10.35GMT

EEEEEEEEEEEEEEEEEEEEEEEEEEEEEEEEEEEEEEEEEEEEEEEEEEEEEEEEE
PL–7

THIRD ADDITION TO PL–4 (WITH FIDEL CASTRO

A YOUNG MAN STARTS A QUESTION TALKING ABOUT THE MOMENT WHEN ALL MATERIAL NECESSITIES WILL HAVE BEEN SOLVED, WHICH BRINGS ON AN INTERRUPTION BY THE PRIME MINISTER: –HOW CAN YOU PUT A LIKMIT ON MATERIAL NECESSITIES? HOW MANY PIECES OF CLOTHING, HOW MANY QUARTS OF MILK, HOW MANY HOSPITALS, HOW MANY LABORATORIES, HOW MANY BUSES, HOW MANY SCHOOLS, HOW MANY UNIVERSITIES, HOW MANY ACADEMIES OF SCIENCE? HOW MANY MUSEUMS, HOW MANY HOTELS, HOW MANY HOTELS, HOW MANY REGRIGERATORS? AND THAT IN A SOCIETY LIKE OURS WHERE NECESSITIES ARE NOT ENCOURAGED OR INVENTED FOR PEOPLE TO SOLVE THE PROBLEMS OF PRODUCTION–.

HOW CAN THE PROBLEM OF PRODUCTIVITY BE SOLVED? –THE ACCEPTANCE BY THE PEOPLE OF THE LAW OF VAGRANCY– SAYS THE CUBAN LEADER, LEGISLATION BY WHICH IT IS CONSIDERED NEAR CRIMINAL NOT TO BE CONNECTED IN A STABLE WAY TO CENTERS OF WORK, –IT HAS BEEN A TREMENDOUS POLITICAL ADVANCE OF THE PEOPLE. BUT THESE SAME WORKERS WHO HAVE UNDERSTOOD PARASITISM AS A CRIME, HAVE STILL NOT UNDERSTOOD IN AN EQUAL WAY THE IMPORTANCE OF PRODUCTIVITY IN WORK, THE TAKING PROPER ADVANTAGE OF WORKING HOURS–.

CONTINUED?TLM?MP10.422.GMT

PL–8

FOURTH ADDITION TO PL–4 (WITH FIDEL CASTRO

AND RIGHT THERE A QUESTION POINTBLANK AT THE STUDENTS CLOSEST BY: –WHAT ABOUT YOU? HOW MUCH DO YOU STUDY? DO YOU

REALLY UNDERSTAND THE PROBLEM THAT YOU HAVE TO GIVE YOUR MAXIMUM TO YOUR STUDIES. AS A MISSION GIVEN YOU BY THE REVOLUTION—?

THE QUESTION BRINGS OUT A FEW AFFIRMATIVE ANSWERS? BUT NOT MARRIED AND THEREFORE SHE HAS OTHER PROBLEMS AFFIRMATIVE ANSWERS, BUT NOT VERY DECISIVE. A GIRL ASKS TO SPEAK, SHE EXPLAINS THAT SHE IS MARRIED AND THEREFORE HAS OTHER PROBLEMS TO RESOLVE AND HAS TROUBLE STUDYING. —WHY DON'T YOU PUT YOUR HUSBAND TO COOKING TOO—? WAS THE PRIME MINISTER'S ANSWER. —WE SPLIT IT UP— THE GIRL SAID, —BUT WE STILL HAVE SOME PROBLEMS TO GET THE MOST OUT OF STUDYING—.

THEN FIDEL CASTRO MADE HIS CURIOSITY EVEN MORE PRECISE: —IF YOU COMPARE YOURSELVES TO THE VIETNAMESE STUDENTS WHO ARE IN CUBA, HOW WOULD YOU DEFINE YOUR SUBMISSION TO STUDY? DO YOU STUDY MORE OR LESS THAN THE VIETNAMESE?—

AFTER SOME CONSULTING THE LARGE GROUP CAME TO THE CONCLUSION THAT THEY REALLY DID STUDY SOMEWHAT LESS THAN THE VIETNAMESE WHO HERE TOO AND AT THE TASK ASSIGNED THEM ARE AN EXAMPLE OF SACRIFICE AND CONCENTRATION IN WORK.

THE PRIME MINISTER THEN ASKED WHETHER OR NOT IT WOULD BE NECESSARY FOR CUBAN STUDENTS ALSO CONSIDER AS A TASK OF FIRST POLITICAL IMPORTANCE THE OBTAINING OF THE MAXIMUM EFFORT IN STUDIES WHICH THE PEOPLE PAY FOR AND WHICH COST MANY SACRIFICES FOR THE POPULATION.

CONTINUED/MP10.50GMT

PL—

FIFTH LAST ADDITION TO PL—4 WITH FIDEL CASTRO

FIDEL CASTRO IMMEDIATELY EXPLAINS THE RESOURCES THAT THE REVOLUTION HAS PUT TO USE IN THE FIELD OF EDUCATION, HEALTH AND CARE OF THE ELDERLY—. SOMETIMES MORE RESOURCES THAN WE COULD REALLY AFFORD, BUT WHICH WERE ABSOLUTELY NECESSARY BECAUSE THEY ARE THINGS NO ONE CAN DO WITHOUT—.

FINALLY HE EXHORTED THE STUDENTS TO CONTRIBUTE TO THE IDEOLOGICAL STRENGTHENING OF THE UNIVERSITY. HE ALSO ADVISED THEM TO BE VERY CAREFUL ABOUT WHOM THEY ELECTED AS MEMBERS OF THE FEDERATION OF UNIVERSITY STUDENTS AND OF THE YOUTH ORGANISMS OF THE COMMUNIST PARTY. —WATCH OUT FOR ARRIVISTES. FOR OPPORTUNISTS WHO SOMETIMES POSE AS REVOLUTIONARIES. KNOW HOW TO TELL THEM. ALWAYS ELECT THE BEST. THOSE WHO DON'T GO AFTER POSITIONS, WHO DON'T THINK ABOUT THEMSELVES AND ARE READY TO GIVE THEIR ALL FOR THE REST—.

A FEW MOMENTS AFTER THREE HOURS AND DOZENS OF QUESTIONS, HE GOT INTO HIS SMALL CAR AGAIN AND WENT AWAY AS RAPIDLY AS HE HAD ARRIVED. HE INVITED SOME OF THE STUDENT LEADERS TO COME TALK WITH HIM. —I'M NOT KIDNAPPING THEM, I'LL GIVE THEM BACK IN A LITTLE WHILE—, THE VISITOR FINALLY SAID.

TLM/MP10.55GMT

Why are you debasing me? Francine had asked going up the boulevard in the midnight undertow, mingling with vague clusters, groups on corners, a lumpen of Algerians and Spaniards and local pimps, offers from the shadows of doorways, *cochon* movie, fortune-tellers, the smell of French fries as rancid as the music from the bars, oh baby, how can I explain that that's not it, that's not how it is, even if you were right because you are besides, logic can't cut in this and that's how precisely out of two opposing reasons who can tell what spark might jump, look at that old woman picking up butts and mouthing God knows what ancient curse of misery, a kind of end-of-the-world balance with these privileged witnesses who are naturally you and I, because it can't be Lanza del Vasto or Señora Puchulu Gándara seeing how that filthy hand picking up butts in order to put together her early morning smoke is the best Western summary of the seventies.

"I know all that," Francine said, "I know all that by heart, you don't have to come on like a dime-store Aquinas to verify all the inevitable filth."

"You said it, baby, your speech was fine but at the end you said that little word that's just as inevitable in your weltanschauung, for your world and mine these things are always inevitable, naturally, but we're wrong, watch out for that black man who sure as hell is going to vomit on the sidewalk, and so you see, that's why I need you tonight, you by my side spitting in my face without knowing it, or wanting to. Look, if I had just a drop of decency left I'd go lie down over there so that black man in his cups could puke on top of me, but when you know the themes of all of Mozart's quartets by heart you realize that it's impossible, what the fuck, and yet and yet and yet."

"You, we are drunk too," Francine said. "Let's go home, Andrés. I know, you'll look at me from the side, you'll say sure, you'll make me some tea and you'll tuck me in. I promise you I won't but let's get out of here, I can't take any more of it."

It was a bar like any other, the whiskey tasted like kerosene, the whores along the bar and everybody feeling so well there in that parenthesis of drinks and low lights, while they were already going up the Rue des Abbesses holding each other around the waist, Francine had asked about the mission, twice she'd slowed down to ask, What mission? and I could have explained it to her, stopping right there and explaining it to her, this is how it is, I have to or I must, either starting with that moment or another moment I'm going to begin to, but finally the bar and our remaining silent as if waiting although there was nothing to wait for, impossible to say anything about that thing that was like a barbed-wire fence in the night, a wall that rose up beyond the field of action of two hands held upward, the black bulk, the halt with his disc brakes on all four wheels, and then just telling her the dream in detail, the movie theater with the screens at right angles, the absurdity of so much light before and then as if to limit the black nothing of the medium better, what had happened before the waiter had come to get me and before I came back to the theater knowing something that precisely I didn't know, the inconceivable absurd, you see, baby, I was in a movie, that's for sure, but what movie, girl, when you come to think of it, a movie is something important at the end of the world, how many things begin for us in a movie theater or on a bus, the things that happened to Dante in a cloister or on the banks of the Arno have changed location, epiphanies happen in a different way, you're on the Bratislava express and right there, over your head, the new mantic holes, the jukebox oracles, the hallucinations on the banks of the TV, how about movies, if you think about it, remember that visual fatigue makes us more receptive, although in this case I was only dreaming but who knows if when we're asleep we don't go on burning the same as when we're awake, wait, don't move, girl, I would say that a fly has fallen into your whiskey."

"How strange, a fly at this hour of the night."

"You're right, it's almost inconceivable because even they have their timetables, but it must be a poet fly or something like that."

"Get it out," Francine asked.

"It would be better if I ordered you another whiskey, my finger isn't any cleaner than the fly in spite of what our self-denying little teachers taught us about the extreme filthiness of these insects. Well, taste it, it's probably better than it was before, everything's a question of proportions; Lonstein told me once that in some of the theaters in his neighborhood the stink of the audience is so horrible that the only way to purify the air around is to cut an enormous fart."

"Yes, it's better than it was before," Francine said. "It's proper for a fly to fall into my glass, it's not worth wasting money on another; everything's fine just the way it is."

"Oh no it isn't, girl, don't force me into the therapeutic slap to invert the pole of hysteria. Sure, it's better this way, you smile between tears like Andromache, except that I haven't got anything of Hector about me, goddamn it."

There, at that moment, precisely at that point, Ludmilla would have said bloop. But each to his own system, Francine lowered her head and rubbed her fingers rapidly across her eyes. Andrés put the fly on the edge of the ashtray, the fly dragged itself along like an expressionist ballerina and gave off a buzzing that was the forerunner of total drunkenness or imminent flight; they studied it in silence until the creature had warmed its turboreactors enough and took off for the back of the neck of a mulatto fairy in the back of the room who was kissing a gentleman with a learned air. Smoking, looking once more into the eyes of Francine who had rationally taken advantage of her pocket Kleenex, Andrés began to retell the dream in great detail, Fritz Lang came into the bar with his Teuton belly, the waiter and the Cuban and the unidentifiable friend were sitting down with them, lasting as in the movies up to the last reel, accompanying them from near and from far, with that being there and not being there of all images, now you can see that I was right, epiphanies take place today in the midst of flies and drinking bouts and smoldering cigarette butts, every day has its dog tonight. Don't look at me that way, I'll explain it to you Cartesianly, there's no use pretending that your diplomas can carry you that far, girl.

"Where's the bottle of milk?" Ludmilla wanted to know in a morning way. "What would you rather have, toast or fried eggs?"

"You're completely mad," Marcos said looking at her with surprise. "Breakfast? Bottle of milk? You've been having auditory and lactic hallucinations, child, no one has ever left a bottle of milk here, be advised."

"A while back something sounded like a bottle of milk against the door, it's a sound that refreshes the soul and what they called *revilo gnik* in Cracow. You don't think I'm going to breakfast on bitter *mate*, I won that war a long time back and it cost me all the legions of Varus, I don't intend to start again."

"Here, Polonette, we breakfast on good black coffee and plenty of it and cup after cup matched by cigarettes. If you want milk there's a stand on the corner, it's no worse in a can than it is fresh. One thing I do know, somewhere there has to be a package of cookies, I'll find it for you."

The first sun of morning was slipping down alongside the bed, began climbing up over their feet. Ludmilla put the blanket and sheet aside—it had almost been cold at dawn, they were lazily coming out of a long skein of heat and dreams—to take a close look at Marcos's stomach and thighs; the mark of the kick deserved Bonnard's signature, all in old gold, perverse reds, and parrot blues. It must have hurt you a lot, something like that isn't just for free/If I didn't die last night it's because I'm immortal, Polonette/Bloop/What about you, now that we're into it, explain that bruise there/Put your hand there, not that way, more open, now close it a little/Oh/You see/But it doesn't hurt you/You've got a guilty conscience, eh/No, but if we go on like this, Lonstein will have work for sure/Why did you get circumcised if you're not Jewish?/Because it hurt me, Polonette, and according to some people you come out losing sensitivity/Did you notice any difference?/At first I did, but it must have been because it hadn't formed scar tissue completely and I saw stars/A man's sex is so strange, I'll never get used to it, when they walk around the room with all that swinging I get the feeling that it must be so heavy, so uncomfortable/You're dying with envy, Freud said so, and something else, Polonette, calling it a sex is silly, anyone would think you'd learned Spanish through a correspondence course/It really was through correspondence but a very personal one/Ah, from mouth to mouth like saving the life of a drowning man, but then please do me the favor of saving the terms sex and act of love for tea with the nice little nuns/Do you think it's so important?/Yes, because that type of vocabulary links us to the Vip/I don't understand/You'll understand, Polonette, you're like the one I told you who still hasn't gotten over a lecture on onanism that Lonstein foisted on him/What about you, why do you say onanism now that we're on it, bloop?/Whap, bullseye, said Marcos laughing, now you can see how the Vip looks after us, it's hard to get away from him but it has to be done, Polonette, we won't get anywhere if we're afraid of him because of these things and lots of others/It's obvious that you're between thirty and forty because damned if the kids today worry about those things, they look at each other without all that paralyzing vocabulary, they laugh like crazy about such problems/We know that, Polonette, but it so happens that things like the Screwery aren't done by them, they're too wrapped up in festivals and the hippie or yippie life or the map to get to Katmandu, they're going to be the heirs if people like us succeed in flipping the pancake, the problem is fated and eternal, it's old-timers like us who take the armored train and get ourselves killed in the jungles of Bolivia or Brazil, at least on the leadership level, understand me well, and so the problem is still ours, it doesn't matter if the kids piss laughing when they listen to what I'm telling you, but what does worry me, the question of the moment, is for us to free ourselves so we won't ruin the stew pot for them when the time comes for us to write our decalogues/*Concha peluda y pija colorada*, said Ludmilla/You bring out that expression every chance you get, but I don't know if you sense that it's rather vulgar/Andrés and Patricio said that it was quite fashionable/Put it away for great occasions, but there you have it, *pija* is better than sex when you're the way we are now, actually there's not too great a need to use those words but if the time comes don't weaken, Polonette, after all, *pija* is a beautiful word, more personal than penis, for example, right out of an anatomical treatise, or virile member, which always made me think of Roman history, probably because of their togas/Yes, *pija* sounds pretty in Argentine, I like it better than the Spanish *polla*/A matter of taste, you know, I think that the Galician *picha* and the Cuban *pinga* are fine, or the Chilean *pico*, which it might be said is a rare case of masculinization because all of the Argentinian or Latin American variants are always feminine, call it *pinchila* or *poronga* or whatever. Now be aware that if I'm right about one thing it's that using those words, I want to say kiss your *concha* and not your vagina, you get kicked into that other reverse, that of the Vip let's say, because there are ants in language too, Polonette, what good is it to bring down the Vips if we're going to keep on being prisoners of the system, that's why in very revolutionary novels from Uruguay, Peru, or Buenos Aires, from the theme up you read for example that a girl had a velvety vulva, as if that word could be pronounced or even thought without accepting at the same time the system on the inside, notice how when all's said and done the one I told you is content with Lonstein's stuff, something came out clear, I think, and besides I don't know how to tell you but you'll have to understand all this without being in the thing itself/Bloop, said Ludmilla, actually only kids keep using sexual terms all the time, they're really not necessary/Of course not, Polonette, but when you come right down to it you can call these balls or nuts and that's that, it's neither better nor worse than testicles, in the same way that *concha* is a most beautiful word and since it means shell the very essence of Botticelli's painting, if you'll notice, and with all the sensual and aesthetic associations you want, and we fuck, you and I fuck, and when I read somewhere that people live together or copulate I wonder if they're the same people or if they have special privileges/Well, I call it making love, I like that better, it comes across in so many languages and it's like a mystery, because we really do it as a challenge to death or something like that, telling it that it's a bad-smelling marsupial, and that's enough for now because I want some coffee even if there isn't any milk and find those cookies for me.

"In our language, and not just on the Rio de la Plata, the great problem lies on the side of the ass," Marcos meditated aloud, looking precisely at Ludmilla's as she in turn was looking out the window and discovering with enormous enthusiasm the presence of a hardware store across the way. "I don't know how they handle it in your country, Polonette, but with us it's a hassle. *Culo*, ass, is generic, its special value is as a popular and stylistically pure improvement on *nalgas*, buttocks, which always has a butcher-shop sound to it, but the problem lies with *ano*, anus, a horrendous term if ever there was one/Once you called it *ojete*, eyelet, Ludmilla said remembering a precise situation and wrinkling her nose a little/Yes, but it doesn't work, there's something about it I don't like although a lot of people probably use it without any problem. The great marvel of the English and Yankees is the question of asshole, which translated into Spanish is lugubrious and too topographical and descriptive, but I suppose that for them the direct meaning gives way to a more manageable and approachable image of the thing. I really don't know what to call it, *siete*, seven, is unsatisfactory, *orto*, sunrise, I like a little better but not entirely, *carozo*, peach pit, has no meaning. *Pocito*, little well, maybe, that's all I need now, setting about to invent terms, but it's O.K., don't you think. Let's see that little well, give me that little well, yeah but in the end I fell headfirst into the asshole since it means the same thing in a more poetic way, *pozo*, well, is prettier than *agujero*, hole, the Yankees could even call it asswell, which is good for wordplays too."

"There's a hardware store across the way," Ludmilla informed.

"You leave me thunderstruck," Marcos said.

It was hard to be aware of much at that hour and after so many drinks, fatigue obliging her to lean on me more and more as I crossed the bridge talking about Fritz Lang and Mademoiselle Antinéa, wondering if they could give us a room in the Hotel Terrass, the problem of no luggage, the obvicouple as the little rabbi would have said, but when the old man caught sight of the tail of the fifty-franc note, your best room with bath of course, on the top floor with a balcony, then you are familiar with the hotel, sir, of course I am and I've sent a whole lot of friends, don't worry, we'll leave before breakfast and the changing of the guard, the change is yours besides the fifty francs but give me the best room and don't forget about the balcony and mineral water, oh, and soap, French avarice knows no limits in these cases, soap and towels for two.

Why, Francine had asked vaguely, a taxi would be better and you come to my apartment, then I had to explain to her, we were crossing the last span of the bridge and I was looking at the balconies of the hotel knowing that Francine couldn't imagine that we were going there, that I was taking her to a room with a balcony overlooking a certain city I wanted to show her, it's better this way, baby, a hotel room from time to time is a kind of minitherapy, unfamiliar furniture, irresponsibility, the dazzling fact that in the morning you go, leaving everything in a mess and behind you, think about the absconsive metaphysics, everything in a mess and behind you and they won't do anything to you, no one will come and tell you you have bad manners, one doesn't leave a proper home with the soap on the night table and the towel on the window latch, understand that when I sleep at your place I'm ever so careful not to spray the mirror when I shower, I hang everything on its own little hook and still I remember very well that one morning you scolded me in a nice way for having got the toothbrushes mixed up, it must have been intolerable for you.

"No, I just thought I had to tell you, that's all, if I put out a toothbrush and a towel for you it was so that you would use them. All right, we'll go to the hotel, I hope it isn't too far."

"We're right in front of it, girl, now we've got the problem of going in without any luggage because this is a come-eel-foe hotel, you can't imagine, the manager maintains a whole stack of Judeo-Christian values and so you see, couples by the hour or the night voll verboten, but now you'll see how the values in question give way before these others which have a little number and a portrait with wig and everything, Voltaire, Louis XIV, or Molière, just watch the effect from this sofa, the ladies always stay behind in these crises and tend to look at the floor."

"At least we'll get some sleep," Francine said, "at this hour any place at all will suit me fine."

I seated her on a sofa before going up to the night clerk in his shadowy cubicle, promising her a long lustral sleep and the morning croissants, and therefore after so much precision concerning the towels and the mineral water he brought up a bottle of cognac and the ice cubes and even that breakfast that belonged to another world because night had still not ended and on this side there was cognac and balconies overlooking the Montmartre cemetery which Francine would not see for a while as the first thing he did was to draw the heavy drapes as if inside he was ashamed of what awaited beneath the balcony. I noticed in the night clerk a tendency to tell me about the 1914 war or something similar, and after checking victuals and hygienic resources (Francine was testing the mattress with both hands, with application and efficiency, sinking in and almost bouncing back to make sure that the foam mattress wasn't full of lumps) I took him out into the corridor and fulfilled that gesture, mechanical for so many people, of double-locking the door, which was not at all mechanical for me now that there was a haven, a room, a delimited zone and Francine and I there precisely where I had wanted us to be that night after the fly in the whiskey and the black stain on what had been Fritz Lang (not to mention the Ludmilla stain, the cold stone at the mouth of the stomach). It's not bad, Francine said, at least the light's good and the bed is perfect, let's go to bed, shall we, I can't take any more.

He was still kind of inspecting the bolt and the lock on the door, looking around momentarily, walking visually about the room; when he heard me he made a vague gesture, came over smiling and sat me down on the edge of the bed, he kneeled down looking at me with the same attention with which he had checked out the room, he began to take off my shoes, to stroke my ankles. You're cold, baby, you still need a drink, let's have a smoke in bed talking about what people talk about when fatigue turns its creatures loose and proposes answers to enigmas.

"Andrés, Andrés," letting him talk as if from so far away, letting him undress me ceremoniously, "Andrés, beyond all sanction, quite simply what's left for me to do is not see you any more, exchange you for some Scandinavian novels or ski vacations."

"But of course," Andrés said as if surprised, his hands on the clasp of the bra, "I know it myself, girl, I know that I'd have to exchange myself for something else, in any case nothing to do with skiing but something else and that's what we've got to talk about, I mean I've got to talk with part of that bottle of cognac to unblock things and a great whack applied to mental stoppers, if it can take it. I wonder why you have such a fuzzy little belly, so delicate, and it makes me tender and I don't want that, tonight I don't want tenderness, baby, I don't know what I need but in any case it's not tenderness, I don't ask for it and I'm not looking for it and in that sense it's fine that Ludmilla broke up with me, it's archwhorishly fine because it couldn't have gone on like that and it's the fault of all of us, you and her who are incapable of changing bookcases and me who all of a sudden is this cretin here in search of some kind of clarity, to erase the black stain, know what that guy in the movies told me."

"Cover me," I asked him trying to get my legs free of his, and Andrés still kneeling looked at me with surprise and started to laugh, poor thing, naked as a corncob and me giving her the cosmic baloney, of course I'll put her to bed, baby, I'll even put two blankets on her so that the vasometer mechanisms or whatever organize their informational circuits and produce the thermic response, without counting that little drink that we're taking right now, the old man had brought up five-star Martell no less and opened it besides, that's a brain. Oh, speaking of black stains

> he was getting undressed, looking at me, unbuttoning his pants very slowly, letting his fingers fall asleep on each button, his hands on their own while he

you probably know where there's a place called Verrières. Yes, of course, it's on the Sceaux line, the Métro you take at Luxembourg, it must be about ten miles south of Paris,

> slowly pulling his shirt out of his pants, without having finished unbuttoning them, beginning to unbutton his shirt

with some rather pretty woods, Andrés. Oh, so that's where it is. Where what? What Ludmilla explained to me this morning at the hour of the twilight of the gods. The gods? But of course, girl, or while Wotan, who I came to be, witnessed the downfall of his kingdom, Ludmilla, a kind of maddened Brünnhilde, was making ready to enter a different world which they've nicknamed the Screwery for lack of a better name. You told me something about that, I don't remember too well. Wait, girl, one more step forward and you'll see it in the papers and you'll be nice and quietly quiet, of course, because the pom-day-tare are going to brule, you know

> taking off his shoes and looking at them one by one, lost on who knows how many simultaneous planes, talking to me, getting undressed, looking at the room as if it were something extraordinary, examining the shoe and putting it on the floor, taking off

Of course, Andrés, although maybe you'd better not tell me anything, it's not so necessary for me to know

his shirt and pants little by little, letting them fall onto the rug like dried leaves, completely unaware of them, putting his thumbs into the elastic of his shorts

Bah, girl, I don't know much either but it would seem that those chumps trust us who knows why, Marcos is like that, Marcos is an incredible madman and now Verrières, well, making the necessary summary I warn you that something big is going to happen, buy the newspaper.

"Go to bed," Francine said, "you've got goose pimples."

"Damned if I don't," Andrés said letting his shorts slip down facing Francine, leaving them on the floor with the rest of his clothes, "the black stain is that, girl, an area of goose flesh that takes in precisely what is most important, a blackout that puts Jung and Pichon Rivière to shame. These glasses aren't bad for the Martell, wait till I put the lamp on the floor so that we can talk with that special grace that a penumbra gives."

"Talking," said Francine, "yes, talking one more time, that is you'll talk and as always I'll serve as a wall for the rebounds, so you can pick up the ball and throw it again, so you can look for yourself in the echo, in my useless answers. The same as when we make love, the other wall, that other search where I don't count, I've known it for a long time and it doesn't bother me much either any more, but I've known it for so long, Andrés, like this hotel and this room and our being drunk or tired, the false bridges, the false dialogues. Come, love, you're going to catch cold."

Two pillows five stars two blankets two glasses the lamp on the floor the almond-like light and the silence; Andrés slid up against Francine, they covered themselves up to the waist, a perfect Etruscan sarcophagus, the couple looking at each other and smiling from a time outside of time, so close to the real tombs down there that Francine had never seen, that were there as if waiting behind the drapes, by the far-down foot of the balcony against the night. Baby, none of this will probably be real for you when you wake up and we leave, there'll be another day and Madame Franck will tell you what happened at the bookstore, you'll buy a new blouse, compensations of that sort, but understand, girl, understand that I'm not debasing you out of evil, I'm going to have to enter that thing they call tomorrow too and especially that thing they call Friday, and before that I had to do something like this, say because I'm a coward or a sadist, but it's not true, say rather balance and inventory, something you should know as a bookseller, a balance sheet of the end of the world, understand that, something that had to come after Fritz Lang and then we have to go through it tonight and know whether we're going to survive or not, whether what I'm going to show you tomorrow is heads or tails and when I say heads, we call it *cruz*, cross, I know what I'm talking about, believe me.

"It's a good-by, right," Francine said. "In your way, with your ritual, with your lamp on the floor, your glass in your hand."

"I don't know, baby, how can I know yet, the black stain is there, every time I get to the door of that room and I stop seeing and knowing, I go into the black stain and I come out changed but without knowing why or for what reason."

"But how can I help you, Andrés, what can I do for you so that you can find it, so that you can remember."

"Just like that, you can do it like that, with that way of looking at me, with everything you're going to give me tonight, your hands and your mouth and every piece of your body and your intelligence weighing in the balance, that's how you'll help me know if we're going to survive Fritz Lang, I'm talking for my part but you're part of the world too even though you stay on this side, we're going to find out whether I have to go alone, whether there's still something for me to do or whether we'll keep on seeing each other like tonight or so many nights, accepting each other out of habit and words, whether the faithful daily dog will be waiting for me wagging its tail, the records and the books and my little apartment that Maple set up, until the first infarction or the gaudy cancer and self-pity, naturally, self-pity."

"You're going to leave, Andrés, you're going to leave," Francine repeated kissing me, slipping her now warm body under the covers. I let her reach the last caress while I sank my hands in her hair guiding her, almost obliging her to go farther down, telling her in her ear the first numbers of the inventory, who could know if it were true or not, whether at dawn we'd wake up alone forever or if we'd go out to the same croissants, the same taxi to start up again the soft play of telephone calls and meetings and the understanding smile of Madame Franck when we went up to the apartment as on so many occasions. I didn't let her continue even though she was moaning and looking for me, I moved her face away and made her sit up again, drink the cognac that brought tears to her eyes. You're going away, Francine repeated, you're going away, you're going away, Andrés. Pick it, he said, that's the end of the ceremony exactly, knowing if it's heads or tails, baby; I can't search with my reason any more, I have to go down these cognac steps with you and see if there's an answer in the basement, if you'll help me come out of the black stain, if you'll kick old Lang in the belly so he'll give up the combination of the safe. Come on, it's time now, come see before going down.

Pulling her because she didn't understand I got her out of bed and took her to the window; she might have been crying, I could feel her resisting, not understanding why I'd opened the drapes with a sweep of the hand, was opening the door to the balcony. I put my hand over her mouth so that she wouldn't cry out, naked we went out onto the balcony, I forced her over to the railing, under the purple light of Montmartre she saw the crosses and the stones, the coagulated geometry of the graves. She cried out, I think, I covered her mouth again, felt her kind of falling apart in my arms, I held her up against the balcony leaning over the cemetery, drinking in every cross and every piece of cast iron, the whole stupid perpetuation of the original mystery. I don't know if I understood then, I don't think I did, it must have been after other things, when I put her back into bed and covered her and made her drink another glass of cognac, opening her tight mouth for her, blowing on her face, falling on top of her with the caress of my whole body so that the warmth would return to her breasts and her thighs, now the inventory would continue, the night was long and there was so much time to witness the death of a petit bourgeois or his confirmation, to know whether the descent led to the other side of the black stain or would wrap it in complacency and nostalgia. Comedian, Francine would probably tell me at some moment, you'll always be what you have been, you'll always play your games with graves and women, comedian. But maybe on the balcony, there where she couldn't know anything else but her fright (because later on she told me between caresses that she'd been afraid I was going to throw her down into the cemetery) maybe while I made her look, made her know that Paris that she and I were denying through lies and routine and the dead cock of every day, yes, maybe it was there that the black stain was erased for an ungraspable instant, was erased and leaped out again with all of its spiders onto my face, but something in me had seen the other side, there was something like the final figure of the inventory, a finished balance, without words or behavior to follow: a brusque fulfilling, a breaking of branches. Now we could begin drinking cognac, we could begin to caress each other with cadence, forget the balcony.

What the one I told you would have liked was to have been able to tell what happened from the fear and trembling of the Vip's jowls in Roland's car, from the face of the Vipess when they let her out on an esplanade on the Pontoise side, an absurd place if ever there was one to go from the Parc Monceau to Verrières but which Lucien Verneuil, copilot and pistol in the trembling belly of the Vip, thought would be rather useful to throw the police off the track since a general although for a moment rather incoherent search had already been launched. A pity but it wouldn't come out, at the moment of taking up the word to tell about the events as is called for in a good narrative, from so much get into the car or I'll blow a hole in your belly, the gaudy grimace on the part of the Vipess as her Dorothy Gray number eight makeup turned to the left as she was convulsed by a colic that put Pacific megatons to shame, Roland piloting like Barney Coldfield a quarter of an inch away from the red taillights and already a whistle that shook their spines down to the coccyx and if you weren't a little more careful below that, out of all that the only thing that came to the one I told you was a general impression of total confusion above or below the absurdity of things minutely synchronized, that scandal in the joy of improvisation that others would have called history, Lonstein escathouse-ology, and Ludmilla, the wisest of all, bloop. So that tiresqueal-turns at fifty, you can't do this to me, Patricio taking a close look at the Vipess as if it were a question of a batrachian especially ignored by Linnaeus, don't let me frighten you, lady, give me your purse, things that the one I told you found a little untellable, we're not going to lift your lipstick, it's just to put in these envelopes in so you'll know what to mail as soon as the post office opens, oh Beto what's going on good Lord, topical and typical phrases, the boredom of the one I told you until the arrival at the chalet, where the transfers were carried out in the midst of fragrant pines, a kind of nightingale singing in the neighboring forest, things only reserved for the panting, sweating Vip since the Vipess was already walking all by herself along an avenue that was rather lacking in businesses and other luminous aids, running insofar as her high heels would permit her until she ended up like a death rattle against the uniform of a watchman who began as was logical thinking that she was a whore running away from an angry pimp, then a greenhorn foreigner incapable of expressing two continuous ideas in the only language worthy of the name, and finally a great distribution of whistles and automatic alarms, a half-hour later the police station at full steam (the one I told you was losing control of his notes, let anything come out, what the fuck), calm yourself, madam, and tell us what happened, nom de Dieu call an interpreter, this old woman must be from some embassy, the clean little room on the first floor of the chalet, Marcos giving the Vip a cigarette, bring him a glass of cognac, he's all jelly, you can't do this to me, and Patricio lowering the pistol and looking at him slowly as in one by Raymond Chandler and telling him son of a bitch, lucky for you we're not the same, there's no parrot perch to string you up on here, Marcos cutting off the psychodrama, explaining to him in a few words the exchange and the alternatives, the Vip cognac gulp thinking Higinio you shitty son of a bitch, this was my protection you goddamned bastard, relative calumnies according to the one I told you because the Gi-ant with an emergency team was already taking care of the matter, a question of time for someone like Higinio so good for crises like this and with connections everywhere.

"They were horrible, horrible," the Vipess shouted, "they dragged us into the car, there were four of them, Beto couldn't do anything and the chauffeur seemed asleep, they must have drugged him with one of those curare darts, something like that, I read about it, yes, wait, let me explain, I've got something here, I swear, there were four of them and Beto's bodyguard is about to take out his revolver and what can I say the skinniest one puts the barrel of his gun to his head, you're not going to let yourself be killed for a hundred thousand francs a month, are you, but wait till I explain, an awful thing, they almost pulled Beto's jacket off, inside there were two more and when we came to, Beto and I were on the floor and those bandits right on top of us, I swear, with all those turns that made their knees and elbows dig in, an outrage, and in Paris, sir, and going through my alligator bag, I wonder if they took my vial of perfume I'm sure I had it when we went to dinner and leaving me like that in a neighborhood nobody knows, you can imagine what can happen to a woman all alone with that riffraff that thinks of only one thing, if at least they'd let me stay with Beto, good heavens, I walked and I walked, you can see the dress shoes I'm wearing and the rude watchman who refused to believe me, he'll have to be punished, wait, there were only these three envelopes, I saw them when they put them in my bag to be delivered, but I demand that

"There were only three envelopes," was all the interpreter translated to the special delight of the inspector. As for the letters, they were in perfect French and at the Quai d'Orsay there was already such a running back and forth that it's best not to talk about it, as well as what was happening in three or four Central and South American embassies, because that not even Dante in five volumes.

"I'd rather you didn't come," Marcos had said, and Ludmilla knew that he knew that it was useless to say so, that Verrières with those pretty woods where once she'd roamed with Andrés, that Verrières forever, bloop, I'm going with you, Marcos/All right, I can't forbid you because the other madwomen would rise up like one man, if I know them/We'll make you men lunch and take care of what hygiene and good habits call for/I don't think you'll have time, kid, this is opening up in exactly twenty-four hours and when we grab the Vip, you'll barely have time to make a few sandwiches/What do you want bologna or pâté/It doesn't make any difference as long as Lucien remembers to lay in a few bottles/Marcos, you still haven't gotten over the kicks you got/Polonette, here you are blaming the kicks after all you've done to me/Oh/Just what I said/What about me with these cramps in my forearms and these bruises, not to mention the dark rings under my eyes?/

> "Canal," said Gómez who used a pseudonym on the telephone, as if his own last name wouldn't have protected him just as well.
> "Yes."
> "They killed Lamarca."

The chalet belonged to Lucien Verneuil's mother, a lady who was taking her semiannual cure with the waters at Royan; Lucien had had more than enough time to prepare what was necessary, Marcos had reconnoitered the terrain at night and Patricio had walked around to fix the parameters as those in the know say. The closest neighbors were enduring their retirement three hundred yards away, with cedars interposed; after leaving the highway from Paris you came out onto a secondary road that led to the village, then little streets going this way and that so as not to run into the woods, a drive where an automobile barely fit, a right turn and the chalet among some pines with a wooden palisade fence and only two entrances. The idea had been to limit attendance as much as possible because retired persons might get nosy out of boredom, but it had soon been seen that the maenads demanded something that neither Oscar nor Gómez nor Patricio nor Marcos now slowly hanging up the telephone and looking at Ludmilla could deny or even prevent; in the Screwery there was no discrimination, why shouldn't the maenads be there making the sandwiches even though the celibates who were not French for nothing gave evidence of a disapproval that was received with general indifference. Let them come, Roland finally said, this is getting to look like a Sunday ball game. And now you, of course, Marcos said looking for another cigarette as if it were difficult for him to continue, now you, Polonette.

"What's wrong? Look at your face."

"I've had one like this several times these last two years, old girl, and I'll probably have one a few more times."

"Tell me," Ludmilla asked. The same as Oscar and Heredia, finishing the last-minute details in Verrières and looking at Susana with *Le Monde* hanging from one hand, limp like her, a saddened little rag.

Brésil

Le dernier grand dirigeant de la guérilla est tué par la police dans l'État de Bahia

Les autorités brésiliennes ont annoncé officiellement la mort du dirigeant révolutionnaire Carlos Lamarca, tué le vendredi 17 septembre au cours d'une fusillade avec les forces de l'ordre à Pintada, à 450 kilomètres de Salvador, dans l'Etat de Bahia.

Traqué depuis quarante et un jours par les services brésiliens de sécurité, Carlos Lamarca se reposait sous un arbre, en compagnie de son lieutenant, José Campos Barretas, et de sa compagne, Iara Iavelberg, lorsqu'il fut entouré par une vingtaine d'agents du centre d'opérations de la défense intérieure.

Selon la version officielle, José Campos a fait feu le premier, mais a été fauché par une rafale de mitraillette. Carlos Lamarca a été tué aussitôt après. Toujours selon les autorités, Iara Iavelberg, se voyant dans l'impossibilité de fuir, s'est suicidée.

Le corps de Lamarca a été transporté samedi à l'aérodrome militaire d'Ipitanga, où il a été identifié grâce à ses empreintes digitales Pour éviter d'être reconnu. le chef guérillero avait subi une operation de chirurgie faciale.

"They killed Lamarca," Susana said, for one time ready to translate without complaints, "Brazilian authorities officially announced the death of the revolutionary leader."

"I'm sorry to say I don't know who he was," Ludmilla said, "but I can read it on your face. I'm sorry, love."

"It can't be, goddamn it all to fucking hell," Heredia said snatching the paper from Susana and giving it back almost at once. "Keep reading, it can't be, but keep reading."

"He was sleeping under a tree along with his lieutenant José Campos Barretas and his companion Iara Iavelberg, when they were surrounded by twenty or so agents from the operations center of internal defense."

"Internal defense," said Heredia turning around and looking at the garden and the cedars through the window curtains.

"Oh," Ludmilla said feeling around for the bottle lost among papers and pillows. "I'm sorry, Marcos."

"According to the official version José Campos opened fire first but was brought down by a burst of machine-gun fire. Carlos Lamarca fell with the second burst. Still according to the version, and on seeing the impossibility of escape, Iara Iavelberg committed suicide."

"So neat, so perfect," Oscar said, "all there, really."

"How could I have known him," Marcos said, "Brazil is a long way from Córdoba, Polonette."

Heredia kept looking at the garden, his back still turned. Oscar thought that the night was going to be long, Susana was cutting out the item and putting it in her purse. But the night wasn't long, first Lucien Verneuil's face when he saw Ludmilla come in, Gladis upset by the lack of *yerba mate* in a suburban French house, things like that were not done, Ludmilla waiting for Gómez to explain Marcos's orders to Lucien Verneuil, chess between Oscar and Heredia, between Heredia and Gómez, between Gómez and Monique, the maenads in the kitchen before it got dark because afterwards general blackout so nothing for the retirees, quiet distribution of chores and posts, Heredia checkmate in eighteen moves, you don't drink it down in one swig, South

American savages, my grandmother gave it to my mother for her birthday, this is savored drop by drop, nom de Dieu, Gómez and Monique stalemate. A car passed along the drive, there was a kind of hit the dirt which was absolutely useless since no one could see them, that second of telling themselves the ants had been ahead of them, what if the police had been trailing them ever since the turquoise penguin and the speeches at Orly, Lucien Verneuil that it was the car of one of the retirees, first round of sandwiches at eight o'clock and with wine, this burgundy has been sleeping in the cellar for five years, don't be heavy on it or you'll be seeing double/O.K., take it easy, everything here is from the time of Pepin the Short, let's see if this salami has lost its taste from the fright it got at Waterloo/A good salami has its taste in the smell as long as one has reached the level of civilization necessary to catch it/There it is, he's better than Larousse for explanations/I shouldn't tell you but if you don't keep an eye on that bishop you're going to lose it, my love/You take care of your pieces and let me lose all by myself/O.K., let's see what you can do now/Oh shit/Light your cigarettes away from the windows, I don't trust the blinds or anything/He's seen all the James Bonds ever made/Come, Susana said to Ludmilla, come into the kitchen.

Gladis and Monique were about to follow them automatically as befit the behavior of the maenads, but something told them that it was better to leave them alone. Oscar watched them leave, lighted a cigarette far from the window but close to Lucien Verneuil in order to show his discipline, and Gladis sat down against him on the rug, accepted another cigarette from him, and they talked watching night come through the one hundred forty-seven slots in the venetian blind; they spoke about themselves most of all, that is about the next day, about Gómez's friend who would get them to Belgium if something went wrong and then Max whom they didn't know but that didn't matter, another crossing or some ship, decisions by Marcos and the Frenchmen, Russian dolls that would open successively until perhaps at some moment the lights of Ezeiza airport or the harbor and then more than ever total clandestineness, unless it were something quite different but still Russian dolls, flight, hiding place, false papers, perhaps separation and in any case always the risk and being alert, walls to leap over, on seeing the impossibility of escape Iara Iavelberg committed suicide, the unforeseeable other side of the wall, hands slashed by broken bottles, José Campos opened fire, and Heredia who knew Lamarca so well had had his back turned to them for a long time, Heredia who was now losing to Gómez in thirty-three moves and Lucien back and forth, a house cat felt-footed and vigilant, the night and the flashlight on the floor between two chairs, a lighthouse at the end of the world so that there wouldn't be so much head-breaking with so many steps and so much furniture inherited from ancestors, suddenly Oscar wondered why Gladis, how was it possible that finally Gladis there with them, in the final Screwery, at no time had he thought whether or not he had the right to get her mixed up in the Screwery and Gladis so sure of herself and like someone going to a party in the suburbs among cedars and drinks, that tranquil decision of Gladis knowing that they would fire her from Aerolíneas Argentinas, that everything could go to hell, a jump and on top even if her hands were bleeding a little, and he'd told her you're great, you're really something as if Paris really was a feast with Gertrude Stein and everything, as if the broken bottles hadn't cut her wrists before the gallop through the brush and the first whiplashes. He asked her in a very low voice, kissing her hair, and Gladis snuggled up against him and only after a while, after four masterful moves by Heredia against Gómez, did she tell him that she didn't know, that it was fine that way, that she was afraid, that it was starting to get cold, that she loved him so much. And besides she'd done well in not following the maenads because in the kitchen there was talk of other things at floor level and vague shadowy bites into a common sandwich, Susana out of pure instinct and not asking anything, rather explaining that Lonstein was taking care of Manuel and she hoped he wouldn't let him get too close to the mushroom because that awful thing is surely poisonous, the worst that could happen would be if the one

I told you or Andrés went up to the little rabbi's apartment, a general distraction and Manuel taking advantage and pouncing like a leopard to gobble up the mushroom or set fire to the closet, biting once more the already nibbled sandwich and passing the end of it with a sigh to Ludmilla who finished it before she was asked to give it back. But the one I told you had no thoughts of attending Lonstein's baby-sitting, and as for me yes but not for that reason but because Lonstein was the only one I had left at the end of the day and at some moment I would go up to see him, to ask him a couple of things.

"I love him," Ludmilla said gathering up a crumb by touch, "things happened terribly fast with the kick and the grappa compresses, but don't think it was a stereotype, Susana."

"I know you two a little, eh," Susana said, "you haven't got the slightest bit of stereotype about you."

"And I think he loves me, and I'm afraid," Ludmilla said, with which there were now two in that house who were afraid, three with Susana because Patricio would be lying in wait seventy-five yards from the place where the Vip was having dinner and Susana knew it and thought about the ants and Manuel and the next day, about Patricio seventy-five yards from the place and it was already seven-fifteen and in less than three hours Patricio and Marcos and Roland will have carried out the plan and be coming with the Vip, or will not have carried it out because they ran into ants or cops and so what's the use of thinking and being still more afraid. Better to keep on talking now that Ludmilla had said it that way, as if it had been another bite of the sandwich, you know, I wanted to take care of where he'd been kicked and when I saw him all black and blue, poor thing, bloop. Marcos accepted of course, Susana said, twisting with laughter. Naturally, said Ludmilla, he did very well. Well, now I understand why you're here, said Susana who really had understood since the word go, you're the kind who puts herself on the line for her man if it comes to that, some girl.

"I want to be wherever he is, and besides this is an off day at the theater."

"The Screwery does things well. I'm glad in the end, you know. Of course if this ends up badly . . . Well, tell me a little bit, I've got a terrible nature for prying and there's so much time till they get here with the Vip, wait till I make some Nescafé and then you can tell me."

"Bloop," said Ludmilla curling up like a kind of floor mop. "Susana, tell me about Lamarca, I'm ashamed, this morning when they told Marcos . . . I've got so much to learn, I still don't understand anything. To think that everything started with a few used matches and a penguin, tell me if that isn't like a happening."

Guerrilla group robs over 9,000 wigs on waterfront

Five people who said that they belonged to a commando of the People's Revolutionary Army (ERP) attacked a truck belonging to a business firm and stole 9,326 wigs valued at 50 million pesos.

The act took place yesterday afternoon at 3:30 at the corner of San Martín and Eduardo Madero in the dock area of this capital city.

At that time a truck belonging to the Refiart Company, driven by Angel Sperati, was boarded by five unknown people who were traveling in a private car. After obliging the driver to get out of the truck and transferring him to the car, two of the guerrillas took the wheel of the truck and fled with the cargo.

The truck was found empty a little while later on the corner of Libertador and Dorrego.

"They really give the impression that they know how to move the pieces," Oscar said at the precise moment in which Heredia saw his king mated and frowning witnessed Gómez's Wellingtonian smile. It was almost night and they were playing by the stump of a candle protected by a number of *La Opinión* which Susana had brought them from Patricio for their amusement.

"Look at that, they ripped off nine thousand wigs," Oscar said trying to mix the story in with the chess. "Explain it to Lucien to see if he'll stop pacing like a St. Bernard, the French need a true Rio de la Plata vision, things like that don't happen in these tired old countries."

As might be imagined, the story of the wigs seemed completely incomprehensible to Lucien, more concerned about the noises outside than the activities of the ERP in a city so abstract at that place and at that time, but Gómez and Heredia agreed with Oscar that the destiny of the wigs was rather uncertain, except that they already had a Japanese buyer assured, or something along those lines, exports with equivocal destinies and unpronounceable ports, Thai whorehouses or Yemenite harems. The distribution of new sandwiches and hot Nescafé brought them together in a corner of the floor where the candle could burn without Lucien's roaring; with nine o'clock past, something like a countdown began to drip its numbers slowly on the nerves, Nicolino Locche's last bout, the nine thousand wigs, the meeting between Nixon and Pompidou in the Azores, Glauber Rocha's films, the shadow of Lucien Verneuil back and forth from window to window, Ludmilla dying with fatigue letting herself be carried along by the cooing of the others, Susana pale and tense making the best jokes, looking at the blinds at every moment, that tendency of couples to get closer, Monique leaning on Gómez, Oscar with a hand lost in Gladis's hair, last-minute birds in the cedars, dogs in the distance, long smoking and asking for more coffee, pursued for forty-one days by Brazilian security services, Carlos Lamarca was resting under a tree in the company of. Nine thousand wigs, Oscar's hand

and soul

trámite la afiliación al Instituto Verificado
CORREO ARGENTINO. Tar. red. Conc. Nº 68 (Central B y S

Buenos Aires, Miércoles 8 de Dicie

Massive turnout for burial of murdered student

Mar del Plata students stage violent demonstrations in center of city

MAR DEL PLATA, 7—Shortly after 7 P.M. at the end of an assembly of the students of the local Faculty of Architecture—where means of protest were voted over the death of the student Silvia Ester Filler—violent demonstrations broke out in the center of this city.

coming and going through Gladis's genuine hair, nine thousand wigs, mother of God, and Monique asking for details, imagine a truck with nine thousand wigs, the truck is nothing, Oscar said, the thing is transferring them and they don't say how, hell, they hired nine thousand baldies who were passing in a column, in Mar del Plata students hold violent demonstrations in the center of the city, translate it for the messieurs dames, Susanita, I don't feel like it, yes, you're so good and consistent and we know you love us, sweetie pie, two shots in the head, Silvia Filler, forty-five caliber pistol, eighteen years old, student of architecture. That paper of yours is amusing, Lucien Verneuil said, oh, that it is, old man, for things like this, wigs and the shooting of an eighteen-year old girl my country is a shining light. Talk more softly, merde, Lucien Verneuil said, the retirees have supersonic ears, I don't even trust my old lady's canary bird. Maybe that's why I found it half-smothered, Monique said, you'd put a quilt over its cage, brute. Silvia, Oscar thought and would have liked to tell Gladis but better not to, Gladis half-asleep purring under the fingers that were slowly petting her hair, Silvia a name like so many others, eighteen years old, two bullets in the head, among the little women maddened by the full moon and carnival dances there must have been some Silvia too, statistically more than probable out of a hundred and fifty girls going over the wall, wait for me, Silvia, give me your hand, Silvia, don't leave me behind, and the broken bottles tearing a clenched fist, the galloping coming closer and closer, Silvia, Silvia, how everything tended to be the same, to be a Screwery far away and nearby, in Verrières or La Plata, Gladis or Silvia, everything was Argentina for Oscar eyes closed, fingers working their way through the warm hair, they ripped off nine thousand wigs, Iara Iavelberg committed suicide, a forty-five caliber pistol, violent demonstrations in the center of the city, Mardelplatalaplatamardelríodelaplata, eh, Oscar protested getting up suddenly, if I fall asleep now I might miss the fight, past nine-thirty, hmm. But before going to make himself another Nescafé he could keep on accepting, almost understanding that mixture in which more and more there was a unity, Silvia and Gladis and Iara, a conspiracy of girls and the Screwery so far away, suddenly even the mushroom had a meaning, the total absurdity of the little rabbi demanding reverence for something that Lucien Verneuil would never understand, but Lucien could in turn be part of a system that nobody knew, perhaps not even himself, rendering obscure obediences to what he thought was pure and practical and dialectical reasons, nine thousand baldies filed slowly in and came out with wigs on, oh no, it's fine now, goddamn it, if I really fall asleep I'll make a fool of myself, what a way to wait for the Vip. Shaken by such a quick decision Gladis looked like him catlike, you gave me start, that's no way to wake a person up, first all that petting and then a shove. They're all alike, Susana told her as she ostentatiously dragged herself over to them with a plate of sandwiches. Shut up, Lucien Verneuil ordered. The best way is to keep them full, Susana added, here comes Ludmilla with rivers of Nescafé, a feast like this has never been seen before in this austere and sad country.

The lamentable disorder of some pages in Manuel's book, everybody giving clippings to Susana who pastes them in with an application that is little appreciated by the methodical one I told you, and nevertheless Gómez and Marcos and even the one alluded to end up recognizing that in the helter-skelter collection there is sufficient clarity if at some time Manuel is capable of making proper use of his ocular apparatus. Put in the items just as they come, grumbles Heredia, the kid will end up learning how to add two plus two, and it won't be a question of giving him a crutch, what the fuck. Upon which Susana gives a fearful squeeze to the tube of mucilage and then

According to an analysis of "The New York Times"

Argentina responsible for worldwide price rise of leather

Result of decisions undertaken in the U.S.

Brignone mission has obtained, in principle, credits of 722 million dollars

As the result of its requests in Washington and New York the financial mission headed by the president of the Central Bank, Dr. Carlos Santiago Brignone, was able to concretize an operation of around 722 million dollars. *La Opinión* was informed of this in a telephone conversation with high functionaries of the New York banking community.

Although certain functional details still have not been made concrete, the credits that the Brignone mission obtained in the United States are made up of the following preliminary figures:

Group	Amount (in millions of dollars)
International Monetary Fund	
a) Gold step of the national quota	110
b) First step of credit quota	110
c) Input of Special Rights of Exchange, in reality already in country	46.6
d) Compensatory fund for stabilization of raw materials from 40 to	60
Approximate total	326.6
World Bank	
Special Credit for countries with difficulties in balance of payments	150
Export-Import Bank of the U.S.	
Special credit for financing of imports	100
Private banks	
First National City Bank	15
Chase Manhattan	15
Bank of America	15
Manufacturers Hanover Trust Co.	13
Morgan Guaranty Trust	13
Continental Bank	9
Bankers Trust	9
Chemical Bank	9
First Nat. Bank of Boston	9
Philadelphia National Bank	9
Irving Trust Co.	5
National Bank of North America	5
Marine Midland Bank	5
Two unconfimed entities	14
Total private banks	145

Letter to God Left Before Dying of Hunger

LA PAZ (Reuters).—The last two letters that a guerrilla fighter left before dying of hunger were to God and to his young wife who was waiting for him in La Paz.

El Diario published yesterday the text of both letters contained in the diary of Néstor Paz Zamora, *nom de guerre* Francisco, whose reremains were turned over to his family.

Omar, Jorge Gustavo Ruiz Paz—the leader of the group of six who was rescued from the jungle and is now in Chile—had turned over this document and other belongings to the relatives of Néstor Paz who were able to see him at the seat of the Apostolic Nunciature.

Francisco, considered the theoretician of the guerrilla group of Teoponte, died on October 8 of malnutrition and his body was carried for three days by his debilitated comrades who finally left it on the banks of a river.

Paz, 24 years old and a former Jesuit seminarian, had won over the love of the six survivors because he was the one who—in spite of a previous fast of one month—deprived himself of the minimal diet he needed for the benefit of his comrades who needed it more.

After thirty-five days of having eaten almost nothing, *Francisco* died in the arms of his desperate comrades in the struggle.

"Lord, today I really feel a need for you and your presence; maybe it's the approach of death or the relative failure of the struggle," he says in his "Letter to God," dated September 12.

"I left what I had and I came. Today is perhaps my Thursday and tonight my Friday," he says in a paragraph of the letter that ends: "So long, Lord, maybe in your heaven we'll find this new land we so yearn for."

The other letter by Paz is for his young bride, Cecilia, and in it he already foresees his death although he still harbors the hope of returning to her and "talking for a long time and looking into each other's eyes."

Francisco, the son of a retired general, came out of a Jesuit high school and followed his career of a seminarian until he decided on marriage.

His presence in the guerrilla group of Teoponte was recently discovered on the same day—July 19—when it was known for certain that a group of rebels led by "Chato" Peredo had taken over the mining operations of a company in Teoponte, subsequently withdrawing into the jungle with two hostages of German nationality.

"That's not true," Francine had answered, (try to remember when, at the beginning most likely, in her apartment the first or second time,

or in Milly-la-Forêt after a Sunday of dry leaves, seafood, and kisses in an inn with a fireplace and Irish coffee)

that's not why, Andrés, there's something else,

(or was it finally on the edge of the graves, at the end of so many negatives once more, scenes that left us dirty from words and clumsy misencounters?)

that's not why, dear, what can I say, I don't want to and I can't but don't think it's a matter of principle

(telling the truth, of course, a truth growing in territory from genealogical lies, slow instillations from childhood and puberty, obscure family references, crime news, the terrifying discoveries —fifteen years old, braids, high school, whispering between two desks, but they can with a boy too, you can see so, talked about at home, a tramp from under the bridges, all that, Lucienne laughing as she told it, Aunt Jenny at mama's ear, the guillotine is too good, such times, poor little thing, Madame Fleurquin's nephew, thirteen years old)

that's not why, Andrés, I just don't want to because

(that may be the way you go through life, voting, choosing a profession, certain headaches, preferences, and displeasures, that may be the way he was being carried to be what he was)

and to tolerate one more hour of intolerance seemed impossible to me

(but I, intolerant of intolerance, what degree of truth and honesty was there in that decision of going beyond, of refusing to accept what so many times at Francine's, at Milly-la-Forêt, and now at the edge of the graves?)

that's not why, believe me, that's not why,

(and without any pretense at honesty, without the pretext of helping her against herself to put an end to a region of lack, but because that night the reiterated retraction, the that's not why, dear, leaped out at me like part of the Fritz Lang nothingness, of the black stain where something had let itself be stolen after a lying moment of not remembering, a repugnant censure that was being paid for by headaches and insomnia and good consciences, for all of that suddenly one single total antagonism, the wire fence between possible reality and me, between possible reality and Francine, the concretion of so much negation, Ludmilla's leaving because of me, that's not why dear, there's someone who wants to speak to you, so many other things over the years, small daily betrayals, the Screwery being avoided, the feeling of having come to the edge precisely when Francine drew back in refusal, arched in a buck, not that, you know not that, her mouth tight, the will not to give in)

that's not why, Andrés, that's not why but

> Two screens at right angles, two films, there's someone who wants to speak to you, the metamorphosis of the body in order to reach the true content, the metamorphosis of something, impossible to remain where he pretended to be just as he was, where he insolently decided to present himself as this or that when someone had transmitted a message, a mission (and a few hours later in Verrières, how could he not think that Ludmilla was probably playing her own metamorphosis, Screwery metamorphosis that could be life on other sides, a purifying explosion, Screwery flower of fire opening up ridiculously, insignificantly, the seeds leaping across the Atlantic, helping a nothing, a little piece of what was happening in our lands, and knowing that it was there on the threshold, that it was still possible to arrive, to transmit the unknown message when its flower would also open in the middle of his stomach and bite with the teeth of words)

I fixed the sheet and made her stretch out little by little alongside me, kissing her breasts, looking for the mouth that was murmuring single words and half-dozing complaints, the tongue to the deepest, mingling salivas in which the cognac had left a distant taste, a perfume that also came from her hair where my hands were lost, pulling her redhaired head back, making her feel my strength, and when she was still, as if resigned, I slipped against her and laid her face down once more, I caressed her extremely white back, the small tight buttocks, the backs of her knees together, her ankles with their roughness from so many shoes, I traveled along her shoulders and her armpits with a slow exploration of tongue and lips while my fingers enfolded her breasts, molded them and woke them up, I heard her murmur a complaint where there was no pain but shame and fear once more because she already must have suspected what I was going to do to her, my mouth went down her back, it opened a way between the soft and secret double skin, my tongue went forward toward the depths that retracted and tightened fleeing my desire. Oh no, no, not that way, I heard her repeat, I don't want it that way, please, please, feeling my leg which enwrapped her thighs, freeing my hands to separate the buttocks and fully see the dark grain, the tiny golden button that was tightened, overcoming the strength of the resisting muscles. Her purse was on the side of the night table, I felt for the tube of face cream and she heard and refused again, trying to get her legs loose, she arched childishly when she felt the tube in her buttocks, she contracted while she repeated no, no, not that way, no please not that way, childishly not that way, I don't want you to do that to me, it's going to hurt, I don't want to, I don't want to, while I opened her buttocks again with my free hands and got on top of her, at the same time I heard her moan and felt the warmth of her skin on my sex, the slippery and precarious resistance of that little ass which no one would prevent me from entering, I spread her legs to hold her down better, resting my hands on her back, doubling slowly over her as she moaned and twisted unable to get out from under my weight, and her own convulsive movement drove me inward to overcome the first resistance, to cross the border of the silky boiling glove where each advance was a new entreaty, because appearances now gave way to a real and fugitive pain which did not deserve pity, and her contraction increased a will not to give in, not to abjure, to respond to each cooperating shake (because I think she knew that) with a new advance until feeling that I was reaching the end as her pain and her shame were reaching their end too and something new was being born in her weeping, the discovery that it was not unbearable, that I was not raping her even though she refused and begged, that my pleasure had a limit there where hers began and precisely for that reason the obstinacy in refusing me, in furiously pulling away from me and denying what she was feeling, guilt, mama, so much eucharist, so much orthodoxy. Collapsed on top of her, weighing her down with all my weight so that I could feel myself at the deepest, I knotted my hands on her breasts again, I bit her hair at the bottom of her neck to make her stay motionless although her back and her rump trembled caressing me against her will and moving under a burning pain that became the repetition of the moan now soaked in admission, and finally when I began to withdraw and enter again, removing myself only to sink in again, possessing her more and more while I heard her saying that I was hurting her, I was raping her, I was destroying her, that I couldn't, I should get out, please I should take it out, please a little, just a minute, it was hurting her so much, please, it was burning her, it was horrible, she couldn't take any more, it was hurting her, please love, please now, now, until I get used to it, love, please a little, take it out please, I ask you, it hurts so much, and her different moan when she felt me come in her, an uncontainable birth of pleasure, a shaking in which all of her, vagina and mouth and legs duplicated the spasm with which I cut through her and impaled her to the limit, her buttocks tight against my groin, so joined to her that all of her skin was my skin, a single falling into the green flame of closed eyes and mingled hair and wrapped legs and the coming of the shadow that slipped as our bodies slipped in a confused skein of caresses and moans, all words abolished in the murmur of that breaking away that freed us and returned us to the individual, to understand again that that hand was her hand and that my mouth was seeking hers to call her to conciliation, to a salty region of babbling encounter, of shared dream.

They really are something, after teasing poor Susana so much every time they see her pasting up the clippings for Manuel's book, suddenly they get an attack of solidarity and epic battles are fought over the only pair of shears or tube of paste, Gómez gets entangled in the Scotch tape in such a way that they have to look for the end of the roll on his left ear and how can I describe how it hurts when Lucien Verneuil pulls it off and along with it a clump of hair full of Indian ancestors. Incredible thinks Ludmilla huddled in a corner near the candle stump, what these South Americans are capable of having accumulated in their pockets, now that the Vip is undergoing inspection in the upstairs room where Heredia wouldn't hide the barrel of the forty-five from him for anything and Marcos, Patricio, and Roland are resting up from their deed eating sandwiches and drinking Madame Verneuil's red wine, it would seem that the night exists especially for Manuel, suddenly everybody ready to be co-author of the book and Susana amazed and extremely happy receiving contributions from all sides, looking at Patricio safe and sound and still a little pale but the wine intravenously raising up in him a smile worthy of the stretching out along the rug he has awarded himself, without letting go of the sandwich, of course and the glass because with Roland nearby one never knows.

The one I told you is moved a little upon seeing Ludmilla's and Susana's pulley systems at work now that the boys are within squeezing and kissing range, although there's been little of that because Patricio prefers the rehabilitating rug and the glass of red for the moment, Marcos has too much to talk about with Lucien Verneuil and Heredia, the telephone rings every three minutes with the anticipatory insertion of a wet towel next to the bell to throw the surrounding retired neighbors off the track, confirmation of the presence of the Vipess at the Quai des Orfèvres ("cop headquarters," Gladis to Oscar) and obviously the messages in the hands of the bewildered or frothing ambassadors, Roland manipulates a shortwave transistor that emits strange borborygmi until around one-thirty the first rebounds start coming out, the universal uproar, and news agencies filling the gaps with hypotheses, unconfirmed telegrams from Rio de Janeiro, authoritative sources in Lima said that an official communiqué is expected from Argentina's foreign office, deep surprise caused in Quito by the news that. Five or six hours still before anything definite, Oscar replaces Heredia on the upper floor, the maenads knocking themselves out over the Nescafé, Lucien Verneuil settles down for an hour's sleep while Roland stands guard over the chalet, incredible how those two mistrust Latin American seriousness, Marcos looks at them tenderly, ironically, just let them alone to play in their end of the field, tired and aching he lies down and looks for a pillow for his head, Ludmilla leans her side against him and ends up rounding herself out like a perfect creation by Knoll or Alvar Aalto, the worthy repose of the warrior, caresses on the hair. I told them I love you, Ludmilla murmurs, I shouted it out, I mean to Susana in the kitchen, and then. Ah, Marcos observes. It isn't true that I shouted it out because Lucien would have kicked me to death, but it comes to the same thing, I was so afraid, I had to say it. Of course, Polonette. Bloop, Marcos, bloop. And Patricio yawning after a four-decker sandwich, looking at Susana who is collating the material spontaneously offered during the last half-hour, because you can't just stick any piece of junk in Manuel's book, first prize to Marcos's clipping which is a lucky one and besides chance does things well and the item comes with two additions that Manuel might enjoy someday, if with all this he hasn't eaten the mushroom for lack of something that tastes better and, Susana thinks with a frown, he's turning green and depositing the first lethal diarrhea on one of the little rabbi's couches.

Guerrillas In Mexico Free PRI Leader

MEXICO CITY, 1—The drama of the second political kidnapping perpetrated in Mexico in the last two months ended today with the freeing of the victim, but the government is still deeply alarmed by the effect such incidents might have on the image of the country abroad.

Jaime Castrejón Díaz, president of the University of the State of Guerrero and a high official of the governing Institutional Revolutionary Party (PRI) returned early this morning to his home in the city of Taxco after twelve days of captivity.

In exchange for the presi-

dent, the kidnappers obtained the freedom of nine leftist opponents of the government who were flown to Cuba on Sunday and 2.5 million pesos (approximately 200,000 dollars) paid by the family, one of the wealthiest in Guerrero.

EJECUTIVOS...
FIN DE SEMANA
INOLVIDABLE.
Con el nuevo buque de
lujo "DON LUIS" y alo-

"I'm going to paste them in one after the other," Susana says; "they're good luck and I believe in things like that"—and ipso facto and in a flash a spurt of Pelikan paste and a great swirl of shears.

"But what the hell is this?" Patricio asks sternly having believed in his duty of supervising the feverish snipping and pasting

of Susana who has a hard time keeping up with the sudden contributions from Heredia, Gómez, and Marcos, who would even give the shirts off their backs for the enrichment of Manuel's book.

"This what?" says Susana who doesn't particularly appreciate the interruption in the rain of manna.

"This shit," Patricio says, showing

New Sleeping Bags Contemplate Four-Square Dimensions

Parallel to the tasks of reconditioning and renovating summer articles are others taking place in a similar way with camping equipment and articles destined for use in campgrounds, a form of summer vacation that is increasing in popularity.

In response to this need, the Ipanema company, specialists in sleeping bags, offers a line of new and very reasonable bags manufactured from synthetic materials.

The main advantage of these lies in the stuffing made with Agrotrop, a polyester fiber processed in such a way as to keep the characteristics of the traditional *duvet,* and which can be washed without crumbling.

The outer fabric is smooth or printed with bright colors and can be turned into regular mattresses. The inner fabric is downy nylon, which gives it softness and strong resistance in the snaps, the most abused part of the sleeping bag.

"I offer this," says the one I told you, who up till now has not stood out for his oral contributions, "just so he can see what's being swallowed at this very moment as vocabulary by more than a handful of fellow-countrymen on the banks of the silver-plated river."

A rather tempestuous dialogue follows broken only by the parlez plus bas, nom d'un chien from Roland who doesn't understand one whit of what's happening sub aespecie bonaerensis and the mocking laughter of Marcos and Patricio who have read the clipping and are pissing soto vochay on the soft *duvet* and the contemplation of the downy nylon, not to mention the fact that according to the clipping, and that's what most delights the one I told you, those that contemplate four-square dimensions are the new sleeping bags, something that casts a disquieting splendor on its possible intelligence. Poor Susana is the only one who doesn't dig the reasons for such an immodest interpolation and is on the point of flinging the clipping at the puss of the one I told you, who with great serenity points out to her that his contribution is purely of a semantic nature, something with which Manuel will have to learn to defend himself from an early age against the advertising soft soap that facilitates other telecommunicated soft soaps, etc., and they are arguing about whether the clipping should be pasted in or not when Patricio takes out another piece of paper and passes it to Susana with a wink first at the one I told you. Oh no, says Susana, a homosexual crime, you just tell me if this is something for Manuel's book. Precisely, old girl, says Patricio to the immense delight of the one I told you who has read the clipping with the John F. Kennedy diagonal system in forty and three-tenths seconds, ah merde, mais qu'est-ce que vous foutez, whispers Lucien Verneuil furiously, suspecting retirees at every window, we're talking about semantics, says the one I told you weeping with laughter, Susana has got to realize that ransoms and freedom are insufficient if they're not accompanied by parallel and complementary clippings, Manuel will thank us for it someday, put your stamp on that.

"You're right," Patricio says, "and besides in that clipping that I bothered Fernando with when he came to our place before he sneaked off to vait it out since the potatoes are burning, not only is there lingvistic instruction but a whole mess of Latin American sadness, old man, so many things to be liquidated. Paste it in, Susana, paste it in with tears, girl, we're still far from the day when a clipping like that will look like a Neanderthal skull or something of the sort, this wine has gone to my head."

Obedient and in the dumps, poor Susana grabs the tube of paste and that's how

HE WAS A WAITER AND HIS NAME WAS MANOLO GONZÁLEZ

HOMOSEXUAL CRIME

MOTIVE: JEALOUSY

Another homicide between homosexuals was reported yesterday by police of the Carlos Valdovinos post with the discovery in the apartment house on 3699 Calle San Manuel of the body of the "gay" waiter Manuel González Ruiz, age 20, who had been strangled during the early hours of the morning by another "fairy."

The discovery was made by his "roommate," the waiter José Reinaldo Núñez Fernández, age 30, who arrived at 9:30 A.M. yesterday to join his "worst is best," coming in rather the worse for wear after spending the night drinking.

According to neighbors José Reinaldo arrived at the apartment staggering back and forth and singing the song that goes:

Forbidden love, impossible love;
black sorrows destroy my soul;
violent, passion, horrible morbid love
take away sleep, take away peeeeeace . . . hic!

And he went through the grillwork door walking slowly until he went into the room.

What happened inside and what José Reinaldo Núñez Fernández himself told to reporters from PURO CHILE was the following:

"The fact is, my friend is a homosexual and I spent the whole night 'cruising' in different places . . . hic! And when I got there I found him lying on the floor with his mouth full of blood and a slash across his throat . . . hic!"

A FAGGOT, BUT AN HONORABLE MAN

The deceased boy (or girl, wow!) had worked at the fountain of Soda City on Blanco Encalada at the corner of Bascuñán for more than six years.

A young and friendly cashier who said her name was Rosita, told PURO CHILE that Manuel González was a somewhat introverted man who continually underwent nervous attacks because of the jealousy among his admirers.

"Last Saturday," Rosita said, "Manolo asked my permission to leave for an hour because he had some important private business to attend to and later I found out that he had been seen on Franklin with a young man, also a "faggot," who wore sideburns and had beautiful honey-colored hair.

"Afterwards they came to tell me that Manolo had been caught Saturday night in some business with a certain Fairy Gerardo in a place called La Punta.

"People also say that there are two jealous guys: one called 'The Nigger' and another nicknamed 'Enrique,' who must know something about Manolo's friends.

"But the police should also question José Reinaldo Núñez Fernández, Manolo's intimate friend, the one who shared the apartment so their lives would be less lonely."

On being questioned, our informant assured us that Manolo was "gay" but honorable; he was hardworking and respectable; only once a month he would go on a binge and miss four or five days . . . nothing else."

LOVER ARRESTED

According to information obtained from unofficial sources, the murder probably took place around four in the morning at a place in the house where repair work was being done a few feet beyond the grill.

There the perpetrator had probably strangled the homosexual using a thin but strong cloth that he placed around his neck and tightened until it killed him.

Immediately afterward the murderer had dragged Manolo González inside the area of repairs where he had probably tried to hang him from a beam to make it look like suicide, but since it was impossible to obtain his objective, the murderer fled leaving behind his dirty work.

Some neighbors, those who like technicolor movies, accuse José Reinaldo Núñez Fernández of having committed the crime and of having returned at 9:30 so that everyone would see him and he would have an alibi to throw the police off the track.

In addition, on talking to the neighbors, it was learned that the mother and other relatives of José Reinaldo Núñez live right next door to the construction work and that it is strange that no one heard any call for help or other noise under circumstances in which both apartments are practically side by side.

In any case, and so as not to appear hoodwinked, the police arrested José Reinaldo Núñez and brought him under guard to turn him over to the Third Superior Court of the Pedro Aguirre Cerda Division.

GAY DISTRICT

"The sector bounded by the Zanjón de La Aguada and San Joaquín and three blocks to the east is plagued by 'queers,' in spite of the fact, sir, that there are females that can give you a toothache."

That is what was reported to PURO CHILE yesterday by the resident Miguel Angel Delgado Romero, who has lived in the district only a short time but knows it rather well.

"I can assure you that Manolo's murderer lives around here . . ."

At once he looks toward the street and points out two strangers walking toward the home of the murdered "faggot."

"Look! . . . Those two 'gay boys' coming along are 'Enrique' and 'The Nigger,' two of the dead man's friends."

The fags go close to the house and seeing it full of police and detectives make the following comments:

"Mercy, girl! . . . I'm going to go mad, absolutely mad. . . . I can't believe that Manolo was done in!"

"Me either, but if it wasn't because of all the big real males there like those cops, I'd never be convinced."

And then, realizing that if they got too close to the scene of the crime they might be arrested, they took half a turn and went off wiggling their hips, which was a sight to see . . . Wow!

"It's strange," Patricio said to Marcos, "tonight's not the way I would have thought it would be, not even snatching the Vip. Things always happen in a different way and it's fine that you're pasting items in Manuel's book that have nothing to do with what you were imagining, Susanita, when you bought that blue scrapbook on the Rue de Sèvres."

"You're a romantic," Heredia said, "but to be quite frank with you I thought this would be spies and violence in Technicolor too and here you see it, everybody cutting paper dolls by candlelight, of course the film isn't over yet. In the meantime, so as to give Manuel something more serious, I donate this and I won't hide from you the fact that if you were to translate it for the ambulatory Frenchies you'd give me a great pleasure on this day which has gone rather badly for me."

URUGUAY

Le prix d'un révolutionnaire et celui d'un ambassadeur

Les Tupamaros ont tenu leurs promesses. Sitôt rétablies les garanties individuelles, suspendues le 8 janvier après le rapt de l'ambassadeur britannique, ils ont relâché un de leurs trois diplomates-otages : Dias Gomide, consul brésilien enlevé le 31 juillet, quelques jours avant Claude Fly, agronome américain, et Dan Mitrione, expert en répression affilié à la C.I.A., qui devait être exécuté par ses ravisseurs, au mois d'août.

A diverses reprises, Maria Aparacida Gomide, épouse du consul brésilien, s'était adressée aux Tupamaros par lettre, radio et télévision, pour les supplier de libérer son mari. Ces appels avaient, à chaque fois, déchaîné le concert éploré des « humanistes » qui s'indignaient que des organisations politiques recourent au rapt pour obtenir la libération des détenus politiques. Nous publions ici une lettre inédite adressée à Mme Gomide, par Mme Borges Vieira Alves, épouse du journaliste Mario Alves de Souza Vieira, dirigeant du parti communiste brésilien révolutionnaire, mort sous la torture au début de 1970. Ce document permettra, pensons-nous, de remettre les choses à leur juste place.

"But it's two tight columns," Susana complained, "and with this rotten light. All right, freeing of Brazilian consul kidnapped by Tupamaros, radio and television pleas by his wife, and disconsolate chorus of humanist frogs indignant that political organizations should resort to kidnapping in order to obtain the freedom of political detainees," Susana said with the iron voice of the little schoolteacher who comes to the hairiest part of the theorem, "it's the letter which the wife of the Brazilian consul received before the Tupas returned her husband, and which says: "Mrs. Aparacida Gomide, everybody knows of your suffering and anguish. News services, written and oral, remind us of your drama every day: your husband, a diplomatic functionary abroad has been kidnapped and thus involved in an event of a political nature. Madam, you are not the only one who weeps. But no one speaks of my suffering and anguish. I weep alone. I have no possibilities for making myself heard, for saying in turn that 'my heart is torn apart' and that 'I want to see my husband again.' Your husband is alive and well treated. He will return to your side. Mine

Le 27 septembre 1970.

Madame Aparacida Gomide,

Tout le monde connaît votre souffrance et votre angoisse. La presse parlée et écrite rappelle tous les jours votre drame : votre mari, fonctionnaire en service à l'extérieur, a été enlevé et mêlé de cette manière à des événements de nature politique. Madame, vous ne pleurez pas toute seule.

Mais personne ne parle de ma souffrance et de mon angoisse. Je pleure toute seule. Je n'ai pas vos possibilités pour me faire entendre, pour dire, moi aussi, que « j'ai le cœur brisé » et que « je veux revoir mon mari ». Votre mari est vivant, bien traité. Il va revenir. Le mien est mort sous la torture, assassiné par la Première Armée. Il a été exécuté sans procès, sans jugement. Je réclame son corps. Personne ne m'a donné satisfaction, pas même la Commission des Droits de la personne humaine. Je ne sais pas ce qu'ils ont fait de lui ni où ils l'on jeté.

Il s'appelait Mario Alves de Souza Vieira, journaliste. Il a été arrêté par la police de la Première Armée le 16 janvier de cette année, à Rio de Janeiro. Il a été emmené à la caserne de la police militaire, sauvagement frappé la nuit durant, empalé sur un bâton taillé en dents de scie, la peau de son corps entièrement arrachée avec une brosse métallique, parce qu'il refusait de donner les informations réclamées par les tortionnaires de la Première Armée et du DOPS. Des prisonniers amenés à la salle de torture pour nettoyer le sol couvert de sang et d'excréments, ont vu mon mari agonisant, du sang coulant par la bouche et par le nez, nu, jeté par terre, oppressé, demandant à boire. En riant, les militaires tortionnaires n'ont pas permis qu'on lui prête le moindre secours.

Je sais, Madame, que vous n'êtes pas en état de comprendre ma souffrance, car la douleur de chacun est toujours plus grande que celle des autres. Mais j'espère que vous comprendrez que les conditions ayant amené à l'enlèvement de votre mari et à la torture du mien jusqu'à en mourir, sont toujours les mêmes ; qu'il est important de savoir que la violence-famine, la violence-misère, la violence-oppression, la violence-sous-développement, la violence-torture mènent à la violence-enlèvement, à la violence-terrorisme, à la violence-guérilla ; qu'il est très important de savoir qui met la violence en pratique : ceux qui provoquent la misère ou ceux qui luttent contre elle ?

Votre désespoir et votre souffrance montrent que votre mari était un bon chef de famille, qu'il vous manque et que sa vie est très importante. Mario Alves, lui aussi, a été un bon chef de famille ; il me manque ; il avait une fille qu'il adorait. Il était intelligent, cultivé, bon ; personnellement, il n'a jamais blessé personne. Il est mort par amour pour les opprimés, les victimes de l'injustice, les sans-voix et les sans-espérance. Il a lutté pour que les immenses ressources matérielles et humaines de notre patrie soient utilisées au bénéfice de tous.

Je souhaite très vivement une solution heureuse pour vous, Madame, et pour les Tupamaros.

Dilma BORGES VIEIRA.

died under torture, murdered by the First Army. He was executed without trial and without being sentenced. I have demanded his body. No one has heard me, not even the Commission on Human Rights. I don't know what they have done with it nor where they have thrown it. His name was Mario Alves de Souza Vieira, journalist. He was arrested by First Army police on January 16 of this year in Rio de Janeiro. He was brought to the military police barracks where they beat him savagely all through the night, they hit him with a club cut with saw-toothed notches, they scraped the skin off all his body with a metal brush because he refused to give the information demanded by the First Army and the DOPS. The prisoners brought to the torture chamber to clean up the floor covered with blood and excrement saw my husband dying, blood coming from his mouth and nose, naked on the floor, choking, asking for something to drink. While laughing, the military torturers would not allow them to give him the slightest help."

"We understand," Roland said, "ça va comme ça."

"Oh no, I'm not going to stop now," Susana said, looking at him furiously. "I know, madam, that you are not in a position to understand my suffering, because each one's suffering is always greater than that of the rest. But you understand, I hope, that the conditions that brought about the kidnapping of your husband and the fatal torture of mine are the very same: that it is important to realize that hunger-violence, misery-violence, oppression-violence, underdevelopment-violence, torture-violence lead to kidnapping-violence, terrorism-violence, guerrilla-violence; and that it is very important to understand who puts the violence into practice: whether it is those who cause misery or those who fight against it. Your despair and your suffering show that your husband is a good head of a family, that you deplore his absence, and that his life is very important. Mário Alves was also a good head of a family, I miss him too. He had a daughter who adored him; he was intelligent, educated, good; he personally never hurt anyone. He died out of love for the oppressed, the victims of injustice, those who have no voice and no hope. He fought so that the immense material and human resources of our country could be used for the benefit of all. I fervently hope that a happy solution will be forthcoming for you, madam, and for the Tupamaros. Signed, Dilma Borges Vieira."

"It's already daylight," Heredia said. "Take the paste, pretty one, I'll make you all some dawn coffee, which is the tastiest, especially when made by a Carioca."

His voice was strange, it wasn't Heredia's voice or his way of walking when almost at a run he turned his back on them to disappear into the kitchen.

Now the bridge will have to be crossed; it's not hard, a few yards after leaving the hotel, the city giving its morning slap in the face with the usual insidiousness, the gray sky low and rainy, the smell of burnt naphtha, the posters raping one's eyes, every week its circus changing a program of electric kitchens, installment furniture, Renault, Phillips, real estate offices, samples corroded by time, old entranceways MANUFACTURE D'INSTRUMENTS DE CHIRURGIE EN CAOUTCHOUC ET PLASTIQUE, the poster on the Hotel Terrass, the bridge leading to the Place Clichy, the other side; it doesn't cost anything to cross the bridge, two sidewalks with railings for pedestrians protected from death on four wheels by municipal articles, fines, and punishments; a matter of crossing looking at the red light and the green light; in some ways it's as if the worst remained behind, summed up in that bill and that tip on the edge of a beat-up bar; it would really be exaggerating to say that crossing the bridge of return raises problems.

He had awakened at nine-thirty, the curtains defended us against daybreak and the noises; neither Francine nor I had a headache even though the Martell bottle was lying on the rug with its five stars belly up; fatigue, Francine putting her hands around my neck and curling up and saying that she was hungry and thirsty, telephone and tray, long showers, everything the same, everything at the beginning of a new consecutive normal foreseen day of life. I have to relieve Madame Franck until one o'clock, we'll have to hurry, I hope there are some taxis around. Of course, girl, you'll get there on time, nothing has changed in the temporality of the bookstore business, I'll drop you at your door like a flower, you'll sell a whole lot of prize-winning novels and two or three dictionaries, you'll see. I was looking for her eyes because there, perhaps, something might give me a direction, a buoy with swells and parentheses, a possible alibi if it was necessary some time to explain why I hadn't crossed the bridge, why I hadn't carried the message to García. What about you, Andrés? I asked him because I had to ask him, because in that way of searching into my eyes there was something like an answer crouching. Well, I don't sell books, he told me sitting up in bed to reach for the cigarettes, I only have to take inventory of these past few hours that I owe to you, I don't know whether they'll help me understand anything but in any case I'll start walking and then start arriving little by little as divine proportion commands. I don't want you to leave like that, I told him, you've told me enough for me to imagine that you're going to do something foolish. The fact is I don't know what I'm going to do, girl, and that's probably where the foolishness lies. In any case there's one thing I do know and it's this.

Francine didn't understand right away, sitting naked on the edge of the bed we were, except for the bed, Adam and Eve at the hour of expulsion, something full of shadows and past, covering our faces so as not to see daylight over the graves down there.

"I'm not asking your forgiveness for so many things, girl, even if there were some way to ask, and don't deny it to me with all your red-haired head because you tickle me and I'm going to laugh, something that's not too suitable to the circumstances. Last night you asked me why I wanted to debase you and maybe now, after that bottle, after your irritated little ass, and other things that you'll probably remember, you feel like that rag on the side of the bidet. Let me tell you that no one has ever done so much for me, in a way that I barely understand and which must seem to be unmanageable madness to you. At worst who knows if there's any counterpart, who knows what I've been able to give you since we got together last night at the café, since Mademoiselle Antinéa, you remember, everything I told you, everything that I've told nobody, girl, nobody the way I told you because there was the other thing too, your skin and your saliva, let me just say this, girl, I haven't debased you making you drink that cognac and raping you, I haven't debased you, everything went away with the shower, because it's true that I raped you, girl, and it's also true that you cried and after sleeping an hour you woke up and called me a swine and a sadist and all that while you curled up like a little caterpillar and it was necessary to start all over again and it was so different, you tell me if it wasn't different, until we slept the sleep of the just and had no nightmares and you see, you see now what's in your eyes, just look at yourself in the mirror and tell me, girl."

"No, you didn't debase me," Francine said almost in a whisper, "but what about you, Andrés, what about you."

"Well, I've already told you that I don't understand anything, the black stain is still there like those curtains, but watch how we're going to open the curtains as soon as you've covered your breasts because we can't lose such a gaudy cemetery with panoramic perspective, don't you think, and it probably just might happen one of these days that the black stain will open up like the curtains and behind it will be something other than a cemetery, there'll be some kind of shit but at least something at last; and that's what I owe you, you and Mademoiselle Antinéa, of course, don't think that you're the exclusive redemptress."

"Silly, silly, why do you laugh when you're really . . . No, Andrés, I won't say it, darling, don't be offended, just let me put this kerchief on, like this."

We didn't say much after that, I watched her dress, I got dressed thinking about Gardel and that a macho shouldn't, etc. She wasn't against going out onto the balcony, we looked at the stupid graves, the ignoble perpetuation of the great scandal. I have to go, Francine said almost at once, Madame Franck is probably waiting for me. For her, of course, there probably wasn't any heads or tails, another working day was beginning, an able day, as they say in Spanish. Able, I tell her kissing her as I'd never kissed her before, what a word, girl. But she couldn't have understood what it meant, for her it had no logical sense, so bookstore and Madame Franck. There were no able days in Paris, there was no heads or tails for Francine sad and silent, getting into the elevator as if it were going to carry her up, vertically, from there to the cemetery across the way. I know, you're going to be depressed, you're going to cry, I told her stroking her hair, your won't get out of yourself or me, another working day is starting, you'll stay completely enclosed in that milky skin, in that sadness with nothing but it, you won't try to understand the depth of this night, selah, amen.

"What about you, what about you."

"Probably just the same, on the other end of the bridge we'll be you and me as always, I've got enough honesty left to suspect that the comedian invents the death of the petit bourgeois, imagining that he's entering a different territory beyond that bridge."

"Are you going to leave?"

"Look, as a first event I'm going to drop you at your place parce que Madame Franck, you see I haven't forgotten, and then I'm going to run to Lonstein's to find out what's what, except that at the kiosk there we're going to buy a paper, there must be something by now about the first wiggle."

"But what about after."

"After, I don't know, girl, I'll probably call you to go to the movies, in any case I don't plan to go back to my place for the moment, it must be widowed and dirty, there'll be leeks all over and Ludmilla's clothes on the floor, I'm an aesthete, girl, the petit bourgeois is making an effort to die but you see, on the other end of the bridge you can't see much difference. So I'll give you a call one of these days, as long as you don't decide to play tennis or something like that."

"You won't call me, I won't go to play tennis, but you won't call me."

She was looking at me as if she suddenly didn't recognize me; I saw her go off toward the newsstand, on the way back she had a cigarette in her mouth and the newspaper opened to the second page; she showed me the article and called a cab. Only then did I think that deep down I had always refused to believe that it was true, and now the headlines ran across the wrinkled page like the fly dragging himself across the café table. She didn't even get out of the taxi to say good-by; I felt her hand stroke my hair, but she still had the cigarette stuck between her lips. As always, when she pulled it out at the last minute, she would also pull off her skin, she would bleed and curse.

"Rue Cambronne, corner of Rue Mademoiselle," Andrés said throwing the newspaper onto the floor of the taxi. Going to Lonstein's could be a mistake, of course apart from smoking and drinking he didn't see that he could do anything else. He got out at the corner and continued on foot, going around the block in order to throw anyone who might have been tabulating the little rabbi's visitors off the track, he went into a bar on the Rue du Commerce precisely as the customers were listening to the bulletin about the surprising kidnapping of the person in charge of the coordination of Latin American affairs in Europe, as the announcer described him to the total indifference of the listeners who were waiting for the weather report and news of the semifinals of the championship, important things. I wondered if Ludmilla would be at home, it would be nothing to call but Ludmilla wouldn't be home, only the leeks and the Xenakis record and the one by Joni Mitchell that he hadn't had time to hear, coffee and Xenakis and Joni Mitchell and the bed, temptation right there, a few blocks and on one of them Ludmilla too because Marcos couldn't have been so unfeeling as to get her mixed up in what filled the second page of *Le Figaro*, but Ludmilla wouldn't be home, those things didn't depend on Marcos, the best thing in any case would be to go up to the little rabbi's and hear the news, after which of course I didn't make a move and another coffee because the five stars from the Martell were making themselves felt on the duodenal side, maybe I even slept a little in that nook where there was nothing but a dog and two retirees, the day was long and able, the governments faced with the ultimatum from the kidnappers will probably announce their decision during the early hours of the afternoon, French time; then heads or tails, for the Screwery heads and even more, it's incredible, Andrés thought stretching and reaching for his cigarettes, suddenly you realize that it's not so strange, it's even chic, it happens in every country not to mention air piracy, I don't understand how it can still continue to come off, of course the coordinator of Latin American affairs isn't a big fish, but just put the case that they don't accept the exchange, that the deadline passes and then. Ludmilla must be at home, it couldn't be that she. Then Marcos or Heredia, they're the ones who'll do it, or Roland. Yes, but afterwards and in this country. Lud. Of course she's sleeping at home, I have to. Of course knowing her, a telephone ringing at home alone, that endless lugubrious sound, that callus. What if I go to Verrières, but that's absurd, I could get them into an even worse bind and one or the other, either Ludmilla's at home or at Lonstein's playing with Manuel, the only intelligent thing would be to go to the little rabbi's, strange I don't have the feeling of having showered, the sticky able day no doubt, but you have to be an imbecile to have imagined there'd be an inventory, there'd be heads or tails, nothing changes, old man, the black stain is there even though poor girl, poor girl looking at the cemetery, what a son of a bitch you are, Andrés Fava, so much heads or tails and the bridge back with her on your arm and there we go, an able day for both even if you don't want it, why so much filth and so much bed, where does the testament of night lie, your nose is flat, face of a cat, where does the heads or tails lie, why does the paste from the black stain stick to you on this worn bench, to the next coffee and cognac you're going to order immediately.

"A coffee and a cognac," Andrés ordered immediately.

In Manuel's book this news item figured with the rather sybilline title of *Tribulations of the Chubby Errand Boy*, the copyright of which would be reserved for Marcos:

Meeting Between Bruno Quijano and Kissinger Not Held

WASHINGTON, 4—The White House denied today information from diplomatic sources according to which the Argentine Minister of Justice Ismael Bruno Quijano had met with presidential adviser Henry Kissinger, according to the Latin Agency.

Spokesmen for the Argentine economic and political mission which has been here since Monday negotiating a loan of more than 1,046 million dollars, told the press at 4 P.M. that the meeting had taken place.

The office of the presidential adviser did say that Quijano had come for the meeting but that Dr. Kissinger could not see him because "it was impossible to take time off from his business at the moment."

It was added that Kissinger tried to have the minister talk to one of his aides, "after which [Quijano] left in anger."

One of the adviser's secretaries confirmed the fact that the meeting with Quijano was on the schedule.

An aide to Kissinger said to the Latin Agency that "it was regrettable that he could not receive the minister but there were urgent and unforeseen presidential matters. We are trying to arrange a new meeting."

The sources from the mission who thought that the meeting had taken place said in their declaration to the press that Kissinger and Quijano had discussed relations between Washington and Buenos Aires in light of the supposedly preferential relations that the United States maintains with Brazil.

They added that both officials had also analyzed the thesis of "ideological pluralism," the role of the current Chilean government on the continent, and the political and institutional future of the Argentine Republic.

The economic mission, which will go on to New York, cancelled a press conference for today where it was to announce the results of its efforts of five days in Washington before the American government, the Monetary Fund, and the World Bank, which had apparently been successful.

The path of these negotiations had been cleared by Quijano—before assuming in October the portfolio of Justice—and Luis Cantilo, a relative of President Lanusse.

It was predictable that Lonstein kept forgetting about Manuel, who was melancholically chewing on the tassels of the window curtain that had never been washed by human hands since 1897, the year in which Madame Lavoisier, owner of the apartment, had hung up such a praiseworthy accessory to protect her eyes from a sun which in the opinion of the little rabbi never let itself be seen in the whorish lifetime of the misnamed city of light. Even before he touched the bell Andrés could hear Lonstein's laughter as he greeted him with his left hand because from the right hung a clipping destined no doubt for Manuel to read some time if the cultures in the tassel ever allowed him to reach literacy.

"Look how beautiful," wheezed the little rabbi, look at the superprexpress, old man, a magazine has a birthday and look what one of our compatriots writes. I don't think anyone has never gone so far in the art of not saying anything."

"The most meaningful part seems to be the little circle you made with your ballpoint," Andrés said stretching out in a chair and at the same time discovering Manuel's legs inextricably entwined in the curtain and in a state of suctionary ecstasy. Applying himself, he finally extracted him from the maelstrom of

<u>3rd anniversary</u>

SOME OPIN

70-71

"Imagen" offers in every number a most intelligent literary picture, placing it, to my mind, among the best written and liveliest in our countries."

Edmundo Valadés
President of the Writers' Association of Mexico and Editor of the magazine "El Cuento"

"I think that among Latin American literary reviews, almost none is so up to date in content of value."

Luis Wainerman
Argentina

"The character of the magazine, its tone, the good taste with which it is put together and illustrated show it to be su-

tassels and fringes, not without a crude battle because Manuel resisted like a dedicated man who still had some ten inches of tassel to suck, and when he had him on his knees and Manuel told him several things like ifctugpi, fenude, and other such belches, he asked Lonstein if he had at least given him some milk and other absurd things that infants are obliged to ingest.

"A lot I didn't give him," the little rabbi admitted with a shamed face, "and with Susana leaving me more than three quarts, you realize that between the news on the radio and the patriotic enthusiasm that such news aroused in me one is no longer up to lactic diets, not to mention the mushroom that's tilting to the right on me and that I think is an ominous sign. In short, think what a piece of beef costs my old lady in her little house in Río Cuarto and these uglies pulling out forty-nine million dollars, but you have to think about it, forty-nine million dollars in airplanes to scare the Brazilians."

Argentine

LE GOUVERNEMENT ARGENTIN S'APPRÊTE A ACHETER 14 MIRAGE FRANÇAIS

Buenos-Aires *(A.P.)*. — Le gouvernement argentin est sur le point d'approuver le contrat d'achat de quatorze chasseurs Mirage-III conclu avec la société Dassault et qui porte sur un total de 49 millions de dollars (269,5 millions de francs).

Un porte-parole officiel a indiqué qu'un décret à cet effet attend la signature du président de la République.

"Come on, old man," Andrés said to Manuel who was beginning to realize that things were going to get better in the environment, "come here while this brute gives me a summary of the news."

"Fiata, fica, fifa, figo," said Manuel, ever so ready.

"He's incredibly mnemonic," Lonstein said startled, "last night he was listening to me straighten out the acronyms of a list of international organizations that Rasmussen gave me, he's a copain who dactyloperates at UNESCO, by the way you ought to know that U Thant lost the chance of his life to solve international problems, just look at the list and tell me."

"The news," Andrés repeated.

"Bah, crap, the same old record, ultimatum expires at noon, governments most indignant, French police on the trail, sniff, sniff, things like that. Did they see you come in, by the way?"

"I don't think so."

"Well, in any case you people are going to have to deal with me, the night you've made me spend with this child, you can't imagine how many times he's wanted to pee or eat."

"You're starving him to death," Andrés said in the middle of a transfusion of milk from bottle to Manuel, "look how the poor thing is sleeping, you've got no shame and I'm going to report you to FAO and UNICEF since we're on acronyms."

They immediately put him to bed with more precautions than would have been expected of them, and along the way boiled water for the Nescafé and the little rabbi was at it with the acronyms until with the second glass of grappa Andrés sat looking at him (*news is awaited on the spectacular kidnapping . . . meanwhile Mireille Mathieu will sing the popular success by*) and he asked him hoarsely what the fuck do acronyms have to do with the present status of things, as if Lonstein were determined not to talk about the Screwery even though he kept the transistor on in spite of the diarrhea of bossa nova and Mireille Mathieu, and back to international syncretism and acronyms because everything seemed to be pouring out in that series of hairy monsters heaving about on the mimeographed sheet of paper that the little rabbi had flung to me with a disdainful look.

"I've got my reasons," Lonstein said, "and by the way I'd like to know why you're so pale, you."

"I didn't sleep well, these things, and besides I'm leaving right now, so give me the precise details."

"Ah, old man, that . . ."

"Let me have them," Andrés repeated.

"Wouldn't you be much more interested in knowing what the CNUURC is, or the SACLANT? The UMOSEA and the AEJI, don't they tell you anything?"

"Please, brother."

"Ah, the usual ending: please, please. First I'm going to explain to you that those phonemes respond no less to the United Nations Commission for the Unfication and Rehabilitation of Korea, the Supreme Allied Commander of Atlantic Forces, the World Union of Organziations for the Protection of Infancy, and get a grip on yourself, the Association of European Jute Industries."

"It means you're not going to give me the details."

"It's not exactly that. I asked you a question, you answered me with a side step, and so."

"I'm leaving, Lonstein."

"Ah, the gentleman is leaving. That's a declaration of aim, but with me, that, you understand."

"It's hard to explain," I told him, "it's so hard, Lonstein, I don't understand it myself or what the devil do I understand. It's an old question, something that happens to me when I'm asleep, and there's Ludmilla and Screwery and a kind of weariness."

"As far as flattened out goes you're flattened out," the little rabbi said, "but all those reasons, I repeat. Very easy for you to stand in line after the bell rings, kiddo, in any case out of all the words you just used the only one that rings true is Ludmilla, or is it once more datoldblacmagicoldlov, as Judy Garland used to sing illo tempore."

"But of course, except that there's that other thing too, it isn't for nothing that Ludmilla went with Marcos and that she's going to get herself killed because of it."

"Foreseeable, in all of you there's a binary functioning, even Pavlov would have fallen asleep watching you move around in the Screwery or in sex, it's not right, I've always been given to be the one who runs his hand the wrong way along the cat's hair, at least they ought to let me have a little fun when I show them the mushroom they get tight on me and when I tell three truths to the one I told you, well, I must honestly admit that he wasn't so bad keeping in mind that the thing is kind of hairy."

Andrés didn't understand a word of what the little rabbi was declaiming vehemently to him. He drank another glass of grappa, things were slowly turning around on him, the window was no longer exactly where Manuel had sucked the tassels, everything was softly tilting from and toward his stomach, if a custard had consciousness, I thought, this is how it would write its memoirs. Lonstein had probably just given me the details, now he was still infuriated and bitter, best to wait looking at the famous mimeographed sheet of paper, encourage him to hand him the roll and give him a little more grappa, close his eyes and listen, after all the little rabbi was so right, except Ludmilla in that nausea of Verrières, that need to get there, see her, be there, the Screwery, yes, of course the Screwery too because Fritz Lang too, unjust to tell me only Ludmilla and still, clear, so clear, at this time listening to the little rabbi go on, how right you were, Francine, how different one triangle is from another to use the old expression, where was it going to stop my easy cheap macho very Argentine theory of the triangle with me at one vertex and the two of them closing the figure, now that Ludmilla and Marcos, the future sketching a triangle where two men and one woman, the hypothesis accepted so many times in theory and now, now. Now, Ludlud, now.

"My method is eminently

ACI International Cooperation Administration, United States.
AEJI Association of European Jute Industries.
AFIA American Association of Foreign Securities Companies.
AIDA International Association for the Distribution of Food Products.
AIGA International Geodesic Association.
ARPA Association for Research in Paradontopathies.
ARO Asian Regional Office.
BEEP European Office of Popular Education.
BIS International Bank of Payments.
CAC Administrative Coordination Committee.
CAT Technical Assistance Committee.
CECA European Coal and Steel Community.

CEFEA Center of Fundamental Education of the Arab States.

CIAO International Conference of Western Africanists.

CLINMAR International Coordinating Center of Sellers of Agricultural and Road Machinery.

CNUURC United Nations Commission for the Unification and Rehabilitation of Korea.

CORSO Corporation for the Development of Production.

ECO European Coal Organization.

EMA European Monetary Accord.

EPA European Office of Productivity.

ESA Regional Office for Eastern South America.

ETC European Tourist Commission.

FAMA Foundation for Mutual Assistance in Sub-Sahara Africa.

FEA International Federation for Artistic Education.

FENUDE United Nations Special Fund for Economic Development.

FIATA International Federation of Transporters and Receivers.

FICA International Federation of Antialcoholic Railway Workers.

FIFA International Federation of Art Films.

rational," Lonstein was saying without taking his eyes off me; "the true coordination and exploitation of these organizations must emanate from the acronyms for purely semantic reasons, because as you will note it's a word that contains the mantic which is what counts, even though that cretin U Thant would never see it."

"All right, Lonstein, I'm sorry I tried to make you work so fast, I'm on the edge of something I'm not sure of, but on the edge, and then."

"It doesn't occur to them that the true fortran is in that combinatory element that gives you precisely the prexpress of the acronyms, and that the first thing to do is forget that they refer to things as absurd as the Special Account for the Eradication of Malaria, don't you think, or Tourist Association of the Pacific Region."

"Yes, old man, of course."

"For example, if you will notice, the acronym for the Account in question is *mesa*, table, and that of the Association is *pata*, leg, so all you have to do is start with the leg

FIGO International Federation of Gynecology and Obstetrics.

IFCTUGPI International Federation of Workers' Unions in Graphic and Paper Industries.

IUFO International Union of Family Organizations.

JULEP Joint Program of Education of Unesco and Liberia.

LIDIA International Union of Food Industries.

LILA International League of Antiquarian Booksellers.

MESA Special Account for the Eradication of Malaria.

METO Middle Eastern Treaty Organization.

OCAS Organization of Central American States.

ORCA European Organization for the Coordination of Investigations of Fluoride and the Prophylaxis of Dental Caries.

PATA Tourist Association of the Pacific Region.

PUAS Postal Union of the Americas and Spain.

TAO Technical Assistance Operations.

UMOSEA World Union of Organizations for the Protection of Infancy.

UNPOC Commission for the Observation of Peace.

UNTA United Nations Technical Assistance.

of the table and from there on the fortran builds up like the diplodocus with a little bone that gives you the whole skeleton in the end."

"I didn't mean to offend you, Lonstein, I would have had to explain so many things to you, that balcony, I don't know."

"Everything would be in attaining the catalyzing conjunctions and letting one's eyes and talent fall along the Rasmussian copy, suddenly the messages like green eagles, prexpress, prexpress! For the moment I admit that I'm rather stuck, but I don't despair of articulating the totomundus of the crefundeum and protoplasmating a new struculture that we will immediately communicate to UNESCO even though it might only be to die laughing when they let Rasmussen go."

"When is the next news broadcast on?"

"Who cares. At twelve-fifty. Here, look here and tell me if one doesn't feel that EMA, AIDA, LIDIA, and LILA are not predestined for a new dance of the hours or

WCC World Council of Churches.

the birth of Venus, and that it would be necessary to bring them together even though the executive councils were to throw themselves off the flat roofs that those organizations always have. Notice how for this dance of true concord and cooperation countless concomitants are counted on, delightful things like the ARPA, the ECO, the FICA, and the FIGO. Of course if you look at what such melodious approaches correspond to," the little rabbi murmured somewhat disconcerted, "you'll realize that the distances are galactic. Now then, if you pay close attention, aside from the League of Antiquarian Booksellers whose meaning is not too well understood, poor Lila, all the rest have their connections, first the gelt from the Monetary Accord, which moves the sun and the other stars, then combustibles, dope, and drinking, the last with its unhealthy consequences although who knows what paradontopathies are. Ah, it's a miracle!" the little rabbi shouted recovering hope, "now I can see the climax and the geyser of conunctions, how could it be otherwise that when one begins with four lovelies like Aida, Lila, and the rest, that he won't end up in Gynecology and Obstetrics. There's posterity, the Great Work marches on, the Egg, the Egg!"

"'It's almost news time, I think. I already asked your forgiveness, old man."

"What do I care about your excuses in view of the almost supernatural fact that FEA, ugly, is the acronym for nothing less than the International Federation for Artistic Education and that WCC designates the World Council of Churches, along these paths I'm heading straight for a revelation that will make Wittgenstein look sick."

"Listen," said Andrés raising the volume on the radio, "three governments have agreed to free the prisoners demanded by the Screwery."

"Obviously," said the little rabbi who didn't weaken easily, "they have no recourse but to pass through the ARO, hoop, and tolerate the CORSO, piracy, I'm going to follow this up until I can descript and decode its ultimate consequences, and believe me that will be the TAO. As for you, why don't you stay here nice and peaceful? You're the perfect baby-sitter, Manuel puts me down completely."

"Give me the address, Lonstein. I don't know what to tell you, I've got to go, that's all. Give it to me, brother."

"I really shouldn't," the little rabbi grumbled. "First because I don't know it, and second because you never had any great involvement in the Screwery. I know, Ludmilla and all that, but you don't even know if she went with Marcos."

"Oh yes, I know," said Andrés running his hands over his face, "I don't have to phone home, it's what she had to do, consider him the complete winner."

"As a reason it doesn't seem sufficient to me, you'd better wait till they get back and then you can play the dostoevsky, why take one of those terribly boring trains."

"Now you see," I told him, trying to make the words have some meaning in that fog where Lonstein was still dropping his clinmars, his orcas, his umoseas, and his etc., "in the end you're not so different from the rest of us, you're asking me for coherence and cohesion, everything I would be asked for by people like Roland or Gómez if they were here. All of a sudden you're on their side, logic and proper reasons, the night I spent doesn't count for you, the incredible number of stupidities I committed to try to know if it's heads or tails, and I won't tell you all that because I'm a difficult guy for such things, so just look at me and decide."

As for looking at him Lonstein looked at him.

"If we could leave off with prolegomena and other ballockries," he said.

Manuel crept over and hung onto Andrés's left cuff, then the right, and using both climbed up with great resolution while proffering things like beep, ifctugpi, igo, afa, and aeji.

"This kid is all pissed up," Andrés said, "what kind of a nanny are you?"

"Susana left me streams of cotton and diapers in the bedroom, lotions and talcum powder and other garbage, but you understand that with the mushroom and the news bulletins, by the way notice the imitative sense the kid has, he said afia and ifctugpi perfectly, and they're not easy."

"And then you talk about leaving off with prolegomena. Come here at least and let's do something so he doesn't throw everything out the window."

The little rabbi seemed to understand and followed Andrés to the bed where they stripped Manuel who had several maps sketched out from the waist down and a perfume that was rather a long way from Chanel. Timid and clumsy, convinced that if they held his legs they would break them and that rubbing a piece of cotton over the affected areas was a chore destined for the worst of catastrophes, they didn't even hear the news that the last South American government in question had just accepted the aerial embarkation of five guerrilla fighters demanded by the Screwery. The operation of washing hands and in Lonstein's case the left cheek and elbow took them as long as changing Manuel, but finally the three returned to the living room with a great feeling of confraternity and good conscience. The one I told you would note later on that that somewhat coprological and urinary interval had its importance because Lonstein gave Andrés a glass of grappa and seriously almost solemnly asked him what the fuck he wanted with the information about Verrières since friendship was one thing and in a certain sense, distant but actual, duty was something else. What kind of duty, Andrés said. I haven't got the slightest idea, said Lonstein, but it wasn't for nothing that they left the child with me and went off to stir up a rotten mess that's going to be costly for all of us, goddamned motherfuckers.

"Ifctugpi," Manuel said, sucking on the part of the tassels he had left.

"I haven't got a clear idea of the reasons either, old man. There's Ludmilla's going to bed with Marcos, something that nobody, starting with me, can reproach her for. The bad part is that as always there comes the moment when you get up and get dressed again, suddenly you find yourself fifty yards above a cemetery or a country house where a son of a bitch kidnapped by the Screwery is going to unleash one of those Francosouthamerican repressions that I don't have to tell you about."

"Ah, so Ludmilla did go with them," said the little rabbi, not at all surprised. "Don't expect me to fall off my chair, it's been some time that your all for the worst has been on the edge of the Río de la Plata awakening. But she's one thing and you're another, little brother."

"Oh, me. Of course."

"And your coming here with the disguised fighting mood of a little pampa bully I can understand, because we all have hearts, what the fuck, but there are several versts standing between that and what you want me to do."

"Agreed," Andrés said emptying his glass with one swallow and refilling it with the same speed, "but the bad part is that you're a Jewish gaucho and when it comes to understanding certain things first the flying balls and then the Talmud. You poor bastard, why don't you really look at me and make an effort to understand."

"Fenude!" shouted Manuel who had found a particularly worn piece of tassel and was sucking it anxiously.

"How about that," the little rabbi said enthusiastically, "it's nothing less than the United Nations Special Fund for Economic Development."

"Fuck," said Andrés, "you wonder why everybody is breaking his ass preparing the album of the future for him when he's already got a weltanshauung that beats all."

"Well, in any case excuse the sudden attack," said Lonstein passing him the cigarettes, "but what did you expect, among us things tend to turn out the way they do in tangos, a simple matter of horns and balls and that's the way we are. My racial wisdom tells me that there's something else, but maybe you'd do well to explain to me that Fritz Lang thing and the other riddles you suggested as a good sign that you belong to the agonizing oligarchy."

"It's very simple," Andrés said, smiling for the first time that morning, "I want to be with Ludmilla, for better or for worse, something that may seem oligarchical to you, and in this case I'm afraid it's the worse because she found the better last night and I won't be the one to argue about it, you know how we Frenchified Argentines lose all virile feeling and according to the national consensus we're fairies without a grandmother. That's clear, I hope."

"In short," Lonstein said, "having dilucidated that masculine aspect of the problem, allow me to put before you the fact that there's still another one just as hairy, or maybe I don't understand too well why you want to inmisculate yourself so spontaneously in a *meresunda* that will certainly end up badly. I know, for worse, I heard you. But you should be aware that the Screwery isn't just Ludmilla, there are no less than several million characters caught up in that tug of war. What will you give in exchange for the information you want from me?"

"Nothing," Andrés said. "Like what Caetano Veloso sings on that record that Heredia made us listen to, *I've got nothing, I don't come from here.* I can't even give you Irene, like in the song."

"The gentleman wants things, but he won't give up anything."

"No, I won't give up anything, old man."

"Not even a little, let's say a delightful author, a Japanese poet that only he knows?"

"No, not even that."

"His Xenakis, his aleatory music, his free jazz, his Joni Mitchell, his abstract lithographs?"

"No, brother. Nothing. I take everything with me wherever it may be that I'm going."

"We're just the way we want to be," Lonstein said. "The sow and her twenty, eh."

"Yes sir," Andrés said, "because nothing deep has happened

to me, you talk about Ludmilla's Río de la Plata awakening and it's probably true and Ludmilla no longer has anything to do with the woman I knew, but the only thing that's happened to me is something like the suspicion, almost the desire that something's happening to me, old man, and in order for you to understand I'd have to talk to you about Fritz Lang and one of these days about a fly or a black stain, things that aren't very palpable as you can see."

"I'll probably be bored stiff," the little rabbi said, "but the fact that the fly and the stains have turned you into a piece of snot is something unquestionable, I can tell you that every night I do the twalay for a few with the same characteristics, a bad comparison."

"Bah, I've spent hours trying to open a whole lot of doors and probably trying to close a lot of others, to shed light on the stain and the fly, and in the end everything goes on more or less the same except that in some place in the Marais there'll be a girl crying, things like that. You know, breaking open the beehives, millions of historical hexagons piled up since Ur, since Lagash, since Agrigentum, since Carthage, since every little leap of history, the hexagonal chromosomes in every one of us, go break that up, Lonstein, suicide is nothing alongside that self-destruction, you think about it and you think you feel it and most of all you imagine that you're going to be able to live it, you stick your hand into the first hexagon, which by the way I call triangle for practical reasons, and right there a counterpunch against you, the self-knockout that hits you in the kidneys with one of those jabs that make Jack Dempsey look weak, ask the Argentines who felt them through the medium of the wild bull of the pampas."

"Oh boy," said the little rabbi with sincere admiration, "I didn't know you had those populist derivations, you with your Xenakis and your little sofa culture and the lamp on the left side. Underneath it all you're a little like the one I told you and like me, of course the three of us get fucked up as soon as we extrapolate ourselves historically, ask Chou En-lai."

"It's of no importance," I told him having had enough now, "just give me the information and I'll go."

"Every fortran is desirable and necessary," Lonstein said, "probably your pampa triangle goes beyond Ludmilla and Marcos and you, what should matter is to know whether at some time you or we will be capable of fortran. In any case it's fine now that you've realized that the mental world of Argentines is not the whole world and that in the second place the whole world is not a privilege of males, geometry can project it any way you want, you thought your scheme was acceptable and now you've come to find out that women have their little triangle to tell too. Well, take the Métro at the Luxembourg station, I'll make a little note, Marcos will kill me, I'm sure, as long as they don't kill him first because the ants you can already imagine and let's not mention the vernacular flics."

"I'll get there after dark," Andrés said, "and I'll be careful."

"If you get there," said Lonstein.

Papers get mixed up on you just the same as life, so you go into the Bazar Dos Mundos if it still exists and after buying screwdrivers, deodorant, and various kinds of nails for the labors of the weekend, at the moment of paying it so happens that the lady at the checkout punches the gaudy keys of her electronic machinery and finally out comes a rather extensive paper tape at the lower end of which one clearly reads the figure 389.45 pesos, in view of which you adopt the air of a tortoise brusquely extracted from his shell and declare that it can't be possible because two screwdrivers and seven nails you're not going to tell me can come to a figure like that. At first these ladies tend to maintain that the figure is exact and the machines don't lie, but a previous manual and ocular investigation on the part of the overseer who is always present in such cases comes to the conclusion that even lunar rockets fail and what a goodly number of dollars they cost, believe me, with which her professional integrity having been maintained, the lady proceeds to play the piano a second time and out comes a little bill for you of 38.94, for which we make payment toot sweet in the midst of several very sorry sirs, these things can happen to anyone, of course madam, that's all you needed, fine. As now that the one I told you could not calculate with too much precision the moment in which Higinio spoke with the Vipess, the instructions Inspector Pillaudin gave to Brigade 56-C with headquarters in Bourg-la-Reine, and the wheezy nocturnal remembrances of the Vipess, including the quite evident fact that human memory has its limits and that no one was under any obligation to remember who the said Higinio was except the Vipess clinging to the telephone while the maid brought the bedpan to her room because the frights of the evening before were being manifested in the form of a diarrhea capable of putting Niagara to shame, with which the one I told you gave himself over to an understandable fatigue, and after collating the material available with a frown he turned it loose pell-mell and the devil take the hindmost. Yes, but what might happen then: after the two dots necessary to establish the interrogative hiatus, the one I told you shrugged his shoulders and looked around dishearteningly, he was putting one scrap of paper here and another one there, on one side Lucien Verneuil informing Marcos objective attained (Radio Montecarlo, 5:30 P.M. news, governments accept ultimatum, confirmation of aerial embarkations awaited), in a separate paragraph Roland and Patricio made it known that the starry night had not so far brought the slightest element of concern and that given those decidedly auspicious circumstances it was the moment for the maenads to put together a special cold platter with a double portion of salami or ham in the sandwiches that had been Spartan up till then, and marginally, but with a marked tendency to converge on the place of the events, Andrés Fava was leaving a suburban subway station and following whimsical orbits, a very unrealistic thing given the fact that the ants with Higinio at their head had had him covered from the word go and that Inspector Pillaudin had just given the necessary instructions to Brigade 56-C that there was no need for haste, quite the contrary since a basic element in the matter indicated that the enemy would probably have a falling out before any intervention in the name of liberty, equality, and fraternity. Ah, sighed the one I told you surrounded by doubts, itineraries, and alternatives, this isn't serious, brother, who's going to believe it someday if there is a someday because at this time of night Bobby Fischer moves the fatal bishop and a bitter *mate*, as corresponds to Argentines, of course the ingenious metaphor or metonymy (the big dummy never understood the difference) was the direct result of Higinio's hanging on a longdistancecall and a voice resounding with tonsils from Los Angeles (of all names) approving the report from the Gi-ant and assuring him everything

O.K. thanks to the C.onnection I.ntelligent A.borigine, in common parlance the liaison officer with the Frenchyflics, so full speed ahead, buddy, don't raise any more cain than necessary because after the Ben Barka affair things ain't what they used to be, with which the one I told you could perfectly well allow himself the audacious syncretism of chess and runaway, don't you think.

"Well," said Oscar, dying with hunger and boredom, "you've been giving me a lot of kisses and all those things, but we've been here a whole day already without a bite of anything come eel foe."

"We're ladies from Mendoza," Gladis said offended, "we spend hours and hours combining in showy and unpublished ways the four tin cans in the kitchen, except that San Martín showed himself to be more grateful for feminine help. Look what Susana found in the newspaper, Monique and Ludmilla are making heroic efforts to put it into practice, but you people with your usual boorishness."

Grilled Sandwiches Indicated For Restful Weekends

Sandwiches as the solution for restful outings or weekends offer infinite combinations which do not neglect dietary variety. Hand coolers allow them to be carried and kept fresh without their changing or losing flavor.

The following recipes, highly nutritious, represent a little-used variety: grilled sandwiches.

Meat: mix chopped beef and white sauce in equal parts and season with salt and pepper to taste. Form sandwiches with this mixture on thin slices of bread and brown them slightly on the outside with hot oil or butter.

Chicken: in a large enough receptacle place the contents of a can of chicken paste, chop ½ medium-sized onion, add a spoonful of

"Up till now we haven't seen much of any solution sandwiches," Heredia said.

"Because there's no meat or chicken," Susana roared, "and in such cases please tell me what shit we can fry. It's Lucien's fault and most of all his mother's, who must be as stuffy as he is, all the fridge had was a half a can of milk and a worm-eaten sausage."

"Of course the Vip gets double rations so that afterwards he won't talk about moral tortures," Oscar said, "don't think I haven't seen them going upstairs with the plates, it's a case of children and stepchildren."

Marcos, who was coming back from the telephone, made a signal to Patricio and Oscar and the fried sandwiches dissolved around them: from somewhere in the Latin Quarter they got the predictable news, Higinio in person with Inspector Pillaudin no less in person, it figures.

"They already know, of course," Patricio said. "They're going to fall on us at any moment, old man."

"But what are the French going to do?" asked Oscar who had no reason to know.

"They'll get here first," said Heredia, who had a streak of Francophilia.

"One of two things," Marcos said, "either they'll let the ants hack it alone and then come to count the casualties, or they'll cut them off on the way and present it as a triumph of order in the face of the savagery of underdeveloped tribes who are trying to turn French soil into an ass-busting place."

"The first," Roland said.

"Bien sûr," Lucien Verneuil backed him up.

"I think so too," Marcos said, "and in that case watch the windows. That's the way things are, now we've got to take care of the Vip like a bride, old man, I don't like that one bit. Telephone René, the car ought to be here now to take him away."

"At eight-fifteen," Roland said looking at his watch, "and it's five after."

"The bride has been told," Lucien Verneuil said, "and he seems to have taken the news with particular enthusiasm. He put on his jacket and said that in spite of everything he has nothing to complain about as long as he doesn't get knocked off at the last minute."

"It's hard for him to break his habits," Marcos said, "the

problem is René's coming here, there must be ants everywhere after the powwow between the Gi-ant and Pillaudin."

"It hasn't been proven that the Gi-ant knows where we are."

"Youth, youth," Heredia murmured looking at Oscar. It was one of those rather useless bridges that the one I told you always took advantage of to go off on, disconcerted and regretful because he too liked to listen to idiotic dialogues, but what do you want, among other things there was me for example after a not at all comfortable trip among office workers crammed into the subway and symbolically represented by an old man who from the Luxembourg station on had stuck the handle of his umbrella between my ribs and who could protest in the midst of that sixthirtyhumanmass, ejaculated finally without the least pleasure at the Antony station along with hundreds of other spermatozoids hurrying to fertilize the daily egg of the exit tunnel, coming out into an unknown region of greater Paris, tired and rather drunk, turning around in his head a kind of poem that the rhythm of the subway car could claim as its own, feeling myself supremely idiotic now that I was getting close to what might result in a definition or a new black stain, maybe an irremediable guilt if reaching that house wasn't precisely what was best for the Screwery. So there, more or less: a hope of feeling better, even going down the stairs at Lonstein's a feeling one gets before an imminent appointment and at the same time still Francine, imagining her in her apartment looking at herself in the mirror, naked or only in her panties looking at herself for no precise reason, wondering whether Andrés would call her, whether he'd really decided to go to Verrières, the transistor on the night table, pop music and from time to time news about the kidnapping of the coordinator of Latin American affairs and the acceptance of the ultimatum. He'll go, of course he'll go, if he was capable of talking to me about the place, if he plays with fire like that he'll go because he loves her and hasn't resigned himself to losing her even if he thinks he's going because of the others, a bad conscience isn't any stronger than jealousy, he'll go because he wants to see her again and he feels like a rag far away and alone while Ludmilla is in danger, and she was accursedly sure that I was going for that reason even though not only because of that, girl, you're forgetting about Fritz Lang more and more a hairy ball in his stomach, there's someone who wants to speak to you, someone in this room, and it's not just you, Polonette, there's Fritz Lang and the petit bourgeois with the cramp in his stomach, there's the one who laughed at the response in movies and cafés, the burned matches, and suddenly everything is Ludmilla and much more, as if the black stain, you realize, except that there'll never be anything to pull me away from this thing I am, the one who listens to free jazz and goes to bed with Francine as a fulfillment of ceremonies that Maoist youth don't approve of, love for ritual, pleasure in the tension of the arc of the blood, the selfishness of all perfect statues, a sketch closing itself off after the last swirl, petit bourgeois versus the Gómezes and the Lucien Verneuils who want to make the revolution to save the proletariat and the peasantry and the colonialized and the alienated by what they so correctly call imperialism but afterwards, afterwards, because there are already countries where they are in the afterwards, where they reach the Moon and Mars and Venus of all places, work like madmen to make and consolidate the revolution and are in the afterwards, have fifty years of afterwards and yet that same afternoon the little rabbi looking at me with the irony that comes to him from the Pentateuch and the Diaspora and four hundred pogroms, looking at me while END OF BUKOVSKY TRIAL SEVEN YEARS PRISON FOR SPREADING UNFAVORABLE INFORMATION ABOUT SOVIET REGIME and Solzhenit-

BULLETIN DE L'ÉTRANGER

La condamnation de Boukovski

Le tribunal de Moscou a la main lourde. Vladimir Boukovski, accusé d' « avoir commis des actes visant à affaiblir le pouvoir soviétique », a été condamné, le 5 janvier, au maximum de la peine prévue pour les opposants : sept ans de privation de liberté, dont deux ans en prison et cinq ans dans un camp à régime sévère. Ensuite il sera assigné à résidence, pendant cinq ans, en dehors de la capitale. L'inculpé, indique l'agence Tass, a reconnu les faits qui lui ont été reprochés.

syn muttering at Tarnovsky's grave phrases that would cover the cheeks of Lenin's mummy with tears if it were not that THE SOVIET MUMMY NEVER WEEPS (for being Soviet, of course), then Marcos, a sluggish boy from Córdoba looking at me as from afar and saying yes, my brother, that's why it's necessary to start all over again, history doesn't repeat itself or in any case we're not going to let it repeat itself, and Patricio approving and Gómez convinced, but of course, certainly, except that Gómez, precisely, Gómez and Roland and Lucian Verneuil are of those who will repeat history, you can spot them from far off, they'll risk their necks for the revolution, they'll give everything but when the afterwards arrives they'll repeat the same definitions that end up with seven years in jail for Bukovsky who over there someday will be named Sánchez or Pereyra, they'll deny the deepest freedom, the one I bourgeoisly call individual and mea culpa, of course, but underneath it's the same thing, the right to listen to free jazz if I feel like it and I don't hurt anyone, the freedom to go to bed with Francine for analogous reasons, and I'm afraid, I'm afraid of the Gómezes and Lucien Verneuils who are the ants of the good side, the fascists of the revolution (watch it, there, you're shifting position, Lonstein's grappa must have had pentothal in it or something like it), this must be the street that goes to Verrières if the little rabbi's sketch isn't too full of fantasy, he forbade me to ask anybody so as not to awaken unhealthy curiosity and he's right, so let's turn right and probably at any minute, because even though it's nightime, as they say, we'll come safely to port, the bitch of it is that two streets go off here and the little rabbi only drew one, the crossroads of Oedipus, the great decision, left or right, left of course since nature imitates art and it will certainly lead me to the ominous forest where conspirators hide victims, this has something of an initiation trip about it, there's nothing left for you to do but choose, Siegfried, in you is the path of life and of death, Ludmilla or the dragon and all reasons why, please tell me, even if yes, everything for Ludmilla and for Marcos too even though it hurts me from the waist down, everything for that madman and that madwoman lost in a dream that makes Fritz Lang pale, a daylight dream that's going to end with cold lead, brother, although one of these days Fritz Lang's too since this idiot takes the subway and comes to stick his nose in precisely where no one has asked him and that's costly, in any case not for the Gómezes or the Rolands or the Lucien Verneuils, only because the testament is written and signed and in his shitoid and diarrheaform way as the little rabbi would say, the petit bourgeois is searching for his way out which is his way in and all of that without softening the Gómezes, poor Panamanian damned if he imagines that I've changed him into the image of what I hate most, people who ring the doorbell in the middle of a Mozart quintet, people who won't let me peacefully read the diary of Anaïs Nin or listen to Joni Mitchell, poor Gómez so good but who's going to be the Gómez Robespierre of tomorrow if the Screwery brings everything off all the way, if they make their necessary and unpostponable revolution, well, let's turn left even if it is night, my dear John of the Cross, sweet poet of my sweet sofa hours, let's go right on even if it is night and the ants are preparing their heaters, old childhood tango, the big shot of the slums, *the heaters flashed, and the poor big shot fell*, I wonder if anyone remembers that tango that made me cry as a kid stuck to the green tin loudspeaker, oh life so long, so full of beauty and rottenness, the life of an Argentine condemned to understand, to understand, except the black stain always because that or Mademoiselle Antinéa or the fly in the whiskey or Francine's weeping, oh shit, why don't you let me understand the reason for this idiocy, of the guy who looks for his path in the midst of whorishness and trembling to be what he should be except happy because not that, for sure, I'll be one more corpse or I'll get there too late and they'll tease me or Marcos will look at me as if asking why the goddamned hell did you come to fuck things up where nobody asked you, anything except the happiness that remained behind on the Rue de l'Ouest in an easy chair with a bottle of whiskey within reach, with that record by Xenakis to listen to and those books to read, anything for me and for my sake except happiness, there will be the Screwery with the foreseeable consequences but not the happiness of Heredia and Ludmilla and Monique, those who go to the end looking ahead, the children of Che as somebody said, there will be shit and a bouquet but not happiness for the petit bourgeois who doesn't want, who doesn't want to renounce what the Maos and the Gómezes are going to sweep away and who in spite of all, who knows for what fucking reason, for what madness, for what black stain of the most whorish mother who bore it going along this road that leads to a wood, to that other black stain getting slowly closer, and the problem is to understand Lonstein's sketch now, first a turn, then a crossroads, you take the right, and you go in between some trees, a chalet hidden in the cedars, idyllic without doubt, perfumed with night, with Ludmilla, with mad beauty. What an urge to throw myself in the ditch, sleep it off until tomorrow, write what was being born while I withstood the old man's umbrella in the subway

When the snails parade
and leave a trail that sketches out the lettuce taste
changing its drivel of delight into the perfume of the full moon

I am the one who listens in Paris
to Joni Mitchell sing

the one who between two smokes
felt time go by for Pichuco
and Roberto Firpo

My grandmother talking to me in a garden in Banfield,
a sleepy suburb of Buenos Aires,
"Snail, snail
let the sun shine on your tail."

Maybe that's why on this suburban night
there are snails, Joni Mitchell, American girl
who sings between two drinks,
between a Falú and a Pedro Maffia
(I haven't got any more time and I don't care for fads,

I mix Jelly Roll Morton and Gardel and Stockhausen,
blessed be the Lamb)

What a strange thing
being Argentine on this night,
knowing I'm going to an appointment
with no one, with a woman who belongs to someone else,
with someone who spoke to me in the dark,
that I'll arrive soon
for what

What a strange thing
being Argentine on this night,
the voice of Joni Mitchell
between a Falú and a Pedro Maffia,
a cocktail of memory, *rare blend of Musetta and Mimi,*
to your health, Delfino, childhood comrade,
being Argentine in a Paris suburb
"Snail, snail, let the sun shine on your tail."
Pichuco's concertina, Joni Mitchell,
Maurice Fanon, girl, *me souvenir de toi,*
de ta loi sur mon corps,
being Argentine, walking
to an appointment with whom and for what reason,
such a strange thing
without renouncing Joni Mitchell
being Argentine in this black stain,
Fritz Lang, I am Andrés, just tell me,
that house behind the trees,
there certainly, the cedars and the silence,
everything falls together, but then
everything begins to be nothing again,
knowing that I will come to an appointment
with a woman who belongs to someone else,
what a strange thing

("Someone wants to speak to you," a waiter
in a white jacket, the gesture pointing

to the room in the dark)—
I'm coming, my friend,
wait till Joni Mitchell finishes,
till Atahualpa's silent, I'm getting there,
open, Ludmilla, they're waiting for me
in a dark room.
it's a Cuban, the waiter said, he has something
to tell you.
I dreamed all that, of course, and suddenly I remember
precisely on arriving here, the black stain opens,

I see a face, I hear a voice, everything that I dreamed Fritz Lang I remember, like a sheet that's torn in half that garden with cedars in the shadows I remember without surprise, the surprising thing is almost not having recognized it before, from the beginning, on waking up, so clear and obvious and even beautiful to remember it while I approach the door of the chalet and raise my hand so they won't kill me without at least knowing who I am and that I'm not coming to sell them out, what a strange thing being Argentine in this garden and at this hour, plunged into madness and remembering Ludmilla and Francine and Joni Mitchell, their laws on my body, women and voices and bodies and books while I raise my arms so they'll see me easily, Gómez or Lucien Verneuil or maybe Marcos crouching behind the windows, they're going to rake me with curses when they recognize me if they recognize me because what the fuck am I coming here for at this hour and at the height of the Screwery, tell me that, Pichuco, explain that fact to me, Falú, unless they drop me with a bullet and the poor big shot fell, big shot reader of Heidegger, tell me if it isn't to piss on the trunks of these majestic cedars, because these cedars really are beautiful in the night, living things and green in the great black stain with something singing up there, probably the legendary nightingale, I never heard a nightingale, I was brought up on lapwings and starlings in Banfield, open up for me Ludlud, let me come in to tell you, girl, come it's Andrés, girl, let me tell you if these punks will give me time because they're certainly going to put a bullet in my belly, don't be dumb bastards, let me in now that it's clear, now that there isn't any black stain, because that's how it is, right now and here, old man, right on reaching the little chalet of the naughty children I catch a glimpse of the antenna as my aunt says, pow there it is, the room with its wicker chairs, the Cuban back and forth in the predictable rocking chair, everything can't be so clear, so neat, that weeks and weeks black stain and Fritz Lang and all of a sudden just when everything is black and cedars and chalet with lights out zap I catch a glimpse of the antenna and reconstruct the sequence, I look at the man who looks at me from the chair slowly rocking, I see my dream as if I'm finally dreaming it and so simple, so idiotic, so clear, so obvious, it was so perfectly foreseeable that tonight and here I should remember all of a sudden that the dream was nothing more than that, that the Cuban was looking at me and saying only two words to me: *Wake up.*

Yes, the one I told you thinks angrily, you can talk about waking up you, on top of the work these others are giving me the only thing I need is for you to appear with your inner drama and all that stuff, I really don't know what I'm going to do with the ending.

It was precisely what Lonstein had asked during the days when the one I told you was beginning to put his notes together again and Susana appeared with the album. The two of them are completely mad, the little rabbi had opined, of course in any case she's a mother and we all know, but you, please explain.

"I haven't got the slightest idea," the one I told you had loyally recognized. "It's like torticollis, something inexplicable but which happens, what can you do, I was there with them watching them live, and little by little I was putting them into writing as the cultured boys of today say, until suddenly just take a look."

"What you're showing me doesn't look like any major case of charisma to me," Lonstein had said. "I really don't give a hoot about the Screwery business, but in any event you can't duck its pathos, eh, while yours on the other hand deserves a goose."

Something the one I told you tended to admit precisely at the moment he witnessed the entrance of Andrés catapulted half gently and half firmly by Marcos, with the door closing again and Lucien Verneuil who threw all the bolts at the same time, the linear measurement falling to pieces in face of a series of simultaneities that rather bored the one I told you although not so much the others present who hurriedly took care to decipher a rather obscure meaning, and then:

"Wake up."

"You," Patricio announced, "really are a hairy beast, look at how you've pulled me out of sleep just when I was managing to catch five minutes on top of this moth-eaten rug."

"Shh," Oscar shshed, "come quick."

As quickly as he could come, Patricio only caught the tail end of the maneuver which consisted of the door closing and Lucien Verneuil's throwing all the bolts at the same time while Marcos, pushing Andrés, a little lost in that dark domicile, made him go into the living room where stupefied maenads, to say the least, at the same time that Roland was coming down the stairs four steps at a time to warn them of shadows on the rear side by the woodshed, with his pistol aimed at Andrés barely visible thanks to the candle stub, a gesture by Marcos for Roland to stop playing with guns, and to what do we owe the honor of your presence. Well, I don't know, old man, I thought I had to come. Of course, with the ants following you, dummy, Patricio said still resentful over the way Oscar had awakened him, Heredia advising them that the shadows had been lost behind the trees, a kind of interregnum in which Ludmilla took Andrés over to a couch and by feel gave him a glass of wine, Marcos as if waiting and Andrés I don't know, I'm sorry if I put my foot in it, I didn't think they'd follow me, the one who put his foot in it was me, said Marcos, with guys like you and Lonstein set on messing up the ending, Monique lighting the candle stub again and Roland from the stairs, they're hiding in the trees waiting for something, there are eight or nine of them, Patricio with the pistol on his knees, we're pretty evenly matched but what will I do with the Vip if René can't get here with the car. We've given our word, Heredia said, no matter what happens we've got to turn him loose in a good state of preservation, if René doesn't get here I'll take him to the door and let him go all by himself to join up with the ants or the flics, he's dressed and washed and he's eaten well, what the fuck, no one can say that we didn't keep our word. Yes, Marcos said, but who knows if they're interested now in receiving the package intact or would rather say that it arrived with all the string broken. That's right, said Heredia, I hadn't thought of that. Goddamn it, we really have to watch out for him like a bride, Oscar said. Marcos is right, Heredia said, it's the outside image, old man, they'll certainly try to falsify it, with Roland pushing the Vip who came downstairs and held his hands up as if someone were aiming at him, Patricio ordering him to sit on the rug, forming a kind of ring of redskins in the quivering light of the candle stump, Lucien Verneuil advising they're ants, the police would have attacked already, but then, Marcos said, I'm sure if they got here first it's because of what we already know, they're going to start the battle in order to do him in and put the blame on us. The funny thing would be to call the cops on the phone, Oscar said. Gentlemen, gentlemen, said the Vip from the floor, I really wanted to say that, he saw Roland's pistol and raised his hands again as if praying in a mosque. Put him in the john, it's the safest place, Marcos told Roland, you people keep watch out the windows, you Polonette go upstairs and keep watch and keep me posted. Let me stay here, Ludmilla said and she hadn't finished saying it when she got up and ran upstairs, shit, stupid, starting an argument with Marcos at this time, and when she got up there a panoramic view of the group dissolving, Roland pushing the Vip, Heredia and Patricio at the living-room windows, Lucien Verneuil watching the door. She got close to a window, slipped until she discovered that it was better sitting down and that she could see what little there was to see in the cedar garden, from below came the sound of readiness, the noise of the toilet door, she imagined the Vip sitting on the only seat capable of receiving him in a worthy manner, there was no time to think about Andrés, seeing him hadn't been a surprise, rather the feeling of something useless and going to ruin, a tardy stubbornness for which the others were now going to pay dearly, and at the same time a kind of happiness that Andrés had come, so many other things. Bloop, shit, they're hiding behind the tree trunks, she couldn't be distracted for one single second, but all the same she could think just as if she were still in the room downstairs, Marcos coming and going, Ludmilla had stopped seeing Andrés, thinking about Andrés, she'd given him the glass of wine and the rest was only Marcos, Polonette sentry of the cedars and of Marcos, all she had left of Andrés was the gesture in the half-light when he had taken the glass of wine and had looked at her smiling a little, from another unreachable side, as if wanting to make her understand why he'd come, and all the rest was Marcos and the waiting, a fear in her stomach and hands clutching her shoes, a silence of cedars in the garden and Marcos.

For his part, trying uselessly to put a little order into himself and maybe into the rest, the one I told you had decided that for the moment the best thing was to sit down beside Andrés and have Monique and Gladis within reach, a feeling of knightly protection which was good for nothing at that moment but if in addition Susana left Patricio alone and came with them one could hope to talk about other things, without mentioning that no one was safe and probably those in the Screwery were letting themselves be pulled along by optical illusions. When the first shot sounded it was as if the whole house had been moved two yards forward or backward, Roland's pistol must have been some kind of cannon, Ludmilla's voice at the top of the stairs, here they come, Marcos, eight or nine of them, another shot from Patricio's side, a shout outside, the tremendous blow against the door, Lucien Verneuil drawing back slowly half a yard and aiming at the chest of the one opening it. Well, they asked for it, Marcos said with the pistol in his hand, telephone the police station in Verrières, whether they like it or not we're going to hand him over alive and kicking to the French. You understand me, Higinio said, if you can use one of their pistols. Of course, chief, said the Sycoph-ant, you leave it up to me, just give me the chance and he won't talk again, in the meantime let me say that the more shooting there is the easier it's going to be for this friend of yours here. Let's go, said the Gi-ant, everybody at the same time. And so, the one I told you recalled, as wingèd multitudes of geese, cranes, and thin-necked swans soar high above Asian meadows beside the Xanthos, making the air tremble with their cries, so ran the countless tribes of Sycoph-ants, Miscre-ants, Attend-ants, and Philosoph-ants like a torrent on the plain that the Scamander bathes, and under their feet the earth rumbled horribly. And the great Gi-ant rose up in the midst of all, likened in eyes and mien to Zeus hurler of the thunderbolt, to Ares in stature, and to Ronald Reagan in breadth of chest. Behind the sofa, said Andrés grabbing Monique by the neck and without any other explanation pushing her into the aforementioned place. Here (a repetition of the procedure with Gladis and Susana), be quiet for me, and you guerrilla girl, tell me where there's a pistol because I may be drunk but in my day I qualified a hundred percent in the Federal Target Shoot, so. Ask Marcos, Susana said not going beyond her powers. Here, said Marcos who had overheard no one knows how, and in Andrés's hand a cold, sweet thing, pleasing to squeeze as it slowly grew warm. From far off a siren could be heard, there's no need to phone with a fire fight like this, Inspector Pillaudin was no Beethoven and the three patrol cars and other gaudy accoutrements drew up two hundred yards away at the precise moment when the most valiant Microphonic-ants who dwelt in Euboeia and Chalcis and Erythrae and Histiaia rich in grapes, and maritime Kerinthos, and the tall citadel of Dion, showed themselves anxious to pierce the breastplates of the foe with their ashen pikes. And along with them advanced the hosts of the Flatul-ants and the Minim-ants, along with the Recre-ants who inhabited Aspledon and Orchomenus of Minyae, chieftained by left-handed Malerba and his ambidextrous brother, sons of Nemesio Yáñez who one day surprised the innocent virgin Astyoche Aceida, who gave them being in the dwelling of Actor, and who knows what else. We have to wait a bit, Pillaudin said, three shots are nothing great, I want the stew well cooked, orders from higher up. As Lucien Verneuil also at the moment the door opened, exactly in the middle of the chest and Philosoph-ant on the ground, a doormat for the two Miscre-ants who walked over him as the last thing in the world for him and for them because Lucien Verneuil bang bang, the second Miscre-ant on going down bang, Lucien Verneuil slowly slipping while Marcos and Heredia almost at the same time bang, Heredia and Marcos closing the door and looking at Lucien Verneuil, put a cupboard in front of it, Monique looking for something, it's nothing, help the others, blood running down Monique's fingers while Andrés and Susana helped her lift Lucien and lay him on the sofa, Gladis's useless handkerchief, hiccup, two shots in succession from the north window, Heredia crouching bang bang bang, and at that moment from behind the cedars those who inhabited the environs of Aegion and great Helice, all that coast, led by the Gi-ant clad in splendid bronze and also valiant, a simultaneous rush at the windows, Patricio bringing down the first, a Defend-ant of hairless skull, the irresistible push on the door, Marcos hand to hand with the Gi-ant himself, too much infighting to get off a shot while Gómez with his clip empty looking for an opening to get in a blow with the butt and Andrés getting between Marcos and the Gi-ant to receive from the latter a pumpkin-blow full in the face that practically returned him to the origin of species, the siren in the garden and the whistles, Higinio dropping back pistol in hand, telling Marcos hand him over right now or I'll blow your head off and Marcos seeing his own pistol in the hand of the Philosoph-ant close to Higinio, understanding, remaining quiet and unwrinkled like a person dreaming as he faced the door full of ants, slowly putting his hands in his pockets and saying come in and look for him if you feel like it, seeing Higinio's pistol rise up to the level of his eyes, wondering whether Ludmilla would stay upstairs long enough for the police to come or whether crazy as always she'd butt in right there in the middle of the stew, Polonette, a pause like the ones in a broken film, don't shoot Don Higinio they're watching you, a report, the headlights in the garden and the rather unnecessary tear-gas grenade bursting at Patricio's feet, hands up everybody. Impossible to continue remembering illustrious descriptions thought the one I told you halfway up the stairs, this isn't true, it hasn't happened, in any case, it hasn't happened and it isn't happening this way, too easy to lean on classical authorities, why pretend to say something that impossibly had happened, to say the impossible that it still should be happening, so much so that he couldn't stop thinking about that stopping of the film which from one second to the next would bring on the hoots of the audience, that pause of the three hosts before the finale might also be his own pause on the stairs, his notorious incapacity for the simultaneous and even the consecutive when it was going too fast, for example the Marcos–Giant–Gómez–Andrés nucleus, where it had been before and now, Higinio retreating pistol in hand, telling Marcos hand him over right now or I'll blow your head off, and at the same time Susana, the diagonal shadow of Susana slipping by to get Patricio wrapped in the smoke of the bomb, grabbing him by the shoulders, it was necessary to decide about something, about Lucien Verneuil lying on the couch with Monique bandaging his shoulder (but how in the midst of shooting and in an almost nonexistent lapse had a bandage appeared a towel really but all the same?). Oh, no, goddamn it, thought the one I told you halfway up the stairs, this can't happen this way and here and tonight and in this country and with these people; it's all over. What about Oscar, where had Oscar and Gladis gone? Tall and energetic, almost smiling, a French inspector at the door, every right to be smiling with two machine guns protecting him, nobody move, a chance that couldn't be lost for Andrés to run in what still remained of the darkness because the spotlights were pouring in everywhere, and slipping past the one I told you who was still halfway up the stairs, half-sitting, half-fallen, passing almost on top of him to reach the landing from where Ludmilla, her mission fulfilled, was loping downstairs; he grabbed her in midflight and brought her over to the window, don't move Ludlud, it's not worth the trouble, you'll see how they'll come for us all by themselves. Marcos, Ludmilla said. He's there, Andrés said, I don't have a very precise idea of where and in what state. Let me go down, I want to see Marcos. Wait, Lud. Let me go down, *let me go down*, but it was best not to let her for the moment, to hold her like that in his arms even though she struggled and shouted, I myself couldn't be sure of what Ludmilla would find at the foot of the stairs in that confusion and the blinding spotlights and the police occupying the ground floor and coming up now, bumping into the one I told you in the middle of the stairs, you see, Lud, they saved you the trouble, they are of a proven friendliness, now yes, my love, now we will have to go down.

MILITARY AID MISSIONS OF THE U. S.

Authorized personnel of advisory groups for military assistance of the United States, military missions and military groups as of July 30, 1970.[1]

SOUTHERN COMMAND **(Southcom)**

Country	U.S. Personnel	Foreign Personnel	Total
Argentina	33	6	39
Bolivia	40	7	47
Brazil	69	33	102
Chile	32	5	37
Colombia	48	5	53
Costa Rica	4	1	5
Dominican Republic	39	2	41
Ecuador	39	5	44
El Salvador	15	2	17
Guatemala	26	3	29
Honduras	14	2	16
Nicaragua	15	2	17
Panama	5	1	6
Paraguay	17	3	20
Peru	38	4	42
Uruguay	20	5	25
Venezuela	51	2	53
Total, SOUTHCOM	505	88	593

1. Source: Department of Defense (table put in Congressional Record, April 1, 1969, p. S3510, by Senator Ellender).

On occasion Andrés would agree that everything that had preceded and followed the entry of the ants into the chalet was a total confusion, not so much because of the intrinsic magma of such situations, but because to him, an observer poorly qualified for the task, fell the job to top it off by organizing the one I told you's material, what the latter called notes but which were anything from burnt matches to plagiarisms of the *Iliad* and confused confrontations in the light of a miserable little stump of a candle, so go try to put the skein all together. People like Gómez and Heredia, for example, would have trod firmly on that ground as proven by the fact that they were looking at each other with a fucking and satisfied air, there where they were because neither Andrés nor Lonstein had the slightest idea of it and it didn't matter much to them, they looked at each other and Heredia passed his cigarette to Gómez who took an eager drag and gave it back, lying face up on a concrete floor and sharing the same and only cigarette underneath a dirty window through which dawn and the shape of an iron cross full of cobwebs were growing, in the end we screwed them coming and going, Gómez said between puffs, and Heredia doubled up a little as if something hurt him and he rubbed his shoulder with his fingers, we sure did, it was the greatest Screwery of all time, old man. To think they wanted to kill him themselves, said Gómez amused, then they would have screwed us up. The external image, Heredia said, go explain in Guatemala or Argentina that it wasn't us, that we'd kept our word. And in some other places there would be no lack of those who remember the Vip's face, coming out of the toilet and throwing himself into the arms of the Gi-ant, thank you, brother, thank you, while Inspector Pillaudin looked at them with an air of disguised raillery, it's the best we could do Don Gualberto, if we didn't attack with everything earlier it's because we wanted to protect you, those devils were capable of killing you in cold blood, slaps on the back and embraces and the Gi-ant looking over the Vip's shoulder to make sure the Miscre-ant had dropped Marcos's pistol, the Vip shouldn't catch on, but no, so emotional while Pillaudin picked up the pistol with which the possible fingerprints, and at the same time Pillaudin's overcompensatory smile, everything turned out the best way possible and in any case, thought the Gi-ant who was a realistic fellow, we couldn't carry out the order but even so they'd be happy back there, this is what's called breaking up those bastards' nest, Don Gualberto, they won't do any more screwing hereabouts. And Gómez and Heredia knew that too but they kept on smoking, silent, watching day come up, imagining the Latin American news reports, it was the greatest Screwery, old man, and that's what counts, the only thing that counts until the next one. Of course, said Heredia, Marcos would have thought the same, don't you think.

It was to be thought that the turquoise penguin had brought them good luck, neither Gladis nor Oscar would have been able to explain why they thought so much about the turquoise penguin and almost never about the royal armadillos, after all how could they know which of them had been the mascot, they constantly remembered the penguin and loved him from afar, at thirty thousand feet altitude between Dakar and Rio they loved him and remembered him, they wondered what could have happened to him and they trusted in proper zoos, lady benefactors with swimming pools and lots of hake, some international circus charging admission to see the penguin, all this by the way so as not to think too much about the mongol-looking character who was sitting in the next seat, so friendly the mongol-looking character, always the first to guess Gladis's wishes or to hand Oscar the pack of cigarettes so he could have a butt and cut the dullness of the flight. You'll see, my beauty, as soon as we reach home soil this one's going to have a sudden change in manners. Bah, Gladis said, I've got a sister who's married to a judge. Do judges get married? Oscar asked in surprise. It might be useful, don't you think. Of course, Oscar said, it's a question of having your sister convince him of the usefulness of exporting penguins to Europe. Well, you've got to talk about something, Gladis said, this gets so long when there's no work to do, I envy those girls with the trays. Me too, Oscar said, especially the redhead who's ready for what Cejas said. What did Cejas say? Answer censored. And there are still two hours to Rio and four to Buenos Aires, let's have another little whiskey, said the mongol-looking fellow-countryman, in a little while they're going to show a color movie. Action, I hope, Oscar said. That's for sure, said the fellow-countryman, the marines killing communists or something like that, John Wayne, old and hairy.

"He doesn't name them, naturally, among other reasons because he has no idea where they are," shouted the little rabbi looking at me as if I were to blame for that mess. "A lot of preliminary organization, they rot your soul with pseudonyms, codes, meetings at three in the morning, and all of a sudden they turn to dust."

"You're talking just for the sake of talking," Andrés said putting one paper in front of the other, comparing them, putting them in opposite order, comparing them, throwing them into a corner and grabbing some others, arranging them in consecutive order, comparing them, shrugging his shoulders, recognizing obscurely that Lonstein was right and that no sequence was of any use as a guiding track, "you're talking just for the sake of talking and because you're a child of the West who needs arrows to point the way."

"You really are taking charge of the heritage," the little rabbi roared, "All converts are the same, you're going to screw me until the end of my days with your flaming fanaticism."

"No, old man," Andrés said choosing a series of notes and pieces of paper that looked a little less confused than the rest, "only you, the game turned out that way, things happened to them and things happened to me that had nothing to do with it, a fly for example, but look, in the end there was a kind of convergence, to give it a name, in the opinion of others I was the one who brought the wolf into the fold."

"A crock," Lonstein said, "Patricio found out afterwards that the Spermatozo-ants had already got there four hours before you, except that when they saw you they thought it wasn't a matter of waiting any longer, you must have got them worked up by walking in as large as life as if you were coming for tea and crumpets."

"What difference does it make now," I told him, "what little difference does all this make alongside of what happened."

"I think that it matters suspiciously too much to you, chum. There's no other reason for such a compilatory fervor."

"I'd say for Manuel, brother."

"What the fuck does Manuel have to do with it at this point?"

"Everything, old man. It might seem that we're wasting our time with so much paperwork, but something tells me that we've got to keep it for Manuel. You grumble when you see me doing something that hurts you because you're left out, because you didn't follow the thing closely and don't think I'm blaming you because I'm more or less in the same situation, and then because you've got the screwed-up feeling that something real and lived is falling apart in your fingers like a wormy cruller. Me too and still I'm going to finish this even though it won't be anything more than going to find Susana and giving her what she needs for the album."

"Ah, because you think these things should go into it too, mixed in with fifty pages of clippings and paste-ups."

"Yes, old man. Here, for example, look what the one I told had in his jacket pocket, when all's said and done we don't have any news item to leave Manuel about Roland, let's say, or Gómez. When it's all over he won't even remember them when he grows up, and on the other hand there's all of this which will be the same thing in another way and that's what we've got to put in Manuel's book."

Press Conference of the Forum for Human Rights testimony of political prisoners with denunciation of cases of torture

What they learned, how they took the lessons to heart, was the objective of the declarations made by veterans of the Vietnam War to the American lawyer Mark Lane. In Sweden, a country where many of them sought asylum after deserting, but also in the United States where they are living again as honorable citizens, 32 American ex-soldiers bore witness into the tape recorder of the cruelties that they witnessed in Vietnam and in which they took part. Lane is the author of a notable investigation into the mistakes made in trying to throw light on the assassination of John Fitzgerald Kennedy, as well as *Conversations with Americans*, published by Simon and Schuster, from which we publish the following extracts. Copyright © 1970 by Mark Lane.

The Stories

In the testimony read during the conference as well as that sent in writing, the prisoners explain in the first person the mistreatment to which they were submitted. Practically all of the statements coincide in revealing the use of electric prods, beatings with fists and truncheons, psychological pressure, etc.

A synthesis of this testimony follows:

Norma Elisa Garelli: Arrested September 15, 1971, in Rosario. She sent her testimony in writing, which was read at the press conference by a family member. It should be pointed out that although the Minister of Interior, Dr. Mor Roig, has recently announced her release, Mrs. Garelli is still under detention.

As she says in her testimony, she was arrested at her home along

[p26] Chuck Onan, from Nebraska

LANE: Were you ever given training in the interrogation of enemy prisoners?

ONAN: Yes.

L. Where?

O. At all of the bases. But during the last month, when I was being prepared for imminent shipment to Vietnam, we got a lot of it. It was Scuba school with jungle-survival courses. We were told how to torture prisoners.

[p27] L. Who gave you those instructions?

O. Mostly the sergeants. But some officers also participated. Lieutenants and sometimes the captain.

L. What were you told to do?

O. To torture prisoners.

with her husband by three or four plainclothes police who—from the very first moment—acted with extreme violence. It seemed that the police connected her with the escape of guerrilla fighters from the Tucumán jail.

From the beginning she was submitted to handling and verbal abuse. Then she was transferred to a place of whose location she was not sure. She was stripped—as she tells it—and an electric prod was applied all over her body, especially on her breasts, her vagina, her teeth, and her mouth.

Simultaneously she was beaten about the face.

In one part of her story, Mrs. Garelli says that one of the torturers—who was called "Fats"—changed his attitude toward her and said that "he had fallen in love with me." The prisoner relates that since she was blindfolded she could not see the torturer's face but she touched it and could tell that he was weeping.

The policeman mentioned—according to the testimony—displayed a great deal of medical knowledge and according to what he told Mrs. Garelli he only needed four more courses to receive his law degree.

Norma Morello: Arrested November 30 by military personnel in the town of Goya and taken to the headquarters of the Second Army Corps in Rosario. A month later she was able to be seen by members of her family. Both her lawyer, Dr. Bellomo, and her brother Rubén Morello state that she had been submitted to torture at military establishments. On the other hand, after she was turned over to the jurisdiction of the police—they said—she was well treated.

Mirta Miguens de Molina: Arrested December 11. Her testimony was read at the press conference by

L. How?

O. Removing a person's shoes and beating him or her on the soles of the feet. That was pretty mild alongside of some of the others.

L. What other methods were taught? Can you give me one more example?

O. We were told to make use of electrical radio equipment. We were told to attach the electrodes to the genitals.

L. Did they demonstrate that technique or just talk about it?

O. They had drawings on the board showing exactly how to clamp the electrodes onto the testicles of a man or the body of a woman.

L. Did one of the non-coms draw it on the blackboard?

O. No. They were printed documents tacked to the blackboard.

L. What else were you taught?

O. How to pull out fingernails.

L. What's the prescribed instrument for that?

O. Radio pliers.

L. Who explained that method?

O. A sergeant.

L. What other methods were taught?

O. Various things you can do with bamboo.

L. Like what?

O. Stick them under the fingernails and into ears.

[p28] L. Did they ever demonstrate, as opposed to lecture, any of these techniques?

O. Yes. One time they hit a guy on the bottom of the feet; ordered him to lie down and hit him with a rifle.

L. Did you receive special instructions on how to interrogate women?

O. Yes.

L. What did they suggest?

her lawyer, Dr. Manuela Santucho. Arrested by 20 men in civilian clothes. As she states in her testimony she was stripped naked and submitted to several sessions with the electric prod. Three men raped her, and on one occasion they inserted a mop handle in her anus.

She was also submitted to mental torture. In a neighboring room her husband was being tortured, and more than once they told her he was dead. In addition, she says that she saw her husband in a deplorable state with his testicles and mouth burned with acid.

Mirta Cortese de All: Arrested July 19 in Rosario. In her written story she tells how she was arrested and transferred to a cell of the regional post of the Federal Police. She was tortured by an electric prod in the most sensitive parts of the body. She was insulted and threatened with death, while one of the policemen said that "it pained him very much to see me in that situation." She goes on to say in her testimony: "They turned to other unknown methods. They put wires around my eyes, which were covered with paper, and around my head, which pressed strongly on my skull. Those wires burned me, I could feel a sharp pain. My body kept resisting less and less; I was hemorrhaging from the effects of the beatings and the prods." She says then that when she fainted "they had recourse to drugs put in cigarettes, injections, and pills that brought me around again so that I could continue with that type of interrogation. They passed a small disc over my skin which gave off heat, producing burns in some places." "During other sessions they applied infrared rays" which "gave me two large burns in the gluteal area.'"

Further on she points out that

O. They're pretty sadistic. I don't like to talk about it. What good does it do to talk about it? I'm trying to forget, to get it out of my head.

L. I'm going to try to report just what you tell me as widely as I can. You heard Nixon say that Song My was an isolated instance, that the American soldiers are generous and kind. If Marines are trained to torture in Vietnam, don't you think that it should be known?

O. Of course, we're trained to torture, but people don't want to know it or believe it. If there is any chance that it can help, though, I'll tell you.

L. How were you trained to torture women prisoners?

O. To strip them, spread them open and drive pointed sticks or bayonets into their vagina. We were also told we could rape the girls all we wanted.

L. What else?

O. We were shown how we could open phosphorous bombs without detonating them and then place the phosphorous any place where it would really hurt.

L. What did they recommend?

O. The eyes—also the vagina.

L. Was it suggested that any other chemical be used?

O. Yes. C.S.

L. How do you use that? Is it a powder?

[p29] O. It's a powder until its detonated. We were shown how to open the container and use C.S. as a poison. To make them eat it.

L. Were you ever given lectures about the use of helicopters?

O. Yes. They also make a joke about how one time in Vietnam they took a prisoner and tied his arms and legs to two dif-

after a week of detention "my body was a shapeless mass, purple, with the skin starting to fall off and a continuous trembling. My hands and feet were paralyzed. They told me that I was in Uruguay and that all of the tortures had been caused by an extremist organization."

Afterwards I was transferred to the Federal Police station in Mercedes and the mistreatment ended. Later on to La Plata and then to DIPA, where I appeared before a judge. "They had to hold me up," she tells, "as I still could not move my feet. They presented me to a member of my family whom I didn't recognize. The forensic doctors were there. The judge asked that I be placed in the Neuro-Psychiatric Hospital, where I stayed for ten days."

Guillermo Oscar Garamona: Arrested November 21, 1971, along with Adriana Mónica Arias and Néstor Pot, in Rosario. According to the testimony they were taken to Police Headquarters and beaten by several policemen. The electric prod was also applied. He was tortured for 24 hours—with short breaks—and he states that "at that point he was burned all over from the prod and bruised from the blows."

Further on he relates: "They pounced on me like enraged beasts. When I began to bleed through the nose it infuriated them all the more and they beat me harder. They showed me an invention of torture that they said the Yankees had made and given them to liquidate those who f—— with the security services. It consisted of a plastic ball with a spring and a placket, which was hooked into the mouth as the plastic ball was pulled out a foot or so and it came back with terrible force."

ferent helicopters. Then they took off and tore him apart.

L. Who told you about that?

O. One of my instructors. He was a sergeant.

L. Did he say he actually witnessed that?

O. He said that he did it.

L. Were you given extensive training regarding the use of helicopters?

O. We were trained by a lot of experts with helicopters. In fact we were trained in several methods of torture with helicopters. There was one way that on a helicopter there is a rope that goes down the outside—it is an automatic rope that goes up and down for pulling people out of water and such things. That is what is intended. We were shown how if you have a prisoner you can hang him from this rope, and also you can attach to his neck another small rope that's for an emergency. You lower him so he sees the rope around his neck tightening and when it gets tight enough it is going to kill him. That is one way of using a helicopter for torture. You can tie prisoners to the bottom of the helicopter rails, let him dangle there, and go along the top of the trees and that cuts him up pretty badly.

L. How much torture-interrogation training did you get?

O. It began in my second duty station and went all the way through to the end. At least, on the average, five hours a week for more than six months.

[p30] L. That's even greater concentration than you would have had in half a year in your major subject had you been going to college. The law school I went

Then, according to what he tells, they brought a woman in, "stripped her, and put her on top of me. They used the prod on both of us together, they told her that they were going to destroy her vagina, that she would never be able to have children." "They told me that if I died they were going to throw me out of the third floor and say that I'd committed suicide." "It was unbearable. I asked them to kill me and they told me that was what they were doing, little by little."

Hugo Marcos Ducca: Arrested September 7, 1971, in Tucumán, presently in wing 37 of the Villa Devoto. He was transferred—as he tells it—to Central Police Headquarters where he was beaten. Then he says he was transferred to the quarters of the Communications Regiment, "where an officer named Quinteros and two torturers beat me repeatedly, showing their faces, they stuck pins under my fingernails, stepped on my toes with their boots." "They kept on lying to me about my wife and children."

Tirso Yáñez: Arrested in Tucumán, the same day as Ducca and also in connection with the escape of the ERP guerrillas. He was also submitted to beatings of all kinds. "I was given proposals to save my life if I would turn in other comrades; they told me that Santillán and Martínez had already been shot."

Roberto Santucho: Arrested in Córdoba, September 2.

He was transferred to Police Headquarters and submitted to tortures "consisting of blows with something hard, possibly a piece of wood, on the soles of the feet; blows to the stomach, among others, continuous, and from different angles; blows on the head

to offered only two credits in criminal law, my major, which meant just two hours a week for five months.

O. Yeah, we were thoroughly prepared to torture, all right. And that's just the formal part. It really went on and on. Our instructors, the sergeants, lived with us. We all ate together and slept in the same area and they were always talking about their experiences in Vietnam.

L. What did they talk about?

O. Killing prisoners, torturing them, raping girls. And they all had photographs of the most gruesome things they had done.

L. How did the Marine recruits react to this training?

O. Positively. They liked the idea. The Marines are made up of volunteers. They were looking forward to going to Vietnam to use all these new skills.

[p50] Richard Dow, from Idaho

L. Could you describe an operation that you saw in which innocent people were killed?

D. Yes, I can. A village north of our position. We got a report—Vietcong in the area, go and interrogate the village and find out. We went up, interrogated the village chief. The village chief was a Cong sympathizer—told us to leave. We left. Came back with a larger force and tore the village apart.

L. How?

D. Napalm, mortar attacks, heavy artillery, land assaults, armored vehicles—a full-scale attack upon a small village.

L. How many people lived there before the attack?

and ears, on the arms, and the application of the electric prod all over the body, especially on the genital organs."

Several times he was subjected to similar torture sessions, until the abuse ceased when—according to his testimony—news of his arrest appeared in the papers.

Ubaldo González: Arrested October 13, 1970, in Mendoza, by personnel of the provincial police. He was tortured—according to what he says—at Police Headquarters in that city. "I can't place the time exactly," but "when they stopped prodding me, they sat me on a chair with a strap or a noose around my head, and with something that I think was a stick made a tourniquet with the noose that began to tighten around my head." "At one time when I was on the floor, they made me sit up and I felt them slowly step on my testicles, with laughter and the prediction that I would be sterile." ". . . They took off the handcuffs and tied me with rope or cords at the four extremities and then several men lifted me up into the air by the ropes and once in the air they put the prod to my anus and testicles." He states that he fainted and that when he came to, "someone was massaging my heart and applying an instrument which I think was a stethoscope. I heard them commenting something about a cardiac arrest and someone they called doctor answered that there wasn't any danger, he was coming out of it. Then I heard them say that this one wouldn't take any more, throw him in a cell, and then we'll get rid of him."

Jorge Agrest: Arrested in Mendoza, October 13, 1970. According to his testimony he was tortured first by the provincial police and

D. About four hundred.
L. How many survived the attack?
[p51] D. One.
L. Who was killed, then?
D. Everybody. Women, children, water buffaloes, chickens, goats, everything.
L. Was this an unusual action?
D. No. We've had other actions like this where we were told to completely burn a village down but not to kill everything. I know of other cases where we have killed people.
L. What village was this?
D. Bau-Tri.
L. Where is that—where was that?
D. About a hundred and fifty miles northeast of Saigon.
L. Have you ever been given an order that you were to take no prisoners?
D. Yes, I have.
L. By whom?
D. The lieutenant. The platoon leader.
L. On more than one occasion?
D. Yes.
L. And what happened then?
D. We didn't take any prisoners.
L. What does that mean?
D. We killed everybody we caught.
L. Wounded?
[p52] D. Wounded too.
L. Were killed?
D. Yes.
L. How were they killed?
D. Forty-fives, M-16, machine guns, stabbed them with bayonets.
L. Wounded lying on the ground?
D. Yes—unable to defend themselves. They were out of action. They couldn't have done any more.

then at establishments of the Federal Police. He says that there he was given the prod and "when I tried to shout they squeezed my trachea with a finger until I couldn't breathe."

Emilio Brigante: Arrested on the same day, also in Mendoza. He is threatened with death and then "they made me run around the room while they applied electric charges." He says in his testimony that the torturers "appeared to be people who were very used to this treatment of people under arrest from their comments and their way of beating."

"The next session began in a room different from the first, where they stripped me and tied me hand and foot, passing the prod over different parts of the body, but most of the time on the testicles.

"The electric shocks were accompanied by threats, saying that my life depended on them, that they would turn me over to the judge when they thought it necessary and that they wouldn't do it if they took my life away and that I'd never be able to have sexual contact with a woman.

"Then they took me to a new session of beating"—the testimony says farther on—"they beat me savagely until I was stretched out on the floor" and "in the midst of the worst insults they stuck a mechanical pencil up my anus.'"
"Every night I slept handcuffed to a chair and at every instant they would come to wake me up, telling me they were going to start the sessions and beating me so that I wouldn't sleep."

Alvaro Centurión: Also arrested in Mendoza on the same day. He says in his testimony: "They constantly put their bestial ideas into

L. Did you see this yourself?
D. I participated.
L. Why?
D. After a while you just become like an animal—you just do it out of instinct, you just don't realize any more.
L. How many prisoners or wounded did you kill? Can you make an estimate?
D. I'd say maybe two hundred and fifty.
L. You personally?
D. Yes.
L. And how many did you witness, do you think?
D. Maybe two, three thousand.
L. Of wounded being killed?
D. Oh, yes, wounded, and civilians being killed without reason. Men, women, children, everything.
L. Have you witnessed any interrogations?
D. Yes, several with prisoners I've caught and brought back in. I've witnessed maybe twenty-five or thirty-five interrogations.
L. Could you describe some?
[p53] D. Well, I caught a boy—maybe seventeen years old. I shot him in the leg. He went down. He was armed. I disarmed him, applied first aid to him, called a medivac helicopter in and went with him back to our company CP. He was given medical aid and then we interrogated him.
L. Did you see the interrogation?
D. Yes, I did. I witnessed it. The Vietnamese national, the CIDG, started. The boy was wounded in the thigh. He had been sewed up and given plasma. During the interrogation I saw the CIDG reach down, take the bandage off his

practice. They burned my fingers with their cigarettes and they threatened me with death, telling me that they would throw me off a cliff and would see to it that I was unrecognizable."

Carlos Guido Stecanella: Arrested under the same procedures, he was tortured by the provincial police and, according to his testimony, subjected then to abuse by the personnel of the local detachment of the Federal Police. As he tells it, the federal police stripped him and tied him to a cot. "After wrapping my ankles and wrists with a feather tick so as not to leave any marks, the interrogation began and they asked me if the Mendozans had beaten me before. I said yes, and they laughed and told me, "They were brutes; we do things better, we're scientific." Later on he says, "They applied the prod to my testicles, armpits, and paps; also on the anus as they told me 'we're going to cure your hemorrhoids.' " "So that the cries could not be heard they pressed down hard with their hands and even covered my nose, I became so desperate that I broke my bindings." "During the period of constant torture we went five days without eating."

Roberto Lehn: Arrested November 4, 1970, he recounts that "they began to interrogate me with threats or verbal pressure, they tied my arms and legs, spread out and separate. The interrogation began making reference to the negative role of judicial power and that my fate was out of its hands." Then they applied the electric prod.

Manuel Alberto González: Arrested September 6, 1971, after escaping from the Villa Urquiza Prison in Tucumán. He was trans- leg and hit it with the stock of the rifle to make it bleed again. The kid's losing a lot of blood. Tell him they'll bandage him up if he'll talk. The kid wouldn't talk. So the CDIG pulled a bayonet out and split the leg wider than what the bullet hole had made. That wasn't bad enough; they went ahead and killed him.

L. How did they kill him?

D. Through torture.

L. How did they torture him?

D. Chopping fingers off—one joint at a time. Sticking a knife just enough to make him bleed.

L. How long did that go on?

D. About three hours. Finally the kid went out. They couldn't get him back to regain consciousness. The CIDG pulled his pistol out and shot him in the head. After he was dead they cut off his scrotum area—they castrated him—and sewed it up in his mouth. Then they stuck him out in the middle of this village where they had a sign on him—anybody touch him and they'll get the same treatment. Nobody touched him. They do women just about the same way.

L. Did you ever witness that?

D. Yes. We were on a beer run to Saigon. One of the guys was upstairs above a bar with a prostitute. We heard him scream. He had been assaulted with a razor blade by the girl. We got an MP to take him to the hospital. We took her to the closest military installation from where we were. They got her, tied her down and split her from her vagina clean to her throat. They killed her im-

ferred to the provincial police headquarters and made to walk through two rows of policemen who beat him violently. He was beaten several times and deprived of food. He affirms that "after a long time they finally take off the handcuffs and blindfolds, and begin to give us food and *mate*. Once I noticed that the soldiers were putting urine into the *mate*."

Athos Mariani: He tells that he was stripped and tied to a bed. "They put a ring on my big toe and ran something like a rake or a wire brush over my body, mostly on the abdomen, pubis, and mouth; then on the genital organs and paps.

"There were a couple of moments when I thought I was going to strangle or choke to death. Then they started to give me some white pills taken from a caramel-colored bottle with an aluminum top about three inches tall. I imagine it was to avoid the electrolysis that the prodding might cause to be shown on some future examination."

Carlos Della Nave: He was arrested on March 16, 1970, accused of being implicated in the kidnapping of the Paraguayan consul Waldemar Sánchez. Immediately upon being taken by eight men who found him in a shed in Luján, he was handcuffed and given the prod by means of an automobile battery.

In that same vehicle he was obliged to lie on the floor next to another person who turned out to be Francisco Páez, a mason who did repair work in the shed.

"After driving for the space of approximately an hour," he says in his testimony, "we came to a rather large place which had very small cells. After a few minutes they took me to a brightly lighted room where

[p54] mediately.

L. You saw that?

D. Yes, I did.

L. Did you see any other mistreatment of women?

D. I saw one young girl caught. They said she was a Vietcong sympathizer. She was caught by the ROK—the Royal Army of Korea. During the interrogation she wouldn't talk. They stripped all her clothes, then they tied her down. Then every man in the battalion had intercourse with her. Finally she said she couldn't take any more, that she'd talk. Then they sewed up her vagina with common wire. They run a brass rod through her head and hung her up. Then the commander of the group, a lieutenant, severed her body from her head with a long saber. And I seen one get burned with a hot bayonet stuck dead into the vagina.

L. Who did that?

D. We did.

L. American soldiers?

D. Yes.

L. How many American soldiers participated in that?

D. Seven.

L. Who was the girl?

D. Daughter of a Vietnamese chief—he was a Cong sympathizer. We stripped her, tied her down and heated a bayonet up with a fire. Run it across her breasts—and into her vaginal area.

L. Did she die?

D. Not right away. We had a man with us. Took a leather shoelace from his boot. Wet it down. Tied it around her throat. Left her hanging in the

they undressed me and tied me to a cot.

"There I had to undergo the prod again, while an individual with a calm voice told me that it would be better if I spoke, because they all do in the end. I think it lasted for around an hour. Then they took me to a cell where I began to feel my right arm was paralyzed. I began to shout demanding that someone come. Nobody answered, but after a while the door was opened and they dragged me back to the cot.

"When I told them I couldn't move my arm," Della Nave's testimony continues, "they applied the device again, but in a light way, it must be said, without producing the convulsions as when they gave it to me with full power."

After telling how he was taken to another place by car again, along with Páez, and to a cell whose floor was covered with wood shavings, Della Nave relates that "shortly after arriving, I was lifted up and placed on a table, where they tied me hand and foot, and after rubbing me with water they turned on a machine that made a sound like a carpenter's saw.

"The refusal to answer questions made them hit me on the ears and increase the application of that prod, which was much more powerful than the ones I had felt up till then.

"When that torture session was over, they threw me onto the floor after tossing water over my body and left me alone for about 15 minutes. Then they tied me to the table again, repeating the same operation until they left me alone—tied down—for the space of a few hours. After that lapse, they came in every 15 or 20 minutes to ask me questions."

sun. Rawhide shrinks after it gets dry. It just slowly strangled her to death.

[p50] L. Did you receive any honors or citations for your conduct in Vietnam.

D. Bronze Star, Army Commendation ribbon, Distinguished Service Medal for Gallantry from the Vietnamese government, the Presidential Citation, which was awarded to my team, several Vietnam ribbons, plus the campaign ribbons and some Purple Hearts.

After telling of various transfers and similar "sessions," Della Nave maintains that he was led to an abandoned-looking place, with a wooden hut built on a kind of promontory.

"On arrival," he says, "they ordered me to get undressed and took me out of the house to stake me down hand and foot, continuing with the interrogation. On my refusal to answer, they started the application of the prod again. But this time in a more scientific way, because every so often I felt someone applying a stethoscope to my left pap and giving an order for the torture to continue or to stop.

"At some moment I asked for a glass of water, since I had not drunk anything for three days. They handed me a glass that contained a hot liquid. As I drank it down in one swallow I could tell that it was urine mixed with *mate*. During the night they came to hit my ears with the palms of their hands, they threw cold water on me and bombarded me with questions. In the morning (I could make out the light through the blindfold that they had left on my eyes), they took me out of the shack and hung me to a brace that must have been left over from the construction.

At some moment they held a fake shooting, tying me to a tree. I heard several shots. Then they took off the ropes and let me rest.

"At night they gave me the prod again, and since my breathing had become difficult and I half fainted, when I recovered consciousness I realized that I had a mask over my nose and mouth, which I supposed was oxygen."

Della Nave's account ends with his transferral to the San Martín post of the Federal Police. "There they left me, stretched out on the sidewalk," he says, "and after a few minutes I was picked up by personnel of that unit."

Homar Valderrama: Arrested May 1, 1971, he states that he was taken at 7:30 P.M. to the San Martín post of the Federal Police. An asthmatic, he asked for some medicine that he had with him when he was picked up and which had been taken away from him. It was not given back to him, nor was any similar remedy supplied. He was placed in a cell where water came in through the window and from a gutter. He was not given a blanket or a canvas to cover himself with in spite of the intense cold. At three in the morning on May 2, he says, they made him recognize as his a group of objects and papers. He states that he did it "so that they would not bother me and so that time would pass, in that way someone might reveal my arrest."

That same morning he was taken to the main building of Federal Coordination (now Federal Security). There he was handcuffed to a spring without a mattress. At 6:10 P.M. (he had still not had anything to eat or drink since his arrest) he was taken by a young man between 25 and 30 to the eighth floor. In the office of the "Delegation Division, Disciplinary Matters," where he was brought, there were three other men. One of them, "the boss," looked on laughing while the others beat him. He was stripped ("So my clothes wouldn't be damaged," he states) and beaten again. When they stopped, "the boss" began to ask him questions, threatening to take him to "the machine." Since he did not answer, "the boss" started to try to hit his genitals with a spring wrapped in a tube. When he was unable to do so, he hit him in the stomach. Then, as he recounts, he was taken outside blindfolded, while they pushed him from behind. He was taken back into the office again where "the boss" announced that "the machine" was waiting for him because he hadn't talked.

He was returned to his cell, it was 7:15 P.M. Twenty minutes later he was taken to the second floor and moved to an office that "is approximately fifteen by twenty feet, it is at the end of the corridor that leads to the elevator, coming out on the right of it; it has closets on the wall opposite the door and also to the left, some leather easy chairs, straight chairs, and a table three and a half by six and a half feet against the right wall, using the door as a point of reference."

There were two men inside. With "the boss" and the man who brought him they came to four. One of them placed a blanket on the table, which had four hooks. Beside it was "a wooden box one foot by two in which were kept some cylindrical objects half a foot high and a quarter foot in diameter: the electric prod.

Valderrama affirms that he was stripped, laid down face up, and tied. They put cotton in his ears, held in by adhesive tape. "The boss," between insults, asked him questions while another brushed different parts of his body with a liquid. When the interrogation halted, on the wet spots and on his lips "they applied something like an electric brush."

"The feeling one has," Valderrama relates, "is that they are pulling off the flesh, and when the brush was taken off I realized that I was all huddled up because I began very slowly to stretch my arms and legs." At 8:30 the session ended and he was taken to a cell on the third floor. There he listened to other prisoners being taken from their cells, and 10 minutes later shouts and kicking were heard coming from the second floor.

On Sunday, the third, he was victim—as he tells it of another "session." He still had not eaten or had any water. On Monday the fourth he was taken to the eighth floor, where "the boss" showed him things that he was to recognize in order to stop the tortures. On the second floor he signed a "spontaneous declaration." Then he was transferred again to San Martín and soon after the 17th the marks of the blows and the prod disappeared from his body. Valderrama states that of the things he identified, only a very few belonged to him.

Listening to Patricio and Susana one could have imagined something else and that was what infuriated Lonstein while Andrés looked at him as if explaining that no one was to blame and that everyone pulled on the ball of yarn in his own way. Agreed, said the little rabbi, but just tell me if it makes any sense for Susana to appear like a newly cut head of lettuce at eleven o'clock in the morning, precisely when I'm listening to the news, and you already know how much this sacrifice has cost me with the mushroom getting worse and Manuel crawling around the floor for no other reason than to leave a stream in the shape of a boustrophedon, if you know what I'm talking about. I know, I said modestly, but in your case I would have been happy for many reasons, even if it was just that she was taking Manuel away. Look, Lonstein said, I don't deny my satisfaction over that fact, but first Susana and after half an hour Patricio cool as a cucumber, asking for a cup of coffee and rolling on the rug with Manuel, I wanted to know something because after all I'd labored as baby-sitter and there's no price for that, brother, and what can I tell you, those two took possession of their son, gathered up the diapers and the food jars and scrammed out so pleased with themselves after telling me it's best not to say anything and thanks for the nursery time. They didn't feel like talking, Andrés said, the same thing happens with me but you can see that we've got to get busy with what's missing, even though who the hell knows what the fuck it is. What's missing, said Lonstein closing his eyes, yes, what's missing, of course there are things that are missing now, old man, you tell me.

TRAINING OF FOREIGN MILITARY PERSONNEL

Summary of Students of MAP*[1]

Country	Period 1950–1963	Period 1964–1968	Total
Argentina	1,190	1,216	2,406
Bolivia	764	1,432	2,196
Brazil	3,416	2,255	5,671
Chile	2,219	1,448	3,667
Colombia	2,516	1,378	3,894
Costa Rica	208	321	529
Cuba	521	—	521
Dominican Republic	955	1,419	2,374
Ecuador	2,246	1,549	3,795
El Salvador	304	528	832
Guatemala	903	1,117	2,020
Haiti	504	—	504
Honduras	746	602	1,348
Mexico	240	306	546
Nicaragua	2,366	1,204	3,570
Panama	768	2,106	2,874
Paraguay	204	564	768
Peru	2,820	1,624	4,444
Uruguay	807	607	1,414
Venezuela	724	2,382	3,106
Total Latin America	24,421	22,058	46,479

* Military Assistant Program

1. Source: Office of the Deputy Secretary of Defense (International Security Affairs), Military Assistance Facts (Washington, D.C., U.S Dept. of Defense, 1969) p. 21.

"Any news?" Susana asked.

"No," said Monique.

"I know the system," Patricio said. "France doesn't want any outside hassles, you've seen that. They'll take them to some border point and one of these days you'll get a postcard and all you'll have to do is hop the train, girl."

"Yes, that's how it is in theory," said Monique. "You two go on to the movies, I'll stay with Manuel."

"Me too," Ludmilla said.

"Come with us," Susana said. "We'll walk a little, it's hot."

"No," said Ludmilla, "let me stay with Manuel."

"Poor kid," Lonstein said, "just answer me if that's any way to prepare him for the future, at the age of thirteen he's going to be a complete spastic."

"That depends," Andrés said passing the shears to Susana who was pasting in the clippings with a highly scientific air, "if you take a look at the album you'll see that it isn't all that way, I for example, when this madwoman wasn't looking, put in a whole lot of funny drawings and news items that weren't too serious in the consensus of the solid citizens, if you take my meaning."

"Wait a minute," Patricio said alarmed, "did you change the arrangement for a Tom and Jerry one or something like that?"

"No, old man, the arrangement is still the one we know, including the little piece we were given to live through."

"That's better," Patricio said, "because with your refined mixtures no one's going to understand a whit of it in the end if the album falls into his hands."

"Manuel will understand," I told him, "Manual will understand someday. And now I'm leaving because it's late, I've got to pick up a Joni Mitchell record they promised me and keep putting some order into what the one I told you left us."

"In that order of priorities?" Patricio said looking him in the eye. "Your Joni what's-her-name and then the other thing?"

"I don't know," Andrés said, "it might be that way or the reverse but it will be both things, always. In any case, before I go I can leave you something you can add for Manuel, it begins with a pitcher of water."

Lonstein slowly filled the water pitcher and put it on one of the empty tables; he was alone in room three, gimpy Tergov wouldn't come to help him until eleven at night. Without taking the butt out of his mouth, he went over to the corpse lying on table five and lifted the sheet. He was so used to undressing them that he had no trouble taking off the soggy jacket, pulling down the pants, changing him into a body that the sponge and the detergent would wash until they left it white and pure, all marks of history erased, all blackish stain now suppressed, all drivel wiped away. As if, ironically, it amused him to watch the little rabbi work, two rays of light filtered between the eyelids, the head on the rubber pillow gave the impression of rising up a little to see better, to tease him slowly. I just fucked up, Lonstein thought, nothing could have changed you, little brother. In any case it won't be me that closes your eyes, let the one who puts you in the drawer do it. Rest easy, there's time. Look at the way we came to meet here, nobody's going to believe it, nobody's going to believe any of all this. It had to be us, that's for certain, you there and me with this sponge, you were so right, they're going to think we made it all up.

Paris, Saignon, 1969/1972

About the Author

Julio Cortázar, an Argentine who was born in Brussels in 1914, has lived and worked in Paris since 1952. He is a poet, translator, and amateur jazz musician as well as the author of several novels and volumes of short stories. Pantheon has published six of his books in English: *The Winners, Hopscotch, End of the Game, Cronopios and Famas, 62: A Model Kit*, and *All Fires the Fire.*

About the Translator

Gregory Rabassa won the National Book Award for his translation of Julio Cortázar's novel *Hopscotch.* He also translated *62: A Model Kit* by the same author. He received the P.E.N. translation prize for *The Autumn of the Patriarch,* by Gabriel García Márquez, and is the translator of *One Hundred Years of Solitude* by that author. He has also translated works by Mario Vargas Llosa, Miguel Angel Asturias, Dalton Treviasan, and Clarice Lispector. He is currently working on Cortázar's latest collection of short stories, which will be published by Pantheon.